INDIRECTION

BOREALIS: WITHOUT A COMPASS

BOOK 1

GREGORY ASHE

H&B

Indirection
Copyright © 2021 Gregory Ashe

Published by Hodgkin & Blount
https://www.hodgkinandblount.com/
contact@hodgkinandblount.com

Published 2021
Printed in the United States of America

This cover has been designed using resources from Freepik.com.

Trade Paperback ISBN: 978-1-63621-015-5
eBook ISBN: 978-1-63621-014-8

Indirection, noun: lack of
straightforwardness; indirect action; lack
of direction.

Shaw's note: Like the time North got wasted at a Sigma Sigma party and tried to walk home and got stuck in the hedge for two hours until I found him.

North's note: (better example) Or like the first time Shaw used a dab pen and got lost inside his own sweater.

Chapter 1

"STAKEOUTS DON'T REQUIRE CHEESE," SHAW SAID to his partner, boyfriend, and best friend since college, North McKinney. They were sitting in a borrowed Ford sedan on a quiet block of Kingshighway. On one side of them, Forest Park opened up, where puddles of safety lights illuminated February-bare branches. On the other side stood businesses, churches, Barnes-Jewish Hospital, condominium buildings, and the glowing façade of The Luxemburg. Still nothing.

"It's not cheese." North's voice was low and deep, with the heat of a fire about to catch. He rattled the can for emphasis.

"It's got cheese in the name."

"No, it's got cheez in the name." North traced the letters with one finger. "See? That's so they can't get sued for false advertising."

"That makes it even worse. You understand that, right? It's probably full of benzoates and carrageenan and that's not even getting started on what dairy does to your body."

"It's not—"

"Because of your dairy allergy."

North's jaw tightened before he spoke again. "That's what I'm trying to tell you: I'm ninety-nine percent sure there's no dairy in this. None. It has cheez, Shaw. Not cheese. So I'm totally safe."

"I really think—"

"No."

"I'm just going to—"

"No," North rumbled, and when Shaw reached for the can, North planted a hand against Shaw's head and shoved him against the driver's window.

"It's killing you," Shaw said, trying to knock North's arm away. "By 2038, I won't have a boyfriend anymore."

"It's going to take that long? God, I need to start buying this in bulk."

"North, I absolutely forbid you to—"

The can's hiss interrupted Shaw. One-handed, North sprayed a mound of the artificial cheez onto a cracker balanced on his knee. The mound got bigger. And bigger. North didn't stop until the pyramid of cheez started to topple, and then he scooped up the cracker and shoved it in his mouth. He grinned, displaying the cheez foam between his teeth, and crunched loudly. Then he coughed.

Shaw watched him for a minute as the coughing continued and tears ran down North's face. North was getting plenty of air. He was also white-knuckling the can of cheez spray as though he thought Shaw might take advantage of this moment of weakness.

"Don't worry," Shaw said, putting his fingers to his temples. "Master Hermes just recognized that I'm now a level-five psychic. I'll dissolve the cracker with my mind, and while I'm in there, I'll fix that acid reflux you've been—"

"Don't you fucking dare," North croaked, swatting Shaw's hands away from his temples. He managed to swallow, cleared his throat, and in a raspy but more normal voice continued, "First of all, that psychic stuff is bullshit Master Hermes sells you when he has to pay the vig to those Bosnian guys he borrowed from."

"Oh, he didn't borrow it. The spirit of George Gershwin showed him where—"

"And second of all, even though I know it's not real, don't you ever fucking dare use that juju to mess around inside me."

"A lesser man would point out that a couple of nights ago you were begging me to mess around inside you."

"And third of all, I don't have acid reflux. I got food poisoning from that fucking toxic nacho cheese—"

"Dairy allergy," Shaw murmured.

Whatever North had been about to say, he didn't finish because instead he screamed with what sounded like frustration. Softly.

Movement at The Luxemburg's front door drew Shaw's attention. In the flood of lights illuminating the building's exterior, Chris Hobson might as well have been standing on a stage. He was in his late twenties, close to North and Shaw's age, cute but on the verge of being rat-faced. He was an investment wunderkind at Aldrich Acquisitions, the company owned and run by Shaw's father, and he'd been responsible for helping Aldrich Acquisitions become a principal investor in several highly valued biotech startups. He was also, Shaw and North were pretty sure, a thief.

"He's moving," Shaw said, taking out his phone. He sent the same message to Pari, their assistant, and to her nonbinary datemate, Truck.

Kingshighway was a busy road during the day, but late on Sunday, the flow of cars was irregular. Twice that night an ambulance had headed into Barnes-Jewish, sirens screaming, and once a Silverado had pulled to the curb ahead of Shaw and North, breaking the crust of old snow so that a troop of frat boys could pile out and piss on the sidewalk. Chouteau boys, undoubtedly—the same college, just up the road, where North and Shaw had met. Other than that, though, the night's entertainment had consisted of Shaw trying to tap into his past lives and North trying to see how many crackers he could sandwich together with spray cheez.

Now, though, Hobson had emerged, and it was time to work.

Hobson turned up the street, walking toward the portion of St. Louis known as the Central West End. It was a ritzy area, with Chouteau College, Washington University, and the hospital creating anchor points for people with way too much money. It had trendy bars and coffee shops, fancy restaurants, and even a handful of clubs. If Hobson stuck to his usual routine, he'd be going to the Jumping Pig, a hipsterish bar that offered pork infusions and bacon-themed everything. If Shaw had to guess, he'd say it would be closed in a couple of months, but for now, it was Hobson's go-to.

As though on cue, Hobson went east at the end of the block.

Shaw and North waited a tense ten minutes; the only sounds were their breathing and the cars whipping past, the whisper of slush churned by tires. Then a message came from Pari: an image of Hobson backing through a men's room door, his hands on Truck's waist.

HE'S TOUCHING MY DATEMATE!!!!!! DURING OUR VALENTINE'S MONTH!

"You're never going to hear the end of that," North said, grabbing the door handle. "You know that, right?"

Shaw sighed, nodded, and got out of the car.

At the next break in traffic, they jogged across Kingshighway, cutting at an angle so they reached the sidewalk at the end of the block. Pari was coming towards them along the cross street. Her long, dark hair was bundled up under a ski cap, and she wore a quilted down coat that came to her knees. The bindi today was raspberry colored.

"He's touching my datemate!" was her first, screeching announcement.

"I think it's sweet," Shaw said. "Having a bisexual villain. I think that's really kind of nice. And progressive. Don't you think, North?"

Pari's head swiveled toward him.

"I mean—" Shaw tried again.

North groaned.

"You think it's sweet? You should have seen Truck's face. That…that new-money prick was groping Truck through hir jeans. Truck was so scared!"

"Truck offered to spank my monkey—those were hir words, by the way—this week, Pari. Twice. Ze's not exactly a sexual shrinking violet."

"We're getting into the weeds here," North said.

"I'm sorry," Pari said. "I'm sorry, did I hear you correctly? Are you slut-shaming my datemate? Hir level of sexual activity is none of your business."

"Well, it's kind of my business when we're talking about my monkey."

"Let's not—" North tried.

"Truck is an unbelievably generous lover," Pari said, shaking the set of keys she'd lifted from Hobson.

"So is North!"

"That's really not—" North said.

"And Truck is extremely well endowed."

"So is—"

"Ok," North said, grabbing the keys from Pari's hands. He caught Shaw's arm and dragged him down the block toward The Luxemburg. Over his shoulder, he called back, "Let us know if we need to hurry."

"I've seen North when he wears those cutoff gray sweatpants," Pari screamed after them. "He might as well have been holding a measuring tape for me."

"Jesus Christ," North muttered.

"It's very difficult to have a conversation with her because she's so—"

North growled and shook Shaw by the arm. "Don't. Start. You two were fucking made for each other."

By then, they were getting close to The Luxemburg. North stopped and released Shaw, and Shaw stumbled a few steps before catching himself. He set off toward the condo building, glanced back, and said, "I don't want you to feel bad, so I just think I should tell you that I think you look really good in those gray cutoffs. They make your whole, you know, business area look very impressive."

"I'm going to murder you," North stage-whispered. "Get the fuck in there so I can be done with this nightmare."

"Very bulge-y."

North packed a snowball faster than Shaw expected, and it caught him in the back of the head as he ran toward the condo building. He was still shaking snow out of his hair, the melt trickling down his nape, when he stepped into the lobby.

It was about what he had expected from The Luxemburg's outside: tile and wainscoting, coffered ceilings, lots of white paint. A mural of the 1904 World's Fair covered one wall; in the bottom-right corner, a young lady looked like she was having an indecent relationship with a waffle cone, although Shaw would have to inspect further to be certain. On the other side of the lobby, a security desk marked the midpoint between the front doors and the elevators.

Two women stood behind the desk: one was white, in a security uniform, a hint of a pink-dyed curl slipping out from under the peaked cap. The other was black and wore scrubs. An ID clipped to the waistband identified her as Dr. Holloway. The women had been looking at something on a phone, and now they both turned their attention to Shaw.

"Hi," Shaw said, wiggling out of his sherpa cloak. "I'm—" He'd gotten his arm stuck, and it took him a moment to get it free. "I'm Max. I'm here to see my cousin. Oh, I like your nails!"

The women exchanged a look as Shaw approached the desk. "Sir," the woman in the security uniform said. Her nametag, now that Shaw was closer, read Weigel. "You said you're here to see your cousin? What's the name and unit number?"

"I told my boyfriend I wanted to get rainbow-painted cat claws for Pride," Shaw said wistfully, staring at Weigel's nails, "and he told me no. Oh, you've got a tattoo! Is it a rose?"

"It's a carnation," Weigel said, rotating her arm to display the underside of her wrist.

"For purity," Holloway said and started to laugh until Weigel slapped her leg.

"My boyfriend won't let me get any tattoos. Or piercings. I told him I wanted to get my nipples pierced, and he said he'd break up with me. He said he's the only one allowed to touch my body."

"Boy," Weigel said, drawing out the word. "What'd you tell him?"

"Oh, I know he just wants what's best for me. Davey's so sweet. He picks out what I'm supposed to wear—well, not my cloak. He told me I couldn't have this, but I bought it anyway. But he made me wear this stuff." He gestured at the long-sleeved tee and jeans. "And I have to hide the cloak at Mom's. But I can't tell her about Davey because when I said something about the diet Davey put me on, she just about lost her mind."

Holloway narrowed her eyes at him; she was picking at her weave with one hand. "You ain't nothing but skin and bones. Why're you on a diet?"

"Davey likes it when he can count my ribs. He says that's when I look best for him. Oh, Coca-Cola. That's my favorite! I don't know when the last time was that Davey let me have one."

"Like a big, white baby," Holloway murmured to herself.

Weigel held out an unopened can of Coke, but instead of taking it, Shaw moved around the desk. "Hey, you've got all sorts of cool stuff back here. Do you really watch all those screens?"

"You know you shouldn't be back here," Weigel said.

"Leave him alone," Holloway said. She reached out and caught some of Shaw's hair. "Now don't tell me Davey makes you wear your hair like this?"

"Oh." Shaw let his expression fall. "I was, um, really bad. One time. And Davey cut my hair. It was for my own good. You know, he had to teach me a lesson."

"Child," Weigel said. "Why don't you call Davey and tell him to come down here?"

"Do you want to see what my hair used to look like? It was really long. Oh, that's a picture of a mole on Davey's back that I think might be cancerous. And that's a carousel horse, but the carousel's gone, so I guess maybe it's just a regular horse now. But out of wood. And that's—"

"Just a big baby," Holloway said to herself again, both women turning away from the lobby to face Shaw, leaning closer to look at the pictures on his phone. He glanced up just once, over their heads, as North sprinted silently across the tile. Then he went back to the patter, dragging it out until North rode the elevator up and Shaw guessed that several minutes had passed.

"Anyway," Shaw said, "I guess I'd better go see Chris. Chris Hobson. He's my cousin; he lives in 8A."

"Sweety pie," Holloway said, "you got to get this Davey out of your life. He's got some bad energy."

"I say call him," Weigel said. "Get him down here and let the two of us talk to him for a few minutes. That boy won't ever trouble you again."

"And drink that Coke," Holloway said. "I think I've got a Kind bar in my purse. You're too thin; don't listen to that boy."

"Drink that Coke right up," Weigel said as she grabbed the desk phone. "What's your cousin know about all this?"

"Oh, he and Davey don't get along at all. That's the whole reason I came over tonight; Chris wants to talk about it."

The women exchanged knowing looks.

"Uh huh," Holloway said, fluffing Shaw's hair again. "Listen to your cousin, Max. You're too pretty to waste on a jerk like Davey."

"Mr. Hobson? Yes, I've got your cousin Max—yes, sir. I'll send him right up."

It took a little longer, but Shaw finally managed to extricate himself and ride the elevator up. He found the door to 8A unlocked and open, and when he stepped inside, North was waiting near the landline phone where he'd answered the call from the security desk and told them to let Shaw into the building.

"What the absolute fuck was all that fuckery?"

"I got a Coke!"

"You've got an abusive boyfriend named Davey? Jesus fucking Christ, Shaw. I didn't say you couldn't buy that stupid fucking cloak. My exact words were, 'I don't think you'll wear it very much, so I don't think it's worth the money.' And I didn't say you couldn't get tattoos or have your nipples pierced. I said maybe you should think about the fact that you don't like needles and having the script of *Memento* tattooed over every inch of your body might be a decision you regret in a few months."

"I—"

"And if you say one more fucking word about that Coke, I'm going to lose my fucking shit."

North's shit looked pretty lost already, so Shaw just sipped the cola and nodded. "It's been a hard night. Your penis. Those cutoffs."

North's fists clenched at his sides. Then he turned slowly and stalked down the hall.

The condo looked like it had come straight out of a CB2 catalogue: sinuously modern furniture, glass and teak, the occasional bleached wicker and white-varnished rattan piece. It even smelled store-bought, like all-purpose cleaner and artificial lavender. Sliding glass doors opened onto a balcony overlooking the park: asphalt ribbons, the arched backs of stone bridges, winter-brown grass rippling like water.

Shaw pulled on disposable gloves to match North, and they moved quickly through the unit. They couldn't toss the place the way they normally would have, but they still managed to work efficiently, dividing the rooms without speaking, each man methodical in his search.

North found the safe hidden on the bookshelf. It had a cover designed to look like a row of books, and it was a surprisingly good deception—from a distance. With the cover pulled back, a keypad and lock were visible. They tested keys on the lock until one of them turned, and the safe's door swung open.

"Computer," North said as he drew several external hard drives from the safe.

"Got it," Shaw said, already powering up Hobson's laptop. A login screen appeared, and Shaw typed in an Aldrich Acquisitions administrator password—provided courtesy of his father, who also happened to be their most valuable client. After an uncertain flicker, the screen changed, and Shaw had access to Chris Hobson's computer.

After scrolling quickly through the files, Shaw said, "Nothing obvious."

"It's corporate espionage," North said as he plugged in the first external hard drive. "He's been smart enough so far not to leave a trail of breadcrumbs. That's why we're here."

"So far," Shaw said with a smirk. A new window popped up, showing the contents of the hard drive that North had just connected. "Porn."

"Tentacle porn," North corrected.

"You really shouldn't judge—oh." Shaw cut off when North double-clicked one of the files. He covered his eyes and then peeked between two fingers. "I didn't know he could fit so many inside him."

North was already disconnecting the drive. He plugged in the next one.

"This is it," Shaw said as he looked at the files.

"Make a nice, obvious folder to stash it all. Something like 'Chris's Secret Stuff – DO NOT TOUCH.'"

Instead, Shaw burrowed into the computer's main drive, created an unnamed folder, altered the properties so that it was hidden, and copied over the contents of the hard drive. It was a lot of data, and it took several minutes. While they waited, he sent a text to their contact at Aldrich Acquisitions—a woman named Haw Ryeo.

Picked up dinner. Heading home.

Haw didn't respond to the nonsense text, but she would understand the message. Hobson's computer, which was technically company property, would be inspected immediately via remote access. The stolen files and documents would be found, providing grounds for a warrant. In their search of the condo, the police would find the hard drives. Hobson would go to prison, and Aldrich Acquisitions would maintain control of millions of dollars' worth of intellectual property.

"Done?" North asked.

Shaw nodded.

While North disconnected the cables and returned the hard drives to the safe, Shaw powered down the computer. They locked up the condo, took the fire stairs, and let themselves out through a service door. Shaw sent another text, and Pari met them on the same street corner.

"He touched Truck's butt," Pari informed them as she accepted Hobson's keys.

"Get back there and claw his eyes out," North said. "Just make sure you put the keys in his pocket while you do."

Pari's grin was vicious; she practically ran toward the Jumping Pig.

Shaw followed North across Kingshighway again. This side of the street was dark, and the air from the park smelled like wet wood and mulched leaves. In the distance, a few artificial lights looked like silver brads fixing the trees against the night sky.

"Is this how you thought things were going to be?" Shaw asked as they approached the Ford.

"I thought it went pretty smoothly."

"No, I mean—corporate work, planting evidence, tracking down the mistresses of high-level executives."

"Is this a morals thing? Are you feeling guilty?"

"What? No. He stole that stuff; we just gave them a way to prove it. No, it's just—I don't know, I didn't think this is what we'd be doing."

"It's work, Shaw. And we're good at it." North opened the door and rested one arm on the roof of the car. "We're fucking fantastic at it."

"Right."

"And Borealis is doing great."

"Right."

"So?"

After a moment, Shaw shrugged and got into the car.

Chapter 2

WHEN THEY PULLED UP in front of North's Southampton duplex, Shaw had one thing in mind.

"Huh?" North said. And then he grunted and spread his legs. "Oh."

The borrowed Ford rumbled quietly beneath them. The inside of the car smelled like the air freshener—shaped like a cluster of cherries, although smelling more like Laffy Taffy than anything else Shaw could name—and like the American Crew gel North still wore in his textured thatch of blond hair. He was hardening rapidly under Shaw's touch, and he leaned back in the seat, eyes hooded as he watched Shaw impassively. Normally his eyes were a remarkably light blue, the predawn color of fresh snowfall, or like light caught on the rim of a sheet of ice. Tonight, in the darkened interior of the Ford, with his pupils blown wide, they might as well have been black.

He made a sound in his throat and tried to spread his legs farther. His knee thumped the door panel.

"This is when you invite your beautiful, sexually prodigious, unbelievably generous boyfriend inside," Shaw whispered, his fingers tracing the length of North's dick through the denim.

North made another of those noises, but he was still relaxed against the seat. With one hand, barely more than a flick of his fingers, he beckoned Shaw closer.

Grinning, Shaw leaned over the center console. North's movement was minimal, only a few inches, making Shaw come to him. He raised up toward North's mouth for a kiss.

At the last moment, though, North veered, his mouth coming to Shaw's ear, and at a normal volume he said, "What about Davey?"

"Ow!" Shaw reared back so fast that he hit the car's headliner. "North, what the hell?"

"I just remembered your crazy, abusive, controlling boyfriend, Davey. I want to make sure he's ok with us messing around."

"You are really taking that the wrong way."

North watched him through hooded eyes. His erection was still visible through the jeans.

"I just took a few details and, you know, made something else up."

"Uh huh."

"You and Davey have absolutely nothing in common."

"Uh huh."

"He was a total figment of my imagination."

"Uh huh." North reached down, pretending to adjust himself, although his hand lingered long enough to suggest something else. "Except those details that you took from real life."

"North, come on!"

"Night, Shaw."

"Hey, hold on." Shaw caught his wrist, drawing North's hand to the bulge in his own jeans. He let out a satisfied noise and rutted softly against North's palm. "It's been too long," Shaw whispered. "And last time, we didn't even get to do a sleepover."

"We're not ten, Shaw." But his fingers curled possessively, rubbing slow and hard against Shaw's dick.

Shaw made another of those appreciative noises; he didn't miss the flush speckling North's throat. Leaning over the console again, he stroked North and found him, if anything, even harder than before. "Please? I want you to fuck me."

The rumble in North's throat was almost a growl. "Is that what you need, baby?"

Shaw nodded.

"Say it," North ordered.

"I need it. I need you to fuck me."

North's grin was sharp and sudden. "Then ask Davey."

"North!"

North's grin got bigger.

Shaw slapped his erection.

"Holy Christ, Shaw!" North folded, covering himself. "What the fuck?"

"You're being a brat."

"Did you just fucking spank my cock? And not even in the fun way, I might add?"

"Quit being so mouthy," Shaw said, "and take me inside and fuck me."

"You're a fucking monster."

Shaw turned off the car and withdrew the keys from the ignition. "Now, North."

North grumbled the whole way to the front door. He let them inside, and the puppy—North's puppy—was there, waiting for them. He immediately started yipping, dancing around their heels, clawing at North's legs.

"Hello," North cooed. "Gotta take care of him first."

"He's a fucking cockblock," Shaw called after him. "This is worse than having children. Children you can just lock in their rooms when daddy needs some dick."

North pointed at the ceiling and glanced back long enough to reply softly, "Keep shouting; I'm sure Mr. Winns is interested in what daddy needs."

Face hot, Shaw locked the front door behind him and headed into North's bedroom. He left the sherpa cloak on a chair, kicked off the engineer boots, and climbed onto the bed. A few minutes later, North was there too, yanking off his Redwings, rucking up the sweatshirt he'd worn. He peeled it off, exposing the dense slabs of muscle, the old scar on his side, his chest and belly covered by thick blond fur. He crawled between Shaw's legs, ran his hands up Shaw's thighs, and kissed him. Then he pulled back, palming Shaw through his jeans, a smirk plastered on his face.

"Why are you being so mean to me tonight?"

"Keep whining," North said, eyebrows shooting up, "and you're going to find out how mean I can be."

Huffing a breath, Shaw reached for North's waistband. He unbuttoned the jeans, worked the fly down, and pulled out North's dick. North shivered and let out a breath. Shaw stroked him slowly, watching North's eyes glaze.

Then Shaw's gut twisted.

North was tugging on Shaw's shirt, trying to turn him out of it, his fingers warm and rough.

"Just a second," Shaw said.

"What?"

"Just a second. I've got to, um, clean up first."

North studied him, kissed him, and fell onto his side. Swatting Shaw's thigh, he said, "Hurry, mister. Now who's being mean?"

Shaw did what he needed to do. Perched on the toilet, he suddenly felt hyperaware that none of the guys in the books he liked ever had to deal with this situation. When he'd finished, he opened the door and called to North, "Just gonna take a quick shower." He stepped under the hot water, found the bar of hemp-milk soap he'd stashed so that he didn't have to use the chemical-laden Irish Spring stuff that North bought in bulk, and cleaned himself up. His hair looked like a cumulus cloud after he toweled it, but North seemed to like his hair more the longer and wilder it got, so he left it the way it was and padded into the bedroom naked.

North was asleep on the bed, jeans still around his thighs, the puppy curled up in the crook of one arm. He yapped at Shaw once.

"I don't know what you're complaining about," Shaw muttered as he walked around to North's side of the bed. "You got exactly what you wanted."

"Shaw?" North mumbled.

"Let's get you out of these," Shaw said, helping North free of the jeans.

"Just give me five minutes. Gonna fuck you…" He made a sleepy noise. "…can't walk."

Sliding under the covers, Shaw found North's hand and squeezed it. Then he kissed him. By the time he was reaching to turn off the lamp, North was asleep again. And in the morning, when Shaw woke, North had already left for work.

Chapter 3

"SHE DOESN'T LOOK like a romance author," Shaw said, studying the picture on the website. It showed a woman still on the young side of middle age, trim, her hair in a severe black bob. She had a cigarette holder in one hand, a wisp of smoke artfully photoshopped into the image, and she wore elbow-length gloves. "If anything, she looks like Audrey Hepburn. Or a flapper. Or Audrey Hepburn playing a flapper."

It was Wednesday. Monday and Tuesday had been nonstop with the work Aldrich Acquisitions sent their way. It wasn't just the investigations that kept North and Shaw busy; it was the paperwork. Shaw's father had mostly kept out of the arrangement, at Shaw's insistence, and although Haw was a reasonable woman, corporations still apparently required massive amounts of paperwork, documentation, and evidence—all of it carefully organized and presented. After their first job, North had insisted on doing the paperwork himself.

Today was a paperwork day. The Borealis offices occupied the main floor of the house Shaw owned in Benton Park, and they consisted of two areas: reception, where Pari pretended to be an administrative assistant and where Truck and Zion occasionally completed reports for the part-time jobs they did for Borealis; and the inner office, where North and Shaw worked. The inner office had seating for clients and two desks placed side by side in the center of the room. North's desk was immaculate: a large, high-definition computer monitor, a lamp, and a stacked chrome inbox-outbox combo that looked like something Don Draper might have used. Shaw's desk did not quite reach the level of immaculate, although it was definitely cleaner than it had been. It currently held a series of four Twinkies that had been dissected to various degrees and pinned open against their cardboard sleeves; volumes one, three, and six of the *Encyclopedia of Environmental Analysis and Remediation*, a Vitruvian Man coffee mug full of water and green onions, and the LP for *The Best of Gallagher*, which was currently being used as a plate for a piece of a child's birthday cake. Shaw didn't remember who the child had been, but the cake still looked edible.

"North?"

North was typing something in a spreadsheet, checking figures against a page he held.

"North, I think she might be lying."

"Hmm."

"I think she might be lying, the woman who called us. She doesn't look like a romance author at all."

"Uh huh." North pecked at the keyboard.

"North!"

"Look at this. It's the middle of February, and we've already billed more than we did in the whole first quarter of 2018. And that's not even counting jobs like last night."

"North, I'm trying to tell you something."

After one last, lingering glance at the spreadsheet, North looked over. "That's her?"

"That's what I'm trying to tell you: I think this is a ruse."

"A ruse."

"A con."

"A con."

"A scam."

North sighed. "Ok. Let's hear it."

"She doesn't look like a romance author at all."

"And just because I feel like my life won't be complete until I hear this: what is a romance author supposed to look like?"

"Well, you know." Shaw gestured vaguely. "A corset. Fishnet stockings. Stiletto heels. Would it kill her to wear a bustier?"

"I don't—"

"Or one of those vinyl bodysuits. And maybe a whip!"

"I think you're thinking of a prostitute—"

"Sex worker."

"—or dominatrix." North pointed to the screen. "This lady just looks like she has too much time on her hands, and maybe she likes playing dress-up."

"Says the man who just ordered an adult Naruto costume—" Shaw cut off at the noise North was making. "I mean, right, yes, whatever you were saying."

A knock came at the door, and a moment later, it opened.

"Ms. Maldonado is here to see you," Pari said, all sweetness and light with a prospective client standing behind her.

"Thank you, Pari."

"And Truck asked me to tell you that hir job is taking hir to East St. Louis."

North nodded; he was obviously trying not to make a face. "Please remind hir that we only reimburse legitimate expenses."

"Ze knows," Pari said, her smile turning brittle.

"That means—"

"Ze knows. We all know."

"All right," Shaw said. "Great. Thank you, Pari. Thanks so much. Ms. Maldonado?"

A soft voice answered, "Yasmin," and then the woman and Pari traded places, and Yasmin Maldonado moved into the office. She had a skunk stripe of gray roots where her hair was parted, and she looked thinner than she had in the picture. She wore a PURE MICHIGAN! sweatshirt, snow pants that crinkled every time she took a step, and ratty Reeboks. The only thing consistent with the picture was the smell of cigarette smoke that moved with her.

They took a few minutes getting her settled, exchanging introductions, and her eyes roved around the office before settling on the LP with its slice of birthday cake. With what looked like a great deal of effort, she dragged her gaze up to look at North and Shaw.

"I know you're going to think I'm fangirling, but I just can't believe you're willing to take this case. The gay detectives! This is so exciting!"

"Well," North said with a sidelong glance at Shaw, "there might have been a miscommunication. I'm interested in hearing about the job you want us to do, but I have to be honest and tell you we're very—"

"Very interested," Shaw said. "Very excited about a chance to do some work with the LGBTQ community."

Yasmin nodded. Then her mouth widened into an O. "You mean us! Oh, right. Yes, that would be great. I mean, you're gay! It would be fantastic."

"Right," North said with another of those sidelong looks. "We're definitely gay."

"And you're boyfriends," Yasmin said, clasping her hands.

Another of those sidelong looks. Shaw discreetly rolled his chair back a few inches and kicked North in the ankle. "Why don't you tell us," Shaw said, ignoring North's murderous glare, "what's going on? You mentioned death threats. Against you, in particular? What's been happening?"

"Well, I don't care what anyone says: we can't cancel the con. We can't. We're on our last legs because of everything that happened last year, and cancelling now would be the end of us. I won't do it. I'm not going to let some pathetic nobody terrorize us. This year has to be a success, or we're finished."

"You're talking about the…" Shaw checked his notes, which he now saw were written on the back of a Jack in the Box receipt. "Queer Expectations Convention? Is that right?"

"Yes. The premiere gay romance literature convention in the world."

"The only," North coughed into his fist.

But Yasmin had heard him, and she shook her head. "Oh no, there's at least one more."

"And this con, Queer Expectations, it's being held in St. Louis this year?"

"That's right." Yasmin squirmed to the edge of her seat, snow pants crinkling. "A few weeks ago, I started getting emails. 'I'm going to get my revenge.' 'You're all going to pay.' That kind of thing. Then the physical letters started showing up. They had the words cut out of magazines, you know. They said the same kind of things. I brought them, in case you want to see them." She gestured to a folder on her lap. "And I checked in at the hotel Monday; Tuesday morning, I had another one. Someone had slipped it under the door while I was asleep. It's crazy. The whole business is insane. And of course, someone leaked it, and our guests are going wild. We already have a lot of people who suffer from anxiety, and this is going to put them in the ground. It really will."

"I'm not sure," North said slowly, "what you want us to do. This sounds like something you need to take to the police."

"I tried! They're not interested. Actually, if I'm being frank, they looked at me like I'm crazy. Very homophobic. It's probably because we're in Missouri."

"The Metropolitan Police aren't always my favorite people, but they wouldn't ignore a credible threat."

"But they did. I mean, they are. They talked on and on about being careful and keeping an eye out for anyone strange or unfamiliar. It's a romance convention! We're all strange! And we love it that way. I tried to explain to them that something horrible is going to happen, but they just won't listen."

"Did the messages you received have any specifics?" Shaw asked.

"Like what?"

"Well, anything, really. Any details."

Yasmin made a face, opened the folder, and spread a half dozen pages on the desk. They were all as she had described them: cut-out words pasted onto copy paper, spelling out a variety of threats: *I'm going to get you, No one is safe, Watch your back.* Shaw sighed and looked at North.

"Oh no," North said. "You're the one who opened this particular door to Batshit Land."

"The problem," Shaw said, "is that even if the police wanted to help, there's nowhere for them to start. You might be the intended target, but you might not be—this one says, 'I'm watching all of you.' There's no sign of when or how someone might be in danger. We're even making the assumption that this is connected to the con. You're giving the police a black hole of possibilities, and they'd need limitless resources in order to even try to make a difference."

"But they can't do this. You're not allowed to threaten people."

"You're right; harassment is against the law, but it's a misdemeanor. Unless you can give them a viable suspect, they just don't have the resources to run down something like this."

Yasmin stared at them, mouth agape, her breath stirring invisible eddies that smelled of cigarette smoke. "Fine. Fine. That's why I'm here, isn't it? I'm going to hire you: private detectives. Gay private detectives."

"If I have to hear about how gay I am one more time," North said to Shaw, "I'm going to shit a unicorn."

"We're not gay detectives," Shaw said to Yasmin. "We're detectives who happen to be gay. And this isn't a gay detective agency. It's a detective agency that helps the LGBTQ community."

"Or anyone who can pay."

"Well," Yasmin said, "I fit both those criteria. I can pay, and I'm part of the LGBTQ community. I mean, I'm straight, but I write about gay men. I'm an ally."

"We know," Shaw said. "And we're really grateful. And we're looking forward to reading your books."

North cleared his throat.

"We really are," Shaw said. "I think North got a little chub just looking at the cover for *Spankin' Angels*, and I really liked the description of *Marcus the Marquis*, especially the part about the Prince Albert—"

"What Shaw is trying to say, in perhaps the most backassward way possible, is that we can't take this case. We'd like to help you, and I'm sorry this is upsetting for you, but you're asking us to do something impossible. We don't have the resources to provide security for an entire convention. Your best bet is to do what the police recommended: remind people to be vigilant, keep hotel staff and security in the loop, and immediately inform the police if anything suspicious happens."

"What if I have a suspect?"

"You just said you have no idea—"

"We had to ban a convention-goer last year. She was way too aggressive with the men who attended. Objectifying. Sexualizing. She hired a young man, a hustler, to seduce a very well-known author, and then the police got involved. It was awful. We had to tell her she was never welcome back at Queer Expectations."

"Why didn't you mention this to the police?" Shaw said.

"Because…because I didn't think of it at the time."

"Very convenient," North said.

"I didn't! A friend just told me that Leslie—she's the woman I'm talking about—Leslie is planning on crashing the con. And sitting here, listening to you, it all suddenly clicked."

"What a wonderful coincidence," North said.

"Exactly," Yasmin said, straightening in her seat with excitement.

"No," Shaw said. "He's being sarcastic."

"Oh." Yasmin's expression fell, then she brightened again. "I can pay you to see if Leslie really is in the area. That's something you can do, right? You can just try to find her. Come to the convention. See if she's hanging around. And if she's not, if she's safely back in Utah or wherever she normally is, your job is done, and you get paid. Although I really hope you'll attend the whole convention because you'll be our local celebrities."

"Would you give us a moment?"

"What? Oh, yes. Of course. We can even pay you for your time at the convention. Your hourly rate. You really don't understand—everyone will be so excited."

When the door shut behind her, North spun in his chair to face Shaw. "No."

"Hold on."

"No way, Shaw. This is amateur hour. We might as well be investigating a high-school mean girls club. Samantha told Sarah who told Megan that the boys' swim team stuffs their speedos."

"First of all, you would know, because I remember you bragging freshman year about that water polo player and telling me, quote, 'Turns out I like the taste of chlorinated balls.'"

North made a disgusted noise. "Shaw, we've got four open jobs from Aldrich right now. Four. And the paperwork keeps piling up, and the jobs keep rolling in. I honestly don't know the last time I slept more than six hours in a night. I'm exhausted, and I've got a dickwad ex who is fighting me for every fucking inch on this divorce, and I've got a lawyer bleeding me dry. If we want extra work, we've got independent clients who are willing to pay obscene hourly rates for us to take pictures of cheating spouses. This is a fan convention for romance readers. Gay romance readers. How are they going to pay us? In poppers?"

"Actually, that's not a bad—"

"This is what we've worked incredibly hard for, Shaw. This. What we've got right now. We built Borealis from nothing, and it's finally paying off. Why can't we just enjoy that things are good right now?"

"We didn't start Borealis to get rich," Shaw said quietly.

"Speak for yourself, you fucking trust-fund baby."

With a shrug, Shaw waited, holding North's gaze.

Outside, a diesel truck lumbered past the house, engine grumbling as the driver struggled to shift up.

North let out a wild growl. "Fine. Fine. Just shut the fuck up. If you say one more fucking word, I'm going to lose my mind."

"All I said was that you like chlorinated balls and that you might want our clients to pay us in poppers."

"You got what you fucking wanted, Shaw, like you always do."

"You—"

North stabbed a finger at Shaw. "Not one. More. Fucking. Word."

Shaw shrugged again.

Wiping his face, North stood. He bent, caught Shaw's hair, and kissed him. Then he gently tugged on the hair, turning Shaw's head, and whispered, "If you ever tell anyone how easily you just made that happen, you're going to need a boatload of poppers to handle what I'll do to you."

"Is that a bad thing or a good thing? It kind of sounds like a good thing."

North scowled, released Shaw, and headed for the door. As he pulled it open, he said, "Ms. Maldonado? We'll take the job. The contract is standard, and we do require a retainer—" North cut off, and when he spoke again, his voice was tight and hard. "I'm with a client."

A man's voice, familiar, carried back to where Shaw sat: "North, North, North. Is that any way to greet your uncle?"

Chapter 4

NORTH STARED AT RONNIE, the man he had called uncle for most of his life. Short, dressed in a Hawaiian-print shirt that accentuated his sagging gut, he looked like a middle-aged tourist who had gotten turned around. Ronnie smiled and scratched the gray fringe of hair above his ears, glancing around the waiting area.

Sweat prickled under North's arms, and he tried to keep his voice normal. "Pari, could you please help Ms. Maldonado with the details? And get any relevant information she can provide about Leslie, including a recent photo, last name, address, email, Facebook—anything and everything."

Pari's dark eyes moved from North to Ronnie and back to North, but all she did was nod, set aside a platter holding a half-eaten king cake, and say, "Ms. Maldonado, come sit right here. We'll get you all taken care of."

"Wonderful," Yasmin said. "And I'd love, really love, to invite you boys to a special dinner—"

"We'll see what we can do," North muttered, his eyes locked on Ronnie. "You can leave the details with Pari."

"And I thought since you and your friend like my books, I could sign a couple of copies—"

"Excuse me, Ms. Maldonado," North said. "This looks like a family emergency."

He turned and headed into the inner office; Ronnie followed, whistling *The Addams Family* theme song. Shaw was standing behind his desk, opening his mouth to ask a question, but North gave a hard shake of his head. Shaw shut his mouth and sat again. North sat too, relieved to have the bulk of the desk between him and Ronnie.

Ronnie, though, didn't sit. He strolled back and forth, studying the walls, the molding, the furniture. The new money from Aldrich Acquisitions had made it possible to transform the ground floor from a shabby suite of rooms into a legitimate office.

"You painted," Ronnie said. "Is it gray or tan? I can't tell."

"It's called greige," Shaw said. "We tried it with a little more gray, and then it was called rock dove."

"Nice, nice, nice. This place sure looks great. You boys are doing a fantastic job." Ronnie plopped down in one of the new client seats, bouncing a few times, his feet barely reaching the floor. "Check this out—this is a heck of a chair. I ought to get a couple of these myself. Say, where'd you get these?"

"What do you want, Ronnie?" North leaned forward. "You want the chair? Take the fucking chair. It's a gift. It's yours. Have a great day."

"You know, I was never really one for 'spare the rod, spoil the child,' North. But some days, I think your dad was a little too easy on you. If I'd talked to my uncle the way you just talked to me, I'd lose a tooth, and that'd just be the appe-teaser. I wouldn't sit down for a month. You ought to think about that in case the two of you want to have kids. Is that something you've talked about? Is that something you want?"

"We've talked about it," Shaw said, "and we agreed that—"

"Shaw," North said softly.

Shaw's teeth clicked together.

"You're not my uncle," North said. "And I paid you back. More than paid you back."

"North," Ronnie said, drawing the name out in a tone of extreme disappointment. The silence that followed made North's skin prickle. In the reception area, Pari said something North couldn't catch, and Yasmin Maldonado laughed. The sound startled North; one of his boots thumped against the chair. With a roll of his eyes, Ronnie smiled. "You are a very ungrateful young man. No wonder you give your dad so much grief. That's just kids, though. They don't appreciate what their parents—or their uncles—do for them. Not until it's too late."

"I didn't ask for that," North said. "So forget it."

"What?" Shaw said.

"Nothing."

"The last time North got himself in trouble—"

"Enough, Ronnie. Drop it."

"Be quiet, North. I won't tell you again." Ronnie settled back, the friendly-neighbor façade sliding away to expose something grim and goblinish underneath. "The last time North got himself in trouble, I bailed him out. To help him. And his father."

"What are you talking about?" Shaw said. "When? North, what does he mean?"

"I mean the Marvin Hanson case. I made sure that North was taken care of—in court, I mean."

"The lawsuit? The civil suit? You're talking about—what? North, is he talking about jury tampering?"

"I really don't think we need to go into the details." Ronnie smiled. "I've got a job I'd like you to do."

"I didn't ask you to do that," North said. "I never would have asked you to do that."

"I was worried, North. My favorite nephew was in trouble. I would have moved heaven and earth to keep you safe; forgive me for a mistake in judgment. But what's done is done, and, of course, if certain people were ever to find out about it, well, I think you'd face a heap of trouble."

"Fuck this. I'm not going to be blackmailed, and I'm not going to let you—"

"What's the job?" Shaw asked.

"No, Shaw. Not on your fucking life. If we do this, then we're going to be doing it forever."

Shaw's hand was warm and soft when it settled on North's arm, and he squeezed once, but his voice was firm when he said, "What's the job?"

"It's simple," Ronnie said. "It's right up your alley. Hate crimes. Someone is doing some good, old-fashioned fag-bashing. Whoopsie." Another roll of his eyes, another neighbor-next-door smile. "Sorry. That's what we used to call it. Someone is attacking young gay men. The ones that stand on the street, waving their peters for God and country to see."

"Hustlers?" North said.

"Sex workers?" Shaw said.

"I know the guy who's doing it. He's a piece of work, a real piece of work. I've had my boys try to catch him, but he gives us the slip every time."

"Then how do you know he's the one doing it?"

"A friend of a friend of a friend."

"This is something for the police," North said. "Take it to the police."

"You want us to get proof that he's doing this?" Shaw said.

"Shaw—"

Shaw squeezed his arm again. "Or do you want us to kill him? Is that what you're asking?"

Ronnie's eyes got huge, and he erupted into a belly laugh. It went on for almost a minute, and when he settled down, he was wiping his eyes. "Oh, Shaw, 'kill him.' You really are too much. No, no, no. Don't be a ninny. I want a video. Or, at the very least, photographs. He'll need to be clearly identifiable in the images, just so you know. You'll have to be creative about that, but I'm sure you boys will figure it out."

"And then what? Then you turn it over to the police?"

"Then my friends and I will handle it. Don't worry your little head about it; I can promise you that this nasty guy won't do anything like it again."

"No," North said, pushing back from the desk and standing. "That's my answer, Ronnie: no."

"Well, North, my lad, I recommend you take a nice long look at these walls, and then I recommend you plow your boy's pussy really well, because you won't see any of this for seven to ten years. Or you can be smart about this situation. I'm not asking you to do anything you wouldn't want to do on your own. This man is hurting people from your community. He's abusing them. He's put several of these young men in the hospital in critical condition. What's so bad about stopping a guy like this and, in the process, working down the debt you owe me?"

"I already said—"

"We'll do it," Shaw said. "North, shut your mouth. We'll do it. Give us the information, and we'll get a recording of him."

Ronnie smiled, but it didn't reach his eyes. "Tony Gillman. Anthony, but he goes by Tony. I'll send over a picture." Then he recited an address in Clayton. North jotted it down out of habit; his brain had overloaded and turned off. "And boys, I'd really like this wrapped up quickly. Before any more young men get hurt, you understand." He squirmed to the edge of the seat, eased himself onto his feet, and beamed at them again. "Bang-up work, North. Really bang-up work on this whole place. You ought to be proud of yourself. And you ought to see your dad more. I know, I know, nobody likes a nag, but it's an uncle's prerogative. I'll see myself out—be sweet to each other, you too. No fighting after I'm gone." He waddled out of the office, humming "Tutti Frutti" as he left.

North rounded on Shaw. "What the fuck do you think—"

"We need time," Shaw said, the words clipped and unexpectedly harsh. "Think, North. Use your head. We need time to figure out what he really wants, and we need time to figure out how to neutralize him."

North struggled to draw a full breath. Adrenaline drained out of him, and he put one hand on the desk to steady himself. After a moment, he managed to nod. "Yes, ok. That's smart, but you don't understand—"

"How the hell am I supposed to understand, North? I can't believe you've been keeping this from me."

"Shaw—"

"How long?"

"I didn't want you—"

"How long?"

"Right after the verdict. He didn't make a thing of it. He just made sure I knew. Then, after everything that happened last year with the Slasher, he brought it up again. It's something to do with your dad's business and..." North stopped. He couldn't bring himself to meet Shaw's eyes.

"This is about working for my dad, and you still didn't tell me?"

"I told him no. I told him I wouldn't help him."

Shaw's breathing was shallow and rapid. He took a step back. "I need to take a walk."

"Shaw, come on. I told him no."

Shaking his head, Shaw left.

Chapter 5

FOR THE REST OF Wednesday, no matter how hard North tried, he couldn't get Shaw to talk to him. The closest he got was a curt conversation when North was in the process of tracking Leslie Hawkins's Facebook presence. The banned convention-goer had her personal account locked down, but she had posted publicly on Yasmin's Facebook page about her plans to crash the con. When North had relayed this information, Shaw replied in short, brittle phrases, agreeing to visit the con the next day in hopes of either tracking down Leslie or getting a lead on where she was staying. After that, North got nothing until a brusque goodnight when Shaw went upstairs at the end of the day. North drove home, played with the puppy, and drank four Schlaflys. He went to sleep and woke at three in the morning with a roaring headache.

On Thursday, North picked Shaw up in his 1968 Pontiac GTO, original Springmist Green, even though Shaw's Mercedes would probably have been more practical in the cold. Shaw was wearing a shearling coat, a tank top that said *My other tank top is ironic*, his Lulu-fucking-lemon yoga pants, and bright pink Nikes. He was also carrying approximately eighteen bags that looked like they were full of books.

"Are you doing a one-man bookmobile operation?"

Instead of answering, Shaw got extremely busy rearranging the bags.

"It was just a joke," North said.

Shaw started rooting through one of the jumbled collections of books.

"All right," North said, sighing as he shifted into gear. "You're still mad at me."

The Queer Expectations Convention was being held downtown at the Royal Excalibur, one of the grand old dames of St. Louis and one of the few remaining independent hotels. In keeping with its name, its décor featured knights and princesses, everything pseudo-medieval, pseudo-European, and pseudo-Arthurian, although North spotted a range of anachronisms, including a replica tapestry featuring an Elizabethan ruff that King Arthur, mythological or not, sure as fuck had never worn.

The Excalibur's lobby was a cavernous room with crystal electroliers, gilding on the molding and column capitals, and a mural on the ceiling depicting a very twinkish King Arthur receiving Excalibur from a very butch Lady of the Lake. Thick red carpet had probably been intended to muffle sound, but the room still echoed with excited voices, laughter, and occasional screams. Several hundred people milled in the lobby; North guessed that ninety percent were women. The scene in front of him was pure chaos. A man was waving flyers, shouting at passersby about his latest circumcision-torture slow burn novel. A woman was trying to lasso another woman with a feather boa. An extremely young man was trying out a new shade of blush, pursing his lips and hollowing his cheeks as he turned his face to be inspected by three women who might have been sisters. A woman at North's elbow burst out laughing at something she had seen on her phone; she threw her head back, clutching at a hat that looked like it was made out of foam penises to keep it from falling off her head. Every available inch of remaining space seemed to have been given over to promoting an author named Scotty Carlson—posters, banners, flyers, even drink coasters.

"Jesus, Mary, and Joseph," North said. "How in the hell are we supposed to find her in this ocean of crazy?"

"Let's start by finding Yasmin," Shaw said, and then he plunged into the maelstrom of bodies.

The third time North had to stop and wait while Shaw adjusted the eighteen bags he was carrying, North growled and snatched half the bags, tearing them away from a protesting Shaw.

"Enough," North said, holding up a finger to forestall more objections. "You can be mad at me. You can ignore me. You can refuse to talk to me. But I will be fucked on a ten-foot pole before you make me look like a bad boyfriend."

Shaw blinked several times. "What?"

"What in the goddamn world is all this shit?" North rifled through one of the bags and came up with a sheaf of wadded pages.

"No, put that back, that's—"

"Is this your library porn?"

"North, put that—"

"'His dominating, engorged, throbbing overdueness filled my book return chute. He yanked my head back, baring my neck so that he could stamp it LATE with his teeth.' Pages and pages of this, huh? Does this poor guy ever— oh, all over 'the inflamed rim of my night depository.' Good for him. Well, at least you seem to have learned how to use commas."

"You can't sex-shame me. We're sex positive." Shaw seemed to struggle for words and settled on, "You can't."

"I'm not sex-shaming you."

"Oh."

"I'm comma-shaming you. Well, retroactively, because this all looks fine. Your diction, on the other hand—"

Shaw snatched the crumpled papers and shoved them into one of his own bags.

"Since you're talking to me, even if it's only until you remember how mad you are, can I just tell you that the book thing is genius?"

Adjusting one of the bags that had slipped down his arm, Shaw gave North a wary look.

"I'm serious. For about five seconds after I saw all these bags, I wondered if you'd lost your goddamn mind. Then I realized there's probably not a better way to blend in at a book con than to be overloaded with books."

"And swag," Shaw said, his eyes meeting North's for a moment before sliding away. "Nobody's going to look twice at us if we're carrying bags of books and swag."

"Genius."

Shaw cleared his throat. "I did, um, bring half of these for you."

"That was really thoughtful of you."

Shaw put his hands on his hips and looked out over the crowd.

"Especially for someone who's so angry at me that he can't say two words to me, not even good morning."

"Good morning," Shaw mumbled. His face colored, and his eyes slid back to North. "I'm not very good at being angry with you."

"Thank God. Even this bad version is really, really fucking upsetting." North cleared his throat. "Shaw, I'm sorry. I will say it as many times as I need to. I know I screwed up, and I promise it won't happen again."

"We're best friends."

North nodded.

"We're more than best friends," Shaw said. "I love you more than anyone, and I can't believe you'd keep something like that from me. Especially when it affects me and my family. We've got to trust each other—"

"One hour."

Shaw narrowed his eyes.

"I will talk about this with you for one full hour," North said, "at the time and place of your choosing. We can talk about every feeling we each had about it. We can talk about what I was thinking and why I made such a bad choice. I'll tell you all about how scared I was, and how I locked this away instead of dealing with it. We'll spend a full, solid hour processing it together. That's my offer, if you'll please forgive me."

"Eight hours," Shaw said. "At a spa. And you have to get a pedicure."

"An hour and a half, at Dave and Buster's, you pay for the tokens."

"Four hours, in a sensory deprivation tank, and we try ayahuasca."

"Two hours, I do a whole yoga thing with you, and you can light that fuck-awful incense."

"The yoga time doesn't count against the two hours. I want the full two hours to be talking. And processing. God, North, we have so much to process about this."

North fought the urge to close his eyes. After a moment, he nodded. Shaw stretched up to peck him on the lips.

"Oh my God! They kissed!" It was the woman in the penis hat, and she was turning her phone toward them. "You guys, they kissed! Do it again!"

"Sweet Jesus," North said, shrugging the bags back up his shoulder. "Let's find Yasmin so we can do this job and get the fuck out of here."

Across the Excalibur's lobby, a registration area was made up of several folding tables labeled with letters of the alphabet. North and Shaw made their way to where Yasmin was seated at one of the tables. Today, she was wearing a sweatshirt with holes at the collar and cuffs; it displayed a monster-truck tire and the words *Your axle goes here* and then an excessively enthusiastic arrow.

"Oh my God," Shaw said, stopping and standing on tiptoe. "It's Scotty Carlson. North, it's Scotty Carlson."

"Great. That's fucking great," North said, stopping as a procession of women passed him, each one holding up an illuminated pair of silicone butt cheeks and a hole that had been totally destroyed. They were screaming with laughter.

"I'm just going to see if I can get him to autograph—" Shaw pawed at the bags he still carried. "This one."

"Which one?"

"This bag. All of these. They're all his."

"Jesus. Fucking. Christ. You read this shit?"

"Um, of course. Where did you think I'd gotten all the books?"

North didn't answer.

"Did you think there was some sort of book-themed spy-gear shop?"

It took North a moment too long. "No."

"Oh my God."

"I just—you're changing the subject."

"I'll be really fast, North. He's my favorite. He's the best. And he and his husband are so sweet. They do all this charity work, and they post these incredible after-workout—" Shaw cut off so suddenly that he actually made a gulping noise.

North waited.

"After-workout shake recipes," Shaw finally finished.

"This is actually too sad to watch. Go find your big-boy crush and get him to sign your books."

"He's not my—"

But North just gave him a tiny shove, and Shaw stumbled off toward the far end of the lobby. An attractive young man, probably close to North and Shaw's age, was holding court. North assumed he was Scotty, and he was reading something out of a book to his admiring audience. An even hotter guy stood to the side and back, in a position North recognized (from all his years going to Tucker's work events) as that of the supporting spouse. The audience was hanging on Scotty's words, bursting into uproarious laughter every few moments. A guy with a very expensive-looking camera was photographing the whole thing.

"Lars?"

It wasn't until North turned around that he realized that he was being addressed. A young man, heavyset and sweating under a rainbow sweater, was staring at him.

"Oh my God, that is a perfect Lars."

"What the fuck is a Lars?" North growled, pushing past the kid as he headed toward the registration tables.

Yasmin was red eyed and twitchy and looked ready to kill for a smoke. She brightened when she spotted North, though, waving him to her end of the row of tables.

"You made it! This is fantastic. Heidi, isn't this fantastic?"

The question was addressed to a black woman who was probably in her early thirties, her ash-blond hair done in an intricate crown of braids. She grinned at North. "A celebrity gay detective. Scotty better watch out, or this crowd might find someone more interesting than him."

"God," Yasmin said, "Don't even say that out loud. Scotty will have an aneurysm, and I'll be the one who has to talk him down. North, this is Heidi. Heidi, North McKinney."

They exchanged pleasantries, and then North said, "Leslie posted on your Facebook page that she plans on crashing the con. I find it interesting that you didn't mention that to us."

Dropping her gaze, Yasmin shuffled papers in front of her.

"If she's here," North said, "I'd like to find her and ask her some questions, but the first step is a photograph so I know what the woman looks like."

Yasmin had the decency to blush. "Your assistant did ask for one, but I got busy."

"Listen, you're the client. If you don't want me looking for her—"

"I do." Yasmin shot him a glare. "I wouldn't be paying you if I didn't. I told you: I just got busy."

"Then I need some recent photos."

After a moment, Yasmin nodded.

"And I want to talk to hotel security. Then I thought I'd take a look around the property. If she's got any friends I can talk to—"

Yasmin waved a hand. "I can do better than all that. Several people have already told me they've seen Leslie here. She's around somewhere. I want you to find her, and then I want her arrested for trespassing."

Heidi's lips thinned, but she didn't say anything.

"I saw Clarence and the whole gang near the restaurant," Yasmin said. "Could you introduce North so he can talk to them? They're Leslie's friends; maybe you can get something useful out of them."

"About those pictures," North said.

"I'll get some for you. And I'll give them to security too; that was a good idea."

"It's what you're paying me for."

Yasmin looked like she might respond, but a woman rushed up, babbling something about the diaper mountain, and Yasmin's face spasmed in horror.

"Come on," Heidi said with a quiet laugh. "Before we get roped in."

"Did I hear diapers?"

Heidi nodded but didn't offer any explanation as she led him down a hallway, leaving the lobby behind them. The crowd thinned out considerably as they went, which meant that the volume of ambient noise dropped as well. The molding and pilasters and gold-leaf flossing continued here, although more subdued. Even though the holiday had been over a week before, Valentine's Day bows and hearts and paper Cupids still hung on the walls; someone had even had a little fun with the paintings, adding Valentine's stickers to the scenes. Lancelot was bringing Guinevere a heart-shaped box of chocolates.

"Leslie really isn't a bad person," Heidi said. "Just so you know."

North nodded. "What makes you say that?"

"This whole thing is ridiculous. I mean, I support Yasmin, and what Leslie did was wrong, but I'm really not convinced anybody got the full story."

One of the best tricks, North had found, was just being quiet. They'd left the crowds behind now, and the only sounds were their footsteps on the thick red carpet.

"I mean, it doesn't make any sense. Ok, Leslie is a little extreme sometimes, but why would she break into Scotty's room and then try to record him and Josue having sex? It just doesn't make sense."

North made a considering noise.

"Does she watch way more gay porn than she should?" Heidi asked. "Yes, probably. Is she hypersexual with the guys she meets? Yes, definitely. But breaking into someone's room? Invading their privacy like that? I just don't get it. Actually, I don't believe it."

"But someone did."

"Oh, sure. Plenty of people. I mean, it was hard not to. Scotty and Josue were furious, and they had hotel security up to their room. I heard they were thinking about suing, and of course, that would have ended Queer Expectations for good."

"This was last year?"

"Right. Indianapolis. Nobody except Scotty and Josue actually saw Leslie in their room; by the time the ruckus started, they were all out in the hallway. Scotty was genuinely furious, though. I mean, scary mad."

"What's Leslie's version?"

Heidi shook her head and said, "You know what? I really shouldn't be talking about this. Leslie's my friend too. I just wanted you to know that she's not a bad person."

North tried the quiet trick again, but it didn't work this time. Ahead of them, the hotel restaurant opened up on one side of the hallway, with a large sign proclaiming it THE ROUND TABLE. A cluster of people sat at a table close to the hallway, separated from the hall only by a half-wall partition. North took them in at a glance: a middle-aged gay man with thinning brown hair and a boxy blazer; a bottle-blond woman with enormous eyes and shlumpy black athleisure gear; a hard-faced older woman, her hair a much more expensively kept-up version of the black bob that Yasmin wore; and a gay couple, men who had to be in their seventies and who had, like so many couples, started to look like siblings with their Brylcreemed ducktails, one man in a pearl-snap shirt and the other in a Western-style black button-up with red stitching and red piping.

"Everyone," Heidi said, "this is North McKinney, the gay detective. Gay detective, this is everyone. Clarence," the man in the boxy blazer, "Mary Angela," the bottle blond, "Serenity," the hard-faced woman, "and Jerry and Rodney." Heidi's tone softened. "Aren't they adorable?"

"If you really meant it," the one in the Western-style shirt said, "you'd buy me a drink."

Everyone burst out laughing. When they'd settled, Heidi said, "Mr. McKinney is trying to track down Leslie. Apparently Yasmin is very serious about the lifetime ban."

"This is about the death threats," Clarence said. "That's what this is really about."

"Oh Lord," Mary Angela said, swirling her mimosa. "Please let's not get started on that again. Did I tell you about my daughter and her dissertation adviser? She asked her to lunch. Have you ever heard of something like that? Like they're equals. Like she wants to be her friend!"

"What death threats?" Jerry asked. Or maybe he was Rodney; North still hadn't pinned them down. "What happened?"

"Leslie went crazy sending death threats to everyone at the con," Serenity said. "Big surprise; she's always been out of her damn mind."

"Not to everyone," Clarence said. "She just wants to kill Yasmin."

"She doesn't want to kill Yasmin," Heidi said. "If anything, she should kill Scotty." She took a breath. "I didn't mean that. I shouldn't have said that. Mr. McKinney is here—"

"We're not going to throw Leslie under the bus," Jerry/Rodney said. "She's our friend."

The other half of Jerry/Rodney added, "Even if she is cuckoo."

"He's not trying to get her in trouble," Mary Angela said. "He's just being Yasmin's muscle. He'll throw her out, and that will be the end of it."

"Unless Yasmin presses charges," Clarence said, staring into his drink. "I'm not even sure how that would work, but I know she's mad as hell. I wouldn't put it past her. I'm not even sure I blame her. I mean, death threats? Really? Leslie went too far this time."

"He's not here to—" Heidi tried again.

"Why don't we let Mr. McKinney tell us why he's here?" Serenity said in a chilly tone.

North smiled. "Right now, I just want to have a talk with Leslie. With Ms. Hawkins, I mean. I know she's in the area, and I understand that you're her friends. If you could point me in her direction, things would be a lot easier."

"For you," Clarence said, adjusting his blazer. "But what about Leslie?"

"Honestly," North said, "it might make things easier for her. I'm not interested in getting her in trouble, and I don't work as anybody's muscle. I was hired to find out if she was the one sending those threatening messages. That's all."

"Bullshit," Mary Angela said, her eyes getting even bigger. "I don't believe you."

North shrugged.

"Do you have a boyfriend?" Clarence asked.

"You old queen," Jerry said with a laugh—North had decided, for the moment anyway, that Jerry was the one in the pearl-snap shirt.

"It's professional curiosity," Clarence said, blushing all the way to the roots of his thinning hair. "For a character. I didn't mean—I wasn't asking—"

"Let's not get into your love life again, Clarence," Serenity said with a barbed smile. "Nobody needs a repeat of last year."

Mary Angela looked down into her drink. Jerry and Rodney shuffled the flatware in front of them. Clarence turned even redder.

"Really nice," Heidi said. "It's getting a lot easier to understand how you write all those bitchy hags who hang all over your protagonists."

"Put it on your blog, sweetheart," Serenity said, standing and settling a black-and-silver shawl across her shoulders. "I'm sure someone still reads it." She set off without waiting for a reply.

"Gurl," Jerry whispered to Rodney.

"I know," Rodney whispered back.

That broke the stillness, and the remaining people at the table began to stand.

"If I could have a few minutes to talk to each of you," North said.

"Not a chance," Mary Angela said, adjusting her lint-covered shirt. "I don't know you, but I know Leslie, and I'm not going to help you hang something around her neck."

Jerry and Rodney shared a look. The one in the Western-style button-up said, "Leslie's a nice lady. She's just a little…unbearable. That's all."

Clarence shook his head. He was counting coins for the check.

When North looked at Heidi, she gave a shrug that was a little too satisfied for North's liking.

"And just so you know," Mary Angela said, hitching up the elastic waistband of her lounge pants. "It's offensive, this whole Lars thing. And it's embarrassing."

"What Lars thing?" North said.

"There he is!" North glanced over his shoulder to see the young man in the rainbow sweater who had stopped him earlier. Gesticulating wildly, the young man was leading a group of at least twenty people toward the restaurant. "I told you. Isn't he perfect? We have to get a picture." He pranced toward them. "Lars, please, we all want a picture!"

"If you really don't know," Clarence said with a dry smile, "it looks like you're about to find out."

"Find out what?" North said, dragging the bags of books in front of himself like a shield.

"You'll see. Oh, and good luck."

Chapter 6

SHAW RECOGNIZED SCOTTY CARLSON even from across the Excalibur's lobby, and after separating from North, he hurried to join the readers and authors thronging Scotty and his husband, Josue. Shaw had to elbow his way through the crowd, ignoring the nasty looks and, once, a shove from behind that made him stumble. He clutched the bags of books. He hadn't been lying when he'd told North that he wanted Scotty to autograph his books. But he hadn't been telling the truth either. Not completely.

By the time Shaw got to the front of the crowd, Scotty was fully immersed in his reading. Every eye was fixed on him, with good reason: Scotty was young, muscular, with red-gold hair and Scandinavian good looks. Josue, as usual, remained in the background. Josue always took second stage, even in their photos and videos on social media, which Shaw found slightly surprising— Josue was, if anything, even more handsome than Scotty, with his knife-sharp jawline and hollow cheeks and mile-long eyelashes. Up close, Shaw could read their paired black t-shirts: Scotty's had huge white letters that said HEA, and Josue's was almost identical except that the letters read HFN.

A chorus of laughter rose from the crowd, and Shaw's attention shifted to Scotty. He was performing a selection from a book, but it wasn't one that Shaw recognized, and something about the words nagged at Shaw.

"—but if you think I'm crazy enough to give up hot, bucking-bronco sex with an older man, you're out of your mind. And let me tell you, bucking bronco doesn't even begin to come close. He had a dick like Donkey Kong, and he ate ass like a death-row inmate hitting the lobster special." A purposeful pause. Another round of laughter. "But it wasn't just his dick and his tongue that I needed. It was his hand." Scotty paused again, eyebrows wriggling, and more laughter followed. "When he'd get up inside me, his fist like a second heart, fingers flexing and stroking, turning me into his velvet puppet—" Here, Scotty lost control, bursting into laughter. The crowd echoed him.

"And that, ladies and gentlemen, is the tip of the horrifying iceberg that is Serenity Silver's latest novel, *My Master Inside Me*." With a smirk, Scotty added, "Proof that women can't write gay men."

Murmurs of agreement ran through the crowd, heads nodding.

"Now, before my psycho stalker hunts me down and kills me," Scotty said, his smile getting even bigger, "I think we've got time for some autographs. Josue will help you get lined up over here, and—" Scotty stopped as his husband touched his shoulder and whispered something. Jerking his head in a negative, Scotty said loudly enough for everyone to hear, "It's a public space, Joshums, and they can fuck off if they find me and my fans inconvenient." Then, raising his voice again, "Right over here, everybody, and Josue will make sure everything is neat and orderly. That's why I keep him around when I'm not pumping him full of my come." He dragged Josue into a too-passionate-for-public kiss. "Isn't that right, lover?"

Josue mumbled something, and although his skin was too dark for Shaw to make out a blush easily, his eyes cut around the room. Scotty whispered something, and Josue leaned in and kissed him again, and this time Scotty's hand slid between Josue's legs, cupping his crotch.

After another, final, drawn-out kiss, the two men separated, and in a shaky voice, Josue said, "Imagine bringing this guy home to your Dominican parents."

Laughter broke the crowd's stillness, and people scrambled for a spot in line. Shaw watched and waited, adjusting the bags on his shoulders. Josue seemed to relax as he moved away from Scotty, laughing quietly at things people said to him, but he also threw lots of glances back at Scotty. Scotty didn't look over at him once; he was already gabbing with the first woman in line, flipping open her book for a place to sign.

"The whole gay-fairy-tale-romance shtick gets old fast," a woman said behind Shaw.

"It's cute," another woman said. "It's about the only thing Scotty does that's cute."

"It's bullshit. Scotty wants everybody to think they're this perfect, soulmate couple like the ones he writes in his books, but you saw how he treats Josue."

"They must be soulmates," the other woman said. "Nobody else would put up with Scotty. Besides, whatever else they're doing, they've definitely got the physical side of it squared away. I shared a wall with them in Sacramento, and I swear to God I didn't sleep all weekend. I wish you could have heard the noises Scotty can get Josue to make." A finger tapped Shaw's shoulder. "Sorry, I'm not trying to intrude, but you look a little lost. If you want Scotty to sign your books, you need to get in line." A hesitant note crept into her voice. "Although I'm not sure he'll sign all of those."

"He won't because he's a total asshat. You should read my books. Here: *Pierced by My Dragon-Mate's Fang: Babysitter Confessionals Volume 12*. It's only fifteen dollars."

By the time Shaw had finished turning around, he was face-to-face with a book. The cover was slightly too close to his eyes for him to be able to focus on it, but he had an impression of something green and scaly. Then his eyes caught the name at the bottom of the cover, and he dropped one of his bags.

"You're JD Hathaway?" He rummaged through the bag, pulling out a stack of paperbacks. "I absolutely loved your *Picking My Pocket, Picking My Bed, Picking My Partner* books. Would you sign these?" He shoved them in her direction, forcing her to pull *Pierced by My Dragon-Mate's Fang* away from his face.

JD Hathaway, like many of the authors Shaw read, didn't have a picture of herself connected to any of her author profiles or social media accounts; instead, she rotated a selection of book covers. The woman in front of him had to be past fifty, her skin leathery, her platinum hair in an ultra-short pixie cut. She hesitated, and then she said, "Absolutely. You hold on to this," she shoved *Pierced by My Dragon-Mate's Fang* into Shaw's hands, "and you can find fifteen dollars while I'm autographing these. Do you want them personalized?"

"Yes, actually. To Shaw. But I'm not sure I want to buy—"

"Ok, Shawn. Fifteen dollars."

"Actually, it's—"

But JD was already digging through her purse, muttering under her breath. The woman next to her was young, her nose and mouth too big for her to be classically beautiful, but she had a smile on her face, and her eyes were clear and bright. When Shaw looked over, she extended a hand. "Karen Prow."

"Oh, I've got some of yours here too! *En Garde*, and, here it is, *Fleche*. Would you?"

"Definitely," she said with a soft laugh. "You're kind of a super fan, aren't you?"

Shaw nodded. "Absolutely. When you had Roderick and James fencing on the waterfall, and Roderick started to fall, and James threw away his epee to save Roderick, oh my God! That was everything."

"You are too sweet," Karen murmured. She accepted the books, drew a pen from her pocket, and signed the title pages. When she passed them back, Shaw noticed that she had gotten his name right. "Oh, bad news. It looks like Josue just turned a few people away; I think you might have missed your chance."

"It's ok," Shaw said as he packed Karen's books away. "I'll just talk to him after."

Karen's eyes slid to JD. JD, who was still autographing the books, glanced up at Shaw and said, "Shawn, don't forget that book you just bought."

"You might not know this," Karen said, "if this is your first time at Queer Expectations, but Scotty isn't always very...receptive to people approaching him at random. He likes to do impromptu things like this to meet people, but he can be abrasive if you approach him outside these kinds of events."

"Abrasive," JD said with a huff.

"I think it'll be fine." Shaw produced his wallet and drew out a twenty. "I've been spraying all the mirrors in my house with rose water, and I put a framed picture of myself in my bedroom, and a framed picture of myself in North's bedroom, only the one in North's bedroom fell off the dresser, and it must have fallen really, really hard because it was broken into, like, a million pieces, and I've stopped wearing white underwear, so I think it'll pretty much be fine."

Karen blinked.

"Because of my aura," Shaw clarified.

"Right."

"Thanks, love," JD said, snatching the twenty out of his hands. "A little something extra is always appreciated."

"Well, I thought you could give me my change—"

"Here you are." She shoved the books toward him, and Shaw barely caught them. He folded back the cover on *Picking My Pocket*, where JD had scribbled, *To Shawn, with much.* The rest of the inscription was missing.

Behind Shaw, a campy voice called out, "It's not fair! This event wasn't announced." Shaw turned around. A man who must have been in his late forties was stomping his feet, facing down Josue. He was wearing a blue union suit with cutesy white embroidery, like an oversized onesie an infant might wear, and he was carrying an enormous lollypop over one shoulder. "I want to sit on Scotty's lap!"

Josue said something quietly, and the overgrown baby shook his head and screamed, "It's not fair, it's not fair, it's not fair. I'm his biggest fan!"

The photographer, tall and lean with Asian features, moved closer, snapping photos of Josue and the overgrown baby.

"Let's all settle down," Scotty said. "I know you missed the signing, but if you're really my biggest fan, you're going to enjoy the next part. We're going to do a pop-up trivia contest. The winner gets a photo with me, and," his voice dipped into good-humored patience, "tell you what, I'll even sign your books if you win."

Behind Scotty, Yasmin had abandoned the registration tables and was standing in the middle of the lobby, arms folded, a scowl on her face as she observed the gathering. Scotty met her gaze and set his jaw, and something Shaw couldn't decipher passed between them.

"All right," Scotty said, turning back to the crowd, "We'll start with something easy. If you think you know the answer, raise your hand, and Josue will come check. In the first Build-Your-Own-Bear book, *Ordinary Stud,* what does Twerpy Twink bring Lars as a moving-in gift?"

At least half the hands shot up in the crowd, Shaw's included. Josue moved from person to person, signaling for some of the people to move to one side, others to move to the other. When Josue approached Shaw, his dark eyes widened, and he said, "You really went all in, didn't you?"

"What?"

"Never mind. I'm guessing you know the answer."

"A cherry pie," Shaw said, "and he offered to let Lars eat it off him naked."

"Bonus points," Josue said with a tiny smile. "Go on over there."

Bags swinging around him, Shaw moved to join the first-round trivia survivors. The photographer bobbed around the group, the flash occasionally catching Shaw by surprise.

"All right, all right, all right," Scotty said. "Look at how many people made it past round one. Very impressive. Let's make things a little more difficult, shall we? In Build-Your-Own-Bear book two, *Jack Stud*, Lars and Jack get into a little bit of trouble when Jack invites Lars to his wedding. What happens?"

Josue made his way through the group of first-round winners. When he reached Shaw, his eyes crinkled.

"He, um, pounds Jack straight through his own wedding cake," Shaw whispered.

"Come on," Josue said. "You can do better than that."

"And when they land on the floor, covered in cake, Jack, uh, finishes, you know, hands free."

"Oh my God," Josue said, flashing a brilliant smile as he moved to the next contestant. "You're shy. That's adorable."

This time, the winners were fewer: only five. Scotty stood with hands on hips, glowing as he looked at the trivia participants and at the growing crowd watching them. "Well, what do you say, folks? Should we make it a little harder this time?"

Cheers and shouts of encouragement came from Scotty's audience.

"In *King Stud*, Lars reminds Preston about the first time he made Preston beg. What did Lars use to dominate the company CEO?"

When Josue reached Shaw, he was grinning again. "You know this one, I bet."

"Jackhammer dildo," Shaw said as quietly as he could.

"God, Scotty is going to eat you up."

When Josue had finished collecting answers, Shaw and the overgrown baby were the only two left. The overgrown baby was tugging on his union suit, and sweat flattened his artificially brown hair. Shaw kept adjusting the bags of books. He concentrated on his aura, just the way Master Hermes had taught him when they'd tried those really strong shrooms.

"Our final two," Scotty called, and another cheer went up. "Wow, look at this level of dedication. I have to say that this is an honor, a real honor. Here we go, for the grand prize: in the final Build-Your-Own-Bear book, *Post Stud*,

Lars walks in on Brick and Jaunty after Brick has just finished wrecking Jaunty. What is Lars's official diagnosis of the situation?"

The overgrown baby's face twisted. The photographer was circling again, camera clicking and flashing.

Josue went to the overgrown baby first. The older man whispered a few frantic words, and Josue shook his head. Then the older man said something else.

Josue's face was expressionless as he moved to join Shaw. Thick, dark eyebrows rose. "Well?"

Shaw shrugged. "Plunger prolapse."

Josue laughed, squeezed Shaw's shoulder, and headed back to Scotty.

At Josue's nod, Scotty shouted, "We have a winner!"

"It's not fair!" the overgrown baby shouted before sprinting into the crowd, just a blur of blue union suit before he disappeared.

"Come on up here," Scotty called to Shaw. When Shaw got closer, he laughed and said, "I know I've written a lot of books, but not that many."

"Just these," Shaw said, lifting the largest tote.

"That looks about right," Scotty said with a smirk. "And you really want me to sign all of them?"

"Well, if it's not—"

"No, no, no. I'll do it. Because I love my fans. I owe you guys everything. I love you so much. If you were Josue, I'd take you upstairs and jack a load into you."

The crowd laughed; Josue shifted his weight and ran a hair over his cropped hair.

"Let's get a picture first. Brendon, come get my picture with—what's your name, buddy?"

"Shaw."

"Come get my picture with Shaw."

Brendon, the photographer, moved closer, snapping photos, issuing instructions on how to stand, ordering Shaw to ditch the bags full of books, and then finally standing up and nodding when he was apparently satisfied.

"All right," Scotty said. "Let's see how bad the damage is going to be." He bent, reaching into the closest bag.

"Not that one—"

But it was too late. Scotty was already pulling the wad of papers from the bag. "What's this?"

"Nothing. That's not—"

Unfolding the pages, Scotty got a tight, sharp grin. "Well, well, well, it looks like you're an author too. How's that, folks? Pretty amazing coincidence, right?"

Uneven laughter ran through the gathered men and women.

"I really didn't mean for you to—"

"No, I insist. Professional interest, you know. You might be my next big rival. Let's take a look here." When Shaw reached for the pages, Scotty held them out of reach, laughing. "Consider this a free critique; people pay five hundred dollars for me to look at their first twenty pages, so you're really getting your money's worth today. Let's see, let's see, 'Oh, Mr. Haversham, the brass handles on the card catalogue drawers are so cold.'" Scotty burst out laughing.

"I don't want you reading it," Shaw said, trying to grab the pages again.

"And then there's 'Please untie my ankles, you wicked librarian, and please give me my bliss and my release,' and then Mr. Haversham says, 'I'm afraid not, young man. No bliss and release for you. This is the only way you'll learn to obey orders and be timely with your book returns.'" Scotty's laughter was wilder this time, color mottling his cheeks, his eyes sharp and lively. "Well, buddy, I'm sorry to say it, but I don't think I have anything to worry about from you."

Shaw grabbed the pages, hoisted the bags onto his shoulders, and broke into a stumbling run.

Chapter 7

NORTH FOUND SHAW IN the hotel bar, which was called, of course, the Camelot Public House. At ten yards out, North spotted the slumped shoulders, the hectic color, the way Shaw's hands twisted and kneaded the shearling coat in his lap. North slid onto the stool next to Shaw, pulled Shaw's drink closer, and sniffed.

"Just Coke?"

Shaw nodded, his gaze still focused on smudged wood of the bar. "I wouldn't put any alcohol in it even if I wanted to. I feel sick enough already."

"I wasn't worried about alcohol; I was worried you wanted a vanilla Coke, and the last time you did that, you got so hopped up you bought half of a Toys "R" Us and spent four hours trying to fit a child-sized ATV in the Mercedes's front seat."

Shaw didn't answer. After a moment, North ran his hand through the crazy, frizzy curls that Shaw was growing out, and Shaw turned to look at him. Once again, even after all these years, North was struck by Shaw's features: by his thin eyebrows and narrow nose, the cheekbones and jaw that at first glance might look foxish, the sharp symmetry of his face, the intense hazel of his eyes. Eyes that were red rimmed now.

"What happened?"

Shaw told him.

"Stay right here," North said, shrugging out of his Carhartt coat. "I'm going to handle this."

"North, stop."

"Buy yourself another Coke. Hell, buy yourself a vanilla Coke."

"Ok, ok, I appreciate this very macho and, if I'm fully honest, kind of arousing display of protectiveness." Shaw caught his sleeve. "Let's go home. And you can say lots of threatening things and make me feel better."

"Sure. We'll go straight home. As soon as I find this fucker, knock out his teeth, and extract them through his asshole."

"He's a jerk. Just let it go. I just—it just sucks, North. It sucks. I really like his books. And he and Josue are so cute in their videos. And then I saw them together, and he says weird, overly explicit things—"

"You thought they were explicit?" North murmured. "The guy who almost faced criminal charges for hanging his peter out to dry when he decided to weed the flower beds?"

"—and he wasn't nice at all, and everybody just...just seemed to think it was ok. I don't know. And he didn't even sign my books."

"This bleeding anal cyst of a human being humiliated you after you had just proved you're one of his biggest fans, and you're upset that he didn't autograph your books?"

"I like autographed books. I like collecting those kinds of things."

North barely heard him. "And on top of everything else, he had to make up this fucking Lars character."

"How do you know about Lars?"

Too late. North tried: "Hm?"

"No way. I heard you. How do you know who Lars is? Have you been reading my books?"

"Christ, no. I'd rather read that four-hundred-and-sixty-page compendium you wrote on your extensive thoughts on which animals would look cutest in which human outfits. And I want to go on record again that a penguin wearing a head mirror and a lab coat is a 9.7, maybe a 9.8, not an 8.4. Your whole fucking algorithm is fucked up."

"North Sephora McKinney—"

"Not my middle name."

"—don't you dare avoid a direct question by bringing up adorable penguins. How do you know about Lars?"

"Apparently I am fucking Lars," North growled, seizing a handful of the mixed nuts and flagging the bartender. "Fuck my fucking life."

"Oh."

"Oh?"

Shaw must have seen something in North's face because he gulped down Coke, wiped his mouth, and said, "So, you, um..."

"Know that Scotty Carlson's main character is a construction worker named Lars with Swedish ancestry who apparently is a walking jerkoff wish-fulfillment for anyone with a Carhartt fetish? Yeah, Shaw. I figured it out when a middle-aged lady groped my ass and asked if I liked finger stuff as much as the real Lars did."

"Oh." Shaw slurped more Coke. "Do you?"

North made another grab for the bar nuts, this time knocking half of them out of the bowl.

"I didn't think it would come up," Shaw said. "The Lars thing, I mean. Well, for that matter, or the finger stuff. In my defense, I would have told you if I'd thought, you know, you'd be assaulted."

North grunted; the bartender had finally made his way over, and North ordered a Sprite. Where the bar was open on one side to one of the hotel's major hallways, a young gay couple was talking animatedly, pointing at North. North considered changing his order to a beer, never mind that it was still mid-morning.

"You know what's weird?"

"That you haven't mentioned Twerpy Twink yet."

Shaw colored. "He's not—when I had my hair long, I didn't—oh my God."

"So here we are, the two of us at a gay porn convention—"

"Romance. Romance convention. Because it's literature."

"—and we look like Scotty's STD-ridden protagonist and his annoying, on-demand fuckboy who's always interfering in his life. That's perfect, Shaw. So much for not getting noticed."

"First of all, I think it was really impressive the way you used 'protagonist' so authoritatively. It was very convincing. If I didn't know you, I would have sworn you'd read a book before."

"I do read books, Shaw. I just don't read a hundred-and-ninety pages of guys banging each other in sex slings and call it high art."

Shaw waved a hand at that. "And second of all, what better way not to be noticed at a romance convention than to blend in? The bags of books, the cosplay."

"Cosplay."

"Oh my God, your eyes just got so happy."

"No, they didn't." North sipped his drink. "I guess if they're focused on the idea that we're just playing dress-up—"

"Cosplay. You know you want to say it."

"—then they won't think about why we might actually be here." After another long drink of Sprite, North said, "I don't suppose you got a glimpse of Leslie?"

Shaw shook his head. "But do you know what's weird? Scotty said something about the death threats."

"That's strange. Heidi said something too. No, wait. It might have been the old guy, Clarence. I don't remember. They were all talking about it."

"Why didn't Yasmin keep it a secret?"

"Well," North said slowly, "keeping the threats secret probably would have been the best idea if she was worried about people cancelling their con attendance. And she seemed to want to keep people from finding out, remember? She told us she was worried about how it would affect the con-goers, and she told us someone had leaked it."

"So we need to know who Yasmin told." Shaw had his head cocked, his attention elsewhere. "Scotty thought the death threats were about him."

"Now that is strange," North said. "The first thing Heidi wanted to tell me was this story about Leslie getting into a huge fight with Scotty at last year's convention."

"I guess we need to talk to Scotty," Shaw said. "Oh God. I think you're going to have to do it; I don't think I can face him again."

"Gladly."

"And we need to see who Yasmin told about the threats."

"Just make sure you get some bail money for after I put Scotty in traction."

Shaw rolled his eyes. He waved at the bartender, signaling for a refill. North put his hand over the glass, waved the bartender off, and then caught the strap of Shaw's tank top. Tugging Shaw to his feet, North said, "And Shaw, about Scotty?"

"North, yes, I get really, um, interested when you tell me how you're going to use physical violence to protect me, but as a level-five psychic I feel like it's my responsibility as a more evolved being—"

"You're not psychic. And this isn't about me breaking Scotty's arms and using a fire hydrant as a butt plug."

"For him or for you?"

With another tug on the tank's strap, North pulled Shaw closer. His fingers rubbed the line of Shaw's clavicle, and he got a whiff of the spiky musk of whatever product Shaw used in his hair. "I just think you should know that your library stories are really, really hot. Fuck that guy for being a pretentious dickwad about them. Your library stories are fucking fantastic."

Shaw's face revealed his doubt.

"For example," North said, his face heating, "I thought we could maybe try that thing on page thirty-seven."

Shaw's eyebrows knitted together. Then, with a note of suppressed excitement, he said, "Oh!" Clearing his throat, he added, "Yeah. I'd like to try that. You know, if you want to."

"You do realize we'll have to buy the library books after? There's no way we can return them."

"If they've got those cover protectors on them, we might be able to wipe them down."

"Dear God," North muttered, tossing cash onto the bar. "This is the more-evolved being I'm stuck with. Trying to return defiled books to the library to save himself five bucks."

Chapter 8

FINDING SCOTTY WASN'T AS easy as North had hoped. They tried the lobby, but Scotty and his group of followers had vanished. In fact, the crowd had died down considerably, and the harried staff looked relieved. Then they backtracked and checked The Round Table and Camelot, but neither the hotel restaurant nor the bar showed any sign that Scotty was currently holding court.

"He could be in his room," North said, eyeing the hotel's front desk, where staff stood at several computers. "Do you want to slip and fall? Or is it my turn?"

"It's your turn. And I really think you'd be more convincing if you accepted those free acting lessons Master Hermes offers…" When North didn't bite, Shaw added, "You're always playing to the back row."

North turned a look on Shaw.

Shaw swallowed and whispered, "Sometimes less is more."

North waited a five count. "And they're not acting lessons, Shaw. He's just trying to lure me down to his sex dungeon. Incidentally, that's the same reason he keeps telling you that you'll be able to see auras more clearly in a very dark room."

"Oh, I don't think he—"

"Yes, he does. Now go away. I'm going to slip and fall and threaten to sue this place for all they're worth. And I'm going to sell the fuck out of it, Shaw, because I'm a great fucking actor."

"Actually," Shaw said, "I don't think Scotty's in his room."

"What? Why?"

"Well, it's a convention. And it's the first full day. And he's a big deal. Some authors avoid anything except the events that feature them—there's this one lady named Serenity Silver who apparently does it every year—but I've never heard anyone say that about Scotty. Why don't we check the schedule and see if he's got an event? And if he doesn't, we'll scope out the different panels and discussions and see if we can find him in the audience."

"You know a shit ton about this convention for someone who'd never mentioned it to me before yesterday."

"Well, I like the Facebook groups. I can talk about the books I like."

North frowned. "But the con was in St. Louis, and you weren't going to go?"

"We've been so busy with work." Shaw shrugged, and color flooded his face. "And I know you think this stuff is silly."

Running a hand through his hair, North took a breath. "I'm only going to say this once, so please listen and internalize it so we never have to have this discussion again: you're literally talking to a guy who owns costumes of his favorite anime characters, so maybe you shouldn't feel, you know, like there's a lot of weight behind my judgment."

Shaw's hazel eyes sparkled.

"And if you like this stuff," North said, "you should go to the con for real. As a guest. Next time, I mean."

"That would be fun if we went together."

"And then maybe we could go to Comic Con. No, don't look at me, and don't acknowledge what I just said. Pretend it didn't happen."

"I would love to go—"

"For fuck's sake, did you not hear a single word I said?" Grabbing Shaw's arm, North blew out an explosive breath and started toward the convention's registration tables.

Yasmin was sitting behind one of the folding tables, surrounded by the invisible cloud of old cigarette smoke. She and another woman were looking over a list, with Yasmin shaking her head increasingly vehemently.

"But he didn't tell us," the other woman was saying, almost in tears now. She kept pushing her hands through her hair, clutching it so that it pulled the skin on her face tight. "We got the special hypoallergenic bedding, and we got the glacier-melt bottled water, and we designated certain rooms fragrance free so that he wouldn't have a headache, but he didn't say anything about vegan meal options, and it's not fair." The last word tipped her over the edge, and she began to cry, head in her hands.

Patting the other woman's shoulder, Yasmin made consoling noises while she rolled her eyes at Shaw and North. When the other woman had recovered, Yasmin said, "It's going to be totally fine. Completely fine. You've done a fantastic job, and nobody thinks this is your fault."

"But the caterers won't—"

"We'll call around. There has to be a vegan place in the city that will do two takeout orders. We'll pick the food up, the caterers will plate it, and Scotty and Josue will never know."

"There's this great vegan takeout place on Grand," Shaw said. "They do a tapioca-starch cheese boiled in coconut milk, and they serve it over elbow noodles that are made out of lentils and chickpeas. It's North's favorite mac and cheese now."

"No," North said. "I told you that even though it looked like boiled strips of newspaper, it was barely edible."

"It's called Free and Clear."

"Because, of course, it has to sound like an acne cream."

"Oh, kind of like that one you asked me to put on your back—"

Yasmin rolled her eyes some more as she interrupted. "Can I help you with something? Oh, I emailed you some pictures of Leslie, and I already gave them to hotel security. Is that what you wanted?"

A quick glance at his phone told North he had missed the email alert; he didn't study the photos at length, but he had a glimpse of a woman who must have been in her early sixties, birdlike, her silver hair in a choppy shag that seemed too trendy for the baggy cardigan and mom jeans.

"That helps," North said, "but actually we're trying to track down Scotty Carlson."

"He's—Francie, where is he?"

The crying woman was wiping under her eyes in big, dramatic sweeps. She sniffled, grabbed an itinerary, and read hoarsely, "Ten-thirty, Superstars Spotlight, Castle Orgulous."

"A castle?" Shaw said.

"That's what they call the ballrooms and convention areas," Yasmin said. "It's a real pain in the butt. Why can't it just be Multipurpose Room C instead of Castle Blanc and Castle of Maidens and all that business."

"So Scotty Carlson is a superstar," North said. "I must have missed him on the cover of *Vogue*."

"That's because you don't read *Vogue*," Shaw said. "And I don't think they feature gay romance authors on the cover of *Cement Mixer Quarterly*."

"What time is his panel over?" North said.

Yasmin checked her watch. "Eleven-thirty, I think, but good luck catching him before the raffle-winner luncheon, and then he's moderating—Francie, what's he moderating?"

"I think it's 'Putting Your Boys to Bed,'" Francie said. "It's the pajama one."

"What the actual fuck," North muttered. "And after that?"

"After that, he's on a Q&A, and then he's running a Q&A, and then he's doing a wine-and-cheese thing, and then he's at the guests-of-honor table at the banquet, and—"

"When is he free?" North managed to cut in. "When can we talk to him."

Francie and Yasmin traded a look. "Never," Francie said simply. "He's Scotty."

"Never mind," North said. "We'll talk to him at the panel. Where's Castle Orgulous or whatever the hell it's called?"

"Up those stairs, then right, at the end of the hall."

"You mentioned a leak," Shaw said. "When we first met. Do you remember?"

Yasmin's posture stiffened, and she looked like she was trying hard not to look at Francie. She nodded.

"Do you have any idea who might have leaked that information?"

"I told two people: Serenity and Mary Angela. That's all."

Shaw nodded and glanced at North. North shrugged.

"All right," Shaw said. "We'll see where that takes us."

North started for Castle Orgulous, with Shaw at his side; behind them, Francie was saying, "What do they mean, a leak? What are they—"

"Francie, right now, I just need you to find me a vegan place. Start with the acne one he was talking about."

Following Francie's directions, North and Shaw found Castle Orgulous easily. Every seat was filled, and even the standing room along the sides and at the back was crowded. If North had to guess, he would have said the room was over capacity, although nobody looked that interested in finding the fire chief. Aside from a single banner proclaiming QUEER EXPECTATIONS, the rest of the decorations seemed to be advertisements for Scotty's books—even the table runner featured the covers of his Build-Your-Own-Bear books. Take out all the mostly naked dudes, and the event could have been picked up and transplanted to any other convention: the too-narrow folding chairs, the smell of wet wool and body odor, the room already warm enough to make North sweat and steadily getting warmer. A table at the front waited for the panelists: five seats, three mics, and bottled water.

"I cannot believe this," a woman was saying. "I just cannot believe this."

North glanced over. A woman with long, auburn hair was standing a few feet away, arms folded, glaring at the table. The right kind of man would find her attractive, North knew, although she wasn't classically pretty. Next to her stood Heidi, North's guide from earlier that morning. Heidi spotted North and gave a discreet wave, her attention mostly focused on whispering something to the woman next to her.

"Karen?" Shaw said. "What's the matter?"

"Of course you know her," North muttered.

"What's that supposed to mean?"

"She looks like trouble, so of course you know her. Fucking hell, Shaw, my weenus!"

Shaw didn't have the decency to look back as he approached the women. North, rubbing his elbow, followed.

"Is something wrong?" Shaw asked. "Are you ok?"

"We're fine," Heidi said.

The auburn-haired woman, who must have been Karen, shook her head. "We're not fine. We're nowhere near fine. This was my event. This was my idea. I told Yasmin it would be amazing if we bookended the con with panels featuring our biggest hitters. The idea was that people don't always get here for the first day, but the really famous authors get their feelings hurt if they aren't featured on the last day. So why not do both? Scotty jumped at it, of course."

"Scotty would jump into a thresher if somebody shone a spotlight on it," Heidi said. "Look, I'm really sorry about this, but I have to get up there."

"I thought you weren't an author," North said, glancing toward the table. During their short conversation, the five seats had been taken, and North recognized four faces: Scotty, Mary Angela, Clarence, and Serenity. The fifth was a leathery woman, her platinum hair in a too-short pixie cut.

"I'm not," Heidi said, squeezing Karen's arm once more. "I'm moderating."

As she slipped away, Karen gave a sniffle. "It's just not fair. It was my idea. I told Yasmin that I ought to be on the panel because I thought of it, and she agreed. Then Scotty said JD had to do it, and it's not JD's fault, so I can't even be mad at her, but it's not fair." The last part sounded close to a wail.

"How'd they make the selection? Are they the bestsellers in the genre?"

A wet laugh bubbled up, and Karen shook her head. "Hardly. Nobody reads Clarence anymore. He's a dinosaur, and they're just nice to him because he's, well, you know."

"Old?" North said.

The next laugh was more solid. "No, gay. A gay man. They're the same way with Scotty, but twenty times worse. Thirty times worse. Because he's young and hot and he's got a young, hot husband."

"So Scotty doesn't sell much either?"

"Oh no," Shaw said, swinging tote bags from his shoulders to display them. "He's very successful. His new books always top the charts."

"What about the others?"

"Mary Angela has been around for a while, but she writes good books, and they sell well. She's pretty professional. And Serenity is, well, I mean she does write a lot of books. And a lot of people like them."

North waited.

After a moment, Karen said, "She thinks she's Nora Roberts or something, so she tries to get away with treating everyone else like dirt. But she's not Nora Roberts, and honestly, the books aren't even that good, but people buy them because she puts a ton of sex in them, and that's all some people care about."

"Lot of big egos for a pretty small genre."

"You're not kidding."

"What about JD?"

Karen was silent. When North glanced at Shaw, he shook his head.

"She looks like she's really successful," Karen finally said.

Then, over the room's sound system, Heidi said, "Excuse me. Hello. Thank you for coming today. We're excited to kick off Queer Expectations 2019 with our first ever Superstars Panel. I'm pretty sure everyone knows our authors, but in case you don't, I'll be pleased to introduce them." She named each panelist, saying a few words about their best-known books or series, although North thought it was obvious she was scraping when she got to Serenity, and with JD, the praise was so vague that it could have applied to anyone. "The format of today's panel should be familiar: I'll begin by asking a few questions to get the conversation started, and while our authors are answering, I'm going to request that anyone in the audience who has a question line up over here, and you'll each have a turn to approach the microphone and ask your question." She waited for a moment and then said, "Wonderful. Let's get started with an easy one: how did you get your start writing romance?"

Four of the panelists shifted in their seats, exchanging glances, obviously trying to decide who would speak first. Scotty didn't seem to share that uncertainty. He leaned forward, grabbed the standing mic that he was obviously supposed to share with Mary Angela, and dragged it in front of him.

"Well, I guess the first thing I should say is that I'm not a romance author. I'm a literary writer. Anybody who's read my work knows that." He then launched into a convoluted story about how he became a writer. In North's completely impartial opinion, Scotty was immensely successful at making himself sound like even more of an asshat. The story meandered through various stages of sexual self-awareness, including an anecdote about being spit-roasted by his two best friends on the baseball coach's desk and a longer, more elaborate sidetrack about his first abusive relationship with a closeted man almost twenty years older than him. He even paused meaningfully, taking long drinks of the bottled water in front of him to underscore the emotions overwhelming him. Most of the audience seemed to swallow the tripe whole, leaning forward in their seats, gasping at the appropriate moments. A few people, men and women, were wiping their eyes.

North turned his attention to the other panelists. Mary Angela's face was rigid with anger, and she sat with her arms crossed, her huge eyes fixed and unseeing on some distant part of the room. Serenity had an ugly flush mottling her face. JD sat with her head cocked; of all the panelists, she seemed to be the only one listening to Scotty. Clarence kept huffing and rolling his eyes, shaking his head when Scotty dove into explicit sex.

"He can't tell a story in a straight line," North murmured, "but he sure knows how to hook people."

"That's kind of how his books are too," Shaw whispered. "All over the place, but lots of really vivid scenes that make you want to keep reading."

"Is he really a literary writer?"

"Um," Shaw looked torn, his gaze moving down the bag full of Scotty's books. "Well, the prose isn't totally mechanical, but I don't think he's going to be having lunch with Saul Bellow anytime soon."

"That's because Saul Bellow is dead."

"No, no, I'm pretty sure I saw him on C-SPAN 2 the other—"

A mousy woman shushed them viciously.

"No, wait," Shaw whispered, "I think that was Orville Redenbacher."

"He's dead too," North whispered. "And they look nothing alike."

A brittle, choppy voice broke out over the microphone: "Well, I don't think there's anything wrong with being a romance writer." Mary Angela pulled the mic back into its spot between her and Scotty. Her eyes were bulging, and she was speaking almost too quickly to be understood. "I'm proud to be a romance writer. I always tell my daughter that you shouldn't do anything in private that you wouldn't do in public, and that's true for me. I love writing romance because I love reading romance."

Scotty was leaning back in his seat, a lazy smile on his face, but his cheeks were flushed, and the look he turned on Mary Angela was hard. The silence that followed was broken only by the sound of restless bodies and the weeping of an older gay man in a sunhat.

"Maybe this question will be a follow-up to some of the answers our panelists gave. What is the current state of the romance genre?"

This time, JD swooped in, grabbing the mic in front of her.

Scotty was still faster. "The current state of the romance genre is what it's always been," he said, the words clipped and fast. "It's a dead end, an escapist fantasy for women and campy fags who can't get anyone in the real world interested in them. It's bullshit—it's total bullshit. The characters are bullshit; they're the same action-figure tops and hairdresser bottoms over and over again. The plots are bullshit; they're the same manufactured arguments, the same clichéd plots, the same tired sex scenes that wouldn't even get a horny teenager hard. And the readers are even more pathetic—I can see one of them in the back, dressed up like one of my characters. What a joke. Romance is this sad little lifeline that all the uglies and wannabes and losers cling to, this little escape hatch that lets them pretend they're special, let's them imagine someone might actually be interested in vacuuming the Oreo crumbs off their face and taking them out in the real world. That's why I don't write romance. I write real literature."

The silence that followed was a thunderclap.

"Holy shit," Shaw whispered.

Someone tittered nervously.

Mary Angela's bug-eyed gaze moved restlessly. Serenity's lips were a thin, white line. JD leaned forward, her too tan face twisted with excitement as she stretched toward the mic.

For the second time, someone else beat her to it.

Clarence patted his thinning hair and said, "I think I have to respectfully disagree with Scotty. While I'm concerned about several issues in the romance genre, notably representation and authentic voices, I think that overall, the genre is doing quite well. And while I would agree that the worst examples of our genre can be exactly what Scotty described—lackluster and formulaic, to put it kindly—the best romance writing is vivid and powerful. Yes, it's about an emotional experience. And yes, it's escapism, and it contains an element of wish fulfillment. But those aren't reasons to dismiss it. We all need to escape from reality for a minute here and there, and we all have wishes we want to see fulfilled. Doing so safely, and experiencing something beautiful in the process, is a way to explore ourselves and what it means to be human."

"I really think—" JD began.

"Spoken like a true wannabe," Scotty said. "And a true loser. It would be funny, Clarence, if it weren't so sad: the lonely little queen, with his tender little heart. No wonder you've never been able to find someone interested in fucking you—" Scotty cut off. He shivered, and he wiped his face with a shaking hand. The blush in his face was a deep scarlet. "Not even—" He seemed to have trouble swallowing, and when he spoke again, his voice was thready and wandering. "Not even with a bag over your head."

And then he arched backward in his seat, his body spasming.

"Fucking hell," North said.

"He's having a seizure," Shaw shouted. He shot forward, twisting to squeeze between people. "Help him onto the floor! Catch him!"

North charged after him, but he couldn't replicate Shaw's moves, and it took him longer to bull through the crowd. All he could do was push his way forward, watching as the participants at the table moved away from Scotty, faces frozen with surprise and horror. The whole room was locked in place, everyone staring as Scotty thrashed and gurgled.

Shaw vaulted the table, grabbing Scotty as the redhead slid from his seat. Shaw grunted, trying to maneuver Scotty's weight as he lowered him. By the time North elbowed past Clarence and Mary Angela, Shaw was on his knees, straining to lift Scotty. North knelt next to him.

"On his right side?" North asked.

Shaw nodded.

Together, they got Scotty onto his side.

"Coat," North said.

Shaw was already slipping out of the shearling coat. He folded it twice and slid it under Scotty's head. "Can you hold him on your own?"

Scotty was still jerking and twisting.

North nodded.

Shaw stood and began moving the chairs and microphone cords, clearing the area around Scotty.

Thirty seconds later, Scotty let out a soft breath, and his body went limp.

North looked around; his eyes locked with Heidi's, but she didn't seem to see him.

"Call a fucking ambulance," North roared.

Chapter 9

IN AN EMPTY BALLROOM called Wormelow Tump, Shaw and North spaced out the surviving panelists.

"We have rights," Serenity said, her bobbed black hair swinging wildly as she stood up from the seat Shaw had directed her to. "You can't keep us here. We know the law."

"We're not keeping you here," Shaw said. "We're just waiting for the police to arrive. As soon as they've talked to you, you'll be free to go."

In a chair spaced farther down the room, JD let out a racking cough and said, "We do have rights, though. We've all written our fair share of mystery novels. And we all know you have to keep the suspects separated."

"Suspects?" Clarence called from the other end of the room, his voice shrill and climbing. "Suspects?"

"But you can't force us to stay here."

"Mystery novel?" Mary Angela said to JD. She kept twisting at the waist, as though trying to make sure no one was sneaking up behind her. "You've never written a mystery novel in your life. You write romantic suspense. The mystery is about an inch deep."

"What do you know? You haven't broken the top twenty in months."

"That's because you and your skeevy friends pay for clicks and I've been so busy with my daughter—"

"Everyone shut the fuck up," North barked. "The whole point of this fucking thing is to keep you from talking to each other."

"I'm a very important woman—" Serenity began.

Heidi called out, her voice cutting through Serenity's, "Let's quietly wait for the police. This will be over soon enough."

"Easy for you to say. Nobody cares about you. I've got readers waiting for me. They won a special lunch with me, and—"

"You don't want us agreeing on details and getting our story straight," Clarence blurted out. "That's why you're trying to separate us. But if we were the killers, we would have already agreed on what to say." Everyone turned to look at him, and Clarence drew into his boxy blazer like a turtle. "Well," he mumbled, "we would have."

"Can you do something about this, please?" North said to Shaw.

"Oh my God, I thought you'd never ask." Shaw cleared his throat and projected his voice. "Wormelow Tump is a very cool name, but it's probably even cooler if you know that the *orme* in Wormelow probably comes from an Old Norse root meaning snake, and the *low* probably comes from a root meaning a rounded hill. Tump, on the other hand, doesn't have the same Norse roots, but it also seems to mean a low hill. So Wormelow Tump actually means Snake Hill Hill. Or maybe Snake Rounded Hill Small Rounded Hill. Or maybe Snake Rounded Hill Clump of Trees. Oh, that's another meaning for Tump. Or maybe Snake Hill—"

"What the fuck is he going on about?" JD screamed.

"I have no idea," North said. "I'm talking about the meditation bullshit. Yoga. Incense. Breathing exercises. Make them stand on their heads or something so they'll shut the fuck up."

"Really?" Shaw wrinkled his brow. "Right now? Doesn't that seem, you know, a little..." He wiggled his fingers.

The wild, growly noise North made in his throat was very satisfying. Shaw hid his own smile.

"I'm having a heart attack," Mary Angela shrieked. She slipped out of her chair and rolled onto the carpet squares. Her black velour leisurewear picked up lint and torn pieces of papers.

"Stay in your fucking seats," North roared.

"That was very loud," Shaw said as he jogged toward Mary Angela; the other panelists were moving toward her too. "You did an excellent job using your diaphragm."

"Jesus Christ," North muttered. "If the rest of you can't stay in your seats, at least hang back so he can take a look at her and she can get some air."

"Is he a doctor?" Clarence asked.

"You're supposed to put heart-attack victims upside down," JD shouted. "Upside down. Bend her over the chair."

"No, no," Heidi yelled. "On her side. Her side!"

"Shut up! All of you shut up!"

Silence blanketed the room. Outside Wormelow Tump, someone was playing tinny music. Selena, all these years later, was still dreaming of you. Mary Angela didn't look good. She was sweating and trembling, her pupils were dilated. She moaned and then farted.

JD's leathery face contorted with a struggle. A giggle slipped free. JD was still giggling when Mary Angela scrambled onto her hands and knees and puked. Everyone else backed up, and several people gagged.

"What's wrong?" Shaw asked as he knelt next to Mary Angela, helping her lie down away from the vomit. "What hurts?"

"My head," Mary Angela said. "And my chest."

"Show me."

"I'm having a heart attack. I'm dying."

Clarence wobbled, but when Shaw looked up, he just waved a hand. "I'm dizzy, that's all. And my head's killing me."

"Me too," JD said on the tail of his words. "And I might throw up."

"Then find a corner and shut up," North said.

JD's shoulders drew up, but she didn't say anything else.

"Show me where it hurts," Shaw said again.

Mary Angela touched her stomach, even though she had said chest, and Shaw glanced up at North and frowned. North shrugged.

"How many of the rest of you are feeling headaches, trembling, stomach or chest pains? Or dizziness?"

A murmur of assents ran through the crowd.

"We've been poisoned," Serenity wailed. "Someone's trying to poison me."

"Oh shut up." Heidi glanced around. "All of us?"

Nods confirmed her words.

"Where did everyone eat breakfast?" Heidi asked. "No, it couldn't be that because Scotty had one of his very specific vegan meals. What about the water?"

"What water?" Clarence said.

"The bottled water at the panelist table. Did we all drink some?"

More nods.

"You weren't a panelist," JD said, pointing at Heidi. "Why would you be feeling sick? That's suspicious."

"For the love of God," North said. "This is not a drawing-room mystery."

"They always provide a bottle of water for the moderator," Heidi said. "Believe it or not, we're human beings too."

Serenity sneered at that, but her gaze went quickly back to Mary Angela.

"It may be a heart attack," Shaw said, "but it doesn't sound like one. It sounds like you were all given some sort of stimulant."

"Like cocaine," Serenity said. Then she flushed, brushing back some of the black bob with a gesture she had probably meant to look casual. "It feels like that. Not the good way, but my heart is pounding, and I'm shaky."

"All right," Shaw said. "We'll tell the police. They'll take you to the hospital anyway, but at least we can help them—"

"I want to know right now." Mary Angela sat upright, reaching for her purse. "I might be dying. I want to know right this minute."

"For a woman just having a heart attack, you're sure hopping around," North said.

She ignored him, digging through her voluminous purse. She emerged with a capped plastic cup and an oblong object in sealed packaging. "If it's just cocaine, I want to know."

"Is that an over-the-counter drug test?" Shaw asked.

"I deserve to know. I have a right to know. If I'm dying, I want to—"

"All right, all right," North said. He glanced at Shaw.

"I don't think it'll hurt," Shaw said. "Although I'm sure they'll test her again when they get her to the hospital."

"I want to go to the bathroom," Mary Angela said.

"I want to be tested too." JD elbowed Serenity out of her way. "I want to know if I was drugged too. I have a right—"

"Unless you're conveniently carrying around your own drug test," North said, "be quiet and sit down."

An unspoken question made everyone look at Mary Angela. Her eyes bulged, and her hands curled protectively around the plastic cup and the foil-wrapped testing device. "It's for my daughter." Her voice was stiff. "I always have to have one on me."

"I'll take her," Shaw said, extending a hand to help Mary Angela to her feet. "If you think you can keep this rowdy bunch under control without me."

North crossed his arms.

"I know it'll be hard, but it's time for you to stand on your own two feet."

North slowly extended a middle finger.

"I believe in you," Shaw said with what he hoped was an encouraging smile.

North was still swearing enough to blister the air when Shaw let the Wormelow Tump door fall shut behind him.

"He's very creative," Mary Angela said hesitantly.

"He spends too much time on Urban Dictionary. Let's find a restroom."

They found a family restroom, which consisted of a single room, and Shaw insisted on keeping Mary Angela's purse when she stepped through the door.

"Just in case," Shaw said.

"In case of what?"

He smiled, and he held on to the purse.

She locked the door. The water ran. A few minutes later, she opened the door. "Well?" she asked, giving her bottle-blond hair another tug. "Want to see?"

The plastic cup had been set aside and capped, and the testing device—a dip panel—lay flat on the countertop. Shaw started a timer on his phone. Four minutes and forty-three seconds had passed when the amphetamines band began to turn pink. Over the course of the next minute, the color deepened. Shaw read the other labels on the panel, twelve in total: THC, Cocaine, Opiate, Methamphetamines, Oxycodone, Amphetamine, Barbiturates, Benzodiazepines,

Methadone, MDMA, PCP, and PPX. Only the amphetamines band changed color.

"All right," a man's voice, familiar, said from outside the bathroom. "Both of you come out of there."

Shaw opened the door and found himself face to face with Jadon Reck, his former boyfriend, lead detective on the Metropolitan Police's LGBTQ crime squad.

Chapter 10

BACK IN WORMELOW TUMP, Shaw waited for the explosion.

Jadon stayed behind while his partner, a woman named Cao, herded the remaining panelists downstairs and into waiting patrol cars. He was watching North and Shaw, hands on his hips, his face an unreadable mask.

"We're not under arrest, are we?" Shaw asked.

Jadon let out a weary breath. His face looked thin, and dark hollows marked his eyes; he'd been beaten and tortured in September, almost killed, and the effects of the attack still showed in his body.

"I know we're not," Shaw said. "Logically, I know you're probably just going to take us down to the station to talk to us. But you look really, really angry. Maybe. Or sad. Or like that one time we listened to deconstructed bluegrass until you told me you had a headache and you needed some quiet. So, you know, it'd be nice to hear you say that we aren't under arrest."

Nothing.

Jadon had very nice eyes; Shaw was currently being reminded of this fact. They were a soft brown, matching the darkly sandy coloring of his hair and skin. Like a very hot beach bum had gotten drafted into the NFL, built up lots and lots of muscle, and then decided to go cop. And the man knew how to wear a suit.

"Eyes off his junk, if it's not too much to ask," North said. His hand settled on Shaw's shoulder in a way that was unmistakably possessive, and Shaw was going to tell him exactly how dehumanizing that was, and how it sprang from a culture of toxic masculinity, as soon as he stopped liking it so much.

"Actually," Shaw said, "I was looking at his legs. His thighs, in particular."

"That's not better."

"Does it help if I tell you it's purely physical?"

"No."

"I'm objectifying him as much as I can, North."

"You know what?" North said, his eyes moving to Jadon. "You can have him."

"Pass," Jadon said, some of the stiffness in his face and posture relaxing into a smile. "Why should I not be surprised to find the two of you caught up in this?"

"Hi, Jadon."

"Hi, Shaw. North. Want to tell me what's going on here?"

So they told him.

"All right," Jadon said. "We'll take it from here."

"Of course," North said. "We wouldn't dream of doing the Metropolitan Police's job for them."

"Guys, come on. You're not going to make me be a hardass about this, are you? Your job's over. You can wrap up and go back to your normal work, the corporate stuff you've been doing."

"A hardass?" North's eyebrows arched. "Gee, Shaw. We don't want that, do we?"

"Be nice. Jadon, our job isn't exactly finished. We were hired to find Leslie Hawkins and see if she's behind the threats Yasmin was receiving. We still haven't been able to track her down."

"And now it's gone beyond a case of harassment," Jadon said. His voice was level. His eyes were not. "If the toxicology tests come back the way we expect, it'll be assault, possibly attempted murder. I'm going to ask you one more time to be professionals about this and let it go. Your part is done."

"Exactly," North said, his hand tightening on Shaw's shoulder. "Our part is done, Shaw. Time to leave it to the Metropolitan boys."

"North," Shaw said quietly.

"No, he's right. We'll just hang back. When they fall assbackward the first time they turn around, we'll just be sitting back and watching."

Shaw groaned.

Jadon opened his mouth, but before he could respond, his phone buzzed. He checked the screen. "Cao's waiting for us; let's go. I'll try to make it as quick as possible."

"One-liners from the Jadon Reck Bedroom Collection," North said.

"Enough," Shaw whispered furiously.

Whether it had been North's remark or simple logistics, they were at the police station for hours. Jadon's partner, Detective Cao, was too thin to be called athletic, practically swallowed up by her polyester suit. Acne scars pitted her cheeks, and the incredibly tight ponytail made things worse somehow. She must have known about their complicated history with Jadon, including the fact that they had been responsible for his last partner's arrest, but she didn't let any of it show in how she treated them. From the beginning, when she informed them that their conversation was being recorded, through the questions about their involvement with Scotty's poisoning, she was quiet and professional. When she had finished the questions, she led them to a desk in the LGBTQ squad room, where they waited. And waited. And waited.

"Fuck this," North said, standing. "Let's call an Uber."

"I don't think we should—"

"I know what you think, but I'm done sitting around with my dick in my hand."

"Freshman year, you were sitting around with your dick in your hand every time I went in your room. You seemed to like it back then."

North grunted.

"Literally every time. I had to start knocking, North. I was visually traumatized."

"Normal people always knock before barging into someone else's bedroom, Shaw. And it was one time, and I was checking myself. For cancer."

Shaw nodded. "With lube."

"God damn it."

They were making their way toward the door when Jadon stepped into the squad room. "Oh. Good." He shook his head. "Sorry about the wait; we had another attack, and I was shuttling your friends back to the hotel. I'll give you a ride."

"Another attack at the con?" Shaw said. "What happened? Who?"

"No, sorry. I'd say it's an ongoing investigation and I can't comment, but you've probably already seen it in the papers: someone is attacking gay youth." Jadon paused. "It's bad. This guy is escalating. He's going to beat one of these boys to death pretty soon."

Shaw and North shared a look. "Hustlers?" North said.

"It's an ongoing investigation," Jadon said with a sharp smile. "I can't comment on that."

"But it's two in the afternoon," Shaw said, glancing at his phone. "Are boys hustling in broad daylight? And someone drove up and attacked one of them?"

"The attacker takes them somewhere else. And this happened last night; someone just found the boy today." Jadon set his jaw.

"Bad?"

"The way the kid looks, it might be a homicide case by tonight."

"Is it always the same kind of boy?" Shaw said. "Dark-haired, fair, redhead, skinny, young?"

Jadon nodded. "I'm tempted to say that's the only good part—random attacks and killings are a cop's nightmare—but there's nothing good about any of it."

"What do they look like?" North asked.

For a moment, Jadon's gaze hovered on Shaw, then he shook his head.

"You don't seem to have any trouble answering Shaw's questions."

"That's because I like him. Come on, I'll drop you at your car. Sorry again it took me so long."

"Another one-liner from the Bedroom Collection."

Jadon drove them back to the Royal Excalibur, and he stopped his car at the GTO. He looked each of them in the eye and said, "Stay out of this. Get in your car and go home, refund these nice ladies whatever money is left over. The next time, I'm not going to be talking to you as a friend."

"Aye aye," North said, opening the car door.

"Shaw, please talk some sense into him."

"Good fucking luck with that one," North said.

Shaw and North made a show of getting into the GTO, starting the engine, and backing out of the parking stall. North took as long as possible to complete each step. By the time the GTO was pointed toward the garage's exit, Jadon seemed to have run out of patience—or another emergency called. He merged out into traffic.

"What a fucking walking ball-blister," North said as he parked the GTO again. They got out, leaving the tote bags full of books in the car this time, and headed toward the Royal Excalibur.

"You're supposed to be nice to him," Shaw said, poking North in the ribs as soon as Jadon was out of sight. "You're supposed to be civil at the bare minimum. He's our friend."

"He's your friend. Or something. And he shouldn't look at you like he's planning on fucking you into your next existence. And he also shouldn't ask for a dick-measuring contest when we've done his job for him God knows how many times over the last few years."

They were approaching the hotel's parking-garage entrance when quick footsteps sounded behind them.

"You have to solve this!" Yasmin scurried toward them, carrying the smell of cigarette smoke with her. "You have to. You have to figure out who did this!"

"What are you—"

"They made me go down for questions too. I just got back." She drew in a shivering breath, glanced around the icy concrete shell, and said, "God, I need a smoke. Do you mind?"

"Well, actually," Shaw began.

"Fantastic." Yasmin worked a pack of Virginia Slims Silver out of her purse. She lit one, turning her back to a gale of freezing wind that whipped through the garage, and drew hard on the cigarette. "Oh. My. God. One pack a day my fanny."

"Yasmin, we're happy to do what you hired us to do." Shaw sidestepped to avoid an eddy of smoke. "Find Leslie, I mean, and figure out if she's behind those threats. But what happened today, the attack on Scotty and the other panelists—"

"What do you mean? Someone tried to kill Scotty."

"But at least one other panelist tested positive for amphetamines," North said. "And they all reported the same symptoms. Someone could have been lying, of course, but what makes the most sense is that all the bottles were tainted. That would be one way to be sure that a target, if there was one, got the drugged water."

"But someone tried to kill Scotty. How can you ask if there was a target?"

"Because maybe they were all the target. Or maybe someone else was, but Scotty was affected more strongly. If all the water bottles were tainted, then a lot of possibilities open up. We don't want to focus exclusively on Scotty. Not yet, anyway."

"You have to solve this," Yasmin muttered around feverish puffs. "You have to."

"And we'll do our best to do what you paid us—" Shaw said.

"Not that. I mean, yes, you need to find Leslie and see if she's behind this. But you have to solve the whole thing."

"That's really something the police—"

"You don't understand." Yasmin's teeth crimped the cigarette's filter so tightly they threatened to shear through it. "We're always one year away from going under. The con, it's not this huge moneymaker. And we're committed to a hotel for next year. People are already talking about not going. If that happens, we're still on the hook for all the expenses, and we'll be bankrupt. No more Queer Expectations."

"They're already talking about not going?" North said. "It's a year away. They'll have forgotten—"

Yasmin was shaking her head, the cigarette's ember flaring. "You don't know this crowd. They're very tight-knit, and they'll turn on you in a flash. On top of that, they're anxious, or sensitive, or delicate little snowflakes. Pick your word. A couple years ago, we almost had to cancel because one crusader was mad we hadn't made an official ban on attendees wearing cologne or perfume. I mean, it's one thing after another." She closed her eyes, waved the cigarette, and made a choked noise. After a moment, when she had mastered herself, she opened her eyes and said, "If we can't turn this around, we're sunk. People are going to freak out, and they'll never come back. But if we can turn it into a publicity stunt—I know I'm an awful human being, I know I am—but if we can turn it around, and have gay private detectives and the whole thing is sensational and exciting, then it might actually work the opposite way. Everybody wins: we find who did this, we keep people safe, and we save Queer Expectations. People will flock to the con next year."

Shaw looked at North.

North shook his head in a no.

Shaw kept looking.

No, North mouthed.

A Volvo drove past, a cloud of exhaust, warm and sweet, in its wake.

"For fuck's sake," North said. "We're going to play it by ear for now. We'll see what we can do. That is not a contract. When it gets to the point that the police have to be involved, we're letting them handle things."

"And we'll do our best to spin it the way you want," Shaw said.

"That is not a verbal contract," North said, "and it is not a guarantee or a promise or in any way a binding offer."

Yasmin blinked. "Yes, of course. Thank you. Oh my God, thank you!"

"Let's start with opportunity," North said.

"The water?" Shaw said.

North nodded. "Who had access? Who did the setup for that panel? If we need to look at the hotel staff—"

But Yasmin was already shaking her head. "I did. And Clarence."

"You set up that multipurpose room? The chairs and all that?"

"I thought hotels did that for you," Shaw said.

"Not the chairs and tables. But we often have very particular authors, and so after a debacle five or six years ago, I started doing all the amenities myself. Well, with some help. Clarence is a sweetheart. And some of the readers like Francie, they usually help. It's like that. So Clarence and I set up the water."

"And Clarence was on the panel." Shaw shoved his hands into the pockets of his shearling coat; his breath was still steaming in the garage's frozen shadows. "That's interesting."

Yasmin shifted her weight, plucking the cigarette from her mouth to wave it around again. "I don't even want you thinking something like that. He's a total sweetheart."

"Call him," North said. "See if he's back from the hospital."

Yasmin tapped her phone a few times and held it to her ear. "Clarence, are you ok? Yes. Yes, I know. I'm so sorry—listen, dear, are you back? Those gay detectives want to talk to us. Ok. Well, if he does that to you, I want you to tell me all about it after. Ok, sweetness, we'll meet you there." Sliding the phone back into her purse, she smirked at North. "You've got an admirer."

"Fantastic. I'll shuffle him into the deck of psychos I already have to deal with."

"Don't worry," Shaw said to Yasmin. "He doesn't mean me."

"I surely fucking do," North growled, grabbing him by the arm and steering him toward the hotel.

Chapter 11

NORTH FOLLOWED YASMIN ALONG one of the hotel's smaller corridors, Shaw trailing at his side. Judging by the lack of artwork and the reduced dimensions, he guessed that this was the updated equivalent of a servants' hallway. They passed a laundry, the air hot and humid and smelling like too-sweet detergent. They passed several offices in a row, with steel security doors, and they passed a kitchen where two skinny white boys were loading a commercial dishwasher, the clatter of ceramic and stainless steel mixing with the rush of running water. A brown-skinned girl in a chef's hat was sitting on a stool, vaping as she read the *New York Times* Lives column. Somewhere along the hall, someone was playing Radiohead.

Shaw ducked into the kitchen and spoke quietly to the girl in the chef's hat. She pointed him deeper into the kitchen, and for a moment, he passed out of North's line of sight.

"What's he doing?" Yasmin said.

"Probably trying to replace all their snack foods with activated charcoal and then hoping they won't notice."

"Did he—"

"Don't ask."

Shaw came back, nodded at North, and they continued down the hall.

"The hotel gives us a small storage space," Yasmin said. "It's really not enough—I have to keep some of the stuff in my trunk, believe it or not—but we try to keep all the food and drink items locked up inside the hotel. Then, if there's still room, we bring in whatever else will fit in the space they give us."

"Did you lock up the food and drink because you were worried someone would tamper with them?"

"No," Yasmin said. "Because some of our visitors have food allergens, and we need to be able to guarantee that something is nut-free or soy-free." Blushing, she added, "And because one year, I kept it in my room, and someone was stealing bottles of wine. That was ten years ago, though, so I don't think it has anything to do with this."

"Fatal last words," North muttered.

Yasmin stopped at an unmarked door. It had a standard latch, the lock built into the handle—the kind of security that was meant as a deterrent, not a genuine safeguard. Above the handle, though, someone had installed a hasp that was secured with a padlock. Yasmin produced a key, removed the padlock, and opened the door.

"The lock on the handle isn't set?" North asked.

Yasmin shook her head. "I think they only use that one when guests aren't using the storage space."

"And who has a key to the padlock?"

"Me. I'm the only one."

"Ok. Let's take a look."

From down the hall, Clarence came towards them. He was carrying a bag over one shoulder that said QUEER EXPECTATIONS 2019 – SPONSORED BY JD HATHAWAY. When he reached them, he ran one hand over his sweaty forehead. "Sorry. Ran all the way. God, I don't know the last time I ran anywhere." He followed North's gaze to the bag he was carrying, gave a mock groan, and adjusted the weight. "Swag. I swear these bags get heavier every year."

"You need to add some strength training to all that cardio," Yasmin said. "Stop torturing yourself running marathons."

"What kind of swag?" Shaw said.

"Buttons, pens, things like that. Hello, Mr. McKinney. Hello, Mr.—I'm sorry, I don't know your name."

"Shaw Aldrich."

"My partner," North added.

Shaw must have sensed the undercurrent in North's words because he wrinkled his brow, but Clarence just nodded, smiled, and shook Shaw's hand.

"We were just confirming with Yasmin that nobody else has a key to the padlock," North said.

"That's true as far as I know." Clarence glanced at Yasmin and continued, "I don't have one, if that's what you're asking."

"And you don't know if anyone else does?"

"No one should."

"Doesn't that get inconvenient?" Shaw said. "Every time you need something, you're the one who has to come down here and get it?"

With a jittery laugh, Yasmin nodded. "Very inconvenient. Very irritating. But if I do it myself, it gets done right."

"Tell me about it," North said. "Try finding an invoice that's about to go into the mail, and the client report only says, 'We watched people having sex. Thank you.'"

"It's polite to say thank you," Shaw said. "That's just good manners."

Sighing, North waved Yasmin aside. He held out a hand, and Shaw passed over a pair of disposable gloves that North knew he'd gotten from the kitchen. North removed the lock from the hasp, touching it as little as possible, and placed it in a plastic bag—also courtesy of the Royal Excalibur's kitchen. When Yasmin raised her eyebrows, he said, "This isn't exactly a masterpiece of sophistication. I could pick it in a few minutes, and if I did it when the hall was empty, I could be in and out of this room without anyone noticing."

"Oh my God," Yasmin whispered.

"Except the security camera," Shaw said, pointing to the ceiling.

North grunted as he pushed the storage room door open.

"North has problems with his vision," Shaw said quietly.

"I can see perfectly fucking well, thank you." When North's fingers caught the switch, he flipped it, and a fluorescent panel flickered to life overhead, buzzing in fits and starts. The storage room was small, and steel shelving lined the walls. The shelves were loaded with housekeeping supplies: rolls of trash bags, toilet paper, and paper towels; gallon jugs of Fabuloso; tiny, individually wrapped bars of soap. An artificial, floral smell hung in the air, which North guessed was somehow related to a stain on the carpet. On one shelf, someone had shoved a threadbare King Arthur costume, complete with a giant plastic head. Opposite the door they entered, a second door led out of the storeroom.

"The first time I realized he needed glasses was when he was squinting incredibly hard to see a boy's nipples."

"That's not what happened. There was a bumper sticker. I had something in my eye. Jesus Christ, Shaw. Can I have five minutes to work in silence?"

"I carry a pair of cheaters with me," Shaw whispered. "Just in case he needs them."

North moved along the shelves until he saw a section stocked with coffee cans, granola bars, foam cups, and most importantly, bottled water. He glanced over at Yasmin.

Nodding, she said, "That's our stuff. They didn't exactly leave us a lot of space."

"Did you keep any water in your car?"

"No, just random stuff that I didn't want someone walking off with from my room. Tablecloths, because sometimes the hotels run out. Or Tide pens, for example. You wouldn't believe how many authors spill on themselves."

"That's not the same brand," Shaw said.

North cocked an eye at him.

"The water on the table. The water the panelists were drinking. It was a different brand."

"He's right," Yasmin said. "Scotty can be very particular. He insisted at the last minute on having a certain kind of water. I'd already bought what you see here, so I ran out yesterday to get a pack just for the panel today. I was planning on buying another before his panel on Saturday."

"How many bottles were in the pack?" North said.

"Six."

"And why did you set one out for every panelist, not just Scotty?"

"You saw how they are." Yasmin waved a hand. "Most of them, their egos are so fragile they'll pop if I breathe on them wrong. Sorry, Clarence."

Clarence grinned, and the expression made him look surprisingly youthful. "You're not wrong. Can you imagine Mary Angela if she knew Scotty was getting his own special water? Or Serenity? Good God."

"Five bottles for the panelists," Shaw counted them on his fingers. "Plus one bottle for Heidi, who was moderating. That's six."

"All right," North said. "Talk us through everything after you picked up the bottled water."

"We have a few activities on Wednesday to kick everything off: registration, a meet-and-greet, and a cocktail hour. That's where I went after hiring you two. There's time between the meet-and-greet and cocktails for people to go get dinner if they want, so that's when I slipped out to buy the water for Scotty."

"By yourself?"

Yasmin shook her head. "Heidi went with me. And Rodney and Jerry."

"And me," Clarence said, raising a hand. When North looked at him, he shrank back and smoothed his thinning hair.

"And they all could have seen you buy the water?"

"They all did see me buy the water. We went into a grocery store. It's in walking distance. Strad's?"

"Straub's," Shaw supplied.

"That's right. Anyway, we all went inside. Rodney and Jerry were picking up a few things—they like to have all their drink supplies stocked in their room—and Heidi and Clarence just tagged along. I bought the water. I brought it back to the hotel because I didn't want to lug it to dinner. I locked it up here, we left, and we got a quick bite at a Korean-fusion place that's just a few minutes away. I didn't come back to the storeroom until this morning."

"What happened this morning?" Shaw asked.

"The hotel gave us a cart. We use it to move water, snacks, coffee urns. Well, usually the hotel staff takes care of the coffee, but I like to handle the rest of it myself. This morning, Clarence and I met here, and we loaded the cart together."

"And we cleaned up an entire bottle of Fabuloso that got knocked off the shelf," Clarence said with a roll of his eyes.

Yasmin barely seemed to hear him. "We took the cart upstairs together and set up Castle Orgulous for the panel, and then we set up the rest of the rooms."

"What time was this?"

"Eight?" Yasmin said, looking to Clarence.

He nodded. "Around then."

"What happens to the convention rooms before the panels start?"

"The doors are locked until the moderator gets there," Yasmin said. "We've had people leave…presents for authors in the past. We try to avoid that now."

"So nobody could have gotten to the water once you put it on the table?"

"Not unless hotel staff unlocked the room for them. Even I don't have a key to those doors; the staff lets me in to set up, and then the doors are locked again until the panel starts."

"And you didn't mind setting up your own panel?" North asked, his gaze shifting to Clarence.

"We're friends." Clarence shrugged. "Besides, it gives me a reason not to get dragged into all the socializing. I enjoy these events, but most of the people are younger and, if I'm being honest, not exactly my school of fish."

"Did either of you leave the storeroom this morning? Did you ever leave the other one alone, even for a minute?"

"Are you suggesting—"

"North's asking what the police are going to ask," Shaw said quietly. "We need to know who had access to the water, and right now, you two look like the only ones who could have gotten to it."

Clarence had bright spots of color in his cheeks. He flattened his thinning hair with one trembling hand. "No. We stayed together the whole time. Even taking the cart upstairs and setting up everything."

"That's right." Yasmin looked ready to cry. Or chain-smoke the hell out of some Virginia Slims. Or both. "We were together. Neither of us could have done it, not unless you think we were in on it together."

That was certainly a possibility North was willing to consider, but for the moment, he said, "Thank you."

"And that door?" Shaw said.

Yasmin shook her head. "It connects to the banquet hall. I can't remember what the room is called—"

"Tintagel," Clarence said.

"—but it's locked, and only hotel staff have a key. I think they use it if they need to get in here when a guest has the other door locked."

North gave the door another considering look. Then he took two steps, touched the handle minimally to avoid disturbing latent prints, and applied pressure.

The handle turned, and the door swung open, revealing the empty, darkened space of Tintagel on the other side.

"It was locked," Clarence said, glancing at Yasmin.

She nodded furiously. "Clarence locked it last night. I was standing right here; I saw him do it. It was locked. I swear it was locked."

"Well," Shaw said, in what he obviously thought was a helpful tone, "it's not locked now."

Chapter 12

THE CONVERSATION WENT NOWHERE after that; no matter how North tried, he couldn't pin Clarence and Yasmin down on any slips or inconsistencies. A brief conversation with the hotel's day manager was peppered with phrases like "inconsistent with policies" and "not in keeping with hotel protocol," but the bottom line was that the manager couldn't guarantee that one of her staff hadn't unlocked the storeroom, and she refused to let North and Shaw look at the security footage.

After finally shaking off Clarence and Yasmin, North and Shaw found a Kayak's Coffee inside the Royal Excalibur. The coffee shop was crowded with men and women wearing Queer Expectation badges on lanyards. The tendency in this crowd, North saw, was toward bright eyed and bushy tailed.

"If these people get any more excited," North muttered, "they're going to start a fire just by rubbing elbows."

"I know," Shaw said, beaming as he looked around. "Isn't it awesome?"

North grunted and looked at his phone.

"Everything ok?"

"Ronnie," was his only answer.

"Well, I think it's great that these people are so excited," Shaw said. "They know what they like, and they're enjoying themselves. That sounds like a really good way to have a happy life."

"Fine. Whatever." Then, because North couldn't help himself: "It wouldn't kill them to be cool about it, though."

"This is the perfect opportunity to talk about how a culture of emotional repression—"

"Mr. McKinney? I thought that was you." It was Rodney or Jerry— whichever one was wearing the pearl-snap shirt. He laughed. "Well, at first I thought it was another Lars cosplayer, but then I recognized you."

"He does look like Lars, doesn't he?" Shaw said.

"No," North said. "I don't."

"He really does," Rodney/Jerry said. "And don't tell me you're—"

Shaw flushed. "I know, I know. Twerpy Twink. He made me dress up this way."

"Hold on," North said. "Never in my life—"

"It's adorable," Rodney/Jerry said. "Do you guys need a table? We're—"

"No," North said. Too quickly. Shaw stepped on his foot.

With a pained smile, Rodney/Jerry continued, "—just leaving."

"Oh," North said.

"One of you guys ought to sit down and save the table," Rodney/Jerry said. "This place is only going to get more crowded."

"Yeah," North said. "Thanks." He ducked under the retractable belt barrier, followed Rodney/Jerry to a two-top where his other half was waiting. The men gathered their belongings, and the one in the pearl-snap shirt offered North a tight smile. "Thanks again," North said. Neither Rodney nor Jerry answered.

North watched the crowd shift and eddy. A few minutes later, Shaw appeared carrying two large coffees.

"I got yours black," Shaw said. "So you can feel extra butch."

"I don't drink my coffee black because it makes me feel butch. I drink it black because that's how my dad drinks it, so that's how I grew up. I just got used to it."

Shaw ignored him. "And I got mine unicorn-style so I can feel extra gay."

"You can't feel extra gay," North said. "You're always the same amount of gay."

"I can always be gayer. And you shouldn't be rude to those guys; they're just trying to be nice." Shaw popped off the lid of his coffee, exposing a rainbow swirl inside the cup. "It's not their fault you choose to dress like a cartoon construction worker or whatever you're supposed to be."

"I'm not supposed to be anything. I'm just me. Wearing my normal clothes. And what the fuck is that?"

"Unicorn style. But you probably wouldn't like it. It's super gay and definitely not cool."

North leaned back in his chair, sighed, and covered his face. Through his hands, he said, "Ok. What do I have to do?"

"I don't know what you're talking about. Besides, I'd hate for you to go out of your comfort zone."

"Great. This is exactly what I need on top of everything else. Can we talk about the case, please?"

"The door was unlocked."

North nodded. "And it could have been unlocked anytime between five pm last night and eight the next morning. That's fifteen hours that the water was accessible."

"So anybody could have slipped away long enough to get inside the storeroom, tamper with the water, and get back to their party or their room. If they went during the middle of the night, they wouldn't even need to worry about an alibi."

"All right." North slid a hand toward the unicorn-style latte. Shaw was off in shawland, hazel eyes dreamy, and North took a quick sip. It was fantastic. Sweet, but not too sweet. It tasted kind of like a sugar cookie had a baby with the best espresso. North returned the cup, wiped his mouth, and said, "That means we have to change our approach. Access to the water isn't going to help us find whoever drugged Scotty and the other panelists."

"And we don't know what drug they used," Shaw said, his voice slow and sleepy from inside shawland. "So that means we can't narrow it down by means either, although it wouldn't hurt to have a look at the drugs people are carrying around."

"So we're back to good, old-fashioned motive," North said before sneaking another sip of the unicorn latte. "And from what I saw, anybody who spent five minutes in the same room as Scotty had a reason to want to hurt him. If that's what they were trying to do."

"I'm not sure it was." Shaw's gaze sharpened, and for some reason, his lips twitched in a smile when he glanced at North. "I'm not sure what they were trying to do. If it was attempted murder, an amphetamine is a strange choice unless there's no other option—or unless Scotty has an underlying condition that would make him vulnerable to a heart attack or stroke or whatever we saw today."

"Josue?"

Shaw nodded. "Statistically, the partner is the most likely killer, although I think those statistics are primarily about women. I think it makes sense to talk to him first." He slid out of his chair. "I'm going to the restroom. Sit here for, oh, about two minutes. Then I'll meet you in the lobby. Please don't drink any more of my latte."

"I didn't—"

"Rainbow foam," Shaw said, tapping the corner of his mouth.

"God damn it." North wiped it away. "Kingsley Shaw Wilder Aldrich, why am I supposed to sit here for two minutes?"

"I love you," Shaw sang as he headed for the Kayak's exit.

Coos and awws followed him as men and women in the crowd gripped each other's hands in excitement. One guy said, "Twerpy Twink" loud enough for everyone else, and then a woman picked up on it with, "And he's with his Lars, oh my God, isn't it adorable?"

"No," North called across the room. "It damn well fucking isn't."

For some reason, that just made them all coo some more.

"North," a barista called from the pickup counter. He flashed a huge smile as he displayed a cup. On the sticker with North's name, someone—presumably this barista with his huge smile—had added rainbows and the words MY SUPERPOWER IS BEING SUPER GAY. North popped the top and saw a unicorn latte waiting for him. He dropped the black coffee in the trash and carried Shaw's latte and his own out into the lobby.

Shaw met his eyes and mimed zipping his lips.

North kissed his cheek.

"Without going into the specifics of what just happened," Shaw said, "this is a great launching point to talk about—"

"Nope," North said.

The compromise, it turned out, was holding Shaw's hand as they went in search of Josue Carlson.

Chapter 13

THEY FOUND JOSUE IN the Royal Excalibur's presidential suite, which was about what Shaw had expected. A roller bag held the door open, and after a glance at North, Shaw stepped inside. Thick, high-quality carpet, green with a damask rose pattern, immediately replaced the worn, red squares from the hallway. The walls were papered with a green-and-white stripe, and the light fixtures were brass with big, electric chandelier bulbs. From deeper in the suite came the sound of low voices, and Shaw headed down a short hall toward them.

The suite's sitting room was done in the same style: chintz sofas, ceramic figurines that were probably meant to be Arthur and his knights, prints of Pre-Raphaelite paintings in huge gold frames. Josue was sitting in an armchair upholstered in a chevron linen that reminded Shaw, like everything else in the suite, of his grandmother's Ladue condo. On Josue's lap rested a leather dopp kit, which Josue was digging through. The photographer, Brendon, was pacing the length of the room behind the chair. He froze when he saw them.

"Josue."

"I don't care if you don't like it," Josue snapped without looking up. "He's my husband, and I—"

"Somebody's here."

Josue's head came up. He drew in a sharp breath, which only accented his hollow cheeks, and his fingers tightened around the dopp kit. The leather dimpled under the force of his grip. "Who are you? Wait. You're the guy from the contest. This isn't—I don't know what you think you're doing, but you need to leave. It was a dumb game, and I'm sorry Scotty treated you like that, but he's not going to make it up to you, and you're not going to be best friends or whatever you're hoping might happen. Jesus, if he saw the two of you dressed like that, he'd lose his mind. You need to go. My husband is in the hospital, and I—I just need you to go."

"Let's start with some introductions," North said. "North McKinney. Shaw Aldrich. We're investigating the assault that happened today."

"You're with the police?" Brendon asked.

"No."

"What assault?" Josue said.

"The tampered water," Shaw said. "That's technically assault."

"Don't talk to them," Brendon said. "They're probably working for—"

"Will you shut up?" Josue released the dopp kit, set it aside, and stood. He eyed Shaw and North. "What do you want? Is this to help Scotty?"

"We're trying to figure out who did this," North said. "Do you think that's what Scotty would want?"

"Obviously. If only to spend the next twenty years crucifying them in public. Can you imagine how happy he's going to be when he starts feeling better? Scotty's the master of spinning a crisis into an opportunity. This is everything he wants handed to him on a silver platter: talk shows, interviews, probably a memoir deal. He's the author that someone tried to poison; *madre de Dios*, if he weren't worried about the PR, he'd probably send whoever did it a thank-you basket."

"I'm telling you," Brendon said, "don't talk to them. Finish packing and get over to the hospital."

"Who are you again?" North asked.

"None of your business. Josue, tell them to leave."

"His name's Brendon," Josue said. "Brendon Va. He's a photographer."

"Va," Shaw said. "Hmong?"

Brendon sneered at him. He was a nice-looking guy, although not pretty the way Josue was: his silky black hair long with a tapered undercut, his eyes dark and big.

"You're a photographer for the convention?" North asked.

Brendon laughed.

"For Scotty?"

"Freelance," Josue said. "Brendon works with a lot of male models. He discovers a lot of new talent. And he sells a lot of his photographs to cover designers who work with authors at the convention."

"Does that include Scotty?"

"Yes, of course. Brendon's pretty much the best. Scotty wouldn't have used anyone else." Josue shifted his weight and glanced at Brendon again. "We're all friends now. Brendon even did our wedding pictures."

"Huh," North said. He glanced at the dopp kit. "Are you going somewhere?"

"To the hospital. I was out doing some sightseeing when Scotty…when he got hurt. And by the time I got back and learned what had happened, the police wanted to talk to me. The hospital still won't let anyone in to see Scotty, but I want to be there anyway. For when he wakes up."

Shaw wandered over to one of the side tables, where he pushed around Arthurian figurines. He grabbed one, held it up, and said, "Do you think he's overcompensating? Because of the sword."

North looked at Brendon and Josue and raised his eyebrows.

After a moment, Josue said, "That's Excalibur."

"Right, right, I know. But doesn't it seem a little, um, phallic?"

"What are you talking about?"

"This place has some crazy sex vibes," Shaw said. "Do you feel them, North?"

"There's no such thing as vibes."

"I'm a level-five psychic." Shaw directed the words at Josue and Brendon. "So I can pick up a lot of things that North can't."

"What level psychic do you have to be to pick up your fucking room? Dirty clothes fucking everywhere. You two wouldn't believe it; it's a sty."

"I think remote levitations start at level thirty-seven, and cotton transmogrifications start at level fifty-nine."

"My fucking luck. He can't do his fucking laundry for another thirty fucking levels, but he can smell sex from a mile away." North turned toward Josue and Brendon. "Do you want to explain this bullshit?"

Josue swallowed. "I mean, Scotty and I have always been very spiritual, and we do have an advisor who reads our auras—"

"Is it Master Hermes?" Shaw broke in. "Master Hermes is the absolute best."

"Why would it be Master Hermes? They don't live here, Shaw. Why would they see your twice-bankrupt accountant-slash-fraudster for spiritual advice?"

"He telecommutes. And he astral projects, although sometimes the connection is bad, and even if he doesn't manifest it's an extra fifty dollars an hour."

"What the fuck is going on right now?" Brendon shouted.

"Oh, I was just curious about the sex vibes," Shaw said. Then, using the King Arthur figurine's ceramic sword, he picked up a pair of spliced fishnet briefs and dangled them above the sofa. "And about these."

Josue gulped. The noise was like something off a kid's show. "Scotty and I, we have—we have a really active sex life. We can't keep our hands off each other."

"So those are yours?" North said.

Josue gave a few jerky nods. He took a few uneven steps, grabbed the briefs, and wadded them up. Then, with those same stilted movements, he crossed to the bedroom and pitched them through the door. For a brief moment, with the door open, Shaw could see through the bedroom and into the en suite bathroom: more brass fixtures, lots of silk flowers, and two wet towels on the floor. Then Josue slammed the door.

"Right," North said. "A bit of advice, for next time: the secret to good acting is that you have to believe it yourself."

"North knows," Shaw said, "because when he was eight, he was the star in an elementary-school production of *Oliver Twist*."

"For fuck's sake," North muttered.

"He played Crumpet. That's a dog. It's not in the original play, but they didn't have enough roles for all the kids."

"The star of *Oliver Twist*," Brendon said, "is Oliver."

"Oh no. Not after you add Crumpet."

"How the fuck do you know that?" North said.

"Because I love you. I know everything about you. Well, not everything, because sometimes, when we're having those awesome, ten-hour-long conversations, all of a sudden you have to go on those really long drives to check something in the GTO, and I'm not sure what you need to check. But I know pretty much everything about you. The same way, I'm guessing, that Josue knows pretty much everything about Scotty."

"How about it, Josue? Want to tell us what's been going on with Scotty lately?"

"What do you mean?"

"Let's start with an easy one: has Scotty rubbed anyone the wrong way recently? Any outstanding grudges? Does he have any enemies?"

"You saw him," Josue said. He moved suddenly and violently toward the window, where he parted the curtains with one finger. The February light made a milky trapezoid on the side of his face. Glancing at Shaw, he added, "How do you feel? Got the urge to kill my husband?"

"No," Shaw said. "But he wasn't nice to me. And I don't think he's very nice to you either."

"He isn't," Brendon said. He took a step toward the window and Josue, and then he stopped again. "He treats Josue like shit, calling him Joshy, Joshums, all those stupid nicknames. Talking about their sex life in public. Never once have I seen him treat Josue with respect."

"It's ok," Josue said.

"It's not ok. That piece of shit talks about you like you're a...a dirty sock he jerks off into. He's a bastard."

"Bren, enough."

Breathing heavily, Brendon swung away and stalked to the other side of the room, where he dropped into a club chair.

"Scotty's complicated," Josue said softly. His fingers fell to his side, and the curtain dropped back into place, cutting off the winter light. "He's got a lot of unresolved issues about being gay. His parents were...were really unsupportive when he came out."

"And yours were?" Brendon said. "Your Dominican grandmother? Was she dancing in the streets when you came out?"

"Most gay guys have some sort of issues around coming out," Shaw said. "It's not just families; it's our whole culture. In fact, I was writing a monograph—"

"With frosting on graham crackers," North muttered.

"—on Big Dairy's role in constructing gendered stereotypes, and—"

"Look, Scotty's got baggage," North said. "He can join the fucking club. If you want my opinion, it doesn't give him the right to treat you like shit, but you know what? That's not my business. Did you put something in the water? Were you trying to get rid of him?"

"What? God, no. I can't even believe you'd say that."

If Josue were acting, Shaw thought, he was good: eyes wide with shock and the beginning of outrage, voice rising with each word.

"Lots of spouses kill their partner," North said. "You'd be in good company."

"Why would I want to—why would I try to hurt him?"

"Stop talking to them," Brendon said. "Kick them out. Or I will, if you want."

"Money," North said.

"Revenge," Shaw said.

"But probably money."

"Probably. Or both."

Josue stared at them. "I didn't put anything in Scotty's water. I wouldn't do something like that. I love him."

"But he does have a lot of money," North said. "Doesn't he?"

"We're comfortable. Scotty's very talented, and he's worked hard. I don't think the details are any of your business."

"Do you know why Scotty thought someone was threatening him?"

Shifting in the club chair, Brendon leaned forward and said, "Because he was a drama queen."

"You mean the messages that Yasmin was getting?" Josue asked.

"For starters," Shaw said. "How'd he hear about those messages? Yasmin says she didn't tell him."

"I don't know. Everybody knew about the messages."

"You don't remember how you heard?"

"Scotty told me."

"And you don't know who told him?" North said.

Josue shook his head.

"Why would Scotty think those threats were about him? We've seen some of them; they don't mention anyone in particular."

"Brendon's not...not wrong." Josue swallowed; on the street below, a horn blared, the sound distant. "Scotty likes drama. And he knows how to use it. To get attention, I mean. To sell books, but also just to..."

"To feel like a big deal," Brendon said.

With a shrug, Josue nodded.

"What are Scotty's underlying health conditions?"

For a moment, Josue just stared. "None."

"You're sure?"

"Of course. He had a physical a few weeks ago; he's totally healthy."

"What drugs does Scotty use?"

"Prescriptions?"

"That's not what I asked," North said.

"He has a scrip for Prozac. He upped his dose lately; he struggles with depression."

North waited. After a moment, Shaw asked quietly, "And?"

"That's all. Some beers. A glass of wine. He's not like the rest of those pillheads."

"What do you mean?"

"The authors. They're all pill poppers."

"What kind of pills are we talking here?"

"Well, if you put ten writers in a room, nine of them probably buy Adderall from a pimply-faced teenager in their subdivision."

North glanced at Shaw, and Shaw said, "Like high-achieving kids who use it to study?"

"Right," Josue said. "They can work longer, stay focused. It's basically a necessity for the hacks who can't do it on their own."

"And Scotty never used it?"

"Never. And some of those women? You could open a pharmacy with all the shit in their bags. That's not even getting started on bitches like Serenity. She does coke in her room with her readers. Did you know that?" Josue's jaw sagged. "Oh God." He looked at North and Shaw. "They had a big fight."

"Who?"

"Serenity and Scotty. They had a huge fight the first night we were here. Tuesday. I was downstairs, getting drinks with—" In what looked like a remarkable display of self-control, he didn't glance over at Brendon, but Shaw could practically feel him fighting the urge. "—with some friends."

"Nice save," North told him.

Scrubbing a hand over his cropped hair, Josue said, "When I came back up, I caught the tail end of it. They were screaming. Throwing things."

"Fighting about what?"

"Serenity's latest book, I think."

"What makes you say that?"

"He kept saying, 'Nobody's going to buy that shit. Nobody's going to buy it. Good fucking luck peddling it.' Stuff like that. Then they saw me, and Serenity took off." Josue pointed at Shaw. "You saw him downstairs today, reading from her book, making fun of it."

Shaw nodded at North's inquiring glance. "He wasn't complimentary, that's for sure. People seemed to find the whole thing funny."

"Jackals," Brendon said abruptly. "That's what Scotty calls them." When Shaw raised an eyebrow, Brendon sat straighter. "He doesn't like them, those people. But he knows how to use them. They like to feel better than other people, and they like to do it by seeing someone else humiliated."

"Have they had any other interactions? Serenity and Scotty. Since the convention began, I mean."

"I don't know," Josue said. "Not that I've seen."

Brendon shook his head.

"What about this woman," Shaw said, "Leslie Hawkins?"

"I heard an interesting story about last year," North said.

"I'm not going to talk about that," Josue said. His gaze fell, and he shoved his hands in his pockets. "If you want to know about that, you can talk to Leslie, or you can talk to Scotty, but I'm not talking about it."

"You could save us a lot of time—" North began.

"I said no."

A man laughed in the hall, great guffaws, and a woman's soprano answered with a snatch of a showtune. *Gypsy*, Shaw thought. Then the voices had moved past the suite, and the only sound was the wind battering the glass.

"If that's all," Josue said, "I want to go see my husband."

"Sure," Shaw said. "We wanted a few minutes with Brendon anyway."

"No, I'm going with him."

"Later, then," North began.

"I don't think so."

The goodbyes were terse, and when Shaw and North found themselves in the hall, North spoke first. "That's a fucking mess in there."

"They probably need a good therapist," Shaw said as he headed to the elevator. "I should recommend Dr. Farr."

"What they need is for somebody to give them hazmat suits for that toxic three-way they've got brewing." North glanced over where Shaw had pressed the down button. "Serenity?"

"Yep. I want to talk to her about her coke habit."

"You do realize he meant cocaine, not Coca-Cola."

Shaw bit his lips. "Oh. God. That's so disappointing. Maybe I should—"

"No," North said, steering him into the elevator car by the shoulder. "You do not need to buy one just to run a taste-test or a double-blind experiment or whatever scam you think you can run on me."

They were halfway to the lobby when Shaw said, "Theoretically, though, a control group—"

"Not a fucking chance."

Chapter 14

YASMIN PROVIDED THEM WITH Serenity's room number and hotel, which turned out to be within walking distance, at a Hyatt overlooking the Gateway Arch.

"She's not staying at the Royal Excalibur?" North asked.

"No," Yasmin said, rolling her eyes. "Francie, can you grab some more swag bags from my car? Thanks, sweetie."

"Why stay somewhere else? It's February. Why go to the trouble of having to venture out in bad weather?"

"Not to mention carting your books and swag," Shaw said, pointing to a heavyset man, red-faced and sweating as he dragged a hand truck across the lobby.

"Ask her yourself," Yasmin said with another roll of her eyes. "I'm dying to know."

Outside, the February air was so cold that it made North's head throb, every breath flash-freezing the inside of his nose. A bus rolled away from the Royal Excalibur with the whoosh of brakes releasing and a miasma of sickly-sweet exhaust. Afternoon was well on its way to evening; the sun hung low in the west, turning the Arch into a ring of fire, scattering embers across the Mississippi. St. Louis's rush hour was just getting started, but it was a small city, and all it meant was that North and Shaw spent an extra two minutes shivering at a crosswalk, with the tomato-basil fragrance from the calzone place up the street making North's stomach rumble.

The Hyatt was just north of the Arch, an orange-brown T of a building, with one wing set perpendicular to the other. They waited in the lobby while an older woman at the front desk rang Serenity's room. A woman in a mink coat was checking in to the hotel. She kept looking at herself in a compact, answering questions distractedly, while two little monsters kicked over a vase and rolled it around, pretending to play soccer and mostly just wanting to raise hell.

"Reggie, Percy," the woman said, her tone suggesting that she was so exhausted that death might be preferable to even the slightest degree of effort. "Stop that right now."

One of the hellions gave the vase a solid whack, and it rolled across the lobby. It struck an older woman in the shins, and she went down with a cry of surprise and pain.

"Reggie's doing club soccer this year," the woman in the mink coat told her compact.

The young woman at the front desk smiled like she had hooks pulling on the corners of her mouth.

"Ms. Silver will be right down," the woman helping North and Shaw said. "You can wait right over there by the elevator."

"Reggie, don't bite her, darling; she's ancient," came the exhausted remonstration behind them.

"They need a good smudge with sage," Shaw whispered.

"They need a sack and a drive upriver," North said. "Handle those two nightmares the way my dad wanted to handle that litter of kittens."

"North!"

"That one has to be eight years old, and he's biting an old lady. They're past saving, Shaw."

"I'm talking about the kittens. You didn't let your dad do that, did you?"

North leaned against the wall, the stone cool even through his Carhartt coat, and watched the hotel staff. A teenager was trying to use a hanger to hook one of the hellions and get him free from the fracas.

"North!"

When North glanced over, Shaw's eyes were wet. North sighed. "No, he didn't drown them."

"You saved them?"

"Jesus, Shaw."

"Well, I have a right to know. I'm emotionally invested now."

"Can we let this go?"

"No way." Shaw dashed at his eyes. "Not a chance."

"The kittens were fine. That's all you need to know."

"Did you let them sleep in your bed with you and hide them during the day?"

"What? God, no. They pissed everywhere."

"Did you find an individual home for each one and then check on them every day to make sure they were growing and getting big and strong?"

"This is why I don't tell you anything. Do you realize that?"

"North!"

"I put them in a fucking laundry basket, and I rode the fucking bus for three miles to the Macklind Humane Society. And everybody on the bus laughed at me, in case that part of the story is pertinent to this whole fucking debacle."

Shaw wiped his eyes again. "Oh."

"I was twelve years old, Shaw. What the fuck was I supposed to do?"

Stretching up, Shaw kissed him on the cheek.

"What the fuck," North muttered, scrubbing at the spot.

"You shouldn't smile when you're trying to pretend you're angry," Shaw said. "Just so you know."

"Great. Any more fucking feedback?"

"Just that you're the best, most wonderful man I've ever met."

North folded his arms, stared across the lobby, and got another kiss. This one with some tongue.

"Well," a woman's voice interrupted them. "Not exactly the reception I usually get, but I'm into it."

Serenity stood in the elevator car, one hand holding the doors open. She was smiling, but it didn't touch her eyes.

"Ms. Silver," North began.

"Serenity is fine." She stepped aside. "Come on; the girls will eat you up."

"Actually, we were hoping to talk to you—" Shaw tried.

"I know, sweetheart. But I want something too, and you're going to give it to me."

Like Scotty and Josue, Serenity occupied a suite, although the Hyatt's décor had clearly been updated more recently than the Royal Excalibur's: black-and-white herringbone drapes, gold and ivory and onyx accent pieces, modern furniture that was sinuous and slightly misshapen like still-cooling wax. The suite's front room held a pair of sofas and several armchairs, which were currently occupied by a gaggle of men and women, all of them in Western apparel. *The girls*, North decided, apparently wasn't a gender-specific term. Rodney and Jerry were part of the group. One of the pair, the one in the red-stitched shirt, waved. The other, in the pearl-snap shirt, smiled and blushed.

"This is the Homebound and Hogtied luncheon," Serenity said. "Based on my books. I'm sure you've read them. We're having it a few hours later than scheduled, thanks to Scotty's little performance. Let me introduce you."

"If we could—" Shaw tried again.

But Serenity ignored him, pointing to each of her guests in turn and naming them as she went. When she'd finished, she said, "Girls, these strapping young men saw the whole thing today. Wouldn't you like them to tell us about it?"

"You were there too," Shaw said.

"But I think they'd like to hear it from a couple of gay detectives."

"Did Scotty really pee himself?" asked an older man wearing a teddy-bear bolo slide.

"We're not talking about this," North said to Serenity.

"Don't be spoilsports."

North shook his head.

"I brought you up here because these are my special guests. I think the least you could do is make an effort to entertain them."

"Clearly there's been an epic fucking misunderstanding," North said. "Let me have the valet get my clown car, and I'll come back up with a shitload of pies. How does that sound?"

"And seltzer, North," Shaw added as he crossed the room, approaching a thin-faced woman who vaguely reminded North of a beagle. "Don't forget the seltzer."

"I've got one of those flowers that shoots water when you lean down to smell it," North said.

"Oh, and I've got one of those never-ending scarves. The one with all the colors."

"And the floppy shoes, Shaw. You've got those floppy shoes."

"Those are my jump training shoes, actually. In case I decide to get back into basketball."

"Whatever they are, they're fucking hilarious."

"And make sure you bring the pancake makeup and the big red nose."

"Balloon animals. We do those too."

"But North only knows how to make two kinds," Shaw said, now close enough to Serenity's guests that he could pitch his voice in a mock whisper. "A worm and a snake. Well, and a schlong, but that was only one time, and not a kid's party."

"I didn't know you were part-time comedians," Serenity said, her face tight.

"Full-time comedians," North said, "part-time detectives."

"North does a set at the Smirking Fork Wednesdays. Not the schlong balloon, though, if that's what you're wondering."

"I wasn't," Serenity said.

"You looked like you might be," Shaw informed her.

"You really did," North said.

"I wasn't! I'm not—what are you doing?"

"That's an amazing crystal," Shaw told the beagle-faced woman. "Quartz?"

She blinked and nodded.

"It's got crazy strong energy."

"Oh," she said quietly, a flush coming into her cheeks as she smiled. "I got it for my gout."

"That's amazing. I thought it was for gout. I could practically sense it. Couldn't I, North?"

"How the fuck should I know?"

"One time, we were following this ancient creep who kept picking up young guys and then collecting their pubes, and he had gout. That's how we caught him, actually."

"What does that mean?" the man with the teddy-bear slide demanded. "You have to explain that."

"Well, he was a pube collector, which is pretty much what it sounds like, and he had this whole storage container, like the kind for sewing, it had hundreds of little drawers, and each drawer had a tiny paper envelope with pubes in it."

"What did he do with them?" a woman with a boxer's jaw shouted.

As Shaw launched into an answer, North met Serenity's chilly gaze. "You got your entertainment," North said quietly. "Now, let's have a conversation. Somewhere private. Before I cut Shaw off, and your guests never get to hear about the 250-piece pube trimming toolkit he carried around."

Serenity lingered for a moment longer, studying her guests, who were firing questions at Shaw and hanging on his answers. Then she glided toward a pair of double doors. Rodney/Jerry—pearl-snap—glanced over at them, and Serenity gave him a tiny wave, just the fingertips. Then she opened one of the doors and gestured North into a bedroom.

The room was neatly made up, and it had the same sleekly modern furniture and geometric designs. There was no sign of Serenity's possessions; either the suite had a second bedroom, or Serenity had packed up everything and stored it in the closet. North took a few steps, considering the room, trying not to make his goal obvious. The lingering smell of baby powder hung in the air. After a few false starts, he got himself in position to glance through the bathroom door. Nothing on the counter, no toiletry bag in sight. Worse, no prescription bottles.

"I didn't have anything to do with it," Serenity said.

"That's an interesting way to start."

"I like to be direct. You don't gain anything by beating around the bush." Her lips flexed stiffly into a smile that she probably meant to be naughty. "So to speak."

"You didn't have anything to do with what?"

"With whoever poisoned Scotty today. Obviously."

"What makes you think it was a poisoning?"

"Well, Mary Angela told us, of course. And we all had to be tested and give our statements. It's really thrilling. I think I might write a mystery series now. I've got all sorts of good ideas."

"You believe someone tried to poison Scotty?"

"He had that horrible reaction, didn't he? Unless—" She frowned. "We all had our water tampered with. Do you think someone else was the target?"

"Do you?"

"You're very good at that, not giving anything away. I bet you're a tremendous lay. Your poor boyfriend probably has to work so hard just to get a noise out of you. Is that right?"

"Earlier," North said, "you called what happened a performance. Scotty's performance. What did you mean by that?"

"I don't know," she said, sounding faintly surprised. "It just came out. I mean, the seizure seemed real, didn't it? But I'm so used to Scotty's little…productions that I guess I said it without thinking about it."

"Why don't you tell me about that?"

Serenity moved to sit on the bed. She was older than she looked, North realized suddenly. The slight shuffle in her step. The way she lowered herself onto the mattress. "You heard about his dramatic reading in the lobby today?"

"I did."

"That kind of thing. Scotty was a second-rate writer but a first-class self-promoter. Think P.T. Barnum; there's nothing Scotty couldn't turn into a publicity stunt. What happened today, for example. He'll come back with a conspiracy theory, with suspects, with a tell-all book and then with a fictionalized version. He'll make a killing off it. Lord, I wouldn't put it past the man to fake his own death just for the attention." She grimaced. "That's in bad taste. Consider it retracted."

"Do you use any drugs? Legal or illegal, prescription or not."

Serenity burst out laughing. Her breath carried a mixture of halitosis and the fading perfume of the baby powder. "Oh my goodness. I really am a suspect, is that it?"

"It's just a question."

"One I'm not going to answer, I'm afraid."

"Any stimulants?"

Serenity's smile thinned and hardened. "No, Mr. McKinney. I'm not interested in playing this game."

"Someone told us that you use cocaine recreationally."

"As opposed to medically? Someone's been talking about me behind my back. Why would I want to hurt Scotty? He's an obnoxious egotist, but that's got nothing to do with me."

"He ripped your latest book apart in public. He said women couldn't write gay fiction."

"Do you think he's right?"

"I have no idea. Shaw's the writer; you'll have to ask him."

"I'm asking you. Do you think women can write realistically about gay men? Or, to put it more broadly: can women write about men? Then switch it up: can men write about women?"

"You can write about whatever you want to write about. I'm more interested in how you felt about Scotty's comments."

"It's an old saw," Serenity said, shrugging as she leaned back. "Women don't understand men. Women particularly don't understand gay men. Women are trampling authentic gay voices. Women are crowding out legitimate gay authors. Women are ruining the genre. Not worth getting angry over."

"Even after he tore your book to pieces?"

"Can I tell you something, Mr. McKinney? A little bit of insight into the publishing business that you can pass on to your boyfriend. It doesn't matter whether or not women can authentically write gay men because that's not what my readers are paying for. My readers are paying for at least five steamy sex scenes, one of which is usually kinky. My readers are paying for me to hit the beats at the right moment: inciting incident, pinch, midpoint, crisis, and climax. My readers are paying me to write what they want to read: daddies this month, piss play next month, tentacles the month after that. My readers are paying for their HEA. Or at least for their HFN. If you can do that, if you can do it reliably, and if you can do it with moderately workable prose, you can have a career. If you can do it fast, you can be a success. Authentic voices? Psychological insight? Those don't have any bearing on it."

"It sounds like you agree with how Scotty described romance."

"No." Serenity cocked her head. She had shark eyes, dark and cool. From the other room came a burst of happy, excited laughter, and then Shaw made a booming noise—where it fit into the story, North had no idea. "I don't share his contempt for the genre and its readers, but he's not completely wrong either. It's a fantasy. A pleasant one. We all need fantasy, don't you think? There's no harm in it, and if you choose the right one, you come back to the real world a little happier, with an itch scratched. That's the idea, anyway."

"I understand you and Scotty had an encounter Tuesday night. In private."

"Ah. There it is. You've been talking to Josue."

"What were you and Scotty fighting about?"

"Nothing. It was trivial. A disagreement."

"It sounded like more than a disagreement. Things were thrown. Shouting."

"You already know he doesn't like my book. He decided to tell me in person."

"In private? Just the two of you? In his hotel room, while his husband was away?"

"That's right." Serenity smiled. "You're wasting your time with me. I'm the best-selling author in the genre. Do you understand that? I hold workshops, and people travel from around the world to learn how I do it. I didn't have any reason to want to hurt Scotty. You're looking at the wrong tier."

"What does that mean?"

"It means Scotty might not have been quite at my level, but we were relatively equal. You need to be looking at the little people. The authors scrambling for his attention, his approval, his blessing. His imprimatur, if you'll pardon the joke. Scotty might not be able to do much damage to me with his rants and stunts, but a newer author, or one who wasn't as well established…" Serenity gave a one-shouldered shrug.

"Do you have someone in mind?"

"As a matter of fact, I do. You're such a good little gay detective. Really well done. Do you know JD Hathaway?"

"She was on the panel. There was some sort of dustup—she wasn't supposed to be, but then she got on somehow."

"Somehow, yes. Scotty insisted we include her, and poor Karen got left by the side of the road. And Tuesday night, I saw JD follow Scotty into the men's room downstairs, right before Yasmin made the changes to the panel. Quite the coincidence, no?"

"You're sure that's what you saw?"

"Positive." Serenity stretched; it must have been intended to be catlike, but her joints popped, and she looked more like an old tree in a strong wind. "Now, let's get you and your boyfriend settled for some really good stories. I hope you have some sexy ones. My readers love some heat."

"No," North said. "We're not going to be doing that."

He made his way to the double doors and pushed them open.

"—had the rent boy tied to the hood of his Buick and—North?"

"Let's go."

"He's just getting to the good part," the man with the teddy-bear slide protested.

"Too bad," North said. "You can read the rest of the story when his book comes out."

"Really?" the beagle-faced woman said. "What's it called? When is the launch party?"

Seizing Shaw by the arm, North turned him toward the door. "Pube-Snatcher Confessions Part I," North said without looking back. "The first Friday of get a fucking clue."

"When does part two come out?" That sounded like Teddy-Bear slide again.

When they were out in the hall, Shaw said, "North, that's genius."

North groaned as they made their way to the elevator.

"I could be like Watson, and you could be like Sherlock Holmes, and I'll document all our adventures."

North jammed the down button.

"Updated for the 21st century, of course. And with some sexy times. Because, you know, everybody likes to read about sexy times. I could even include some details, you know, to make them unique. Like, how you like it when I touch that spot between your—" Shaw glanced up and must have seen something on North's face because he swallowed. "Um, you know what? Maybe I need to do some more brainstorming."

"Do that," North said. "Silently."

Chapter 15

THE ROYAL EXCALIBUR'S LARGEST convention hall was called Pendragon, and Shaw smiled as he tapped the plaque. "That's kind of cute, right?"

North grunted. "Pendragon is a person, not a place. They need to read a little more fucking closely."

"But it's perfect for authors. Pen, you know? And some of them write about dragons."

"All of them write about dragons," Heidi said, stopping at the doors next to them. Her T-shirt was a Black Power fist that had been designed to look like the Infinity Gauntlet. "They just don't all admit it."

"How are you?" Shaw asked. "Feeling any better?"

"Police and hospital administration are a very time-consuming combo. They told me to drink a lot of water; how's that for medical advice? It does seem to be helping. I feel more normal, anyway, or maybe that's just the effects wearing off on their own."

"How did everyone else seem?" North asked.

"Did I notice any suspicious behavior, you mean? Do I have any suspects?" Heidi smiled. "Unfortunately, everyone acted the same: freaked out. And then, when the freak-out wore off, they all acted annoyed. They're paying to be here, after all, and they wanted to get back as quickly as possible."

North just grunted again.

"Have you been to one of these before?" Heidi asked, nodding at the doors to Pendragon. "Things can get interesting."

"I got the general idea in the lobby this morning."

Laughing softly, Heidi shook her head. "You're in for a treat."

She opened the doors and headed into the convention hall, and North and Shaw followed. A wall of stimuli met them, and Shaw's immediate reaction was overload. The room was huge, but it was still packed with milling bodies. The smell of sweat, overheated flesh, and wet footwear floated like an almost-visible funk. Voices clamored, competing to be heard. A man shouted out the sales copy for his book. Another man was yodeling. People seemed determined to outdo each other: Shaw spotted several more Lars cosplayers, although so far, nobody else had decided to dress up as Twerpy Twink, while a man who had to be well over six feet tall stomped through the crowd in a leather blacksmith's apron, with a puffy blouse and hotpants underneath it. A woman was swinging a six-foot-long blow-up penis like a sword; it took Shaw a moment to realize she was fencing with another woman, who carried an identical phallic weapon. A man in a rainbow-sequin ball gown waltzed with an invisible partner. At the closest author booth, a woman was strapped to a Wheel of Death and being spun while men and women threw penis-shaped darts at her.

"Good Lord," North muttered.

"Told you," Heidi said with a smirk. "Actually, most of these people are really, really cool. They're just wild and creative, and this is an outlet for them."

North opened his mouth, obviously intending to respond at great length to this proposition. Before he could, though, a blast of louder-than-usual yodeling cut him off.

Shaw seized the opportunity. "Do you know where JD's booth is?"

Heidi cupped her ear, and Shaw shouted the question.

Nodding, Heidi beckoned for them to follow.

The crowd was so dense that there was barely room for Heidi and Shaw to wriggle between people. Shaw wondered how North was going to manage it until he saw North shoulder his way between a pair of men who were holding rainbow tights up to the light.

"Rude," one of the men called.

"Bitch," the other shouted, wielding the tights like a bullwhip. "You wish you were Lars, you fucking wannabe."

North started to turn.

"Oh no," Shaw said, catching his hand. "Come on."

"That's right," the man with the rainbow tights shrieked after them. "Run away with your Twerpy Twink."

"Hold on," North said, trying to disengage Shaw's grip. "I forgot something back at the car."

Laughing, Shaw towed him through the crowd.

Pendragon was a maze of tables and booths. The authors seemed to be cut from the same cloth as the readers, and while Shaw saw a few sedate specimens—one woman, for example, was sitting at an undecorated folding table, a single book in front of her, while she knitted what looked like a T-back—for the most part, the authors might have been even more extreme. A woman who had clearly been through a few hundred rounds of cosmetic surgery was wearing a steampunk headpiece that was a nightmare concoction of hypodermic needles, syringes filled with colorful liquids, and leather straps. A man in a gimp suit was signing copies of *In the Reverend's Basement*. At one booth, a man wearing a navy blue sherwani was auctioning off a stainless-steel dabba; behind him, a massive poster announced the upcoming release of *The Sikh and the Maharaja.*

When Shaw veered toward the booth, North caught him by one strap of his tank.

"But I have the same kurta," Shaw said.

"Great," North said, yanking so hard that for a moment, Shaw thought the strap would tear. "Put it in your newsletter."

By the time they reached JD's booth, Shaw had added almost a hundred books to his to-read list.

JD's display was, for Shaw anyway, something of a letdown: it had a white table runner, several books displayed on plastic stands, and a massive poster behind her that featured a very well-built man who had lost most of his clothes. At the bottom of the display ran a row of book covers that clearly belonged to the same series: *Uffe Goes to West Point, Uffe Goes to the Naval Academy, Uffe goes to the Commandant's Office.* Judging by the covers, Shaw guessed that military life involved a lot of spanking and paddling. At the front of the table, printed in black-and-white on a standard piece of paper, JD had listed a kind of authorial menu: *Photographs: $5 – Autographs: $10 – Autographed Photograph: $12 – BUY FOURTEEN BOOKS AND GET THE FIFTEENTH FREE – ALL PRICES AS MARKED – PLEASE DO NOT ASK FOR REVIEW COPIES, THIS IS MY LIVELIHOOD. RESPECT THAT.* There was no sign of the dragon books she had made Shaw buy in the lobby earlier that day.

"We'll have two of the autographed photographs," Shaw said to JD, who was prowling behind the table, eyes flicking over the faces of passersby.

"No," North said. "We won't."

"It's a great deal, North. We'll save three dollars. Times two, that's six."

"No."

"You were just telling me that business is going great this year, and I really think we can afford it. Besides, we have to reward ourselves for all our hard work, or what's the point?"

"Do you have a few minutes to talk?" North said to JD.

"No," she said. The fluorescents shellacked her platinum-colored pixie cut with a yellowish tinge. "I'm working."

"Let me rephrase that," North said. "We're going to talk. Right now. Nobody's beating down your door, and you can't walk away from…whatever this is, so we're going to have a conversation."

JD shot him a furious look, her leathery features twisted.

Shaw tapped North's arm. "Why don't you take a break? Look around." Fishing out his wallet, Shaw added, "Buy yourself something nice." He held out a dollar bill. "But don't spend it all in one place."

North stared at him.

"I'm serious, North. Don't spend it all on comic books and horehound candy and Necco wafers."

"I'm taking this dollar because you're a spoiled fucking brat who doesn't know the real value of money," North said as he snatched the bill. "Not because I'm going to—"

"Spend it all on Moon Pies and butterscotch discs."

North spun around and stalked away. Heidi gave North a bemused look and went after him.

"Sorry," Shaw said. "He gets really grumpy when he sees all these half-naked guys. Plus he can't read, so you know, it's very stressful."

JD was still prowling, her eyes only occasionally flitting toward Shaw.

"So," Shaw said, "I really love *Pierced by My Dragon-Mate's Fang: Babysitter Confessionals Volume 12*. Like, I'm only about eight pages in, when the babysitter gets bred on top of the playhouse, but it's really, really good."

Whatever JD mumbled, Shaw didn't catch it.

"And I was wondering if you could sign my book?"

"Autographs are ten dollars," JD muttered, waving a hand at the sign.

"Of course." Shaw produced a bill, passed it over, and then handed her the paperback. As JD scribbled something on the page, he said, "So, you really make your living this way? I thought for most authors it was more of a hobby."

"It's not a hobby," JD snapped, her eyes coming to Shaw as though seeing him for the first time. "I'm a professional. Does this look like something an amateur would produce?" She grabbed a book and waved it in Shaw's face. *Uffe Goes to the Firing Range*. Uffe was straddling an M4 and looked in danger of getting some of his dangly bits caught in the ejector. "That's the work of a professional."

"Yes, right," Shaw said, gently moving the book away from his nose. "But there just isn't that much money left in publishing—"

"Don't get started on that," JD said. She dropped the book in its stand. "People who say that have no idea what they're talking about. They don't understand that publishing is a business, like any business. We're selling an experience; that's all. The experience happens to come in the form of a book, but it's still a sale, and sales are the same whether you're selling an airplane or Tiddlywinks."

"How do you sell something?"

"You hustle," JD said. She paused her pacing again and fixed him with a look. Shaw must have passed the test because she said, "You work your ass off, you never stop looking for the next customer, and you don't take no for an answer."

"That's interesting. Serenity said something about selling a fantasy too."

"Serenity. Mary Angela. They have no idea what they're doing. They play with their spreadsheets and they talk about their PAs and their marketing consultants, but bottom line, they're just lucky. They got in when the genre was starting to explode, and they never had to work for their success."

"Right place, right time."

"Exactly. Not like me. I've had to claw my way up the charts. I'm the only one on that panel who deserved to be there."

"Oh, I don't know about that," Shaw said. "I mean, really? Because I'm sure the convention organizers were very careful about how they selected the authors for the Superstar Panel. I know they picked you for a good reason, but Scotty, Mary Angela, Serenity, and Clarence—well, they all have a lot more—"

"Nothing. They don't have more of anything. They don't work as hard as I do, they don't hustle, they don't make sales. They were just lucky. Well, not Clarence. I mean, he's a has-been. They only keep him around because they feel sorry for him. I was on that panel because I went to Scotty and I told him—" JD stopped. "You've been talking to Karen."

"Not really," Shaw said. "She just mentioned something at the panel."

"That ungrateful bitch. She had a good idea for a panel; fine. That doesn't mean that she should have been on it. She's not a superstar. She's not even a regular star. She's a nice girl who writes nice books, end of story."

"But she seemed to think that she was going to be on the panel until Scotty insisted that you take her place."

JD set her jaw, put her hands on her hips, and looked away.

Shaw began counting silently.

A middle-aged man and woman skipped through the crowd holding hands. The woman was squeezing the bulb of an old-fashioned atomizer, spewing something sickly sweet into the air, and the man was shouting, "We're the candy fairies! We're the candy fairies!"

"I was doing her a favor," JD said, her voice hushed. "That's what I was doing. I didn't mean for her to get bumped. Scotty and I were talking business, and he realized that I've got a good head, and he asked me to be on the panel. I never meant for her to lose her seat."

"When was this?"

JD set her jaw again.

"We're trying to figure out who might have wanted to hurt Scotty," Shaw said. "And I've got to be honest, anything would be helpful right now. When did you have this conversation with Scotty?"

"I don't remember. Weeks ago."

"Really? Because Karen seemed to be under the impression that the changes to the panel had happened very recently."

"I'm telling you it was weeks ago. Maybe months ago."

"I see. And when you've talked to Scotty over the last few days, have you noticed anything unusual?"

"I haven't talked to Scotty at all. Not in person. Not once, not during the whole convention. The first time we came close to interacting was today at the panel when he launched into his spiel about romance and our readers."

"Really?" Shaw said.

"What's that supposed to mean?"

"Well, someone did see you follow Scotty into a men's room."

Behind her tanned hide, JD's color dropped. "I didn't—that's not—"

"And they got it on camera," Shaw lied.

"Oh my God," JD moaned. "Oh my God. I didn't—I didn't do anything, ok? He was avoiding me. He was making me mad. I wanted to talk to him, and he ducked in there to avoid me. I wasn't going to stand for it, so I said screw this, and I went in after him. We were the only two in there; it's not like I was trying to peep on anybody."

"Never take no for an answer," Shaw said.

"Right," JD said desperately. "That's exactly right. I was just…you know, being determined."

"When was this?"

"Tuesday, late afternoon. It was technically before the con started, so I wasn't lying when I told you I haven't talked to him during the con. I just didn't want to get into all this."

"What did you need to talk to him about?"

"It's none of your business."

"Well, that doesn't sound very good."

"I was standing up for a friend, if you have to know."

"What does that mean?"

"Scotty was a liar!" The words burst free before JD seemed to realize she was saying them. A look of horror flitted across her face, but the words kept coming. "He promised Karen he'd help her with a book. He said he'd edit it for her, make sure it was perfect, and then give it to his agent. He basically guaranteed that she'd get a book deal."

"And?" Shaw said.

"And he didn't do any of it. Karen told me about the promise; we were talking about how to build a career, and she pretended she didn't want to say anything about it, made me drag it out of her. I was jealous, of course, but I was happy for her too. When I asked her about it a few weeks later, she laughed it off. When I asked her a few weeks after that, she made excuses. A few weeks after that, and she said it wasn't going to happen. Things had changed. She put on a brave face, of course, but I could tell she was devastated. I emailed Scotty, and he didn't reply. I tried messaging him, and he didn't answer those either. This was my first chance to talk to him in person, and he was going out of his way to avoid me, so I took the initiative." JD raised her head and issued a challenging stare. "It's not like I broke the law or anything."

"And that's all?" Shaw said. "You just talked about Karen's book?"

"Yes. Exactly."

"Not about your own career?

"Please. I don't need any help from the golden boy."

"And then?"

"And then I left. He went to the urinal for a pee; that's the last thing I saw. And I didn't see him again until today."

A string of swearing broke Shaw's concentration, and he glanced to the right. North was using shoulders and elbows liberally to clear a path through the crowd. One overweight man in a pink boa and a tiara let out a shriek as North stomped on his foot. Shaw winced; the Redwings could do some serious damage. North barely seemed to register the noise, though. He was too busy wiping his face and turning the air blue.

"The goddamn candy fairies blasted me right in the fucking face," North said. "I'm going to be lucky if I don't get chlamydia in my eye or a raging infection of giardia."

"I'm not sure you can get chlamydia in your eye," Shaw said, "but I do have a potion that will help the giardia."

Glaring with only one eye—his hand covered the other—North growled, "Pass."

"I brewed it myself."

"Shaw, so help me God, now is not the time for whatever ant-piss-and-chrysanthemum-stamen bullshit you want to force down my throat."

"Oh no, I would never use chrysanthemums. Well, not for this. This has whole fennel seeds, peppermint leaves, carob, ginger oil—"

"Are we done?" JD said. "I've got a reader who wants to talk to me."

"Really?" North said. He was actually scarier, Shaw thought, with just one eye. Even JD seemed to think so because she flinched. "Where? Because nobody's coming within a mile of this fucking booth."

"Over there," JD said. "I've got to go. I'm a professional!" The last was delivered in a nervous, quavering shout as she trotted away.

"—and I think some of Pari's cotton candy actually fell into the potion while I was brewing it, which normally I would object to because sugar is a poison and is even more addictive than—North, where are you going? North, wait up!"

Chapter 16

NORTH FLUSHED HIS EYE with water in the Royal Excalibur's men's room. Whatever had been in that fucking atomizer, it still stung like hell, although it was getting better.

"The tile makes this place really echoey," Shaw said, strolling around the room as he tested the sound of his voice. "Hello, hello, hello. Nessun dorma. Jolene, Jolene, Jolene."

Laving his face, North blew out a breath, spraying water into the sink. Then he waved a hand.

"Out on the wiley, windy moors—"

"Shaw!"

"Oh, right." Paper towels filled North's hand, and he dried his face. He blinked a few times, tested his eye, and grunted. "Well?"

"You're still very handsome. Even if you lose that eye. In fact, you might want to consider wearing a patch. I already think you're way too masculine, but a pirate patch—"

"Too masculine? Give me a fucking break. You're the one who asked me to wear a tool belt to bed a few weeks ago."

"I didn't—"

"What did she say?"

Shaw told him, and North digested as much of it as he could.

"I don't think she was lying," Shaw said. "Or not lying about the parts she told me, anyway."

"That sounds about right. As soon as we got away from her, Heidi said something about the 'click-farm queen.' Before I could ask her what that meant, she saw some of her friends, and they ran off together." Studying himself in the mirror, North ran a hand through the mess of short blond hair once, decided it was good enough, and asked, "What do you want to do now?"

"Find Karen."

"That's exactly what I was thinking."

They went back to the registration table, where Yasmin was now wearing a bulky coat. The smell of cigarette smoke was even stronger, and North felt a twinge of sympathy; he wanted to scratch that itch too.

"Let me text her," Yasmin said.

"Shouldn't she be in the convention hall with all the other authors?"

Yasmin shook her head as she tapped on the phone's screen. "Different tier."

"What does that mean?" North asked.

"She didn't pay for that. She'll have a booth tomorrow." Message sent, Yasmin lowered the phone and glanced at them. "So, I'm glad you stopped by because I needed to talk to you. I just got off the phone with an author who was furious. She threatened to pull out of the con and take her readers with her if I didn't fire the two of you."

"Serenity's got her tits in a twist—" North began, but he cut off when Shaw elbowed him.

"You can't say tits," Shaw said. "And it wasn't Serenity."

North gauged Yasmin's expression and saw that Shaw was right. "Who the fuck was it?"

"I shouldn't say."

"You smell even more like cigarettes than usual," Shaw said, "which means you either had to go for a smoke break because you're so stressed, or you go to the same drycleaner that North uses."

Yasmin's eyes narrowed. "Huh?"

"What?" North said.

"Remember? One time I was reading a list of every possible chess move to you, and then cross-indexing them with every time they've been used in a grandmaster tournament, and all of a sudden you stood up really fast and said you had to pick up something from the drycleaner, and you came back smelling like smoke. It was really, really strong. And we agreed you'd go to a different drycleaner from now on."

Yasmin's eyes slid to North, and his face heated as he said, "We're losing focus. I think Shaw's on to something. It has to be a big-name author, or you wouldn't be so worried about it, and it's not Serenity. Scotty's out because he's in the hospital. So, who was it?"

After a quick glance to make sure no one was close enough to overhear—Francie was cutting out paper swords and pasting plastic gems on them—Yasmin whispered, "Mary Angela."

"Why is she so upset?" Shaw rolled a shoulder and looked at North. "We haven't even talked to her."

"She said she thinks I'm turning a tragedy into a publicity stunt, and that this is disgusting, and—and—" Yasmin started to cry. "And we're really good friends, or I thought we were, and she just kept saying horrible things."

Shaw vaulted the table, making it look surprisingly easy, and wrapped Yasmin in a hug. For some reason, she started to cry harder.

"Hey," Shaw said as he patted her shoulder. "Things are going to work out. We're going to find who tried to hurt Scotty, and the con is going to be a great success because you have real, live gay detectives, and I'm going to cure North's diarrhea with a potion. Everything's going to be fine."

Yasmin hiccoughed. Watery eyes settled on North.

"I don't have diarrhea," North said. "Just so we're all clear on that."

"Giardia," Shaw told Yasmin.

"I don't have giardia," North snapped. A little too loudly, maybe, because people turned to look. In a more controlled voice, he said, "Do you have any idea why Mary Angela would react so strongly?"

"No," Yasmin said through her sniffles. "I don't. Honestly, it doesn't make any sense. We talked about it, even before anything happened to Scotty. We agreed that the threats could be a fun, exciting part of the con if we played it right. They could add an edge. And then Leslie said she was going to be here, and you guys agreed to take the case, and everything was really going fine until Scotty got hurt."

"Will Mary Angela leave, do you think?" Shaw said.

Shaking her head, Yasmin said, "Probably not. She was just mad, and she wanted to vent. I don't know why, though. That's what bothers me so much. I thought you'd talked to her, maybe been rude or something."

"North probably would have said something cis-hetero-machista about her, you know." Shaw mimed breasts.

"For fuck's sake. It's an expression. And I'm gay."

"She'll cool down," Yasmin said. "I hope." Her phone dinged, and she checked the screen. "Karen's at the pub."

"Thank you," North said. "Keep us posted about Mary Angela. If she still seems agitated, or if she contacts you again, let us know."

"But she couldn't be—" Yasmin swallowed. "You don't think she…"

"Keep us informed, please," North said, cocking his head for Shaw to follow him.

Chapter 17

THE CAMELOT PUBLIC HOUSE was much rowdier than the first time Shaw had been here. In the late afternoon, every table was packed with men and women from the con, and most of the available floor space was covered by swag bags, tote bags, purses, man-purses (murses?), carryalls, a single Dierberg's shopping bag, and fanny packs. Voices swelled, punctuated by laughter. At a corner table, a man in a kilt was singing "One More Angel in Heaven" in a falsetto.

"I know you're going to roll your eyes," Shaw said, "but I honestly think I've found my people."

North didn't roll his eyes, and it took a moment for Shaw to realize this was very suspicious. Instead, North was scenting the air, his head coming up and his attention moving toward the door to the kitchen.

"My tribe," Shaw said and waited for the explosion.

Still nothing. North was still taking those tiny sniffs.

"My family. North, will you—" Then Shaw smelled the fried onions. "Oh no. No, sir. We've been doing so good about fried foods."

"They have onion rings, Shaw. Beer-battered onion rings. And I haven't eaten all day."

"But we agreed that we'd try that full-keto, inverted-keto, trans-keto body-psych-out rotation until—"

"You agreed," North said, catching the arm of a harried young man in a waiter's apron. "Onion rings. As many as you can. And the biggest bacon cheeseburger you've got. And—" He glanced at Shaw.

"How many kinds of kale do you have?" Shaw asked.

"Ignore that. A bacon cheeseburger for him too, but in one of those lettuce buns instead of a real, delicious, honest, full-of-gluten regular bun."

"I really don't—"

"And a Coke. We'll be at that table over there."

"In terms of nitrates and nitrites as preservatives," Shaw tried to say, "have you considered subbing sea salt and raw cane—"

He didn't have a chance to finish because North gave a tug that almost launched him off his feet, and Shaw stumbled after him into the maze of tables and backpacks. Karen was sitting at a table behind a support column, talking to someone out of sight. She froze when she saw North and said something, her expression urgent, to whoever she was sitting with.

"Get ready for a runner," North said over his shoulder.

The other person must have said something back, though, because Karen relaxed, and she even offered a small wave as North and Shaw approached. As Shaw came around the column, he recognized the woman Karen was sitting with: in her early sixties, birdlike, the choppy shag of silver hair.

"We've been looking for you," North told Leslie Hawkins.

"So I hear," Leslie said. "God, you're gorgeous. And huge. Is your dick as big as I think it is?"

North blinked.

"Probably bigger," Shaw said.

For some reason, North blushed and shot a look at Shaw.

"Well, you didn't answer, and I thought maybe you didn't want to brag. Although, to be fair, the answer really depends on how big she thinks your dick is. If she thinks you're enormous, then the answer is probably 'Not that big, actually,' and if she thinks you're average sized, the answer is—"

"No more helping," North said, pulling out a chair for Shaw first and then seating himself.

"You're adorable," Leslie said, her gaze moving from one to the other. "I'd pay five hundred bucks to see you two fuck. A thousand, if one of you tied the other up and made him scream. Nothing mean-spirited. Just really get out of control, you know?"

"I'll keep that in mind," North said.

"Which one of you tops? I bet the little squirrelly one can make the big one howl."

"I'm sorry," Karen said wearily as she covered her eyes. "I want to apologize fully and completely for this unacceptable behavior. She's usually not this bad, but she's been bottling it up, and it's kind of like an overload." Lowering her hand, she said to Leslie, "Did you get it all out of your system?"

Leslie offered a tiny smile and a shrug. She picked up her napkin and folded it neatly, her eyes sliding to North again. For some reason Shaw couldn't understand, North blushed even redder.

"So," Shaw said, "you're a lot of trouble."

"Thank you," Leslie said.

"I thought you were banned from the convention."

"What convention?" Leslie's eyes were wide and innocent. "I'm in St. Louis visiting an amateur pornographer. A friend of mine. I happened to pick the Royal Excalibur. I happened to decide to have a drink and a bite to eat in the pub. And by the sheerest of coincidences, here are all my convention friends. Now, since I'm not attending the convention this year—"

"You were banned for life," Karen murmured before taking a drink from a massive margarita.

"—I can't attend any of the panels or discussions, and I can't go into the exhibition hall. But nobody can stop me from having a drink in a pub."

"I guess you heard about what happened to Scotty," North said.

"Karen was just telling me. I can't say I'm surprised; someone obviously has it out for him, and he deserves it."

"Because he got you banned for life."

Another of those unreadable smiles.

"What exactly happened last year?" North said. "We've heard two versions now. In one, you hired a sex worker to seduce an author. In another, you broke into Scotty and Josue's hotel room, hid, and tried to film them having sex."

"I don't know what you're talking about," Leslie said, straightening the napkin again, trying to line up the edges perfectly.

"Are you sure?" Shaw said. "Because I bet that would be hot. Like, really, really hot. I've seen Josue and Scotty's workout videos, and watching the two of them go at it—well, I mean, if writing doesn't work out, they could always make money that way."

"That's exactly what I said." Leslie's gaze shifted to Shaw. "Especially the way Josue makes those breathy noises when Scotty gropes him in public, and— oh no. Very nice try. But I'm not going to talk about any of that. There could be...legal ramifications, you understand."

"That sounds shady as shit," North said.

Leslie shrugged.

"What do you think about all this?" Shaw said to Karen.

"I don't know what happened last year." She gulped more margarita. "It's none of my business; whatever it was, it's between the three of them."

"And I suppose it's just a coincidence," North had his ice-rim gaze fixed on Leslie, "what happened last year, and the threatening messages, and then you showing up and Scotty being poisoned."

"It is a coincidence," Leslie said quietly. "I had nothing to do with that, although, as I said, I can certainly understand why someone would want to." Her gaze moved toward the far side of the bar, where it opened onto the hotel corridor. A woman in a rainbow-colored leotard was staring at her. "I think it's time for me to go. That bitch is going to run and tell Yasmin I'm here, and I'm having too nice a day for a catfight."

Without waiting for an answer, Leslie scurried toward the exit. The woman in the rainbow leotard said something, holding out a hand, but Leslie shoved her out of the way.

"You let her go?" Shaw said.

"Me?" North said. "You just sat there, tugging your own balls."

"I'm not going to dignify that with a response," Shaw said. Then, unable to stop himself: "I had an itch."

North opened his mouth to say something, but before he could, the harried-looking waiter arrived, setting down burgers and onion rings. Shaw had already taken two big bites before he remembered the nitrates, but when he glanced over, the waiter was trying to get a pair of twinks down from the two-top they were dancing on.

The burger was good; the Coke was even better. The sugary, caffeinated rush jolted Shaw's brain to wakefulness, and he took Karen in again, noticing the clues that had escaped him the first time: the hint of redness in her eyes, the shredded edge of the napkin in her lap, her restless shifting in the chair.

"That must have been really scary today," Shaw said.

"Oh my God," Karen said. "It was terrible. He's still in the hospital, do you realize that? One minute he was just Scotty being Scotty, and now he's—he might die."

"I didn't realize you and Scotty were so close."

Karen started. Then she gulped her margarita again. "We're not," she said, returning the nearly empty glass to the table with a wobble. "All I mean is, it's scary, seeing that happen to someone you know. And it could have been any of us."

"Do you really believe that?" North asked.

"Of course. I was supposed to be on that panel."

"But do you believe you were the target? Or the other authors? Or could someone have a reason to target Scotty in particular?"

Karen flushed in splotches. "You've been talking to people already."

Shaw nodded. North bit savagely into an onion ring.

"I don't know what you expect me to say. Scotty was who he was. He rubbed a lot of people the wrong way. I stayed clear of him as much as I could, although it's hard at a place like this. Scotty's like—what's that thing in science? He expands to fill the space available. Does that make sense?"

"So," Shaw said quietly, "you did have a few run-ins with Scotty at the con? Before today, I mean."

More splotches, red and angry, showed in Karen's face and neck. "I mean, I couldn't exactly avoid him. Not completely."

"What was your relationship with Scotty?"

"What? None." But her knee bounced, whacking the underside of the table. "I'm sorry, I—"

"It's going to be a hell of a lot easier if you stop lying," North said.

"And you'll feel better," Shaw said. "Let's start with an easy one: we already know that you and Scotty had an agreement about your next book. Why don't you tell us about that?"

"He…he was going to read it. Give me some feedback. I'm a good writer, I think, and I've got a fan base that's small but loyal. I just can't seem to break out on the charts." She toyed with the stem of the margarita glass. "It's really frustrating after a while. I write these books. They're really good, better than a lot of the dreck that gets churned out. And then I hover at five or six hundred in the rankings. Serenity could put together a hundred and fifty pages of porn, and it would stay at number one for a week. It's…it's insulting."

"Now the rest of it," North said.

"Scotty changed his mind."

Shaw raised his eyebrows. He slid one hand along the table toward the mound of onion rings in front of North.

"That's it," Karen said. "That's all that happened. I don't know why you're looking at me like that."

"Hold on," North said, "I have to stab this fork between the bones of his wrist so this fucker learns not to steal my onion rings."

Drawing his hand back and rubbing his wrist preemptively, Shaw said, "But Scotty was very public about helping you with your book, wasn't he?"

"How'd you know that?"

Shaw waited. A woman at the next table was in a belly-dancer costume, apparently trying to recreate a dance for a TikTok video. She was panting as she tried to repeat the moves.

"Scotty took this job as an editor at Bolingbroke. They're a specialty press, LGBTQ literature. And Scotty made a big deal out of it, of course. And part of that was announcing that he was going to be providing personalized editorial services. He claimed he could make anyone a bestseller. I was going to be his guinea pig. Then, poof." She opened one hand. "He stopped answering emails. I figured he got busy with the new job and with his own writing. I was disappointed, but no skin off my nose."

"That's not exactly how we heard it," North said. "It sounded like you were furious, and you weren't shy about telling other people Scotty had broken his promise."

"Who told you that?"

North shook his head. The belly-dancer missed a step, stumbled, and went ass-over-teakettle when she hit the chair behind her. Shaw got to his feet to help her, but her friends were already there, crowding around her. One of them cheered. While North was still staring, Shaw helped himself to an onion ring. Just one.

"I guess it doesn't matter," Karen said. "As you said, Scotty had been very public about swearing he could make me a bestseller. Everybody in the genre knew about it. And people wanted to know how it was going, what kind of advice he was giving me, that kind of thing. I put them off as long as I could, but I didn't go out of my way to tell the whole world that Scotty had dumped me. Finally I had to tell people the truth: he wasn't responding to my messages, and I figured it had all been a hoax, some kind of publicity stunt. I...I might have acted angrier than I was, but only because I knew that's what people expected. Honestly, I was kind of relieved. That's the author's dilemma, you know: you want feedback, but you dread it at the same time. Once the disappointment wore off, I stopped thinking about it at all."

"But you can understand how it looks," Shaw said, breaking off a piece of the onion ring and popping it in his mouth. "Scotty broke a promise to you. Then, he broke another one today, by putting JD on the panel instead of you. And then we find you and Leslie having drinks: two women who have been publicly humiliated by Scotty Carlson, celebrating after Scotty's been poisoned."

"Do I look like I'm celebrating?"

"No," Shaw said. "I guess not."

"I'm freaking out. Someone tried to poison a group of authors, and now Scotty's alone at the hospital, fighting for his life, and—and it's not right." In what sounded like an afterthought, she added, "Even if he is an asshole."

"Do you believe Leslie when she says she has nothing to do with this?" North asked.

Karen snorted and sipped the last slush from her drink. "You met her. She's kind of got a one-track mind. I honestly don't think she'd have time to plan something like this; she's too busy searching for new double-penetration videos."

Shaw choked on a piece of breading.

"Well," North said, eyes hooded. "That is very fucking interesting."

"I don't—" Shaw gasped. "I'm not—"

"Uh huh."

"North, I'm dying!"

North just shook his head.

After a swig of Coke, Shaw managed to say, "I don't even know what that term means. That was purely an allergic reaction to the gluten."

"You're pathetic," North informed him.

"If not Leslie," Shaw said desperately to Karen, who was watching them with a small smile, "then who?"

"Honestly? It could have been anybody. You saw how Scotty is. After this morning, even you've got a motive to want him dead."

"That's an exaggeration." North frowned. "Wanting someone dead and being willing to poison them, and with a fairly elaborate plan, are two different things. A lot of people think they want someone else dead; very few of them have the guts to commit to it, let alone the smarts to come up with something like this."

"What about someone on the panel?" Shaw asked.

"I thought about that, but I was in the room before any of the panelists, and I was watching them pretty carefully. Well, looking daggers at them, if I'm being honest. None of them touched the others' water. They only drank from their own. And the bottles were still sealed; I could hear the seal break when Scotty opened his. Plus there were almost a hundred people watching; if one of them had started tampering with the bottles, someone would have noticed."

"No, that's not what I mean. I'm getting the sense that the superstars on the panel weren't exactly best friends. And weren't exactly nice people, either, if I'm being honest."

"They're a nest of vipers," North put in.

"That's…true, I guess," Karen said. "Scotty and Serenity are outrageous in their own ways, but the others can be difficult too. JD is a bitch as soon as she feels threatened, and Mary Angela is all sugar and nice until something doesn't go her way. Even Clarence can dig in his heels. You should have seen him and Scotty go at it last year."

"Someone else mentioned that. What happened?"

"Well, you heard Scotty's views on the genre and what he perceives as the general readership. You'd think saying things like that would be terminal for a career, but it just seems to make Scotty more popular. He can look right into people's faces, describe them in the most offensive and insulting ways, and they smile and nod and think he's talking about everyone in the room except them." Karen shook her head. "It's unreal."

"Where does Clarence come in?" Shaw asked.

"Oh, Clarence got tired of hearing the same thing every year. He's started standing up for the genre. He's very eloquent about it. Very passionate too. And honestly, someone needs to say it. We all write this genre because we love it—well, some people write it to make money, but most of us write it because we love it. And it's awful to hear Scotty go on and on about how stupid we all are, how pathetic we are, and how he's really a literary writer."

"This is the same guy," North said, "who has an ongoing series about a character named Lars the Construction Worker who fucks his way through a parade of skilled tradesmen?"

Karen grinned. "That's right. Literary genius. Anyway, last year, Scotty went on his usual spiel, and Clarence stood up to him. Scotty didn't like that, so he went after Clarence. It got really nasty. And personal. Clarence is single, and Scotty kept throwing that in his face, comparing Clarence to him and Josue, talking about how Clarence is a dried-up old queen. He blamed it on Clarence being a romance writer. He said it flat-out—something about how Clarence couldn't have a real relationship because he had turned himself into a masturbatory echo of a human being, or something like that."

"Jesus," Shaw said.

"Yeah, it was awful. And nobody said anything. We all sat there. I couldn't believe what was happening, and then it was over, and Clarence ran out of the room."

"Next time," North said, "I say we help somebody finish the job."

"Not funny." Shaw slurped on the straw a few more times, got nothing, and looked around for the waiter. In the process, he caught North's eye and the warning look there. Setting down the cup, Shaw said, "I don't suppose you have anything in writing, do you? Between you and Scotty, I mean. An agreement. A contract. That kind of thing."

Karen shook her head. Opening her purse, she said, "I'm sorry. Today has been awful, and I want to go lie down. I've told you everything I know. More than I wanted to, actually, although I guess it's for the best." She counted out cash, weighted it down with her glass, and stood. "I don't want you to take this the wrong way, but I hope I don't ever have to see you again."

She wove a path toward the exit, dodging a middle-aged gay man who was trying to tap dance while using a breadstick as an improvised cane.

"This place is fucking bananas," North said.

"A breadstick isn't the worst idea for a cane replacement."

North scowled at him. "I mean the fact that all these people pretend to be friends and secretly want to kill each other."

"Oh. That." Shaw rattled the ice in his cup. "Do you think we have time—"

"No," North said, pushing the cup down. "Let's go find Clarence. I want to hear his side of things."

Shaw wedged cash under the plate, and they headed out of the pub.

"So," North said as they made their way down the hall. "That does something for you, huh? Double—Mother of Christ, Shaw!"

Shaw shook out a fist, smiling to himself as North massaged his arm.

Chapter 18

YASMIN GAVE THEM CLARENCE'S room number, and when they got to 1407, a pinprick of yellow light showed through the peephole. North rapped on the door.

Footsteps moved on the other side, a low voice spoke, and then the deadbolt thundered loose. The door opened a few inches. The woman on the other side was performing a vanishing act inside her cheap polyester suit.

"Detective Cao," North said.

"Hiya, boys. Reck, it's them."

From deeper in the room came a muffled, "For the love of—"

Cerise disappeared, and Jadon took her place, catching the door as it began to swing shut. "Go away. Go home. I told you to stay out of this."

"Hi, Jadon," Shaw said. He had the same huge, goofy smile he always wore for Jadon. It was a kind of proportionate inversion, North guessed, to his own desire to smash Jadon's head in the door a few dozen times. "Good to see you again."

"Hi, Shaw. It is not good to see you again."

"That's kind of rude."

"I'm going to close the door now. Please be gone by the next time I open it, and please stay out of this case."

"Tell you what—" North began.

Shaw grabbed his arm and tugged him toward the elevators, while Jadon sighed and shut the door.

"I'm not letting him run us off like we're mangy dogs," North said, twisting to free his arm. Shaw could be annoyingly tenacious sometimes, though, and now seemed like one of those moments.

"I was wondering about mange," Shaw said. "You have this scabby little bald patch back here."

"I do not—" North yanked his arm free and tried to reassemble his dignity. He felt like he might have lost ground, though, when he touched the back of his head. "That's from the one and only time I let you near me with a pair of clippers. I'm lucky you didn't gouge me to the bone. Now stay here while I go rearrange your ex-boyfriend's dentures."

"Jadon doesn't have dentures."

"He will soon enough."

Sighing, Shaw took North by the wrist this time and led him to the bank of elevators. He drew out his phone and tapped the screen several times.

"We need to talk to Clarence, Shaw. Whether Jadon likes it or not." North thought about this and added, "Preferably not."

"You do realize that jealousy is one of my ten biggest turnoffs, right?" Shaw studied the phone's screen. "Along with yogurt enemas, Republican National Conventions, Port-A-Potties—"

"Ok, ok, ok. Just stop talking, please."

"—that one time I had to see your toenails—"

"For the love of Christ, I will cut it out about Jadon if you'll stop talking."

"Phone."

North handed it over, and Shaw opened a video call app. North saw an image being transmitted from Shaw's phone. Shaw passed North's phone back and nestled his own in a plastic fern sitting at the end of the row of elevators. He watched the image on North's screen until he was satisfied with the angle, and then he nodded.

"Turn off your mic," he instructed, and when North had, he took the lead again. They passed Clarence's room and ducked into the ice machine alcove. The small space was warmer than the rest of the hallway, which North judged had something to do with the heat that the ice maker put off. It smelled like someone had just run a mop over the tile, and not a particularly clean mop. Shaw looked around, shrugged, and sat on the floor. When he patted the space next to him, North grumbled and joined him. He set the phone on his leg where they could both see it, and then he tried to relax.

Minutes dragged by.

The ice machine rumbled, and ice clattered into the bin.

More minutes dragged by.

A TV came on in the room next to them. North couldn't make out the details, but his imagination told him it was Wolf Blitzer shouting about tuna prices.

"I guess we don't know how long it will take," Shaw said, resting his head on North's shoulder.

"I don't have anywhere better to be," North said, "and we're getting paid."

"And you get to spend this time with your amazing boyfriend."

"And that."

Shaw lifted his head, turned, and kissed North's neck. He had missed a patch shaving, and the stubble tickled North's sensitive skin there. He shifted.

"Stay still," Shaw whispered. "This is a stakeout."

Then he kissed North again, and this time the little shit did it on purpose, scraping the stubble back and forth. North tried to convert his groan into a slowly released breath, but he wasn't sure how well he succeeded. Shaw reached down, took North's hand, and pressed it between his legs. He was hard as a rock, stretching the Lululemon pants obscenely.

"Somebody's horny," North said, massaging Shaw lightly.

"Not horny," Shaw murmured. "I think my root chakra is blocked. And my sacral chakra is imbalanced. Also, no talking. This is a stakeout."

North pulled back slightly from the next kiss and raised his eyebrows.

"Ok," Shaw whispered. "I'm also really, really horny."

"Too bad this is a public place," North said, withdrawing his touch. "Too bad we're working a case."

"I said stay still," Shaw whispered, snatching North's hand and pressing it against him again. He rutted into it with tiny thrusts of his pelvis. "God, North. I've been going crazy. My chakras are so messed up."

"You're going crazy because you need some sex," North said, not bothering to fight his smirk. "That's what you're trying to say, isn't it? Try it in plain English."

"North."

"That didn't really answer my question. I have to admit, I'm a little worried that I don't know what you need. I guess I can't tell what the problem is."

"North," Shaw said, the whine edged with desperation this time.

"Not that I don't like getting you all hot and bothered, but do you want to tell me how far we're going? Because I'm not taking you home to change underwear."

"I'm not wearing underwear." Shaw stifled a moan, barely, as North closed his fingers around him.

"I know," North said. "Everybody at this whole con knows."

A door opened down the hall, the sound like a gunshot, and Shaw scrambled back.

"You have a raging erection," North said, pointing to the tent in the Lululemons.

"Look who's talking," Shaw whispered furiously, and North smirked some more and adjusted himself in the Levi's.

Low voices carried down the hall, and a moment later, the sound shifted, emerging from the speakers on North's phone. He watched as first Jadon and then Cerise appeared on screen. Cerise was carrying a plastic evidence bag with a prescription vial in it, but even though she was standing right next to the camera, the angle made it impossible to read what was printed on the label. Their conversation, whatever it had been, was over, and the two detectives stood side by side as they waited for an elevator car to arrive.

"I need to call Dhan," Cerise said, "and cancel."

"You can go if you need to," Jadon said.

"Just because you're pathetic and alone," Cerise said, "doesn't mean you've got to do the job by yourself." The elevator dinged, and the doors opened. "Besides, I don't want to spend my evening in the hospital after you and McKinney finally go at it."

Whatever Jadon said was distorted beyond recognition as he stepped into the car, and as Cerise followed, the bag twisted just enough to bring the prescription label on the vial into focus: Adderall, thirty milligrams.

"There we go," North whispered as the elevator doors slid shut.

"Yes, right, fine," Shaw said, grabbing his hand again, "but if you could just—"

"Let's go talk to Clarence," North said, getting to his feet.

"North, I could really use a hand here."

"Sure," North said, grabbing Shaw's arm and dragging him upright. "Now stick your dick in the ice maker until you're presentable."

"My aura is going to be jacked for weeks because of this. You realize that, right?"

"Remember when you were a nice little virgin who wouldn't dream of humping his boyfriend in a public place?"

Shaw grumbled something that sounded shockingly profane.

"What was that?" North asked.

"I said," Shaw said, eyes coming up clear and innocent, "did you hear that Jadon is single?"

"I surely fucking did," North said. "And did you hear that Cerise thinks I'd put him in the hospital?"

"Oh my God," Shaw said, covering his face.

North headed down the hallway; behind him, he heard Shaw mutter something that sounded like *going to be unbearable now.*

Chapter 19

SHAW FOLLOWED NORTH TO Clarence's room, and North knocked. Clarence answered the door almost immediately.

"I was hoping it'd be you," he said. He'd ditched the boxy blazer, and now he was wearing a mustardy pinstriped button-down that looked twenty years old. He smoothed his thinning hair, opened his mouth, and seemed to notice Shaw. "Oh. And it's you."

"We'd like to talk to you," North said. "If you have a few minutes, that is."

"Of course, of course. Although I have a touch of social anxiety, so maybe your colleague could wait—"

"No," North said. "And he's my boyfriend."

"Oh, yes, of course," Clarence said in muffled tones. Shoulders slumped, he slunk back into the room.

Shaw followed North into what must have been one of the Royal Excalibur's economy rooms: two full beds squeezed into a tiny space, with barely enough room for Clarence to shuffle sideways and sit in an armchair that had been jammed into the corner of the room. North settled onto the bed. Shaw took up position at the ancient CRT television and adjusted the bunny-ear antennas.

"Did you know that the soul actually exists on the electromagnetic spectrum?" Shaw said, turning the bunny-ears toward Clarence. "They've done studies."

"Sweet Lord," North muttered.

"No," Clarence said. "I didn't know that."

"Really powerful souls actually interfere with television and radio broadcasts," Shaw said. "Terrestrial broadcast, I mean."

"Oh," Clarence said.

"Of course, if you're a trained psychic, you can mitigate the interference."

"That's great, Shaw," North said, "call me when your soul stops interfering with my *90 Day Fiancé* episodes."

"No," Shaw said, "that's just because you have a bad cable hookup because you steal it from your neighbor."

"I'm sorry," Clarence said, "I thought you wanted to talk to me about what happened today, but I'm very busy, and—"

"Yes," North cut in. "We do. We're looking into what happened with Scotty, and of course, as an eyewitness, we wanted to get your take on things."

"And," Clarence said drily, a flash of humor animating his façade, "because I'm the primary suspect. Isn't that right?"

"We're private investigators," North said. "Are you a suspect in a criminal investigation?"

"It seems so." Clarence retrieved a bag from the floor and set it on the bed, which was about two inches from his knees. He withdrew a laptop from the bag, opened it, and began typing. "It's very exciting, actually. I'm going to take notes on our conversation. And, of course, jot down my impressions from the police interview. It was my first one." He blushed after saying this, his eyes skating to North and then jolting away again. "And it's all going to be very useful material. Primary research, you understand."

"You're writing a crime novel?" Shaw said, drifting a few steps away from the bunny-ears so he could glance into the bathroom. A polyester dopp kit lay on the counter, and nothing suspicious was immediately visible. "I thought you wrote romance. I know you write romance, in fact. I have some of your books, the early ones."

"That's right," Clarence said, "but I'm shifting into romantic suspense. They're starting a new imprint at Bolingbroke, and it's going to be exclusively romantic suspense. It's a growing market, by the way. You wouldn't mind if I ask you a few questions, just to get started?"

"Maybe later," North said. "Is this the same Bolingbroke where Scotty is working as an editor?"

"It would really help me feel more comfortable in this interview," Clarence said. "If I could ask you a few questions first. Get my mind in the right place before we talk about the unpleasantness from this morning."

North was silent; Shaw knew it was one of his best tricks. But this time, it didn't work. Clarence remained poised at the laptop, his gaze bright and anticipatory, and finally North threw a sidelong look at Shaw. Shaw shrugged.

"Why don't we trade questions," North said, "to keep things moving?"

"I can live with that," Clarence said. "You asked about Bolingbroke; yes, that's the same press where Scotty works. If you can call it that."

"What does that mean?"

"My turn," Clarence said. "I'm very interested in writing a novel about a private investigator—a gay private investigator—"

"Why the fuck wouldn't he be," North muttered.

"—and I find myself incredibly fortunate to have this opportunity. The character is the most important part, and so I'd like to know a little bit about you first. Tell me your background, if you would. Your childhood. Your coming-out story. Your first sexual experience."

"No."

"I'll tell you about my background," Shaw said.

Clarence glanced at him and then looked back at North. "It's very important to understand—"

"Make something up," North said. "If you want to ask a legitimate question, fine. But I'm not telling you about the first time little Timmy felt me up under a blanket at a sleepover."

Clarence's fingers flew over the keyboard.

"That wasn't—" North tried.

"Very interesting," Clarence murmured.

"Who's Timmy?" Shaw said.

North threw him a furious glance.

"What are the most important traits for a private detective?" Clarence asked.

"No, it's my turn. What did you mean about Scotty?"

"You didn't answer my question, so I get to ask another. What would the quintessential private detective be like? Or, if you prefer, what are your own strengths and weaknesses?"

"Analytical reasoning, critical thinking, attention to detail. Now—"

"And running," Shaw put in. "And squats. All those leg days. To catch criminals. And to pick up heavy things."

"Stay out of this," North said through gritted teeth.

"Powerful haunches," Clarence murmured as he tapped away at the keyboard.

"Don't write one fucking word about my haunches," North said. "About my legs, I mean."

"Haunches like tree trunks," Shaw suggested.

"Like tree trunks," Clarence repeated to himself.

"Ok," North said, "that's about enough of this."

"My turn," Shaw said. "I'm much more graceful than North. Part of that's because I don't wear steel-toed footwear wrapped in dead animals on my feet. But part of it is that I'm built more like a gazelle. A list of possible adjectives to describe me would include: able, blade-like, cat-like, darting, elegant, fulvous, graceful, hot—of course—impeccable, jurisprudent, keen, lissome, lithe, loping—lots of good L ones, actually—"

"Mentally defective," North said.

"North!"

"That's very good," Clarence said, his gaze already moving back to North, "but really, my readership tends to prefer a more traditionally masculine protagonist."

"Shaw didn't graduate college," North said to Clarence, "so I'll translate for you: Clarence wants me for his story because I'm butcher."

"That's not exactly what—"

"I'm butch," Shaw said, hands twisting the hem of his tank. "I'm very butch."

"Sure you are, princess," North said.

"North, tell him how butch I can be. Tell him how I saved you from that spider."

"He carried it outside on a piece of paper because he was thinking about converting to Jainism that week, but I'm pretty sure it was already dead."

"Tell him about—you know…"

North shrugged. "What?"

"The sex."

"I'm sorry, let me get this straight: you're asking me to expose the private, intimate details of our sex life to a stranger because you want him to think you're butch enough to star in his B-grade detective fiction?"

"I have to object to the label B-grade—" Clarence tried to say.

"Yes," Shaw said. "Exactly. Tell him!"

"I cannot do this without a beer," North said, pinching the bridge of his nose.

"I'm very traditionally masculine," Shaw said. "I chopped down a tree once."

"It was a sapling, and he ran over it with a lawn mower, and afterwards, he cried so hard that he threw up a little bit and I had to hose the whole fucking mess into the street."

"I own a Cardinals jersey. Oh! And I own ratty gray sweatpants that I wear on the weekends. And last weekend I told North to 'beer me.'"

"He does own a Cardinals jersey," North said. "Several, actually. Including one he had custom-made out of a rainbow fabric. And he cut out the crotch of those sweatpants with pinking shears because he thought they gave him syphilis."

"I thought they gave me crabs!"

"And the full sentence was, 'North, beer me my nipple cream,' and then he laughed for forty-five minutes."

Clarence's eyes were huge, his hands frozen about the keyboard. Down the hall, the ice maker rumbled another load into the bin.

"It's for my hands," Shaw said into the silence. "They get very chapped in the winter."

"Ok," North said, "now you've got enough information for the rest of your fucking career."

"I didn't ask about any of that," Clarence said. "I didn't want to know about any of that."

"Playtime is over. It's time to—what are you doing?"

"That is a fantastic catchphrase. 'Playtime is over.' He could say that every time he dusts a bad guy.'"

North stared wordlessly.

"You probably need to talk about his musk," Shaw said.

"Musk," Clarence murmured, fingers flying over the keyboard.

"Oh, and he could use his catchphrase during sex too. Like he's completely closed off emotionally, so all his relationships are purely physical, a series of one-offs with pretty, vulnerable college boys."

"Thin ice, Shaw," North growled.

"And he could be plowing into one, rattling the cheap dorm bed, and then he flips the rent boy over—"

"He's not a rent boy!"

"—and says, 'Playtime is over,' and then he mounts him and breeds him doggy style. Those are good verbs, by the way. You should use those."

North was taking shallow, rapid breaths through his nose.

Clarence was typing manically.

With one hand, North forced the laptop shut. Clarence squawked as he freed his hands at the last moment.

"Why," North said, his voice grating and sounding only marginally under control, "did the police just walk out of your room with an Adderall scrip?"

"Because—because they think I did that. What happened to Scotty."

"Go on."

Swallowing, Clarence glanced at his laptop, which North still had a hand on. "Scotty and I don't have the best history. Last year, there was an incident. We were on a panel together, and we disagreed about something, and he said some genuinely awful things to me. I got rattled, if I'm being honest, and he laughed at me about that, talked about how I was a fluttering old queen. Something like that. It was a year ago; I can't be expected to remember every awful thing he said. Someone must have told the police about it during the interviews this afternoon because they showed up at my room an hour ago and we had to go through the whole song and dance again. They asked if they could see my prescriptions, and I said yes—"

"Did they have a warrant?"

"No. They just asked."

North nodded. "Keep going."

"And they found the bottle of Adderall, which I have a perfectly legal prescription for, and they asked if they could take it. I tried to say no, but they kept asking, and they kept saying they didn't understand why I wouldn't want to help the investigation, and on and on like that. So I let them."

"That's it?"

"I mean, they asked me a million questions, but it all came down to the same thing: I didn't want to hurt Scotty, and even if I'd wanted to, I never had an opportunity. I don't have a key to the storeroom, and I was with Yasmin the whole time we were inside it. I told them about the service door, the one that the staff use sometimes, and they didn't seem to care. They just wanted to talk to me."

North grunted and looked at Shaw.

"If you want us to help you," Shaw said, "you need to be completely honest."

"I am being honest! And I'm tired of people telling me that. I didn't want to hurt Scotty, and even if I had, I couldn't have done it."

"Technically," Shaw said, "you could have. The service door was unlocked at some point during the night after Yasmin bought the water and placed it in the storeroom. That means you had access to that room and to the bottled water."

"But so did everyone else!"

Shaw nodded. "I know. You need to keep that in mind, though. If the police come back, you might want to have a lawyer. And you might not want to let them take anything else without a warrant."

Clarence smoothed his thinning hair with a trembling hand. His face was ashen. "Oh my God. Oh my God."

"What kind of interactions have you had with Scotty over the last year? Since last year's Queer Expectations, I mean."

"None." He must have read Shaw's disbelief in his expression because he added, "None, I swear to you. I unfriended him on social media, and now he doesn't even pop up in my feed. Every once in a while I'll see his books on the Amazon charts, but I don't spend a lot of time looking at that stuff."

"What about Bolingbroke?" North asked.

"It's all up in the air. And Scotty's not my editor there anyway." He glanced around the room. "I want to go home. I'm going to go home. I can't stay here."

"I'm not sure that's the best idea," Shaw said. "How do you think that's going to look?"

"I don't care how it looks! I didn't do anything. Someone drugged me too, and I'm scared. I want to go home." His gaze settled on a roller bag in the corner. Then he looked at North. "I want you to go. I'm going to pack my bags, and I'm getting the first flight out of here."

"That's really not a good idea," North said.

"I want you to go. Please leave."

North stood slowly. Shaw shared a look with him.

"Get out of my room!" Clarence shouted.

"We're going," Shaw said, "but if you want to do yourself a favor, you'll start thinking about two things: first, a timeline that accounts for where you were, every minute of the day, after Yasmin bought that water; and second, somebody who might have wanted to hurt Scotty even more than you do."

"I don't—I didn't want that. Scotty's a jerk, but that's not worth going to prison over."

"You can give us that information," North said. "Or not. But one way or another, you'll want to be ready the next time the police talk to you."

Clarence didn't seem to hear him; he slid two fingers under the mustardy shirt's collar, wheezing.

Shaw met North's eyes again, and when North nodded, he headed to the door.

Behind them, Clarence's voice was a croak. "The staff."

"What?" Shaw said.

"The staff. The hotel staff. Scotty was horrible to them. Shouting. Demanding. Humiliating. He tried to get one of them fired—we all just sat there and watched like a bunch of cowards." Clarence's voice got stronger, and he said, "It was the service door that was unlocked. The door the staff uses. That means something, doesn't it?"

"Keep thinking about that timeline," Shaw said, and he led North out of the room.

Chapter 20

ON THE ELEVATOR RIDE down, North said, "I don't like that he's so quick to run."

"He's freaking out," Shaw said. "It's a natural response, even if he didn't have anything to do with what happened to Scotty."

"It's also a natural response if he did."

"There's that too."

North tried not to. Then it burst out: "My musk?"

"You have a very appealing fragrance."

"Stop talking."

"Not your foot funk."

North stared straight ahead.

"But the American Crew gel. And the Irish Spring soap. And the leather."

"I said stop talking."

He couldn't be sure—the car's steel-sheet walls gave back a dull, wavery reflection—but he thought Shaw was smiling.

"Ow! My hip!"

"Oops," North muttered as the doors slid open. "My fist must have slipped."

They headed to the front desk, asked for a manager, and waited. It took a long time before a woman showed up. She looked Latina, her glossy black hair in a complicated braid, and she was wearing heels that put her eye to eye with North. Her name tag said Silvia.

"I'm sorry, sir. That's not in keeping with hotel policy," seemed to be the only functional line in her coding.

"Fine," North kept saying. And then he'd offer an alternative or a compromise.

"I'm sorry, sir. That's not in keeping with hotel policy."

Shaw finally dragged him away.

"I was being polite," North said as he ripped his arm free.

"I noticed. You were being polite at about a hundred and twenty decibels."

North's face heated.

"She was just doing her job," Shaw said. "Come on, there's got to be another way to talk to the staff."

"Sure," North said. "We just wander the service areas and start yammering at them."

Shaw turned and looked at him, and North's face got even hotter.

"Oh," North said. "That's what we're going to do?"

"I honestly don't know how you do this job without me sometimes."

It wasn't exactly that easy. Most of the housekeeping staff was gone for the day, and the one woman North did see pushing a cart became suddenly and extremely interested in going the other direction. A loose caster squeaked wildly as she flew down the corridor.

"Maybe don't walk faster and faster shouting, 'Hey, hey, yes, you,' at a woman who doesn't know you." Shaw seemed to consider this and added, "Especially in a deserted hallway."

"Well, you and Clarence fucked up my rhythm. Everything feels off."

"Shake it off; we've got a job to do. Let's split up. Maybe you'll do better without an audience."

North's face was hot again, but he made himself fix Shaw with a glare.

"See?" Shaw said, smiling. "You're already looking more like yourself."

The first lucky hit was two guys, one black and one white, smoking and talking quietly at the back of the loading dock. The rollup door was open, and they huddled in the opening, blowing streamers of smoke out into the early-evening gloom. The cold was intense; North's breath plumed in front of him as he walked toward them.

"Can I help you?" the black guy asked. He was wearing black Dickies, a black tee, and a hairnet.

"Any chance I can bum one of those? Rough fucking day."

The black guy looked at the white guy, who was wearing a black polyester jacket and trousers that reminded North of the staff at the front desk. The white guy shrugged, opened a pack of Camels, and held it out. North took one, accepted a light, and puffed a few times. When the wind howled down the alley, the freezing air made his eyes water; he barely felt it.

"Thank the good fucking Lord," North muttered through wreaths of smoke. "I was about to murder someone."

The two guys eyed each other.

"My boyfriend," North said to the unspoken question.

"You're here for that convention?"

"Kind of. Private investigators."

"That's tough," the black guy said. "Like Luther. That guy is the shit."

"Luther was a police detective," the white guy said.

"Shut the fuck up, Maurice."

The white boy, who was apparently called Maurice, just grinned. "I never heard of any gay detectives before."

"We exist," North said and then drew hard on the Camel. Exhaling, he added, "Apparently."

For some reason, that made the black guy laugh incredibly hard until Maurice said, "Ignore Deshawn. He's dumb as shit."

"Motherfucker," Deshawn said before bursting out laughing again.

A few more quiet moments passed, and North savored the silence and the smoke.

"You don't seem real faggy," Maurice said.

"You are one ignorant son of a bitch," Deshawn said.

"He doesn't! I'm just saying, that's all."

"You're making yourself look like a fucking fool. That's what you're doing."

North just smoked. Down the alley, at the perimeter of the cone cast by the security light overhead, a homeless man was relieving himself against the side of a dumpster. The tinkling sound was musical in the winter night's frozen clarity.

"So what are you guys doing here?" Maurice said.

"They're here about that shit with the police. Don't be so fucking stupid." Deshawn looked at North, his mouth twisted with indecision, and he ashed his cigarette. "You are, aren't you?"

North nodded.

"That writer guy? Fuck. What the fuck are you going to do about some guy having a seizure?"

North took a drag and eyed the men. He calculated the risk, and then he said, "Somebody put something in his water."

"Oh fuck," Deshawn said, "no fucking way."

"Shit," Maurice said through a puff of smoke. "That's messed up."

A minute limped past. Then another.

"So you and your boyfriend are, what?" Maurice said. "Trying to figure out who did it?"

"More or less."

"How's it going?"

"It's going so well I'm bumming smokes on the loading dock."

Deshawn barely seemed to hear him. He nodded the words away even as he was already speaking. "Nacho sucked that guy's cock in the service elevator."

"Bullshit," Maurice said.

"He did. You know Nacho is a—" Deshawn glanced at North. "You know he's into dudes. He bragged about it for a whole shift, like he ought to get a medal or something."

"Who's Nacho?"

"Nacho didn't suck no cocks," Maurice said, dropping the butt. He ground it out, checking himself for ash, and added, "Nacho's full of shit."

"I'm just telling you what he said."

"Who is he?"

"He works in the kitchen with me. Mostly he does dishes, but sometimes he does room service."

"And he's full of shit," Maurice said. "I've got to get back. Good luck catching a murderer or whatever."

"He's not dead," North said. "Just doing really bad."

"Yeah, ok. Fucker screamed his head off because he didn't like the soap in his room. What do I care how he's doing?"

Without waiting for an answer, Maurice trudged back into the hotel. The wind picked up, blowing hard enough to carry a crumpled Natty Light can along the broken asphalt, the aluminum singing out.

"You want to meet Nacho?" Deshawn said, flicking his butt out into the street.

North nodded, drew hard, and killed the Camel against the concrete wall. He pocketed the remaining half and nodded again.

After lowering the rolling door, Deshawn led him across the dimly lit dock and through the warehouse.

"Anybody else talking about this guy?" North asked as they went. "Scotty Carlson is his name, although I bet most people just call him asshole."

"Just stuff like Maurice said. You know, throwing fits because things aren't the way he likes them. And Nacho, I guess." Deshawn threw a look, taking in the empty warehouse, and lowered his voice. "Look, man, my buddy and I used to do each other in high school. Just, you know. I'm cool with it or whatever."

"Cool," North said.

Deshawn straightened his shoulders, nodded as though something very significant and masculine had passed between them, and took the lead again.

God save me, North thought, from bi-curious men.

When they got to the kitchen, North said, "And what new fuckery is this?"

Shaw was sitting on the edge of a stainless-steel countertop, drumming his heels against the cabinet underneath, which made shivering booms as his heels tapped it. Next to him, leaning on one elbow, was a very good-looking man: he had dark hair, dark eyes, a strong jaw, and a tattoo of a rose on one bicep. The black t-shirt he was wearing strained to cover his well-developed arms and shoulders. In one hand, he held a spoon, and he was using it to toy with the whipped cream on top of a banana split.

"Oy, papi," he was saying to Shaw, "te voy a dar mi banana, ¿sí?"

Neither man seemed to have noticed North, and Shaw bobbed and ducked, avoiding the spoonful of whipped cream that the man was trying to force into his mouth.

"That's really nice of you," Shaw kept saying, "but I know how a spoon works, and I'd really rather do it myself."

"Me vas a chupar la polla," the man, presumably Nacho, was telling Shaw as he smeared whipped cream along Shaw's lower lip. "Y te va a encantar."

"No, dairy really isn't good for you, and my stomach is particularly sensitive—oh no, in our country we don't put our hands there. Not on people we don't know, anyway. For example, I could put my hand there on North because we're dating, unless he's trying to watch TV, like one time he told me he didn't need a hand job during the *Game of Games*. Oh, North! There you are."

"Here I am," North said.

"Chavo, te voy a dar un beso negro, ¿no? Te voy a hacer gritar mi nombre."

"I just met Ignacio, and I think he's new to the United States because we've been teaching each other about our different cultures." Shaw frowned. "It's not working that well. He keeps trying to demonstrate how a spoon works."

"And he's trying to give you a fiver through your Lululemon pants."

"And he's trying to give me a—" Horror flooded Shaw's face. "No, that's not—"

"I see that's a theme with you today."

"No, I didn't—I wouldn't—Latin cultures are often very physically affectionate—"

Nacho seemed to take this as an invitation to shove a spoonful of the banana split into Shaw's mouth and run his hand up the inside of Shaw's thigh.

"Touch my boyfriend again," North said, "and I'll use that spoon to scrape out the lining of your rectum and feed it to you. ¿Me entiendes?"

"Dude," Nacho said, dropping the spoon and backing up, hands patting the air. "We're cool. I didn't know he had a boyfriend. I just thought he was some dumb twink I could pound it out with."

"Ok," Deshawn said, "you've met Nacho. Nacho, these guys are private detectives. Investigators. Something like that. They want to talk to you about that guy you blew in the elevator the other day."

"Oh shit."

"And you guys need to do it somewhere else," Deshawn said, glancing around the kitchen. "As soon as Marisa comes back from her smoke break, we've got to get back to work."

Nacho was staring at a door on the far side of the kitchen.

"Go ahead," North said. "Try."

Nacho made a noise that sounded suspiciously close to a whimper. He undermined a lot of his stud credentials by tugging on the hem of his tee as he looked around for help. "This way," he finally said, shoulders slumping as he led them out of the kitchen. The hallway was empty, and Nacho picked a spot twenty feet from the kitchen door. He glanced at Shaw. "Dude, you couldn't have told me you had a boyfriend?"

"You were only speaking Spanish. I don't speak perfect Spanish—"

"You don't speak any Spanish," North said. "You failed Spanish 1."

"I dropped out of Spanish 1—"

"With a failing grade."

"—which is different. But I picked up a lot on my own."

"Right," North said. "So you got that part about him eating you out?"

"Well, I didn't—I mean, my education wasn't comprehensive—certain parts had to be omitted because of curricular requirements—"

"Be quiet now."

"Yes," Shaw whispered, "thank God."

"Well?"

"Look, man," Nacho said, "I had no idea he was—"

"Jesus Christ, not that. Scotty Carlson."

"Oh. Yeah. That."

North stood a little straighter. He folded his arms.

Nacho looked at his shoes, rubbing the back of his neck.

"You didn't blow him," North finally said.

"Look, he's cute, he's a big deal, he's been an asshole to everybody. I thought it'd be cool if I told everybody that. Besides, I've got a reputation to maintain. I'm the hot, slutty chacal. I've got to keep that up."

"What a fucking waste of time," North said to Shaw.

"Yeah," Nacho said, "I mean, all I did was sell him some weed and then smoke it with him."

North's attention slid back to Nacho.

"Um, I mean, I don't smoke weed because it's illegal and—"

"Tell me exactly what happened."

"Ok." Nacho rubbed the back of his neck some more. He seemed really interested in the black Reeboks he was wearing. "So, he asked me if I had any weed—"

"Back up. From the very beginning."

"Like, when I was born?"

North waited.

"Um, sorry, bad joke. Ok, so, I was upstairs, collecting room-service trays."

"When?"

"Tuesday night."

"Ok."

"So I'm up there, and he comes out of his room and closes the door. Someone's still shouting at him. He leans against the door, and I'm looking at him because he's hot and it doesn't hurt to look. You'd be surprised how many of these supposedly straight white guys want me to—"

"Who was yelling at him?"

"I don't know."

"Man or woman," North said with exaggerated slowness.

"A man. Wait, I remember. He called him 'comemierda cundango,' so, like, a shit-eating fag, and I remember because then I definitely thought I was going to get some action."

"You're sure it wasn't a woman?" Shaw said.

"Yeah, I mean, it was his husband."

"You recognized his husband's voice?"

"No, but that's who it had to be, right?" North's incomprehension must have shown on his face because Nacho said, "It'll make sense in a minute, I promise." When North nodded, Nacho continued, "I said something like, 'Rough night,' and he smiled. He looked tired. And kind of sad, actually. And he said something like, 'Try rough five years.' And I said something like, 'You look like you need to loosen up,' which I meant as 'choke me on your dick,' but he must not have gotten the vibe because he said, 'I'd kill for a joint right now.' And I said I could hook him up. He met me at the dock about fifteen minutes later, and he was really cool about it. Paid me straight up, and then he asked me if I wanted a toke. I thought that meant maybe he'd caught the vibe after all, so I hung around, and we smoked for a while."

"Nobody cared that you weren't back in the kitchen?" Shaw said.

Nacho rolled his eyes. "They can fire me if they want; they can't keep anybody here doing this shit work, so Marisa will hire me back in a week or so."

"Scotty?"

"Oh, so we're smoking, and he starts moving his cock through his pants, at first like he's adjusting himself, then it's a little bit more than that. He says, 'Weed makes me so fucking horny, sorry.' But he's looking at me, right in the eyes, smiling, and he's not sorry at all. So I reach over and touch him, and yeah, he's hard. He lets me do it for a minute or so, and then he pushes my hand away. 'You want me to suck you off?' I ask him, and he gets this huge, shit-eating grin on his face. 'You'd love that, wouldn't you?' And it sounds kind of mean, but honestly, that's hot sometimes, so I just shrug. 'What do you think my husband would say about me sticking my dick in one of your holes?' That definitely felt weird. And mean. So I shrug again. 'He'd fucking love it.' By now, he's mostly talking to himself, but then he looks at me and says, 'What if I just want to jerk off? What if I just want you to kneel there, and I jizz all over your face? Do you know what my husband would do if I sent him a picture of your face covered in my jizz?' By that point, the weed wasn't doing it for me, so I say, 'I'll catch you later, man.'"

"That's it?"

"Pretty much. On the way back to the kitchen, I ran into Deshawn, and I wasn't sure if he'd seen me with Scotty or not. That's why I told him that line about blowing Scotty in the service elevator. They know I hook up there sometimes—you can get the car stuck between floors—and like I said, I've got a reputation to maintain." Nacho glanced up from his Reeboks. "You see what I mean about the thing with his husband? They were definitely fighting when I heard them upstairs, right, and then he kept bringing him up like he wanted to make the guy jealous."

North nodded and glanced at Shaw.

"Did Scotty say anything else? Anything about the fight? Or about why the last five years had been rough?"

"No way. I told you everything he said."

"Did you see him again?"

"What? Fuck no. He was creeping me out. I don't mind couples..." Nacho let the pause hang while he gave North and then Shaw the eye, "but I mean, I want them both to be into it. The whole cuckold thing, or the jealousy thing, or whatever kink that guy was playing, I'm not down with it."

"Did that make you angry?" Shaw asked. "How Scotty treated you, I mean?"

"It was messed up; that's what it was."

"Did you want to get back at him?"

After a moment, Nacho shook his head. "Oh no. Hell no. I didn't have anything to do with that."

"Really?" North said. "Because he talked about you like you were a Kleenex he'd picked up off the bedroom floor. That can mess with a guy's head. Wounded pride can make a guy do a lot of stupid things."

"No way. No goddamn way. I didn't even start my shift until two."

"Where were you this morning?"

"Home. And yeah, my mom was there, my three sisters, my abuelita. Fuck this, man."

As Nacho launched himself toward the kitchen, Shaw slid into his path. "What about the storeroom?"

Nacho veered, trying to circumnavigate Shaw, and came up short when North blocked his way. He cast a look over his shoulder.

"That's the second time you've thought about running," North said. "It's not any smarter now."

"What about the storeroom?" Nacho said sullenly.

"Who has keys to it?" Shaw asked.

"Nobody. The guests put a padlock on it. We can't get in."

"The other door, shitbird," North said.

"Oh, from Tintagel? I don't know, man. I think it's one of the standard locks." At North and Shaw's shared look, he added, "Anywhere the staff has to access—anywhere that isn't, you know, special, like the manager's office— has the same key. Not everybody has one. I don't, actually. But a lot of people do."

"So you could bum one if you wanted to."

"Man, I didn't—"

"Or somebody else could have," Shaw said. "That's right, isn't it?"

"Yeah, yeah, anybody could have gotten in there. Housekeeping, they've all got keys because they've got to unlock the supply closets, and the front desk has keys, and Marisa and a few of the other kitchen staff. Anybody could have gotten in there. Anybody."

"Including you," North said.

"I swear to Christ—"

"Nacho?" The voice came from behind North: a brown-skinned young woman in a chef's hat. Marisa, North guessed. "What's going on?"

"Nothing."

From the kitchen came the clatter of pans and the hiss of a commercial sprayer.

"Then get your ass in here," Marisa said.

Nobody moved. A timer beeped, and North smelled something chocolatey. Something with a lot of carbs. Nacho swallowed nervously, angled his body sideways, and squeezed between Shaw and North. North let him go.

As Marisa followed Nacho into the kitchen, her voice carried into the corridor: "Don't go bringing your trouble into my kitchen, Nacho. Do you hear me? Whatever you're doing, cut it out."

"I wasn't doing anything, Marisa. Swear to God!"

Then the timer beeped again, and more pans clanged.

Shaw was trying very hard to avoid North's gaze.

"I know that looked bad—" Shaw began.

"Really, Shaw?"

"—but I was pursuing an important avenue of investigation—"

"And that avenue included being felt up while a fucking chacal fed you an ice cream sundae?"

"—and although I'm not exactly sure what a chacal is—"

North spun away.

"—for the sake of accuracy," Shaw said as he jogged after him, "and because I think it has bearing on my decisions—"

North's long strides ate up the carpet.

"—it was, just technically, I mean, a banana split."

Chapter 21

THEY SPENT ANOTHER HOUR trying to run down possible leads at the con while, at the same time, avoiding Jadon and Cerise. The reality, though, was that they didn't have any more leads. They tried to find Heidi and Mary Angela, the only two from the panel who had escaped an interview so far, but they came up empty. Then they tried to find Leslie, but the hotel wouldn't give out guest information, and nobody seemed to know if Leslie really was staying at the Royal Excalibur—as she had claimed—or if she was even still at the convention. Finally, Shaw suggested a quick meal at the Round Table where, out of the sheerest of coincidences, they could keep an eye on Clarence and a group of older gay men. Rodney and Jerry, in 70s attire now, gave small waves. The other three men were wearing replicas of different glasses from various periods in Elton John's career; Shaw knew because he owned the same glasses himself.

"I want to get into her room," North said for approximately the millionth time.

"Well, we don't even know if Leslie is staying here. Also, I think your cocktail sauce has gone over."

North's phone buzzed, and he grabbed it. As he read something on the screen, he said, "First, those are my shrimp; quit stealing them. Second, that's because it's not cocktail sauce."

"Shrimps. Plural."

North tapped the screen of his phone, grabbed a napkin and a pen, and jotted something down.

"What is it?" Shaw said.

"Martinez wants us to tail wife number six. I'm just doing guesswork, but I bet that will put us at almost twenty-percent more billable hours than last month."

"Gross. I'm tired of helping him kick those poor girls to the curb."

"Those poor girls marry him for his money, and if they're dumb enough to believe that they're the one he's going to spend the rest of his miserable life with, they haven't been paying attention. Besides, it's their own fault for signing a prenup."

"We don't need the work, North. We're plenty busy with Aldrich stuff. And—"

"He pays three times our rates plus expenses, and last time, you included a fourteen-layer cake as an expense."

"It was for your disguise as sexy baked-goods-delivery-man."

North grunted and did some more figures on the napkin.

"What is it?"

"I just told you."

"No, the cocktail sauce."

Brow furrowed, North frowned at the napkin and scratched out a line.

"North?"

"I don't know. Some kind of chutney, I think."

"It's foul."

"I know, right?" he mumbled.

Shaw slumped in his seat, sending a lone shrimp swimming through chutney. At the next table, three sensibly dressed women were laughing and talking about the highlights of the day: authors they'd met, new books they'd acquired, panels and Q&As where the conversations had been interesting. They seemed nice and sensible and fun; Shaw kept glancing over, hoping they'd notice and invite him to join them.

From across the room, two women approached Shaw and North's table. They were dressed in what was obviously a cosplay take on the Japanese schoolgirl uniform, although both looked like they'd hit thirty hard.

"Oh my gosh," one of them said, "your Lars costume is a-mazing."

"Could we get a picture with you?"

North's pen tore through the napkin, but he didn't look up. "No."

"Please? You and Twerpy Twink are so cute, and maybe we could get one where you're making him suck on your fingers like in book three when—"

"What the fuck," North said, glancing up now, ice-rim eyes ablaze, "did you not understand about no?"

The women scurried off. One of them was saying something breathlessly titillated to the other that sounded like, "Just like the real Lars."

Shaw sighed.

"Not one word," North muttered.

His phone buzzed again.

"What is it now?" Shaw said. "Does an evil billionaire want us to bring down a troublesome orphanage?"

"Shit," North muttered. "Shit, shit, shit." He waved at their plates, shoved fried shrimp in his mouth, and managed to get out, "Do you have cash?"

"Yes, but—"

"Come on, I completely forgot we're supposed to be following Ronnie's guy tonight."

After trapping some bills under a plate, Shaw followed North to the parking garage. They retrieved the GTO and headed out into the city. At this hour, on a weeknight, downtown St. Louis looked abandoned: the empty streets, the skyscrapers frosted with light, the Old Courthouse dusty with a sodium haze, the Arch gleamingly futuristic and alien. North and Shaw drove west into Clayton, one of the innermost suburbs. It was only a short distance, a few miles, fifteen minutes in a car. The difference, though, was significant. In many ways, Clayton was what St. Louis aspired to be: affluent, well kept, with a night life that attracted the young and the wealthy.

The Sussex Downs was a six-story condominium building that looked squat and plain against the newer construction around it. Shaw guessed that its primary draws, in this crowded area, came down to two things: more reasonable rent, and an attached parking structure. They didn't have an access pass to get into the garage, so North parked on the street. Shaw fed coins into the ancient meter while North scrolled through something on his phone.

"Ok," North said, "Tony Gillman drives a yellow Camaro. Ronnie sent over the license plate and a picture of Gillman. He lives in unit 412. Want to be FedEx or AAA?"

"What about UPS?"

"Didn't bring my brown shorts."

Shivering inside the shearling coat, Shaw blew out a breath. "AAA, I guess."

North read off the license plate and showed Shaw a picture of a man who might have been in his mid-forties, although he was well built and obviously took care of himself. Then they jogged across the street when traffic slowed. On the opposite sidewalk, they split: North headed toward the front of the building, and Shaw walked into the parking structure. Aside from the parking control barrier at the front, the only security seemed to be cameras stationed in the corners of each level. The structure felt even colder than outside, with the freezing chill locked into the cement, and the air smelled like urine and motor oil. Shaw jogged up each ramp, his breath steaming as he watched the yellow numbers of each parking stall. The paint was flaking and, in many cases, gone completely, but it was obvious that each stall corresponded to a condo.

On the fourth level, he moved up and down the rows until he found 412. Empty. He texted a thumbs-down emoji to North and headed back to the GTO.

North was already sitting in the driver's seat. "Nobody answered when I buzzed. Got a weird look from a woman walking her dog, but that's it."

"Probably because of your Lars costume."

North grunted. He studied the building. "Why don't you get an Uber? I'll take tonight."

"Why does Ronnie even care about this guy?"

"I don't know."

"It's not because of that stuff he told us. Ronnie doesn't care if this guy beats every hustler to death between here and Kansas City."

North's eyes looked flat in the weak ambient light.

"So what's his real reason?" Shaw asked. "What does he really want?"

"I don't know, Shaw."

"Well, why are we helping him?"

"All right," North said. "You want to fight about this? Fine. Round two. Give it to me."

Shaw took a few deep breaths. His aura flickered like a kid messing with a light switch, and the tightness in his chest made it hard to think, but he managed to say, "No. I'm sorry. I'm not trying to pick a fight. I'm scared because he's threatening you with something awful, and I'm scared because it has something to do with my dad, and I'm scared because I want to figure out what's really going on, but you won't talk to me. And yeah, actually, I'm still really mad you didn't tell me in the first place, but I'm trying to get over that."

North collapsed against the seat, staring up at the headliner, and wiped his face with both hands. "Yeah, well, I'm scared too. About all of it. I'm not trying to shut you out. I'm just—embarrassed is way too small a word. I'm fucking humiliated that I'm in this situation. I didn't do anything wrong. I didn't do anything wrong when we went after Marvin Hanson, and I didn't do anything wrong in the civil suit he threw at us. But Ronnie's still squeezing my nuts, and it's hurting you, and it might come back and hurt your dad, and I can't even stand how you're looking at me right now."

"I like looking at you."

North's jaw worked silently; he was still slumped in the seat, staring up.

Shaw leaned over and kissed his cheek. "And I'll squeeze your nuts if you want. In a good way."

A tiny smile tugged at the corner of North's mouth, so Shaw kissed that too.

North's head rolled to the side, and he kissed Shaw back.

"We'll figure it out," Shaw said. "And you don't have to be embarrassed. Well, except for the part where you hid this from me."

"You're beating a dead horse," North growled, fingers curling around the shearling collar. He tugged Shaw closer, kissed him again, and said, "Message received: no more hiding things from you."

"It's just very important for a relationship to have open and honest—"

North kissed him again.

"—and very," Shaw continued, a bit breathless now, "very, very extensive and long conversations—"

North kissed him again. Harder.

"—and, um." Shaw bit his lip. "Yeah. Good talk."

North smirked, petted the shearling coat, and pressed Shaw back into his seat.

"The thing about Ronnie is that he always has an angle. He wants something. And the logical assumption is that it has something to do with your dad's business, since that was Ronnie's opening move when he started this bullshit."

"So is Tony Gillman himself the angle?" Shaw frowned. "Or does it have something to do with these boys he's abusing?"

"Good thing we're sitting in a cold car with nothing to do. Plenty of time for research."

"Actually, I was thinking about this blocked chakra—"

"Sure," North said. "Go jerk off behind a trash can like a homeless man and then get your ass back here and do some research."

"North."

North's blond eyebrows went up.

"Your boyfriendly duties—"

"Phone," North said. "Now. Or go squat behind that dumpster and get your rocks off."

Shaw muttered something.

"What was that?"

"Nothing."

"I thought I heard the phrase 'bad boyfriend' in there."

"No," Shaw said with a saccharine smile. "Your hearing must be going. Just like your eyes."

North was silent for what felt like a very long time. Then he took out his phone and began tapping and swiping. "I'll see what I can dig up on the victims. You check out Tony."

With a sigh, Shaw dug out his phone and started to search. It didn't take long; LinkedIn helped him narrow down the results to four Anthony Gillmans in the greater metro area, and only one of them looked remotely like the man in the picture Ronnie had sent. His profile listed him as an external auditor at Sheila G. Rush and Associates, which more basic searching told Shaw was an accounting firm that was much, much bigger than the name implied—their website boasted about Fortune 500 clients.

"I'm getting nothing," North said. "Nobody reports the victims' names. In fact, I've only found a couple of stubs about the assaults—this isn't getting much news, so either it's not as big as Ronnie made it sound, or something more interesting is happening in the news cycle." He flashed his screen toward Shaw, where a headline read *Algeria's President Seeks Fifth Term*.

"That actually is kind of a big deal," Shaw said, "President Bouteflika has been president for almost twenty years, but he just had a stroke, so—"

"What did you find?"

Shaw told him.

"I think you'd better ask your dad if Aldrich Acquisitions is having an external audit."

Frowning, Shaw placed the call. When his dad answered, jazz was playing in the background, and Shaw could practically smell the cloud of marijuana smoke that would be perfuming the air at Gaslight Square.

"Wild," his dad said, "you've got to get down here. You would not believe this woman's voice. It's like road tar on a hot day, and God, it's better than sex. Don't tell your mother I said that."

"Oh my God," Shaw said. "Dad, I really need you to focus." Then he told him what they suspected, although he left North out of it.

At some point in the call, the music in the background stopped, and Shaw's father's voice was surprisingly clear when he spoke again. "Let me call you back."

Shaw looked at North and shrugged.

They waited. Cars went in and out of the parking garage, but none of them was a yellow Camaro. Traffic dwindled. The light from the streetlamps coiled like yellow ribbons on the asphalt.

"Gillman must be good," North said.

"We'll catch up to him."

"I know, but I'm saying, he must be good. He's managed to stay ahead of Ronnie's guys so far, and Ronnie doesn't hire schlumps. The fact that Ronnie came to us and twisted my arm means his normal guys couldn't do the job. And I don't think Gillman knows he's in Ronnie's crosshairs, so that means he's been taking a lot of precautions already."

"But we're the best," Shaw said. "So we'll catch up to him."

His phone buzzed, and he answered.

"Wild, you're a genius. We're not currently doing an external audit at Aldrich, but one of the biotech startups we've invested in pretty heavily has one in the works. I'm firing Gillman first thing in the morning. Hell, I'm firing Rush and Associates."

"No," Shaw said, and North gave him a thumbs-up. "Gillman isn't the one you need to worry about."

"Unless you're a hustler," North whispered.

"If you pull Gillman, whoever is trying to manipulate him is just going to switch targets. This is our chance to get ahead and figure out what they want. What's the startup?"

"Nonavie. They do something with aging. I think there's a supplement. I'll have to look at my files." His voice took on a slightly chagrined note. "I'm pretty messed up right now."

"Ok," Shaw said. "More information would be good, but don't do anything to Gillman yet."

"Wild, what in the world is going on?"

"We're trying to figure that out."

"Shit," North muttered, pointing to a yellow Camaro turning into the garage.

"Your mother and I haven't seen you in ages, and, of course, it goes without saying that we'd be happy to see North as well—"

"Gotta go," Shaw called, jamming the screen with his thumb to disconnect the call.

"Five minutes?" North said.

"I think that's plenty."

They watched the clock on Shaw's phone. A Buick crept past, going at least ten under the speed limit, and through the tinted window the driver looked all of ten years old. An Aldi circular fluttered up the street and pasted itself against a lamppost. Avocados, Hass, sixty-nine cents. At the next corner, a tavern door opened, and a crowd of mid-twenties yuppies stumbled out. Their laughter broke the night's crystalline silence.

Shaw followed North out of the car. The wind nipped at exposed skin, carrying his breath away in frozen streamers; the yuppies were holding the tavern door open, and Shaw caught a whiff of hops and malt and too much perfume.

North and Shaw separated again, and Shaw jogged up the ramps of the parking garage. The pink Nikes whispered against the concrete. When he got to the fourth level, he stopped and listened. Nothing. An engine started, but that was below him. He moved down the aisle until he got to the stall for 412, where the yellow Camaro was parked and empty. He texted North a thumbs-up, shivered, and wrapped the shearling coat tighter as he headed back to the GTO.

North was already there, standing by the passenger door, shifting his weight. His fists were balled inside the Carhartt coat. "He's not there."

"What?"

"I sat on that button for a full minute, and nobody answered. Either he's not there, or he's deaf."

"His car is in the garage."

"He's not in that condo, Shaw."

"Maybe he stopped by a friend's unit. Maybe a talkative neighbor caught him at the mailboxes."

North grimaced. "I knew this was too easy."

"Do you want to get inside and take a look?"

After a moment, North shook his head. "This guy is slippery. And cautious. And I don't want to walk into something blind. Let's wait, and we'll try again in fifteen minutes."

But in fifteen minutes, the Camaro was still in the parking garage, and nobody answered the buzzer for 412.

"It's the right unit," Shaw said. "He's parked in the stall for 412."

"It's his," North said, his expression dark as they returned to the GTO, "he just gave us the slip somehow."

They tried again half an hour later. When they still got nothing, they checked the parking unit for back exits—pedestrian or vehicular. They found nothing; the only way in or out was through the condo building or the main entrance they'd been watching. North swore a streak as they made their way back to the GTO.

"How the fuck," North said as he started the car, "did he do it?"

Chapter 22

WHEN THEY GOT TO Shaw's house in Benton Park, North parked the GTO and killed the engine. The street was quiet. The night was so cold and clear that the shadows were like spiderwebs.

"You're coming in?" Shaw asked as he unbuckled himself.

"Exactly what every boyfriend dreams of hearing."

"No, I meant—"

"Those invoices aren't going to get in the mail by themselves, Shaw." North heaved himself out of the car, his voice carrying back before the door slammed shut. "I'd planned on catching up today and tomorrow, when things were supposed to be slow, but now we've got this batshit case and Ronnie riding my ass."

Shaw sat for a moment, took a few deep breaths, and imagined an inferno burning his aura clean. Then he grabbed the bags of books and went inside. The reception area was dark, broken only by a beam of yellow light that slanted out from the cracked door to their office. North was moving around inside; keys clicked on his computer. On Pari's desk, an enormous basket held lollipops that had been displayed to look like a flower arrangement. The whole thing was wrapped in cellophane, a red ribbon tied around it. When Shaw checked the card, childlike letters proclaimed: *Love, Truck*. Shaw and North had agreed to combine Valentine's with Shaw's birthday (which was the day before). They had agreed. It had been perfectly reasonable, the way North had laid it all out. Pari and Truck, on the other hand, had decided to celebrate their first Valentine's together by extending it to the entire month.

Shaw deposited the bags full of books, ditched the shearling coat, and considered the lollipops. No, he told himself. Sternly. He went to the office door and nudged it. North's mess of blond hair was bent low over papers, and he was typing slowly as he copied the information.

"Can I help?"

"No, thanks."

"I know I messed up last time, but I'll go more slowly, and I'll be really careful."

North didn't answer this time; he swore under his breath, double-checked something, and backspaced several times.

"I think you're exhausted and need to sleep," Shaw said, "and if I can help—"

"No, Shaw." North drew a breath, straightened, and looked over his shoulder. He smiled. "No, baby. I've got this. Thank you, though. Go to bed; you're beat."

"Do you want a beer? A snack?"

But North was already bent over the papers again, grimacing about something as he pounded keys.

At least something was getting pounded tonight.

Shaw made his way back to the reception area, collected his bags and the shearling coat, and carried everything through the kitchen and upstairs to his bedroom. He lay on the bed for a while. He remembered freshman year, the first time North had climbed on top of him, pinning him to the thin dorm mattress, and held Shaw down until Shaw agreed that Sam was hotter than Dean. Shaw palmed himself through the Lululemons. He thought about being cockblocked by QuickBooks.

Sleep seemed very far away, so he rummaged through the bags until he came up with *Cursed by the Billionaire: A Shifter-Second Chances-Secretary Romance.* Propping himself up with pillows, he got comfortable on the bed, and then he read. By page two, the twinkie candidate for the secretarial position was bent over his billionaire boss's desk, a ballpoint pen clenched between his teeth to keep from alerting the other applicants, who were waiting outside. Either it was a very long interview or the boss had an amazing refractory period, because the twink got both *speared aloft by his turgid skyscraper* and then, later, more gently had his insides *inked by the indelible secretion of his masterful plume.*

By that point, the Lululemons were forming their own turgid skyscraper.

Shaw dropped the book. He spent two minutes in a flash of meditation, blowing open his chakra gates and using one hand to…get ready. Then he went downstairs. He padded past Pari's gift basket, stopped, backtracked, and considered the lollipops again. No, he told himself. Absolutely not.

When he stepped into the office, North had added a desktop calculator to the process, and he seemed to be checking numbers—using a pen to focus his gaze on each line of the document, then tapping on the calculator, and then growling and looking at the document again.

"Truck might be even worse at paperwork than you," he said without looking up. "I think we're going to have to forbid him from touching any of this stuff. Pari's going to have to do it for him; she's surprisingly decent at it." When Shaw reached his side, he glanced up, "I thought you were going to bed."

Shaw picked up the pile of papers.

"I'm using those."

Shaw shifted the pile so that it rested on top of the keyboard.

"I'm typing with that."

Shaw perched on the edge of the desk, knees wide, erection standing straight out under the thin fabric of the yoga pants. With what he very, very, very much hoped was a sensual gaze, he plucked the pen from North's hand. He bit down lightly on the end.

"Huh," North said, rocking back in his chair. His own legs were spread now, and denim hugged his hard dick.

"Excuse me," Shaw whispered, pausing to lick the pen. "Are you the famous detective North McKinney? Because I'm in terrible trouble, and I need your help."

North's eyes narrowed, but a gleam of amusement still showed. "Maybe," he drawled. "Who's asking?"

"My name is Kane. Kaneson. Kane Kaneson."

The gleam in North's eyes got brighter.

"And I'm the only witness to a terrible crime," Shaw continued. "I'm afraid I'm in terrible danger."

"Really?" One of North's heavy hands came to rest on Shaw's leg, his touch hot through the nylon. "I'm sorry to hear that. But I should tell you up front that I only work if I get paid."

After giving the pen a few more sultry—he hoped—licks, Shaw whispered, "I don't have any money, but I'm sure I could find a way to make it worth your while."

North raked the fingers of his free hand through his hair. His other hand slid up, thumb tracing the tip of Shaw's dick through the fabric. "Looks like you already have something in mind."

Shuddering at the touch, Shaw nodded. "I'm going to put this between my teeth," he said, tapping the pen. "I get noisy, and I don't want your secretary to hear us."

North's eyebrows arched at this, but all he said was "Huh" again, in the exact same tone. His fingers curled around the waistband of the yoga pants, and he hitched them down to Shaw's ankles in a few rough yanks. The cool air was torture against Shaw's fever-hot dick. North took him in hand and gave long, rasping licks before taking him in his mouth completely.

"Oh my fucking Lord," Shaw moaned, the words mangled by the pen between his teeth.

North worked for a while, Shaw whimpering the whole time, and then he pulled off and licked his lips loudly. "You're trying so hard to be quiet," he said. "You're trying so hard not to be the noisy slut I think you want to be."

"Jesus Christ," Shaw tried to say around the pen.

"Let's see if I can't get some good sounds out of you."

Shaw moaned and bit down harder on the pen. He moaned again when North's thumb came to the base of his balls and slid back farther and applied pressure. North went back to work with his mouth. One of Shaw's legs started to twitch, his heel bouncing against the desk drawers. North was slow and patient and teasing.

It felt like a long time since North had touched him like this, and Shaw made a simultaneously horrified and satisfied noise as he realized what was happening all too soon. He bit down harder on the pen.

Then the pen exploded, and red ink went everywhere.

"Fuck, fuck, fuck," North shouted, wiping his mouth as he pulled off Shaw.

"I didn't know," Shaw said muzzily from the brink of orgasm. "I didn't mean to—"

"Jesus Christ. These reports are ruined." North sat back, ran his hand over his face again, smearing the mist of red ink that had caught him. "This is, like, two weeks' of work."

Shaw blinked. He was vaguely aware that most of him was spattered in red ink. Spitting the ruined pen from his mouth, he leaned forward for a kiss.

Warding him off with a hand, North shook his head, eyes still fixed on the droplets of ink soaking into the stack of pages.

"I'm sorry," Shaw said, fighting to keep disappointment and frustration from his voice. "I thought it'd be hot. Well, it was hot, and—"

"Yeah, Shaw. That was really fucking hot. Can you get down? God damn, I've got to clean this up. Maybe I can still save something."

"North, I'm really sorry. I'll clean it up, I'll—" Before Shaw could finish, though, his phone rang, and he fished it out of the pockets puddled around his ankles. Yasmin's name flashed on the screen; the clock said it was almost midnight.

When Shaw answered, Yasmin sounded on the brink of tears: "He did it again. That fucking lunatic did it again."

"What?" Shaw said, putting the call on speakerphone. "What happened?"

"He's a maniac. I don't know who he is, but you have to find him. You have to stop him." Yasmin took a breath, as though steadying herself, and said, "Someone pushed Clarence, Karen, and Leslie down the stairs."

Chapter 23

NORTH DROVE THEM TO Barnes-Jewish, and because it was almost midnight on Thursday, he only had to drive halfway up the parking structure before he found a spot. The fluorescents were too bright; their hum settled at the base of his skull like the beginning of a migraine. Inside, the emergency department wasn't much better, the smell of body odor and old smoke mixing with the chemical perfume of a cleaner. It all added to the buzzing banks of lights—and, to the flashbacks of red ink splashing all over the reports, to the taste of dick in North's mouth.

The ER crowd was small tonight, but they were the usual motley collection of St. Louis's finest: a woman in a 90s-era neon-yellow suit, holding a bloody cloth over one eye; an overweight man on a scooter, a screwdriver still buried in the hanging meat of one batwing arm, wearing a t-shirt that said LORENA BOBBIT WAS RIGHT; two Latino boys, one of them hunched over and being supported by the other; a man holding a little girl, presumably his daughter, and speaking to the triage nurse in what sounded like Bosnian. Double doors with crash bars and safety-glass windows led deeper into the department. Presumably, Clarence, Karen, and Leslie were still being treated in the examination rooms before they were released or, if necessary, transferred to another floor to stay overnight.

"Can you keep everyone busy for a few minutes?" North asked.

Shaw nodded jerkily. Instead of talking and joking and dragging the whole thing on five minutes longer than necessary, he hurried forward. He was halfway across when he glanced at the double doors. The changes to his body language were microscopic: a slight tightening to his shoulders, the twitch of a finger. He looped back to North.

"Jadon and Cerise are having a conversation on the other side of those doors." The words were stiff. "I'm lucky they didn't see me."

"Fuck. I was hoping we'd beat them here. Jadon must have absolutely nothing going on in his life if he's working this case so hard. Probably looking for an excuse not to be home."

"Everybody goes through patches like that."

"Yeah, ok."

"You probably know how he feels better than just about anyone."

"Wow. Pissy much?"

"I'm tired of you being mean to him."

"No," North said slowly, studying Shaw's face: the rapid blinks to keep his eyes from filling, the hot spots in the sharp triangle of his face. "I'm always a dick to Jadon, and he's fine with it. This is something else. You're mad at me. What'd I do?"

"Hold on; I've got an idea."

"Oh no, you're not getting out of this—"

But Shaw slipped away before North could get a decent grip, and all he could do was watch as Shaw crossed the room again. The triage nurse was still busy with the man and his daughter, and although North imagined there was probably supposed to be someone administrative handling the clerical side of things, the desk was empty. Shaw glanced around once, grabbed the phone, and pressed a number. He spoke quietly, waited, and spoke again. Then he hung up the phone and made his way back to North.

"If you're mad at me—"

"It's a bad night. It's an awful night. Let's just let it go, and we'll start over tomorrow."

"You don't want to talk about this? You don't want to process it? You don't want to have an agonizingly long conversation about our feelings?"

"No," Shaw said. "And you should probably stand over here so they don't see you."

North had barely stepped up against the wall when the double doors burst open. Jadon and Cerise set off at a brisk walk, heading toward a pair of doors on the opposite side of the waiting room. The placement of the doors and the detectives' haste kept them from noticing North and Shaw, and a moment later, they had passed through the doors on the other side of the room. Shaw caught one of the double doors before it could swing shut, and North followed.

"What did you do?"

"Dr. Gamal spotted two men trying to break into the medical records office. One was in a Carhartt jacket. The other was wearing a pink, faux-fur coat. He asked security to contact the police who were in the emergency room."

"That's genius," North said, squeezing Shaw's arm. Shaw pulled free. "Who's Dr. Gamal?"

"I don't know; I saw his name on a form on the desk."

They walked down the hall, pausing to check the names on the paperwork outside each exam room. Shaw kept a minimum of eighteen inches between himself and North the whole time.

"It would have gone with your Nikes," North said after they'd made it halfway down the hall.

Shaw was scanning a page. "What?"

"The pink fur coat."

"Faux fur."

"Right, the pink, faux-fur coat. It would have gone great with those kicks."

"Yeah," Shaw said, and he returned the papers to the plastic holder outside the exam room and moved on.

They found Leslie first. When North twitched aside the curtain, she was watching something on her phone. The masculine grunts and the rhythmic slap of flesh made it obvious what held her interest. She wore a sequined Team USA gymnastics leotard, and she had, to North's surprise, killer legs. A bruise was darkening along one cheek, and her right arm was in a sling, but on the whole, she looked surprisingly good for someone who had been pushed down the stairs.

"Oh," she said when she noticed them. She tapped a few buttons on the phone, and the noises stopped. With a shrug and a smile, she said, "Prison gangbang domination video. They've had this guy's balls tied up for forty-five minutes."

"Sounds like he's going to have some chafing," North said.

"Oh, what he should really be worried about is they're using these police batons—"

"Ms. Hawkins, we need to talk to you about what happened tonight, and we don't have a lot of time."

"Someone pushed us down the stairs." She flashed a huge smile. "Bet you don't think I'm the crazy psycho now."

North offered a half-smile in return. "Can you tell us about it in detail?"

"I have that leotard," Shaw said. Then, as though conceding something, he added, "It looks better on you."

Leslie tossed her shag of graying hair in what was probably supposed to be a flirtatious manner. "Tonight was the costume party. Well, the first one. On Saturday I'll put on my fake cock and go as one of my favorite daddy porn stars."

"Is this a tradition?"

"Of course. They used to just do one costume party. Well, I think they called it a masquerade ball, and it was after the closing banquet. But everyone loved it so much that we decided to add another one. A costume party, I mean. This one isn't organized by the convention; it's just something that we like to do." She gave another toss of her hair. "That's how I was able to get in."

"So everyone would have been planning on a party tonight, with most of the guests in costume?" North said.

"Isn't that what I just said?"

"And what happened?" Shaw asked.

"Well, we were having a great time. Karen and I usually have so much fun together, but today, you know, after the panel, well, she was really down. She almost didn't go to the party, but I convinced her it would be better than feeling sorry for herself in her hotel room. Clarence didn't want to go either, actually, and I had to drag him along too. He's not nearly as much fun as Karen. Honestly," her voice dipped, "he's kind of a disappointment. You know. For a gay."

"Well," North said in what he hoped was a philosophical tone, "we can't all shit rainbow glitter."

"Yet," Shaw added.

"He's not any fun at a party," Leslie said, "and just between us gals, I think it's been a million years since he's had sex. I don't even know if he's ever even deepthroated a cock. I feel kind of sorry for him; that's why I always go out of my way to make sure he feels included."

"So you went to the party with Clarence and Karen," North prompted.

"Right. And we had a really good time. Well, I did. Karen moped. And Clarence sat with her and drank. We only had the hotel space until midnight, and then one of my reader friends invited us to an after-party in her room, so we headed up there. The elevators were clogged, so we took the stairs. And that's when someone ran past and pushed us."

"All three of you?"

"Well…yes. I mean, I think so. We all fell, but we were standing close together, so I guess—I guess whoever did it might have only meant to push one of us."

"I don't understand," Shaw said. "You were going up the stairs. How did someone run past you and push you down them?"

"We weren't on the stairs yet; we were still on the second-floor landing. We were right in front of the steps going down when someone pushed us."

"Did you see who it was? Anything, even a glimpse?"

Leslie shook her head. "I don't even know if it would help if I had; everybody was in costume, and a lot of people were wearing masks. Whoever it was, though, he was strong. We practically flew off that landing."

They tried a few more questions, but Leslie couldn't tell them anything else. When they left, she was already on her phone again, a man moaning in the background.

In the next examination room, they found Clarence. He was lying on the exam table, a bandage on his temple, and he was wearing a Super Mario onesie that revealed how thin he was. North was first into the room, and at the sound of his steps, Clarence rolled his head to look. First shock, then a shy smile crossed his face. "Mr. McKinney, I mean, North. It's so thoughtful of you to check on me. I was hoping I wasn't the only one who felt our connection earlier, and—oh."

"Hi," Shaw said cheerfully. "How's your head?"

Clarence sagged back against the exam table, deflating inside his onesie.

"Did you have to get stitches?' Shaw asked. Then somehow Shaw got caught up in one of the molded-plastic chairs, and he stumbled for a few paces, dragging it with him and almost falling, until North sorted him out. "I had to get stitches once after a dog attacked me."

"His aunt's puppy," North said. "It was twelve weeks old."

"A natural-born killer. Like certain other puppies, I might add."

"I thought—well, I suppose I don't know why the two of you are here," Clarence said.

"I'm a candy striper," Shaw said.

"I'm a candy—God damn it, Shaw. You knew I was going to say that one."

Shaw shrugged. "I'm collecting for the St. Giles Collective Breastfeeding Charitable Fund and Ladies' Society."

"I'm—" North stopped. "God damn it," he said again.

"You definitely weren't going to use that one."

"No, but you got in my head." North struggled and settled for "I'm selling Butterfingers as a fundraiser for my youth basketball league. This is bullshit. I had a really good one, and then you stole candy striper, and now I can't think of anything."

"What is going on?" Clarence said, a shrill note inflecting the last word.

"Let's talk about tonight."

"A man in a gimp mask pushed us down a flight of stairs. I'm lucky I don't have a concussion or a brain hemorrhage or internal bleeding."

"Hold up," North said. "You saw him?"

"Yes, of course. I was looking right over my shoulder. He put his hand on Leslie and shoved. She crashed into me, and I crashed into Karen, and we went right down the stairs. He could have killed us. Oh my God." Clarence swallowed, his Adam's apple bobbing. "He was trying to kill us, wasn't he?"

"It sounds like it, but let's not jump to any conclusions. You're sure it was a man?"

"I mean, he was in a costume and a gimp mask. That's a rubber or vinyl mask that usually covers the whole head, often with zippers or other fastenings and obstructions for the eyes, mouth, and sometimes even the nose—"

"We obviously know what a gimp mask is," North said. "I'm still traumatized from the time I found one under Shaw's mattress junior year."

"No," Shaw said, his face suddenly infused with red. "No. No. That wasn't mine. We'd had a Halloween party, and people were putting their coats on my bed, and—"

"Yeah," North said. "Thanks for coming to our party. Coats? Right in there. Oh, and if you'd be so kind as to shove your gimp masks under the mattress." He made a disgusted noise. "So it could have been a woman?"

"I…I suppose so. She'd have to be strong and, you know, built like a man." Coloring, Clarence added, "I do know what men look like, after all. I don't think I'd mistake a woman for a man, even in a mask."

"But it might have been."

"I suppose so," Clarence repeated.

"Had you seen that person at the party?"

"It's impossible to say. It is!" he said, his voice rising in response to what he must have perceived as disbelief. "Plenty of people were wearing gimp masks. I think they used to be shocking, but now nobody looks twice."

"Ok," North said. "And you're sure he pushed Leslie."

"Yes, but—but I don't think that means she was the target."

"Why not?"

"Well, she might have been. But it could have just been simple practicality: she was closest to the crowd on the landing, and the attacker might have thought it was safer to keep his distance rather than get closer to, say, me or Karen."

"Let's go back to the beginning of the night."

"I didn't want to go to the party," Clarence said. "And obviously, I was right not to. We were all tired. It had been a horrible day, being drugged, seeing what happened to Scotty, the hours at the hospital, and then the police showing up at my room to interrogate me. I wasn't going to go, only Leslie showed up, and she can be very persistent. I changed into my costume, and we went to the party with Karen."

"Super Mario?" North said.

"It's a…a bit of a joke. Scotty's Lars book—there's a plumber character. I started dressing up as Mario a few years ago."

"What does Scotty think about that?"

"Honestly, he's never said anything. I'm not even sure he gets the connection."

"Why didn't you leave?" Shaw asked abruptly from where he was examining a pamphlet on BLOOD PRESSURE: THE SILENT KILLER.

"I was leaving the party," Clarence said. "It was over, and we were heading to a friend's room—"

"No, why didn't you go to the airport and fly home?" Shaw passed the pamphlet to North. "There's a lot in there about French fries, which I think you need to read very carefully. You told us you were going to leave the convention, remember? You said you didn't care if the police thought you were a suspect, and you might be in danger, and you were going to leave. So why didn't you?"

"Not that it's any of your business," Clarence said stiffly, although the words were directed to North, "and not that I feel any obligation to answer your questions, but I changed my mind."

"But," Shaw said, "you'll definitely be leaving after this, right? I mean, two brushes with death. That's got to be a sign, right?"

"No. No, I actually don't think it is. In fact, I'm not leaving. I think someone is terrorizing me, and I'm not going to give in. I got some good news: I'm going to receive the Queer Expectations lifetime achievement award. I'm staying for the ceremony the final night."

"You think you're being targeted because you're the recipient of an award?" North asked.

"Not necessarily. But I'm not going to let one interfere with the other."

"And you still don't have any idea who might be behind this?"

"Honestly? As crazy as it sounds? I'm starting to think Scotty's orchestrated the whole thing as publicity stunt."

North nodded. "Anything's possible."

In the third exam room, they found Karen. The pert, intelligent, bright-eyed woman North had met earlier that day looked like she had petrified in the last few hours, her face hollow, her too-wide mouth rigid. Cotton still packed one nostril, and her nose was swollen to almost twice its size.

Her story matched the others'. She answered their questions dully, in monosyllables when possible, her eyes fixed on her hands.

"I didn't see him myself," she said when North asked. "I wasn't looking in that direction. But there were lots of people wearing those masks. I have no idea who they were, of course." A brittle laugh. "No point asking me."

"Karen," Shaw said softly, sitting next to her in one of the molded-plastic chairs. He put his hand on top of hers, and she started to cry, turning her head away.

"It's so horrible. What someone did to Scotty. And now me. That's not a coincidence. And it's one of those horrible women, I just know it, they're—they're insane, all of them."

"Which women?" North asked. "And what do you mean, it's not a coincidence?"

"The other authors," Karen said, flapping a hand. She drew a deep breath and scrubbed her face once more. "They hate him so much. God, I don't know what I'm saying, but it's not a coincidence, right? I mean, first, they drug the water, and I was supposed to be on that panel. And now I'm—I mean, someone pushed me down a flight of stairs, and I could have died."

"Why would someone have wanted to hurt you?" Shaw asked. "If you're right, and if someone was expecting you to be on that panel, why would someone want to hurt you?"

Hunching her shoulders, Karen let her gaze slide to the floor.

"What's going on, Karen?" Shaw asked quietly as he rubbed her back. "What do you need to tell us?"

She shook her head; she was crying again.

The curtain rings shrieked along the hang rod, and Jadon stood in the doorway, Cerise behind him. The female detective was wearing a tiny grimace. Jadon looked furious.

"Let's go," he said. "Right now."

"Hi, Jadon," North said. "I thought I saw you earlier. What were you…" North pretended to think and snapped his fingers. "You were chasing your own tail—was that it?"

"Right. Now."

"Karen," Shaw said, "whatever it is, you'll feel better telling us."

"Shaw," Jadon snapped.

"Don't talk to him like that," North said, surging a step toward Jadon.

"I'm coming," Shaw said. He gave Karen's shoulder a final pat, stood, and positioned himself between North and Jadon. To Cerise, he said, "Ok, let's leave before the junkyard dogs start going at it."

If anything, Cerise's grimace just got deeper, but she turned and led the way out of the emergency department. Outside, the February air was razor sharp. Still, too; the only sound was their steps across the frozen cement. Something fluttered in the oblong panels of light cast by the halide lamps. Snow, North realized.

"You're burning a bridge here," Jadon said. The words were crisp and clear in the frozen night. "I'm not going to tell you again to stay out of my investigation. I respect what you do; I know, better than just about anybody, how good you are. But this is my investigation, and you're threatening to compromise it."

"This," North said, tracing an invisible line between himself and Jadon, "this is about you wanting to mark your territory like a fucking dog."

Shaw muttered something that sounded suspiciously like *pot* and *kettle*.

"You're making a huge fucking deal about how we're compromising your case. Give me a break. You've got two assault cases at a gay romance literature convention. They might not even be related. It's not exactly the Zodiac Killer you're trying to track down."

"You know what, North?" Jadon said, pausing to blow out a thin streamer of breath. "You'd be a lot easier to like if you weren't always trying to prove something. You'd probably be a better detective too."

"What the fuck is that supposed to mean?"

"It's a murder investigation," Cerise said. "Scotty died shortly after he arrived at the hospital this afternoon."

Chapter 24

INSTEAD OF A SLEEPOVER, North went back to his Southampton duplex. Truck was asleep on the couch—puppy-sitting had obviously worn hir out, because neither ze nor the puppy stirred when North let himself into the house. North showered, brushed his teeth, dropped onto the bed, and woke when his alarm went off at half-past five. He decided to skip working out, slept another hour, and still felt like he was running on fumes when he dragged himself out of bed. He texted Shaw. He made a quick pit stop to get ready for the day. He texted Shaw again. When he headed out, Truck was still snoring on the couch, the puppy asleep on hir shoulder.

North made three stops before he got to Shaw's place, and when he pulled up, Shaw came out dressed in an eye-wateringly green Aran sweater, harem pants banded in geometric patterns, and quilted snow boots. The duffle coat he was wearing was at least two sizes too big.

"Is that camel hair?" he asked when Shaw dropped into the GTO's passenger seat.

In answer, Shaw sniffed the coat and sneezed violently. "I guess so."

"That seems about right," North said as he pulled away from the curb.

Shaw sniffed again—this time, the air in the car instead of his coat.

Retrieving a cup from the cardboard carrier between his feet, North said, "I got you lesbian tea."

"Made out of real lesbians?" Shaw sipped and made a face. "It's, um, good."

"No, I meant it's from that lesbian coffee shop you always want to drag me to. It's hyssop. It's good for liver, gallbladder, the common cold, sore throat, and whatever other bullshit the lesbians could fit on their chalkboard. It's also—" North shifted his hands on the steering wheel. "—forgiveness tea. Because I'm sorry. About yesterday. For yelling at you about the reports."

Shaw was sipping the tea again—apparently knowing that it was hyssop had suddenly made it drinkable. He pulled the cup away, furrowed his brow, and said, "What?"

"You were mad at me. Last night. At the hospital. And I know I was a jerk about the papers, but it's just paperwork, and I shouldn't have yelled at you. I was in the wrong, completely, and I apologize."

"I don't care if you yell at me. You yelled at me for forty-five minutes the other day because I emptied your freezer of all those poisons. I'm used to you yelling at me; you've been yelling at me for eight years, starting with when I did your laundry for the first time freshman year. It's kind of endearing, actually, like when the puppy barks."

"Ok, well, first of all, it's not endearing, and second of all, you didn't do my laundry. You gave a bag of my clothes to someone you assumed was from a laundry pickup service, and I spent the next six months buying an entirely new wardrobe. Third of all, you weren't clearing my freezer of poisons. You threw away a thirty-six pack of Fat Boys that I was looking forward to eating—"

"And you're highly sensitive to dairy."

"No, I'm not."

"You are. When I was listening to my Kurdish folk music the other night, you kept groaning, and that was right after you'd had one of those ice cream sandwiches, so I figured you'd be better off without all those toxins."

"Shaw, I'm not—" North made a strangled noise. "I'm trying to apologize. I'm sorry I made you mad. The end. No more talking."

"Most people don't sound quite so hostile when they apologize," Shaw said. Whatever he saw on North's face made him shrink into the seat, and he added, "That's my only note."

"Here," North said, shoving a pastry box at him.

With an appreciative noise, Shaw opened the box. "Oh my God, it's. beautiful." Then, more slowly, "What is it?"

"It's a celeriac-flour dessert cracker with a sweet potato reduction."

"That sounds amazing."

"Uh huh. Well, it's from that super bougie vegan bakery that you wanted to buy."

"I didn't want to buy—" Shaw stopped, sniffing the air yet again. "But I thought I smelled…"

"Oh, yeah, I got something for myself too. A couple of those vanilla-glazed long johns from Donut Drive In. Don't worry, though; I made sure to keep them away from your dessert cracker."

With what sounded like a struggle for cheerfulness, Shaw said, "Oh. Good."

They drove another mile. They passed the Anheuser-Busch brewery and its perpetual, yeasty miasma. Shaw bit gingerly into the cracker and made an appreciative noise. Then he started to gag.

North kept his eyes on the road.

"That's delicious," Shaw said, the words almost unintelligible as he scraped his tongue with his fingernails. The dessert cracker had disappeared back into its pastry box.

"I'm really glad to hear that. I think they make vegan birthday cakes, so next year for your birthday—"

"No!" After a strangled breath, Shaw said, "I mean, we talked about the Cakery for next year."

"God, I almost forgot. Your half birthday, then."

Shaw had the wide, wild eyes of a desperate man.

"You aren't going to finish your breakfast?"

"I'm savoring it."

"Wow, so you really do like it. That's amazing. I was so worried I was going to pick the one thing at that bakery that you wouldn't like."

"Of course I like it." But Shaw threw a glance at the back seat, where the Donut Drive In box waited. Facing forward again, in what was obviously an attempt at casualness, he said, "You know, the brain needs glucose. Diets that are super low in carbohydrates—"

"Like that bullshit Pure 15 or whatever you told me I had to do."

"—can actually force the body into ketosis, in an attempt to manufacture glucose for the brain. So, you know, sometimes eating some carbs might actually be justified."

North made a considering noise.

"Especially on an early morning," Shaw pointed out, "when you've had very little sleep, and things are really stressful."

"Good thing I got us breakfast."

"Right, yes, well," Shaw was trying to cram the pastry box, with the dessert cracker still inside, between the door and the seat, apparently in the hopes that North would forget it ever existed. "The thing is, I'm not sure a celery cracker—"

"Celeriac-flour dessert cracker," North corrected.

"I'm not sure it has enough glucose. I'm worried about low blood sugar. It could make it hard to think clearly and regulate our emotions."

"Uh huh. And how well do you think I will regulate my emotions if I find sweet potato reduction smashed into the carpet?"

Shaw stopped trying to jam the box behind the seat and considered this question for almost a quarter of a mile. The Arch rose ahead of them, a silver bird frozen in the act of launching into flight. "I think you would be vexed."

"That is very fucking accurate." Reaching back, North grabbed the Donut Drive In box and said, "I got four long johns, and if you don't leave me at least one and a half of them, I am going to be beyond vexed."

When North parked in the Royal Excalibur's garage, one and a quarter were left, which was close enough.

"God," Shaw said, studying the doors that led into the hotel. "I can't believe Scotty's dead."

"I can't believe no one told us."

"Right." Shaw frowned. "I don't think anyone knew. Not when we talked to them, anyway. Josue must have found out after we talked to him; I don't think he would have tried to hide Scotty's death."

"What would be the point?"

"I'm more curious about why he didn't let anyone else know at the convention. It seems like Jadon and Cerise kept that out of their interviews as well."

"What about the attack?"

"The typical reason for something like that would be that one of the potential victims knew something—or the killer was worried that they knew something. Or it could be what Karen suggested: someone else was the real target, and Scotty was an unfortunate bystander. In either case, the killer will probably try again."

"Start with Josue?"

Shaw nodded. Chewing, North beckoned Shaw closer and thumbed glaze from the corner of his mouth. He sucked his thumb and shoved the rest of the long john in his mouth.

"You took that down like a champ," Shaw told him and then kissed his cheek. "Very inspiring. Especially after last night."

Still chewing, North gave Shaw the finger and got out of the car. Shaw came after him.

The mood in the Royal Excalibur was drastically different from the day before. A line of men and women with luggage snaked away from the front desk—early checkouts, North assumed, leaving now that the convention had become the site of a murder. No laughing. No screaming. No grotesquely oversized inflatable penises. The ads—banners and flyers and posters—for Scotty's books had vanished. One woman cried silently into a wad of tissues. A slack-jawed young guy, the kind who looked like Mom still wrote his name on his lunch, was reading *Ordinary Stud*, the first book in Scotty's Build-Your-Own-Bear series. He glanced up, and his eyes widened when he saw North.

North grabbed Shaw's arm and walked faster.

"It would help," Shaw murmured, "if it didn't look like you were trying so hard."

"Thank you so goddamn much."

"Even just a pair of sneakers would go a long way."

Yasmin was at the registration desk, eyes red, a crumpled pack of cigarettes on the table next to her. She was fielding questions from a pack of feral convention goers, who seemed determined to get the price of their registration back—or else the equivalent value in Yasmin's flesh.

"Word spreads fast," North said.

Shaw nodded.

When they got to Josue's room, Brendon answered the door.

"He doesn't want to talk to you." The photographer looked like a wreck: eyes dark with lack of sleep, hair mussed, the same clothes as the day before now wrinkled from wear and, North guessed, sleep. "Go away."

"He might not want to talk to us," North said, "but he needs to. This is now a murder investigation—or, at the very least, manslaughter."

"He's grieving, and he sobbed all night, and I barely got him to sleep. I'm not waking him up. Besides, you're not even police." More firmly, Brendon repeated, "Go away," and then he shut the door.

"Ok," North said. "How far do you want to press this?"

Shaking his head, Shaw said, "We still haven't talked to Mary Angela or Heidi. They were part of that panel yesterday, and I want to see if they can tell us anything."

But Yasmin was still swamped with readers, and she shook her head once when North managed to catch her eye. The front desk staff was working frantically to keep the line of fleeing guests moving, and North figured that even if they weren't busy, they would have refused to give out Mary Angela's information.

"I don't suppose a level-five psychic can divine what room Mary Angela's in?"

"I can definitely try. I'm going to need five uninterrupted hours of complete silence. And how much weed do you have on you?"

North let out a heavy breath.

"Or we could just send her an email," Shaw said.

"Yes, God, that. I do not have time to watch you get high, try to explain the physics of a *Scooby Doo* episode, and then nap the rest of the day." North pulled out his phone. He found Mary Angela's website, filled out the 'Contact Me' form, and sent it. When he'd finished, he saw Shaw holding a convention schedule.

"Anything good this morning?"

"The first panel started at eight, so we're going to be late, but you get one guess who's on it."

"Heidi?"

Shaw nodded. "It's a panel for top industry critics and reviewers."

"Let's see what she has to say."

They found her in a room called Quimper. It was one of the smaller convention rooms, but even so, the audience didn't come close to filling it— fewer than twenty people sat in the straggly lines of chairs. Apparently a murder combined with an eight o'clock panel of reviewers was not the crowd magnet North had anticipated. Heidi sat at the front of the room with two other women, both middle-aged, both white, both sensibly dressed. The moderator was a stout man in a bowtie.

"—nature of the genre," one of the women was saying in a patient tone. "I don't know why people have to talk bad about it. I'm so tired of people shaming me for what I like. I'm tired of all the sex-negative people who are so repressed and ignorant that all they want to do is kink-shame."

The other white woman was frowning, her mouth a thin, hard line.

"I like daddies drilling their boys," the first woman continued. "I like whips and cages. I like guys leaking slick all over themselves when they go into heat. I like one guy getting another guy pregnant. I like what I like—I'm tired of people trying to make me feel bad about it."

"And I think you should be ashamed of yourself," the second woman burst out. "I think it's disgusting. The fantasies are one thing. But writing and reading about a grown man going to the bathroom in a diaper? That's gross. I'm sorry, but it is. And incest is even worse. There's a reason incest is illegal. There's a reason that adults having intercourse with minors is punished. It's abuse. If it gets you hot and bothered, fine, that's your own business, but we shouldn't legitimize it and validate it by writing books about it and then celebrating those books."

"I'm going to cut in here," the moderator said. "Heidi, you haven't had a chance to say anything on this topic yet. Do you want to weigh in?"

Today, Heidi's ash-blond hair was pulled back in a simple braid, and she wore just a touch of makeup that made her dark skin glow. She frowned and leaned forward. "It's a difficult question. Some of it, when it steps over the line into abuse and molestation and bestiality, I think that's a clear-cut issue. We shouldn't allow that. But kink in general—kink is tricky. One problem I see is that kink and fetish stories are almost always dehumanizing and objectifying, no matter how hard the author tries to make the characters three-dimensional. Another problem is that it becomes very difficult to separate those stories out from pornography or erotica. But romance, as a genre, isn't meant to be pornography. They're different kinds of stories, and they're different kinds of writing. I think that's something we should consider when we think about the books we include in our genre, although that's out of our hands, to a certain degree, because of how self-publishing is set up."

The first woman looked ready to launch into self-defense again, but the moderator said something else, and the conversation moved on. North kept an ear tuned, but mostly he replayed the events from last night. He still wasn't sure how Tony Gillman had gotten away from them, but now he understood why Ronnie had hired them: Tony had apparently planned very carefully to keep anyone from linking him to the attacks on hustlers. He was smart and clever and prepared, but everybody slipped up, and North would be ready when he did. He walked himself through everything that had happened at the Clayton condo building. And then he did it again. And then again.

He was still thinking about it when Shaw's elbow dug into his ribs.

"—highly critical of Scotty's books," the moderator was saying, "in a genre where it seems like Scotty could do no wrong. Can you talk a little about that? You've set yourself up as the anti-Scotty Carlson, I think, and that's a very bold thing to do in this arena."

"First of all," Heidi said slowly, "I'm very sorry to hear about Scotty's passing. I know many people loved his books, and I'm sure many people loved him. I think it would be inappropriate to talk about this today; I'm sorry. The only thing I want to make clear is that I didn't bear Scotty any ill will. Unlike many reviewers and critics, I simply held him to the same standard as the other authors I read—I didn't let him slide on character and plot and prose just because he was an attractive gay man. And I honestly think Scotty appreciated that; he wanted to be treated like everyone else, and that's to his credit."

Both the other reviewers jumped in, praising Scotty and mixing in sniping comments that were clearly directed at Heidi. Before the situation could escalate any further, the moderator cut in, and the panel ended. Instead of the rush and throng that North had seen before, the audience members got to their feet slowly, picking up tote bags and sweaters and coffees. A heavyset older woman shouldered her way into a shawl. A thirtyish guy leaned heavily on a cane. One by one, they trudged toward the doors. At the front of the room, the moderator and the two white women had formed a cluster, talking in low, animated voices.

Heidi glanced up from a tablet as North and Shaw approached. She offered a small smile. "You're really getting to see the underbelly of this little world, aren't you?"

"It's like any group," Shaw said. "Strong people, weak people. Kind people and bullies. Power dynamics and politics. Humans are pretty much the same wherever you go."

"That's a bleak way of looking at it." She glanced at her tablet. "Since I'm currently being eviscerated for every bad review I ever gave Scotty, though, I think there's probably some truth to it. One woman just told me she hoped someone raped me to death. That's because last year I said I thought *Post Stud* was uneven—not Scotty's best work."

"As long as you didn't bad-mouth Lars," North said. "I've got an image to maintain."

Heidi's smile was a little stronger this time, but it faded quickly. "God, these last two days have been horrible. I honestly can't believe it; last night, I didn't sleep because it all seemed so unreal, and I just kept running through it again and again, trying to make sense of it."

"Scotty's death?"

"What? No. Josue put that on Facebook this morning around six. Nobody knew until then. Just—the drugged water, the hospital, the police, that horrible thing with Clarence and Karen and Leslie on the stairs."

"You knew about that?" Shaw asked.

"Of course. I was going to the same after-party; I was behind them on the landing. I heard Leslie scream, and I looked down—" She cut off, and her throat moved reflexively. When she spoke again, her voice was thick. "I mean, I saw them fall. It was awful."

"So you saw who pushed them?" Shaw said.

Heidi shook her head. "I was talking to a friend; it was the scream that made me look, and by then, they were already falling."

"You know the con," North said. "You know these people. What do you think about all this?"

"It's awful," she repeated, eyes wide. "What am I supposed to think?"

"What do you think's really happening?" Shaw asked.

"I don't know what you mean."

"Let's start with yesterday," North said. "Someone spiked the water with an amphetamine, and the odds are that it was Adderall. Why would someone do that?"

"To hurt someone, obviously."

"More specifically? Does anyone on the panel come to mind as the obvious target? Including you?"

"Me?" A laugh burst out of Heidi before she could lock it down. Smiling grimly, she shook her head. "I mean, I've made plenty of people angry over the years, but I don't think anyone would care enough to come after me."

"You'd be surprised," Shaw said.

But Heidi shook her head again. "Bad reviews don't tank books. You'd think that's how it would work, but it isn't. A good review helps, sure. A good review can launch a book, give it a new audience, that kind of thing. But a bad review? It might deter a few people, but the ones who want to read that book, they'll read it anyway. Authors take the reviews personally, of course, but that's another matter." Her fingers traced the tablet's frame. "I would have said that someone had targeted Scotty. Especially since he, well, you know. But then there was that attack last night, and the only one of those three who was on the panel was Clarence. Honestly, he's the least objectionable one from that panel. The rest of them don't exactly spend their time making friends and playing nice."

"We got that impression," North said. "We haven't been able to pin down Mary Angela yet, but the others all seem like they could push someone's buttons."

"I love Mary Angela," Heidi said with a shrug, "but she can do it too. It comes with the success, I think. They get a big head."

"We heard about some conflict between the authors," Shaw said, "including Scotty."

Heidi flinched, her eyes squeezing shut for an instant.

If North hadn't been watching her so closely, he would have missed it. Now he leaned forward, channeled the same bullshit look of conviction he used when he suspected Shaw had been fucking around in his fridge, and said, "Yeah. That."

"Oh God," Heidi whispered.

Shaw was too good at this to break character, but North could feel his curiosity. The slender man leaned down, patted Heidi's arm, and said, "Look, we just want to hear your side of it."

"For now," North said.

Heidi flinched again. "I didn't tell anyone," she said. "How can anybody even know? I swear to God, I didn't say a word. This is my—this is my professional integrity on the line, you understand? And I don't want to speak ill of the dead, and—"

"You're stalling," North said. "When Shaw stalls, he does the same thing: unfurls this list of excuses a mile long. You should have heard him when I made him clean his bathroom. There was something about alligators in toilets."

"It's a real thing! It happens. In Florida."

"Please," Heidi said, "can you just tell me how you—how you found out? Because I did not say a word."

"No," North said. "And no more stalling."

"Ok, well." Heidi sank down in the seat. Then, tapping on the tablet, she began to talk. "I'm very upfront with authors. I make sure they understand that I'll only review exactly what they ask me to review. That covers my butt; some authors, especially indie authors, are revising their manuscripts right up until the book goes live on ebook retailers. In the past, I'd review a book, and if I mentioned spelling and grammar errors, the author would fill up the comments section complaining that I reviewed the wrong edition, and the right one doesn't have any of those problems, and I'm so unfair—on and on like that. So I finally made it a policy: I review exactly what you give me, and if you come back before I've done a review and give me a different version, I'll delete the first copy and review the revised one. Usually it's not a big deal because I don't have time to read ahead, so if the author sends me eighteen updated versions before I get to their review, all I do is delete the first seventeen and read the one she sent me most recently."

North nodded. "Sounds fair."

"It's a bit of a pain, but yeah, it's fair, and it's better than listening to all that complaining." Heidi stopped tapping; now she gripped the tablet in both hands. "A few months ago, Scotty sends me an ARC—"

"What's an ARC?"

"Advance review copy," Shaw said. "Authors give them to readers and reviewers before the book is actually on sale."

"So he sends me the ARC," Heidi said, "only it's not the title I'm expecting. He was supposed to send me his Christmas one so that I could get it reviewed before the holidays. Instead, he sent me *Cheap Stud.*"

"Scotty doesn't have a book called *Cheap Stud*," Shaw said slowly. "The four books in the Build-Your-Own-Bear series are *Ordinary Stud*, *Jack Stud*, *King Stud*, and *Post Stud*."

Heidi met his eyes and nodded.

"Oh. Wow."

"What?" North said. "It's another book. More fucking Lars and Twinky Twerpy or whatever his name is."

"Twerpy Twink," Shaw corrected absently. "And it's a really big deal. Scotty swore he was done with that series. But it's his absolute bestseller. People are still crazy about it."

"Yeah, I kind of got that when three guys grabbed my ass and one of them asked Lars to 'pound him through the wall.'"

"Some of that is just because you have a grabbable ass, but yes, that's pretty much the idea. People love the books, and…" Shaw slowed.

"And none of Scotty's other books have been nearly as good," Heidi finished for him. "It's not just that they haven't been as successful—they're not as well written. Some of them are just plain bad. Even *Post Stud*, the last one in the series, was significantly weaker than the others."

"So, people would be excited about this, right?" North asked.

"Not just excited," Shaw said. "People would go crazy. This would have been all over social media. Even just a hint of it would have spread like wildfire."

"That's what I mean," Heidi said. "I didn't tell anyone, so I don't know how the two of you heard."

"What happened? I never saw any rumors about another Build-Your-Own-Bear book, and I'm on all the fan pages."

"Scotty wrote me early the next morning. He said he'd sent the wrong manuscript, and he asked me not to say anything about the project and to delete the file." Heidi shifted in her seat, her gaze moving to a distant spot. "I never told anyone about it."

"But you didn't destroy the file," North said.

For a moment, it looked like she might argue. Then, slumping forward, she nodded. "This is what I meant when I said my professional reputation is on the line. Authors trust me not to go blabbing if they send me the wrong version, which happens more than you'd expect. Normally, I would have deleted the file and forgotten about it. But I'd started reading it almost as soon as I got it. I…I have a love-hate thing with Scotty's work. When it's good, it's so, so good. And this one was good. He sucked me in on the first page, and I read all night. I'd finished it by the time Scotty sent me that email in the morning."

Laughter burbled from the reviewers and the moderators, who were still chatting on the other side of the room. One of the women threw her head back, roaring. The other said, "I'll drink to that." The moderator held open the door, made a prissy flourish with one hand, and the three exited.

"You wouldn't be this upset," Shaw said into the silence that followed, "if it had ended there."

Heidi shook her head. "For a few weeks, I waited, watching Scotty's social media accounts, hoping to see that he'd announced the next Build-Your-Own-Bear book. But he just kept posting the same stuff: trolling female authors in the genre, workout videos with Josue, self-promotion. Then the holidays rolled around, and I was busy. I forgot about it, honestly. Until—until I got another manuscript from another author. Read this."

She spun the tablet; a document was displayed, with a paragraph highlighted in yellow:

The neighbor boy kept running through his head. Club groaned, stroking his namesake under the hot spray of the shower. The neighbor boy had been doing that a lot lately, getting inside Club's head no matter how many times Club told himself no. Whenever Club let himself think about K, his glutes tensed, his hips flexed, and his balls boiled. It was like K turned him into a fucking machine. Just the thought of K. Just the memory of the eighteen-year-old's smooth, developing muscles. Just the thought of his brother's foster son.

"It's not exactly high literature," North began, "and the pseudo-incest angle—"

"I'd read the hell out of that," Shaw said.

North rubbed his temples. "Ok. So what am I supposed to get from this?"

"A woody," Shaw said.

"Jesus Christ," North muttered.

"Now take a look at this," Heidi said, tapping the screen twice. A different document appeared with another paragraph highlighted in yellow:

The kid kept running through his head. Lars groaned, stroking his favorite tool under the hot spray of the shower. The kid had been doing that a lot lately, getting inside Lars's head no matter how many times Lars told himself no. Whenever Lars let himself think about Kris, his glutes tensed, his hips flexed, and his balls boiled. It was like Kris turned him into a fucking machine. Just the thought of Kris. Just the memory of the eighteen-year-old's smooth, developing muscles. Just the thought of his brother's on-call babysitter.

"Huh," North said.

"No way," Shaw said. "There's got to be a mistake."

"The mistake is fucking the babysitter. It's hard enough to get someone you can trust without adding your favorite tool into the mix."

"North, Scotty isn't a plagiarist. He's a great writer. Well, he was. This has to be a mistake. Some weird coincidence."

Frowning, Heidi turned off the tablet's screen. "It's the whole book, I'm afraid. Someone obviously did a find and replace to swap out the names, but it's the same book."

"Ok, so, what?" North said. "Are we talking a lawsuit? Wouldn't the other author just sue Scotty?"

"At the least," Shaw said. "But it would be worse than that. Scotty would lose a lot of readers. Not all of them, but a lot. Probably most. It would ruin his reputation."

"He'd lose the editor job at Bolingbroke?"

Shaw nodded. "He'd be finished. He could probably start up again under a pen name, but as Scotty Carlson, he'd be finished."

North cocked his head. Then he looked at Heidi. "The timeline doesn't make sense. You made it sound like Scotty plagiarized it, but you said you got this manuscript later."

"I did."

"So wouldn't it make more sense that someone else plagiarized Scotty's work?"

"Yes, but…"

"But?"

"But it doesn't sound like Scotty," Shaw said.

Heidi shrugged and nodded. "Exactly. I mean, most people probably wouldn't notice, but it's not quite his style. It starts faster. The sex is less…authentic, although I'm not sure if I'm saying that right. I said it's a great book, and it is, but it's not great the way the first few Lars books were. It doesn't have the same intensity, the same shine. Also, little things in Scotty's version don't quite make sense if it's the original. There's a sentence where Lars says something about clubbing a guy to death, and it's obviously supposed to be a joke, but I didn't get it. Then, a few months later when I read this other version, I realized it was a pun on the main character's nickname, Club. It doesn't make any sense for Scotty to write that line the way it is, but it makes a lot of sense if he got a hold of the manuscript and just did a find-and-replace to change the names."

"So he got an early version of another author's manuscript," North said slowly, "plagiarized it, got cold feet, and backed off. Then, a few months later, the original author finally gets around to publishing her version. Apparently without ever realizing what had almost happened with Scotty."

Heidi nodded. "I think so. Something like that."

"Who's the author?" Shaw asked.

Clicking on the screen, Heidi turned the tablet again.

Clubbing, the title read. By JD Hathaway.

Chapter 25

SHAW FOUND JD THROUGH her Facebook page: she was selling her services, offering to listen to book pitches and provide critiques. *Meet me in the Kayak's Coffee.*

"Fifty dollars for a fifteen-minute pitch?" North said. "That's fucking highway robbery."

"All the slots are full, so apparently some people think it's a good deal."

Shaw and North rode down in an empty elevator car. It smelled like overdone roast beef and wet carpet. The steel panels muddled Shaw's reflection.

"That's two hundred dollars an hour," North said. "We don't make two hundred dollars an hour."

"Sometimes we do. When you jack up our rates for those creepy Ladue doctors who want us to spy on their wives."

"You aren't spending enough time on your library porn."

Shaw tried to figure out if his reflection was as surprised as he was. "What?"

"Shaw, two hundred dollars an hour. Just to listen to people tell you about Alpha A jamming his dingdong into Beta B."

"Actually, there is a whole snack cake series where someone does shove a dingdong—"

"How many library porn books have you written?"

"North, they're not—"

"Are you ready to publish them?"

"I really mostly write drabbles—"

"Maybe I should take you to the library and fuck you. For inspiration." North ran a hand through his mess of blond hair. The faint perfume of American Crew gel wafted off him. "Or you should tie me up in the stacks and leave a vibrator in me until I'm sobbing for you to take me apart with your dick."

The elevator dinged.

Shaw shouldered off the camel hair duffle coat, folded it, and held it in front of him.

"Really?" North said.

"I'm very attracted to you. And these harem pants are, um, revealing."

To Shaw's surprise, North wrapped him in one arm, kissed his neck, and then muttered, "God, I love you."

"Because you gave me a stiffy?" Shaw asked as the doors slid open.

A horde of children stared up at them.

North looked at the children; judging by their matching t-shirts, they seemed to be on some sort of field trip. Then he looked at Shaw.

"Oh," Shaw said. "Right." He cleared his throat. "A stiffy is a natural thing the body does when—"

Sighing, North steered Shaw away from a situation that, Shaw suspected, might have been going downhill.

Outside the Kayak's Coffee, a line snaked down the hall: men and women with sheafs of pages, tablets, laptops, notebooks with flowery covers. One woman, holding her hair as though afraid it might slip off, had a poster with a tripod display. In black Sharpie were the words: *Beta C*ck Learns to Code*.

North was still shaking his head as they moved inside. The fragrance of brewing coffee met them; an espresso machine hissed sharply while a terrified-looking young man jabbed buttons. The line of people continued here, and now Shaw realized that they were not waiting for coffee.

"Seriously?" North said. "Fifty bucks?"

The line terminated near a rack of Vickie's potato chips. A lost-looking man, his sweater unraveling at the hem, was poking the salt-and-vinegar bags. Next to him, a printed sheet of paper announced PITCH CRITIQUES - $50 – LINE FORMS HERE.

"It's kind of like those cooking shows," Shaw said. "For whatever reason, authors desperately want someone to tell them what's wrong with their book. The crueler someone is, the more a reader respects their judgment."

"That sounds like an abusive relationship."

"Well, yeah."

At a table in the far corner, JD was speaking rapidly, but too low for Shaw to make out the words. Her leathery skin looked jaundiced under the Kayak's fluorescent lights, and the platinum pixie cut had a yellowish tinge to it. She was leaning across the table, stabbing a finger at a fortyish man who wore a thinning combover and a cardigan with the NASA logo on the back. NASA guy was getting smaller and smaller. If he kept up his *Alice and Wonderland* trick for five more minutes, he was going to disappear.

"—and if you had said 'empowering' one more time," JD said, "I would have puked on your face."

"Scram," North said when they reached the table.

The man stared up at him from under his combover. "But I paid fifty dollars—"

"Do what all these hacks do: put eight more cocks in it, a shower gang bang scene, and some sort of ball depilation fetish. Now get lost."

"Actually," Shaw said, reading over the man's shoulder, "I think he's writing a picture book."

North flushed.

"Maybe only six more cocks," Shaw said helpfully.

"Do not," North growled at him. To the man, he said, "What don't you understand about scram? JD is going to refund your money; she doesn't have time to talk right now."

"I don't do refunds," JD said, "and whatever you think—"

"I paid for this time," the man insisted.

"You want a critique?" North said. "I'll give you a critique. You get fifteen minutes over Facetime. It's a courtesy critique because I need to talk to her."

"I don't have Facetime," the man said hesitantly. "But my mom has Google Hangouts."

"Fine. Whatever. Go."

"I don't do refunds," JD said, the pitch rising.

"And first free piece of advice," North said, gesturing at the pile of papers, "get rid of that cover with the teddy bear humping the spaceship."

"My mom drew that!"

"Maybe you should frame it," Shaw suggested. "And then you can tell her how mean the cover design artists are, and they wouldn't let you use it, and it'll give you something to commiserate about."

Standing, the man gathered the pages. "How will I contact—"

"Go!" North roared.

The man scurried away, and conversation buzzed to life when he reached the line. Shaw was fairly sure he heard the man say something like, "That's the most helpful critique I've ever gotten."

Dropping into a chair, Shaw met JD's eyes. North sat next to him.

"I'm not sitting here for my health," JD snapped. "Fifty dollars gets you fifteen minutes. You pay in advance."

"When did you realize Scotty Carlson had stolen your manuscript?"

JD's hands curled around the tablet. She seemed to be holding her breath. Then she smiled. "God, how'd you hear that?"

"We've seen the manuscripts."

"Did Josue let you look? He must not have blabbed about the whole thing, though. He idolizes Scotty. I don't know why; Scotty treated him like a jerkoff toy." Her lips parted to expose faintly yellow teeth. "I guess that's what they call real love."

"When did you realize what had happened, JD?" Shaw asked.

She laughed. "Is this the motive? You two really are something. Did you come down here to confront me and get my alibi? Jesus. I killed Scotty because he stole my book?"

"You still haven't answered the question," North said.

"That's because you're asking the wrong question. I never 'realized Scotty stole my manuscript.' I sold it to him."

Shaw threw a sideways glance at North. "Why?"

"Because he was done. Finished. He'd barely eked out the last Lars book, and he didn't have anything left to write. Inspiration all dried up, although you wouldn't know it from how he and Josue carry on about their all-night sex marathons."

"I thought he had some other books after the Build-Your-Own-Bear books," North said, glancing at Shaw for confirmation. Shaw nodded. "What about those?"

"Bought," JD said. "He bought all of them, I think. I mean, I don't know that for sure, but after he approached me, I went back and looked at his work. You can see the difference almost immediately, once you know what to look for."

North was silent for a moment. "He approached you?"

"That's right. I had to sign a non-disclosure agreement just to hear the offer, which makes sense in hindsight. I mean, Scotty had an image to maintain: the perfect gay, the perfect lover, the perfect physical specimen, the perfect writer. I was curious, so I signed, and he told me what he wanted: another book in the Lars series, written by me, delivered in six weeks."

"And?" Shaw said.

"And I said yes." JD shrugged. "I already had a draft of *Clubbing* sitting on my hard drive. I did a find-and-replace for the names and a few of the descriptions, and I sent it off. Scotty liked it. He paid me. The end."

"He didn't contact you about the manuscript again after that?"

"Not until I got an email telling me that he no longer wanted to use the manuscript. I've got to tell you, I just about shit myself. I thought he was going to ask for the money back, and I'd already spent the fifty thousand."

"He paid you fifty thousand dollars to write a book?"

Another shrug. "He'd make it back. The Lars series is extremely popular, and on top of that, he had just taken that editor job at Bolingbroke. I guess he was worried about keeping his credentials current, and he wanted to put out another book to prove he could still write."

"And?"

JD stared blankly.

"The money?" Shaw said.

"Oh. He didn't even bring it up. He said he wasn't going to use the manuscript, and nobody else had seen it, so I was free to publish it myself provided I changed the names of characters. That was easy; I still had the original sitting there. I got a cover, put it up, and the rest is history."

"And this conversation had nothing to do with why you followed him into the restroom a few nights ago?"

For a moment, JD was very still. "I already told you about that."

"You sure did. And there's nothing you want to add?"

"Not a thing. Now, if you'll excuse me, I've got people who paid for my time."

"I don't suppose you can tell us where you were Wednesday night?"

"I was at dinner with some readers. I do a raffle for all my meals and coffees so readers can win a chance to spend time with me."

"So they can pay to spend time with you."

"They want to do it," she said, lip curling. "You wouldn't understand."

"I understand," North said. "Where were you after dinner?"

"In my room. Alone. Now will you please leave? You've already put me behind schedule."

North and Shaw shared a look, and they stood.

"Not that it's any of your business," JD said, her tone suggesting an afterthought. "But I did see something Wednesday night. I treated myself to some cake and ice cream, and I was putting the tray in the hall when I saw Karen sneaking out of her room."

"Sneaking?" Shaw said. "Are you sure she wasn't creeping?"

"Or lurking?"

"Or slinking?"

"Or pussyfooting?"

"Pussyfooting doesn't count," Shaw said. "Try again."

"Excuse me," JD said. "What the hell is going on?"

"Pussyfooting sure as fuck counts," North said. "It's like a cat burglar. Pussyfooting."

"That's not what that means at all. It means, you know, walking around a subject instead of talking about it."

"It can mean walking softly and quietly too. Like a cat. Or a cat burglar."

"I'm going to check."

"You don't need to check," North said, pushing Shaw's phone down. "I just told you, so you don't need to check."

"It's not that I don't trust you—"

"Excuse me," JD was screeching, "excuse me!"

"—but I just want to check."

"And I told you," North pushed the phone down again, "you don't need to check. I'm the one who graduated college. Me."

"Right, but, see, I remember, you kind of had a limited vocabulary when you started college. You were doing all those remedial worksheets. They'd have pictures of musical instruments, and you'd be trying desperately to figure out the name. Or pictures of fruit. Or days of the week. I mean, I'm really amazed that you stuck with it and tried so hard. It was really impressive. And I'm sure you know what a tromboner is now. But, you know—"

"I was learning Spanish, you fucking imbecile. And it's a trombone. Not a tromboner. Not that you would know, because you didn't graduate college."

"I didn't need to graduate college to know what a boner is. You had a whomper cock rocket that time I walked in on you watching those home gym commercials—"

"Excuse me!" JD shrieked.

"What?" North rounded on her. "Jesus Christ, can't you see we're in the middle of something?"

"You're really being kind of rude," Shaw told her. "Just a little."

"She was wearing a trench coat. And a hat. And she kept checking the hallway to make sure nobody saw her. She was sneaking. That's who you should be talking to."

"Who?" Shaw asked North.

"Christ, I don't know. She's been blathering on for what feels like hours."

"Karen! Karen! Karen, you dumb fucks! Now get the fuck out of here!"

As North and Shaw made their way out of the Kayak's, North gave the wide-eyed people in line a double thumbs up. "Best critique I've ever gotten," he whispered.

In the hall, Shaw slid his arm through North's. "Feel better?"

"God," North said, ruffling Shaw's poof of chestnut-colored hair before kissing his temple. "You have no idea."

Chapter 26

SHAW AND NORTH MADE a loop of the hotel's public areas in search of Karen. The playfulness and wild excitement of the previous day had evaporated; people moved quietly in small knots, and judging by the empty halls and sparse audiences Shaw saw in the convention rooms, he guessed that at least half of the convention attendees had gone home. One young woman, who looked barely out of her teens, stood forlornly at the intersection of two hallways. In her hand, she held a drooping silicone cock.

When Shaw made a noise, North looked over at him. "I feel bad for them," Shaw said. "They look forward to this all year, and now it's been ruined."

"Yeah, murder is a real boner-killer."

"A lot of them are probably grieving. Or dealing with the trauma of a near-death experience. Or in shock. I should see if Dr. Farr could set up some emergency sessions for people here. I bet she could really help them start processing their loss."

North looked at him again.

"Sorry." Shaw flushed. "I know how silly that sounded."

"No. Well, maybe a little. But I love that you care about people like that."

"Oh."

"God, you're beautiful." North leaned over to whisper, "Keep smiling like that, and you're going to give me a tromboner."

Shaw didn't know what the right answer was to that, so he settled for squeezing North's ass, which made North laugh so hard he had to sit down.

"I don't know what's so funny," Shaw said, hands on hips, aware that the harem pants weren't exactly doing him any favors.

North just laughed harder.

When he'd recovered, Shaw ignored his request for a hand up—slapping at North's fingers when North tried to grab him—and they started to make another loop.

This time, they found Karen in the Royal Excalibur's lobby. Jadon and Cerise were there too, the three of them forming a tight triangle. Karen looked wrecked from the night before: dark circles under her eyes, a sallow cast to her skin, her hair greasy in the mess of a bun she had attempted. Her nose was still huge and puffy from the fall, and Shaw guessed that it was broken. Jadon was in a fresh suit and shirt, but he had the look of raw exhaustion that Shaw remembered from when they'd been dating and cases had taken over Jadon's life for days at a time. Even so, he still managed to look fantastic—somehow, the fabric gave the illusion of being soaking wet, hugging every inch of defined muscle. Cerise looked thinner than ever in her too-big magician's suit, but her sharp eyes never stopped moving.

Whatever Jadon and Cerise were selling, Karen wasn't buying. She shook her head and stalked away, and when Jadon started after her, Cerise laid a restraining hand on his arm. She said something, and Jadon's gaze shot toward North and Shaw.

"Don't engage," North muttered, nudging Shaw with one shoulder so that they turned to follow Karen. "You're going to make him soup and give him a sponge bath and the next thing I know, you'll be married to him and having his babies."

Shaw allowed himself a few seconds to process that as they cut across the lobby's thick red carpet. "I'm sorry," he finally managed. "What?"

"You heard me. The last thing I need is you feeling sorry for Jadon Reck and trying to take care of him."

"But that part about the babies…"

With a wild noise, North caught Shaw's shoulder and forced him into a trot. "You heard me," he bit out.

They caught up to Karen in one of the hotel's main hallways, halfway to The Round Table. She was crying, her head down, and power walking.

When North squeezed Shaw's shoulder, Shaw hurried to catch up. "Karen? Hey, it's Shaw. Karen, hold on."

She stopped, covered her eyes, and her whole body shook with another suppressed sob. "I'm sorry. Now's not a good time—"

"Karen, what's wrong?"

That opened the floodgates, and sobs poured out. She cried so hard that she was trembling, and Shaw helped her to a bench. The flow of traffic was thin today, and although people slowed to stare, nobody made any move to approach them. Some of that might have had something to do with North, who was standing in front of Shaw and Karen, arms crossed, glaring.

"Take a fucking picture," he told an old man in a rainbow ball cap. "Next hour, we'll have the Elephant Man."

The poor guy ran away so fast that he hit the railing outside The Round Table and almost flipped over it.

After a couple of minutes, Karen's crying slowed, and she wiped her face. "Oh God, that makes my nose hurt ten times worse. I'm all congested, and just touching it is so awful."

"Hot shower," North said over his shoulder.

"Huh?"

"He knows what he's talking about," Shaw said. "Probably. I mean, he worked construction, and he grew up in a middle-class neighborhood, and it's very important that you understand how butch he is, you know, with the boots and all—"

North was making one of those wild noises again, but he didn't look back at them.

"—so he probably knows what he's talking about."

Karen sniffled, winced, and managed to say, "Ok. Yeah."

"Want to tell us what that was about?"

Shaking her head, Karen got to her feet. She took a step away from the bench, casting North a nervous glance, but he only shrugged and moved out of her way. She took another step.

"Whatever they think they have on you," Shaw said, "they don't have it yet. Otherwise they wouldn't have let you walk away. But they're going to come back. And they'll keep coming back."

"I'm not—" Karen tried.

"Even if you didn't have anything to do with Scotty, you've got something that you want to keep a secret. I'm telling you—"

"You're just like them," she said. Her too-wide mouth hardened. Her lips were white where she clamped them together. "You're telling me as a friend, is that it? And if I just tell you what's wrong, you can make everything better? Did I pretty much get it?"

"I'd like to be your friend," Shaw said softly. "I'd like to help you."

Tears flooded Karen's eyes again; she dashed them away. "I'm sorry. You seem very sweet, but I'm exhausted, and I'm in pain, and I can't stop thinking about how horrible yesterday was and what happened to Scotty—" She cut off with a sob, mastered herself, and then managed to say, "But I don't know you. Not really. And I'm tired of everyone here thinking I'm stupid just because I don't sell as many books as they do. Do you know how tiresome it is to have these self-important, self-absorbed people telling you all day what you're doing wrong, and if you'd just do things the way they do, you'd be a bestseller? Only, the reality is, they've just been lucky, and there's nothing you can do about that."

"Does this have something to do with the book Scotty was supposed to help you with?" North asked.

Karen started to shake her head and then caught herself. "Please don't follow me; I don't want to have to ask hotel security to make you leave me alone."

"Karen, you're only making things worse," Shaw said.

"Funny. Detective Cao said the same thing. But you know what? Things can't be any worse. Scotty's dead. Things don't get any worse than that."

Standing, Shaw shook his head. He moved to stand next to North. "I'm sorry we upset you."

"You didn't upset me," she said, but she gave the words the lie by wiping her eyes again. "You know who you should talk to, if you're so keen on figuring this out? You should talk to Mary Angela. Sweet, dumpy-frumpy Mary Angela. I heard her tell Scotty right to his face she was going to end him. Those were her words: end him. And somebody did, didn't they? Why don't you think about that?"

She whirled and hurried in the other direction, but halfway down the hall, stumbled over some irregularity in the carpeting and went down on hands and knees.

When Shaw took a step forward, North caught his arm. "Better if you don't."

Karen was crying openly now as she got to her feet. She massaged her knee for a moment before hobbling away.

Sighing, Shaw nodded. "Mary Angela?"

"Yep," North said, and they went to find a convention program.

Chapter 27

IN THE HOTEL'S LAUNDRY room, Shaw was getting dinner and a show. Or a snack and a show. Or dessert and a show. Dessert was chocolate ice cream, prepared by Chef Marisa, who had taken one look at Shaw and decided he needed a bowl of ice cream with toasted almonds and raspberry sauce. The show was North; Shaw adjusted his seat on top of a commercial washing machine, stretched his legs, and said, "Now spin around."

"Eat me," North bit out as he tried to pull on the hotel uniform trousers.

Nacho was trying to help, swearing steadily in a stream of Spanish, to which North occasionally responded.

"It's your ass, isn't it?" Shaw asked.

"It's not my ass. It's—" He yanked on the waistband, trying to hike the pants up to cover the remaining few inches of his boxers (white with an erector-set Ferris wheel print, purchased by Shaw). "Don't you have a bigger size of pants?"

Nacho replied with another blistering line in Spanish, of which the only part Shaw caught was the end: "Hijo de puta." Then Nacho said in English, "I already told you: these are the biggest pair we have, and you're lucky I could find them. We don't normally have to put chunky-thighed white boys in uniform." To Shaw he added, "And it's not his ass. It's his thighs. What the fuck does he do for exercise? Pure squats and lunges?"

"Actually, that's very interesting because sometimes North likes to—"

"What's interesting," North said firmly, "is that it's not my ass. It's my thighs. They're too muscular."

Shaw watched him over another spoonful of ice cream, raspberry sauce, and toasted almonds.

"I hate you so much sometimes," North muttered. He gave another yank, and a seam popped, and the trousers slid into place. His face was red as he focused on doing the button, and he didn't look up as he mumbled, "Not one fucking word, Shaw." Then, "You're about to lose that fucking hand."

Grinning, Nacho danced back, his fingers dropping from where he'd been caressing North's ass. "Just making sure they fit, papi. Hey, do you guys ever do threesomes? Because I'm really good at them."

"Really?" Shaw slurped more of the melting ice cream. "How can you be good at a threesome?"

"Well, picture a detective sandwich. I have no gag reflex, so—"

"No," North said, grabbing Shaw's arm and taking the bowl of ice cream with his other hand. "Go find some innocent twink to debauch."

"I tried," Nacho said, "and then he turned out to be your boyfriend."

"If I had a dollar," North said as he dragged Shaw from the room, "for every time I heard that."

They had found Mary Angela speaking at a panel that had just started, which meant a sudden change of plans. The schedule suggested they had at least an hour of time to work undisturbed, and so they'd gone hunting for Nacho. They'd found him in the kitchen with Marisa, and aside from the ice cream—which had been a bonus—everything had gone smoothly.

In the lobby, they separated, Shaw rubbing his arm and casting wounded looks at North. North ignored him, cutting toward the front door. The gray polyester hugged him like a second skin, delineating the powerful lines of his shoulders, his ass, his thighs. Shaw wondered if a little drool would ruin his part of their performance.

Wiping his mouth to be safe, he made his way to the front desk. The exit rush from earlier that day had dried up, and since it wasn't even noon, today's check-ins hadn't started to arrive. The lobby was mostly empty, and the lone woman behind the front desk looked worn out under a helmet of hair-sprayed curls. When Shaw got closer, he caught a whiff of the product she'd used. Green apple something.

"Hi," he said with a huge smile, "I wanted to ask about—"

And then he went down, half jumping, half falling. He crashed into the front desk, doing his best to sell the fall without actually hurting himself. He landed on the ground, something sticky on the carpet beneath his head, staring up at the lobby's gold filigree.

"Oh my God, oh my God, oh my God." The woman showed up in his field of vision, hands pressed to her cheeks like she was straight out of a bad drama class. Her name tag said Claudette. "Not again, not again, not again."

And then she passed out.

Shaw, who was still lying on the ground, could do nothing except watch. She had a boneless grace, and when she ended up on the floor, she looked surprisingly comfortable. From around the lobby came the murmur of worried voices.

"What the fuck did you do to her?" North whispered from behind the front desk, where he was typing and clicking rapidly at the computer.

"Nothing," Shaw sat up, tried to wipe the stickiness from his hair, and ended up only spreading it around. "She freaked out, and then bang."

"You probably killed her with that fucking debacle of a fall. Did I see you try to do ballet?"

On his knees, Shaw inspected Claudette, who was snoring softly. He helped her onto her back. Only then did he trust his voice to say, "Obviously not. I don't even know what you're talking about."

"It's that fucking sissonne video, isn't it? You've watched it a million times."

"Ballet is a remarkable combination of grace and strength, and I think it's fascinating—"

From behind the front desk came the sound of furious tapping. "You like the crotch shot of that guy right when he jumps."

"—how precisely controlled their movements—"

"Crotch shot."

"—and the jumps are—"

"Crotch shot. You added a sissonne to your little performance because you liked looking at a guy's flagpole wrapped in two microns of nylon, and now a woman is dead because of it."

"She's definitely not dead. And if anything, it was more of a jeté because I only jumped from one foot, and—

"Got it," North said. Then, in a slightly softer tone, "You're ok, right?"

"Oh, yeah, absolutely."

"Then handle this shit. And be grateful I don't jeté you off the top of the building."

"That's not how it works. That's like saying, 'Be grateful I don't jump you—' Oh, hi. Yes, she's fine. I think. Well, she's sleeping. Or something."

By that point the doorman had reached Shaw, and he was bending down to check on Claudette while North hurried away. It took Shaw several minutes of explaining what had happened, and by then, Claudette was wiping her eyes and sitting up.

"Thank Jesus," she said, wrapping Shaw in an enormous hug, which he returned. "I thought you'd cracked your noggin and gone to heaven just like the last one."

Shaw considered asking which last one, but over Claudette's shoulder he could see North waiting with hands on hips.

"Anything else you'd like to do before we, you know, get to fucking work?" North asked when Shaw joined him. "Do you want to shave each other's legs? Do you want to exchange top ten nail tips?"

"You do need a manicure. I'm so glad you're the one who brought it up."

"I don't—" North had ditched the jacket, and under his crossed arms, the uniform's thin white button-down was practically translucent. He took Shaw's head in his hands, inspected him, and grunted. "You're really ok?"

Shaw nodded as best he could and then tapped his lips.

North kissed him.

"Maybe just one more," Shaw said when North pulled back. "I might have hit my head a tiny bit."

A barely visible smirk pulled at the corner of North's mouth, and he leaned in, stopping just short of the kiss, and whispered, "Then you shouldn't gild the lily, sweetheart."

"Is that, you know, what you did a couple weeks ago when you had my legs up like—"

North turned and walked away.

"North, if that's what it was, I was into it."

North walked faster.

"We can gild the lily whenever you want." An elderly couple had stopped to stare, and Shaw told them, "We really can. He has amazing stamina, and his refractory period is—"

"Stop talking," North called back in a strangled scream.

Shaw grinned and ran after him.

They rode the elevator to the twelfth floor, and they knocked at 1206, just to be safe. When no one answered, they let themselves into the room. Shaw produced the disposable gloves he'd requisitioned from Marisa, and they each put on a pair before beginning their search. The room was a standard: bathroom near the front of the unit, and then, farther back, the sleeping area with a queen-sized bed, a desk, and a cramped window. The wallpaper featured a blackberry pattern with flowers that had probably once been crisply white but were now yellowed. A hint of perfume hung in the air, slightly astringent, like it was the CVS knockoff of whatever scent Mary Angela preferred.

"Adderall," North said from the bathroom. "Thirty milligrams."

"In a prescription vial?" Shaw asked as he sat at the desk. Mary Angela's MacBook was in front of him; it was an older model, which was perfect as far as Shaw was concerned.

North's grunt sounded like a yes.

Shaw opened the MacBook, booted it up, and entered the computer's recovery mode. Designed to help the hapless consumer who had forgotten his or her password, recovery mode was also a useful backdoor in situations like this one. Shaw reset the password to *tootightpants*, logged into Mary Angela's account, and started his search.

He found it in her email.

"North, you're going to want to see this."

North emerged from the bathroom and joined Shaw at the desk. He frowned, leaned closer, and squinted.

"If you'd just try a pair of cheaters," Shaw began.

"What's Josue going to think about this?" North read from the screen. "And it's to Scotty with a video attached. Want to make any bets about what we're going to see?"

"Scotty having an affair, I assume."

"Any bets about who's getting cornholed by Scotty? Or doing the cornholing, I guess?"

"That was very forward-thinking of you," Shaw said.

North looked at him.

"Very open-minded."

North's gaze flattened.

"Very 21st-century."

"Isn't this laryngitis season?"

"Possibly."

"How would you feel about licking some handrails?"

Shaw bit the inside of his cheek. "Based on the people we know, it could be Clarence. He was on the panel."

"Or it could be a rando that he picked up, right? Someone off an app?"

Shaw nodded. He clicked the video, and it began to play.

A high-pitched moan echoed in the small room.

"Oh." Shaw said. He squeezed his eyes shut, opened one a fraction, and repeated in a slightly more curious tone, "Oh!"

"That is definitely not Clarence," North muttered.

And it wasn't. It wasn't a rando either. Their faces were perfectly visible on camera, and Shaw recognized them both.

Scotty was having sex with Karen.

Chapter 28

"HOLD ON," North said. "He's bi? The guy was a major homo."

"Well, the Kinsey scale—"

"Shaw, he was pounding her like he wanted to turn her into Hamburger Helper. Don't talk to me about the Kinsey scale."

Shaw clicked something, typed something, and clicked again. North's phone vibrated, and he saw an email had just arrived.

"Just in case this copy mysteriously vanishes," Shaw said with a shrug. "Also, I thought you could reply to that email and let Mary Angela know we'd like to talk to her. She'll see the attachment that was somehow sent from her own email address, and she'll freak out."

North blinked. "God, you are surprisingly devious sometimes."

"Deviousness isn't really a trait I want to—"

"It is so fucking hot."

"—cultivate because I'm trying to embrace a harmonious existence—wait, really?"

"Guess you'll find out the next time I gild your lily. Come on."

As North left the room, he heard Shaw scrambling free from the desk. "I knew that's what that was called!"

While they waited for the elevator, North's phone buzzed again. Mary Angela's reply said, *I don't know who this is, but I'm calling the police. Don't contact me again.*

Don't bother, North wrote back. *I've scheduled an email forward to them in fifteen minutes.*

The phone buzzed almost immediately. *No.*

The elevator doors dinged and slid open. A pair of young men dressed like a couple of the Village People—one was a construction worker in jean cut-offs, the other was bare-chested under a plasticky leather jacket and a peaked cap—stepped out of the car.

"Hi, Lars," the construction worker camped as they passed North and Shaw.

"Bye, Lars," the one in the peaked cap sang back, twiddling his fingers.

"Jesus fucking Christ," North said to his phone.

The pub, Mary Angela's next message said. *Fifteen minutes.*

"You probably should send that video to Jadon," Shaw said, "just so he doesn't murder us when he realizes we found it first."

"Jadon can eat me," North said as he pressed the button for the lobby.

"Oh, yeah, he's really good at that."

The elevator car lurched down.

"Or," Shaw said slowly, carefully, "so I've heard."

North drew in a slow breath. The elevator car smelled like fake leather.

"All us gals talk about it when we're sitting under the hair dryers at the Wash 'n Set."

"Shaw?"

"Yes?"

"Sweetheart?"

"Yes?"

"Love of my life?"

"That's so beautiful. You're the love of my life too, North, even though last time I asked Master Hermes to do our astrology charts, he warned me that—"

"You have no idea the Pandora's box you just opened."

"Um..."

North met his eyes, gaze level, until Shaw was bright red.

"Uh huh," North grunted, and then turned back to his phone to forward the video to Jadon. "That's what I thought."

The Camelot Public House was still busy with the lunch rush; many of the con-goers obviously preferred not to leave the hotel premises, which meant that a line snaked down the hall outside the pub. Flatware chimed. A hub of voices rumbled. The fryer was obviously being put to good use again, the familiar aroma of hops and yeasty beer made North willing to kill for a drink. The pub was so busy that North had to force a path between the crowded chairs; their feet scraped and stuttered across the tile, often accompanied by protests and shouts. Rodney and Jerry were having drinks at the bar with a pair of women in sensible shoes. A group of pleasant-looking ladies, all in their fifties, were laughing and chatting as they argued good-naturedly about the bill. A thirty-something man with cat's-eye contact lenses swiped at North. His nails, which had been filed into claws, rasped against the Carhartt coat.

"Remember how I said we could go to a con together?" North said over his shoulder. "Never mind. I'm done. I'm out. I want to go to a private beach instead and spend a week getting wasted and fucking around."

"I respect your choices," Shaw said. "We can do cons for when I get to pick our vacations."

"You never get to pick our vacations because last time, you had me rescuing endangered rocks, and I spent three fucking days with my knees killing me. And not for the fun reason."

"Prayer," Shaw said with a solemn nod.

North had to face forward again before the smile slipped free.

Mary Angela was sitting alone at a table in the back. Plates with food scraps indicated that she hadn't been alone for long. Instead of yesterday's shlumpy black athleisure wear, today she wore a sweater and yoga pants, both spotted with something—food or coffee, North guessed. Her enormous eyes roved the room.

"I knew it," she whispered when they sat. "I knew it was you two. You're ruining everything."

"Like your blackmail scam?" North said.

"I don't know what you're talking about. I meant the con. It's ruined. You ruined it."

"Whoever murdered Scotty ruined it," Shaw said, "although you don't seem too torn up about that."

"I'm upset. I'm very upset." One hand played against the edge of the table, inches from a nasty-looking steak knife. North caught Shaw's eyes and looked back at her hand. Shaw nodded and glanced down. In one hand, he held a can of pepper gel he had produced from somewhere, presumably the harem pants.

"Let's start—" North said.

"I don't have anything to say to you. I just—I just wanted to know who was harassing me. I'm going to report you to the police. I don't know anything about anything and—"

"Shut the fuck up," North said gently. "You are in way over your head, and you're making it worse."

Mary Angela's eyes got bigger. She seemed to shrivel up: shoulders contracted, arms drew in.

"Start from the beginning," Shaw said.

"I…I came out of the bar, and they were standing right there. Kissing. I couldn't believe it. I thought I was seeing something. Or that it was a joke. This was last year at the con. It was late, and the hotel was close to empty. They were both very drunk. They seemed to realize they weren't being smart because they separated and went in different directions, but after that, I watched them. And all the signs were there: they were always around each other, always talking to each other, always looking at each other."

"You didn't just watch them, though."

"No…no, I needed to know. I snuck into his room. I planted the camera. I had to—I'd done it before. My daughter. For her own good. It's not difficult, and it's not expensive." Mary Angela's bug-eyes rolled wildly. "Scotty loved to rip women apart for writing gay fiction, but he never brought up Karen's name.

I couldn't believe I'd missed it for so long. And the only reason I'd figured it out was because they'd gotten wasted and made a dumb mistake."

"How did that make you feel?"

"Furious. I was so angry I wanted to kill him." She seemed to hear what she had said, swallowed, and looked at them with huge, pleading eyes. "I didn't, though. I didn't have anything to do with what happened to Scotty."

"Were you angry because you were jealous?" Shaw asked.

"Don't be stupid. I didn't want anything to do with Scotty. He was an attention whore, a jerk, a scumbag. I was furious because he was such a hypocrite. He acted like he was better than everyone, and part of what made him better than anyone—according to him—was that he was a gay man writing in a gay genre. And then, secretly, he was—I don't know. Bi. Demi. Pan. Whatever label you want to put on it, he was fake."

"But not you."

Mary Angela grabbed a remaining French fry and dragged it through a drying patch of ketchup. She looked at the limp piece of potato, grimaced, and dropped it on the plate again. "Do you know who I am? I mean, I know you're not in the genre, but do you know?"

"You're very successful," Shaw said with a smile. "I like your books, and I'm not just saying that."

"I write good books. I'm smart. I took classes. I went to workshops. I learned the craft, and I write about things that I care about, things that I love. My daughter is gay, not that it matters. My first book? I broke the top ten. Book two? I hit number one, and I held on to it for over a day. That's basically unheard of. And for Scotty, it all happens magically, easily, with a wave of his gay magic wand. These dumb, stupid bitches who read this genre, they get their motors cranked knowing that an authentic gay man is writing this stuff, and that's all that matters. I bust my butt writing good books, and they do well, and I'm proud of that. But Scotty? He could shit in a bag, and these bitches would buy ten thousand copies of it."

"And you decided Scotty didn't deserve all that success," North said. "Not if he was faking it. You decided he ought to be punished."

"He did need to be punished! He's awful. You heard about what he did yesterday with Serenity's book? He did that to everyone. He humiliated us. He was a literary writer, in his own opinion, and the rest of us were hacks. And the whole time, he was a fake. You saw the email; I asked him what he thought Josue would do if he saw that video, and he freaked out." She was silent for a moment, her expression thoughtful. Somewhere behind North, a woman was cackling, her laughter drowning out the clink of knives and forks and glasses. "I don't know if he really loved Josue or if he just needed him to keep his image alive, but I know he was scared enough to pay. Until this week. He told me he was out of money. He said he wasn't going to pay anymore. He said Josue was bleeding him dry, and he didn't care what I did. I wasn't so sure about that, so after our fight, I sent him the video again, just as a reminder."

"What about the death threats?"

"What about them?"

"Who did you tell about them? Yasmin said she only confided in—"

"God, you can't believe a word Yasmin says. She told everyone. Everyone. Anyone who would listen. She thought it was so exciting. She thought it would bring up the con's attendance."

"Ok. So you sent that video to Scotty as a threat," Shaw said, "and then the death threats started, and then, what?"

"And then Scotty died," Mary Angela said with a ghoulish grin. "Not that I had anything to do with it, you understand. I preferred him alive. Dead men can't pay."

"That's not much of an alibi," North told her. "It sounds like you had a serious motive: you tried to blackmail Scotty, you failed, and now you were vulnerable. If he went to the police, you'd be ruined. Who would pay for all that expensive rehab your daughter needs? Better to get rid of him."

"No," Mary Angela said. "No, I didn't. And you can't prove that I did."

"What do you think he meant about Josue?" Shaw asked.

With a bitter smile, Mary Angela said, "Do you know what romance is? Whatever makes them buy the book. That's what Scotty was selling, and Josue was part of it. Every workout video they did together. Every public appearance. Every time Scotty pretended to jerk Josue off in public. Every kiss. That was Scotty doing his marketing, his branding. At some point, Josue must have realized that Scotty was a piece of shit, and he started demanding his cut." She shrugged. "That's what I think, anyway. Now, what do I have to do to convince you to leave this alone? I know we can work something out. A little help with your retirement planning, maybe? Or a trip? Somewhere you've always wanted to go? I could—"

North stood, pushing back his chair so that it squealed on the tile. He glanced at Shaw. "How do you feel about blackmailers?"

"Not great," Shaw said as he rose. With an apologetic grimace, he said to Mary Angela, "Bad history."

"Yeah. I fucking hate them. So, Mary Angela, here's the good news: we're not going to do a single fucking thing about this from here on out."

The relief in her face was transparent, almost glowing.

"And here's the bad news," North said through a hard smile. "We already forwarded your email and the video to the police. Have a great fucking life."

"No," Mary Angela said, "hold on, you can't—"

By then, North and Shaw were already making their way through the press of bodies. When they emerged from the pub, Shaw caught North's arm and kissed him on the cheek.

"That was amazing," Shaw said.

The flush started in North's chest.

"You are amazing," Shaw said.

"You didn't do too bad yourself."

"And the part when you said, 'And here's the bad news.' You sounded so trade. My little gay-boy heart just about exploded."

North rolled his eyes, trying to work his arm free.

Laughing, Shaw pulled him down and peppered him with kisses, and for some reason, North found it hard to mind.

Chapter 29

THEY FOUND KAREN IN her room. A roller bag propped the door open, and from where Shaw stood in the hallway, he could see Karen fumbling with the strap of a garment bag. When North raised his eyebrows, Shaw nodded, and North rapped on the door.

Karen jumped, and a tiny squeak escaped her. Dropping the garment bag, she glanced over at them, automatically retreating a step. Then she seemed to recognize them. She swayed, leaned heavily against the bed, and then shook her head.

"Go away." The words sounded a little mushy. "I'm leaving."

"You might not want to do that," Shaw said. "I think the police are going to want to talk to you."

She shook her head, gave another faltering step, and had to catch herself again. "No. No way. I'm leaving."

"Everybody says they're leaving," North said, "and then they stick around. The whole lot of you can clear the fuck out for all I care."

He grunted when Shaw poked him in the side.

"We know about you and Scotty," Shaw said quietly.

Karen was trying to yank a zipper tight, and she shook her head furiously at the words. She gave another yank. The zipper refused to budge. And then she began to sob.

Shaw looked at North.

"This is your goddamn mess," North said.

Sighing, Shaw headed into the room. He stopped in the bathroom long enough to pluck several tissues from the box, and then he made his way to the sleeping area. He sat on one of the beds; Karen had fallen to her knees, the upper half of her body supported by the mattress, the whole frame shaking with her crying. Up close, Shaw could smell the alcohol on her breath.

"Do you know about pressure points?" Shaw asked her. He took the hand that was closest to him, and he spoke as he used his thumb and forefinger to gently apply pressure. "You've got a lot of them in your hands. This one is for your eye, so maybe it'll help you stop crying. And this one is for shoulder strain, because I don't think this bed was ergonomically designed for crying. And this one is to help you refresh your aura. And this one is to help you relax. Oh, and this one is to help you relax too! North, I forgot there were two."

North's face was strangely unreadable. After a moment, he rolled a shoulder, as though that were some kind of acknowledgment.

"And this one is for your pancreas," Shaw said. "Or gallbladder. Sometimes I mix them up."

Sniffling, Karen raised her head. "That feels nice," she whispered.

"North doesn't like it. He wouldn't even let me try."

"That," North said, his voice surprisingly rough, "is because you came at me with those needles that are a mile long."

"It works better with the needles," Shaw said. He took a tissue and wiped under Karen's eyes. "I'm very sorry for your loss."

She nodded and accepted a clean tissue, cleaning her face as she spoke. "Thank you." A silent sob rippled through her, but she held herself together. "It doesn't seem real. And I'm not…I'm not handling it very well. As you can tell." A burpy laugh escaped her.

"Why don't you sit down," Shaw said, "and tell us about it?"

Karen sat on the bed next to Shaw, and after a moment, she leaned her head on his shoulder. "He was so shy at first. In private, I mean. We were at a workshop, and he got assigned to be my mentor, and as soon as we were behind a closed door, he was a different person. That annoying overconfidence disappeared. He looked nervous. He talked in spurts—like he'd been holding it in for a long time, and all of a sudden it was escaping. We were supposed to workshop a short story for two hours, but instead, we just talked, and by the end, he'd told me all of it: he thought he might be bi, he was deeply unhappy, he didn't know how to stop being this asshole public persona he'd gotten trapped in." Unable to see her face, Shaw could still feel the smile. "I was probably sixty-percent in love with him by the time we went back to the main group. We stayed in touch. We talked on the phone because he was so worried about email and text, about someone finding out. And then I really did fall in love."

"It sounds like you had something very special with him."

She nodded into his shoulder. "He was such a good guy. He didn't know how to get out of the trap he'd made for himself, but we were figuring it out. We were working on it."

"How long were you together?"

"Seventeen months. We met at the workshop, like I told you. Then, at last year's Queer Expectations, we…we moved forward with our relationship. It was the first time we'd seen each other in person since the workshop, and we couldn't keep our hands off each other. We were like teenagers."

"What about Josue?"

"I felt terrible about that. Josue loves him, he really does. And Scotty loved Josue. I mean, not in the way Josue wanted, I think. That was always the problem. They had a connection, but Scotty knew he wasn't just gay, and he needed to explore, grow, learn more about himself."

"Stick his dick in everything that moved," North said, "and make sure he kept sticking his dick in things that worshipped him."

"That's not what Scotty was like," Karen snapped, her too-wide mouth hanging open in outrage. "You don't understand. You have no idea what we experienced—love, true love, with all the passion and all the power, something neither of us could deny. He was trapped in a loveless marriage, and then we found each other, and what we felt was beyond anything either of us had ever experienced."

"I know a little something about loveless marriages. And I know that the one who cheats, he's usually fifty-one percent of the problem. You thought he was hot. You liked that he was into you. Fine. But save the rest of it, all the soulmates bullshit, for a book pitch with JD. Scotty had an affair with you, plain and simple."

Sniffling again, Karen pulled her long, auburn hair over one shoulder. She studied North. Then she said, "I told Scotty that people would react like this. People would never forgive him for being bi."

"The problem isn't that he was bi. The problem is that he was a cheating, manipulative, abusive—"

Shaw closed a hand around North's wrist. North cut off, swallowing, and looked away.

"We're getting off topic," Shaw said. "What happened after last year's Queer Expectations?"

"We were in love." Karen cast a defiant look at North, but the blond man was still fixated on the particleboard dresser. "We knew we had to make arrangements so that Scotty could end his marriage gracefully and keep his career going. He was having a really hard time with his writing; the stress made it impossible for him to create something new. He was even talking about hiring a ghost writer. Buying a manuscript. I wouldn't let him do that; he's a genius, and I didn't want him to sully his reputation. I offered to give him one of my manuscripts instead, and he could do whatever he wanted with it."

"Wouldn't that sully his reputation too?"

"Not at all. It was just raw material; he could do whatever he wanted with it."

"Is that why you told everyone that he was editing one of your books?"

A tiny smile pulled at her mouth. "That was Scotty's idea. He wanted us to be able to see each other without anyone asking questions."

"And he wanted you to write a book for him," North said. His gaze moved back to Karen. His eyes were clear, his face unreadable again. "Right?"

Karen ignored the question. "We concocted that story about him editing my book so that we could visit each other, spend more time together. Then he was worried someone might figure out what we were doing, so we had to pretend to call the whole thing off."

"So you saw each other how many times over the last year?" Shaw asked.

"Half a dozen, I think."

"Did Josue know what was happening?"

"I don't know." She touched her puffy nose. "He…might have. I've thought about that a lot since last night. Someone wanted me dead. Someone wanted to punish me, just like someone wanted to punish Scotty. I heard them fighting."

"Wednesday night," Shaw said. "When you snuck out of your room."

"We were going to…spend some time together. Josue was supposed to be getting drinks with friends. But I got there, and I could hear them screaming at each other through the door. Scotty had already told me about several fights they'd had. Oregon isn't a community property state, and Scotty was determined to hold on to his books and the royalties, no matter what else he had to give up."

"You're talking about their divorce?"

"Right, they live in Portland, and Scotty knew Josue would argue that he had contributed significantly to Scotty's work because Josue is greedy; all he does is spend Scotty's money. Scotty hoped he could walk away with his book rights intact at the very least."

"So you want us to believe, what?" North said. "That Josue killed Scotty rather than let Scotty walk off with all that money?"

She nodded, wiping gingerly at her swollen nose with a tissue.

"And what did you do after you heard them fighting?" Shaw said.

"I went back to my room."

"You didn't go downstairs?"

She was still for a moment, the tissues still pressed under her nose. Then she said, "I don't know what you mean."

"Well, I'm wondering if you realized Scotty wasn't ever going to leave Josue, and maybe you decided to punish him."

This time, she was quicker. "Get out of my room."

"Do you have any Adderall?" North said. "Other amphetamines? What am I going to find if I poke around in your bathroom?"

"I want you to get out of my room. Leave. Right now. Or I'm calling security."

"Sure," North said, "right after I have a peek in your bathroom."

"Get out," Karen screamed, stumbling to the phone on the desk. "Get out, get out, get out!"

"We all need to—" Shaw began.

A knock interrupted him. The roller bag still held the door open, and in the doorway stood Jadon and Cerise.

"Detectives," Karen said, "thank God, I want these men—"

"Leave this hotel right now," Jadon said to Shaw, "or I'm placing you and North under arrest for obstruction. Do you understand?"

"Josue—"

"Josue is sitting in an interview room right now," Jadon said. He was clearly trying to control himself, but the volume had slipped up in his voice. "I won't tell you again."

"Obstruction," North said. "Obstruction, obstruction, obstruction. Oh, wait. You mean, that charge that's practically impossible to prove?"

"Let's go," Shaw said.

"The one that's a misdemeanor."

"North, enough."

Ugly red patches colored North's face, but he followed Shaw from the room. When they passed Jadon, Shaw waited for the collision, but Jadon turned sideways to clear a path.

On the elevator ride down, North shouted and punched the elevator wall. The steel panel flexed and buckled, and then he swore and shook out his hand.

"We were so goddamn close. Fucking Jadon fucking Reck."

"I want you to know how proud I am of you," Shaw said. "Particularly that last part, when you summoned the emotional maturity of a toddler and managed not to smack Jadon with your shoulder."

After a moment, the flush climbing higher in his fair skin, North said, "I miscalculated. I thought he was going to get in my way again at the last moment, and then I realized too late that he was going to act like a fucking adult."

Shaw considered this. "Is it weird that I'm actually relieved? I thought maybe something was wrong with you."

"What the fuck are we supposed to do? We need to talk to Josue, but they'll have him in that interview room all night. They've got Karen. I bet they have Brendon too. The little love triangle finally collapsed, and I'd bet money one of them killed Scotty, but we can't get at them. Christ, I'm so foggy I can't think. Maybe I should get an Adderall scrip."

"Quadrangle," Shaw said.

"Huh?"

"Not triangle."

North grunted. "Well?"

"First, no Adderall scrip. Second, what are we supposed to do? I think we need to get you mildly drunk." Shaw prepared a list of reasons, including North's nonstop work over the last several months.

To Shaw's surprise, though, North didn't object. He dry-washed his face, nodded, and said, "That sounds fucking amazing."

Chapter 30

THEY WENT TO RIVETS, a marginally gay bar in Lafayette Square. It sprawled across the main floor of what had originally been several distinct storefronts. The result was a maze of rooms and narrow hallways and two separate bars: one near the front entrance, and the other in a back room that had probably once been designed for storage. The décor was accent walls of exposed brick, plaster painted in muted shades, hot-water radiators, and dark-stained wood. And, of course, rivets. Tarnished rivets glinted in the upholstery, along the edge of the bar, in decorative patterns on the walls.

North and Shaw chose the bar at the back, where the weak light of a winter afternoon didn't reach. The electric lighting was buttery and sparse, and Shaw drank four Cokes before North noticed and cut him off. After that, he traced his design for rocket shoes (why had nobody thought of those before—nobody except Wile E. Coyote, that was?) on the bar, his fingers leaving streaks on the epoxy-resin surface. North nursed two beers and looked like he might fall asleep sitting upright.

"Let's go back to your place," Shaw said. "We'll give Pari a break from puppy-sitting, and you can get comfy, and we'll call it an early night. We'll pick up tomorrow."

The words seemed to startle North. He blinked owlishly at his phone, swore, and waved at the bartender to settle up. As he counted out cash, he said, "Tony Gillman is going to be off work any minute. I want to beat him to his condo."

"Tony can wait a night."

"Great. I'll call the hospital and tell them to expect another boy beaten within an inch of his life."

Shaw hid his hands under his arms.

"Sorry," North said, although his tone was flat. "I'm tired."

"You're tired because you've been working nonstop and because you don't trust anyone else to do anything."

"Can we not do this right now?"

Shaw didn't answer, which was its own kind of answer.

They drove to Clayton and found a spot across from the Sussex Downs building on the rapidly emptying street. For the next hour, traffic in and out of the condo building's parking garage was steady, but there was no sign of the yellow Camaro. They traded off after that; Shaw suggested that North rest, but instead, North found a golf pencil and the back of a QuikTrip receipt and started scribbling something, muttering numbers under his breath. When it was North's turn to watch, Shaw used the ebook app on his phone to skim new books that he'd picked up.

Some of them were pretty good—Mary Angela had released her next *My Alpha Billionaire,* which was set in Dubai and featured what Shaw was fairly sure was an illegal use of a popsicle. He marked that one as a definite 'must read.' Clarence had released a standalone called *Street Wars* that, like much of his recent work, seemed passable without being inspired: a slapped-together cover, a plethora of editing errors, and an abundance of exposition. The main character had just explained to the reader for the third time why he was involved in a prank war with his gruff, sexy neighbor—the first round of battle had involved a laxative in a post-workout shake (one side) and flaming dog poop (the other side). And Karen had released *The Prisoner's Ex,* which was about an insane ex-wife, her prison-made-me-gay former husband, and the nerdy but sexy criminal-law tyro who had proved the husband had been wrongfully accused (framed by his crazy ex, Shaw guessed). The ex-wife was obsessive and murderous, but more importantly, she seemed to share a couple of interesting traits with Josue: both were Dominican, and both were black.

"What are you reading?" North asked, voice gravelly from disuse.

The city had fallen into night. The lamps up and down the street hung cones of sickly, yellow-orange light across the pavement. Weeks-old snow, packed and melted and refrozen, was black with trapped dirt and pollutants. Two couples were heading into the tavern up the street. A date night, Shaw guessed. What normal couples did.

"Just some new books."

North shifted. His hand, heavy and warm, came to rest on Shaw's leg. "So, I was a dick and now you're going to stonewall me?"

"No." Shaw looked over his phone and met North's gaze long enough to say, "You were a dick, so I'm cold-shouldering you."

North looked like he tried to fight it, but he gave in and smiled.

"They're books from the authors at the con."

"I thought you bought a bunch in paperback."

"Yeah. Those are for my bookshelves. These are to read."

North's smile got bigger. "Run that past me again."

"No. You heard me fine; you just want to tease me. Listen to this one, though." He told him about Karen's book and the Josue-like character.

"So in that scenario, is Karen the wrongfully accused convict who learned to love dick? Or is she the idealistic Harvard law graduate who's charmingly befuddled by real-world situations?"

"I didn't tell you he often got confused—North!"

"Easy guess."

"I don't know what the parallels are supposed to be, but it's weird, right?"

"Write what you know. Isn't that the advice?"

"Speaking of which," Shaw said, sliding down in the seat. "If I'm ever going to be a multi-billionaire author like JK Rowling, I'm going to need to write some very convincing apology and make-up sex scenes. You know. After the sexy reference librarian gets in a fight with the sexy, but often very rude and inconsiderate, jack-of-all-trades handyman who keeps the library running."

North's eyebrows rose. "This jack-of-all-trades character sounds dreamy."

"He's not. He gets snappy when he doesn't get enough sleep, and he hooked up the cable box wrong so that all they get is scrambled Korean porn."

"It was a Korean cooking show, but I'm glad to know where your imagination goes first." North's hand slid higher. "I bet even though this jack-of-all-trades guy gets a little snappy, he feels sorry about it later, and then he throws a killer fuck to make up for it."

Shaw pushed North's hand off his leg and raised his phone again. "Maybe. Or maybe he's got ED. I haven't written that part yet."

When Shaw thought it was safe, he sneaked a look; North was still trying to wipe the grin away.

The yellow Camaro appeared fifteen minutes later, and as soon as it turned into the garage, they were out of the GTO. Shaw sprinted toward the garage ramp, slipped around the barrier, and headed up into the frozen cement block and the darkness reeking of piss and motor oil. By the time he got to the fourth floor, the blood was pounding in his ears.

The Camaro was dark and empty.

A text came from North: *???*

Nothing, Shaw replied.

Stay put.

Chafing his arms, Shaw paced near the access door to the condo building. He was freezing even inside the duffel coat. A boat of a Lincoln, probably thirty years old and floating like a cloud, rolled past him and climbed another level. The driver had to be near eighty, shrunken so that the top of his head barely cleared the steering wheel. In that car, Shaw guessed, he probably could have crashed into a school bus without noticing. An engine roared to life somewhere below Shaw. He shivered and walked faster.

The old man in the Lincoln had gotten in his head. Would Shaw still be driving when he was eighty? Or would he be taking one of those Call-a-Ride services? Would he and North be living in a place like this—nice, safe, minimal upkeep? Or would he and North still have their respective homes in Benton

Park and the Southampton area? Even if North wasn't driving, Shaw couldn't imagine him giving up the GTO. He'd probably park it in their assigned stall and let it sit there, even though the smart thing in a dense area like Clayton, where the need for off-street parking was high, would be to rent out the spot to someone who could use it—

The access door to the condo building opened, and North emerged. He had changed clothes; he still wore the Redwings and the worn jeans, but he'd pulled on an orange Spire Energy shirt, and over that he wore a hi-vis vest. The reflective tape shimmered under the fluorescents.

"Please tell me you always keep a hard hat in your trunk," Shaw said.

"It's part of the disguise," North said, glaring as he whipped it off. His thatch of blond hair was mussed worse than usual underneath.

"Sexy gas man? That doesn't exactly roll off the tongue."

"It's not sexy anything. What happened?"

"It's definitely sexy. That's always your angle: sexy dogwalker, sexy meter maid—"

"That's a sexist term. I'm really disappointed in you."

"—sexy carwash jockey—"

"Carwash jockey?"

"—sexy bootblack—"

"We're not in Victorian fucking London, Shaw."

"—sexy upscale denim salesperson. That kind of thing. Sexy everything."

"Not this. I'm just a drone from the utility company. Now, what did you—"

"What size is that shirt?"

North colored. It might have been the cold, but Shaw knew it wasn't. "We need to focus, Shaw."

"I'm very focused. That shirt might be a medium, but judging by your nipples, I'd say it's a small. And you normally wear a large. Hence, sexy gas man."

"This is the size I always wear."

Shaw moved forward. "Great. Let me see the tag."

North retreated a step and pointed. "Take one more fucking step."

Grinning, Shaw raised both hands in surrender.

"I told the neighbors I needed to get into Gillman's apartment for a routine check, and they both said he doesn't come home until late. Often past midnight. I asked if he didn't stop in after work some days, and they both looked at me like I was crazy. Whatever he's doing, he's not going inside his condo."

"Oh, that? I figured that out."

North's hands tightened slowly into fists. "What?"

"Yeah, I figured that out while I was waiting for you. It's pretty obvious, actually."

With what sounded like a great deal of effort at controlling his voice, North asked, "Do you want to explain it?"

"He rents a second stall from someone else in the building, and he's got another car there. He parks, runs downstairs, probably puts on a basic disguise, and leaves immediately. He's probably out of the garage by the time anyone's starting to look for him."

"Mother. Fucker."

"North, I know now is a difficult time for you, but I've been meaning to talk to you about your nipples."

North stalked away.

"Frostbite is real, North!"

Chapter 31

THEY WENT BACK TO North's Southampton house, where Pari was eager to give them an agonizingly detailed accounting of the puppy's misbehaving.

"And he growled at me," she said. "And he barked at a bird that landed on the windowsill. And he's a menace to society. I don't know why you put up with him. And I'm not doing this again unless you pay me double. Oh. And hazard pay."

"The threats lose some of their force," North said, "when you keep interrupting yourself to cover him in kisses."

By the time Pari left, the puppy had wiggled into his crate. To escape more kisses from Pari, Shaw guessed. When the door finally shut behind Pari, North stood one-legged in the hall, unlacing the Redwings. Shaw moved to stand in his line of sight.

As the second boot hit the floor, North glanced up. "Mmm," he said. He pressed a hand against Shaw's erection, and a tiny smile lit up his face as Shaw rolled his hips. "Yeah?"

"God," Shaw nodded, "all day. I've wanted this all day."

"You've wanted it all week."

Shaw nodded faster.

North made a considering noise as he guided Shaw toward the closest wall, hand applying just enough pressure to chafe sparks of pleasure up into Shaw's belly. When Shaw hit the wall, North slid his hand to that spot just above Shaw's dick, rubbing hard circles into the sensitive flesh there, and Shaw let out a thirsty little pant.

North kissed him and whispered, "All week."

The blush was hot in Shaw's face, but he said, "Longer."

"Longer?" North drawled. "Sounds like I've been slacking."

"No—ah!" Shaw shuddered as North forced the harem pants and his briefs down to mid-thigh. The cotton dragged against sensitive skin, and then cold air brushed him, and Shaw shuddered again. "You're just—you're just busy."

"I am."

"You're a busy guy," Shaw said. Then North's hand closed around his dick, and he threw his head back, where it thunked against the wall. "Jesus Christ!"

"Shush," North said with a laugh. "You're going to wake up Mr. Winns."

"Oh fuck," Shaw whispered. North's callused hand tightened, dragged, twisted. Shaw tried to squirm—back, forward, he wasn't sure—and North's other hand caught Shaw's sweater and hauled him back into place. "Oh, North, no, I'm so close—I don't want to—not yet—"

"You're not quite there yet," North said; underneath the perpetual smolder of his voice lay a note of what might have been amusement, but his pupils were huge, and his breathing had accelerated. "Are you?"

Shaw whined.

"Are you?" North insisted.

"North."

"That's what I thought," North whispered and then kissed a line down Shaw's neck, his hand still moving. Sometimes North could be shockingly gentle. Sometimes—sometimes not. Tonight, he was rough, and the firm, callused grip and the hard, tight, unrelenting movements began to blur with the possessive kisses, the nips, North's mouth restless on Shaw's neck and jaw and lips.

"Oh shit," Shaw chanted, "oh shit, oh shit, oh shit."

North's hand sprang open; the other hand, the one gripping the sweater, gave Shaw a shake. "Uh uh. Not yet."

Squeezing his eyes shut, Shaw managed. Barely. He gulped air.

The next kiss, on his jaw, was a question, and Shaw nodded with his eyes still shut.

"Off," North said, tugging on the sweater and turning Shaw out of it. He dragged the harem pants off next, then the briefs. Shaw hopped to peel off the ragg-wool socks. North ditched his own clothes. As soon as Shaw had both feet on the ground again, North caught his balls and tugged him into another kiss. "Bed. Now." Then he gave a squeeze that made Shaw grunt, and he slapped him on the ass as Shaw turned for North's bedroom.

As Shaw's bare feet slapped the boards, a phone buzzed behind him.

"At this fucking hour," North said.

Shaw stopped and looked back. "Leave it."

"What if someone's in the hospital again?"

"Honestly, North? At this point, I need fifteen minutes with your dick, and then I can solve world hunger or invent faster-than-light travel or solve this damn case. But dick first. It has to be in that order."

A spectral smile crossed North's face as he retrieved his phone and checked it. It was either a text or an email because he stared at the screen. For a moment, North was lost in whatever he was reading: leaning against the wall, one arm curled so he could push at the mess of short blond hair, the hard lines of his chest and abdomen on display. Then his face changed: practical, focused, another problem to solve.

"Damn it. I've got to do this right now." He looked up at Shaw, made a face, and said, "Sorry."

"Did my house burn down?"

"What? No."

"Did a foreign power launch a nuclear missile?"

North shook his head; he was staring at the phone again, tapping the screen.

"Did something happen to your dad or my parents, God forbid?"

"Um, no. Wait. What?"

"North, if it wasn't any of those things, you can put your phone down and fuck me and then take care of whatever memo or invoice or blind carbon copy you forgot to send."

North's head came up, and for a moment, irritation stormed across his features. Then, with what looked like effort, he smoothed out his features. "It's an Energizer exec. He's willing to pay triple our rates for us to do some short-term corporate work. Six months, but he says it could be renewed."

"That does not constitute an emergency."

"He wants a whole sales kit, whatever the fuck that is, tomorrow morning. He says they've got to make a decision this weekend and get started. Jesus Christ, what the hell is a sales kit? A pamphlet? A slideshow?"

"We've got plenty of work. We've got more work than we can handle. We've got all the Aldrich stuff, plus the one-off jobs, plus—"

"I'm going to have to put the whole thing together from scratch," North was saying to himself as he fished his underwear out of the jeans puddled on the floor. "And my good computer is at your office. Do I drive over? Fuck it."

"North—"

In boxer briefs, North jogged to Shaw, kissed him on the cheek, and said, "Sorry, baby. This is going to take me all night."

"North—"

"You get some sleep; I'll be quiet, I promise."

And then he was gone, moving toward the kitchen, the smell of American Crew hair gel lingering in his wake.

Shaw closed his eyes. Opened them. He showered, considered jerking off, and instead leaned his forehead against the tile. The cool, sharp edges were a lifeline. He dried off, wrapped himself in a towel, and paused in the hallway. Still in his underwear, North hunched over the kitchen table, pecking away at a laptop. Shaw turned away and went to the bedroom.

In the dark, stretched out on sheets that smelled like North's soap and North's hair, Shaw tried to sleep. Then he sat up, groped for his phone, and read. He tried to get back into Clarence's prank-war book. He tried one of

Yasmin's slave-prince books. He tried another of Karen's, this one about a vegan baker and an organic rancher. None of them could hold his attention. Finally, he found himself starting the next book in one of Serenity's popular series.

Fourth and Down: Alpha Jock Learns to Score was a quasi-BDSM power fantasy. The protagonist Lu Tomlinson, a college running back, had spent the last three books learning how much he loved gay sex thanks to a domineering teammate. Now, in book four, Lu's buddy-slash-dom had graduated, and Lu was learning to run the show.

Bradford is slender but muscular, like those Greek statues we had to memorize in Civ 1, and kneeling on the tile in front of me, he's more beautiful than anything I've ever seen. The locker room is silent now, but we both know that could change at any moment; it adds a thrill to the moment, not that my dick, burping pre, needs any more incentive. As though thinking the same thing, Bradford leans forward, hands obediently on his thighs the way I taught him. Boys like Bradford—rich, spoiled, pampered, who have spent their lives thinking they have to run the show—boys like that are the ones who need an alpha jock like me the most. They're so grateful for somebody else to take charge. They're so grateful for somebody to tell them what to do. What they need, more than anything else, is for someone to put them in their place.

Grabbing a handful of those pretty blond curls, I yank Bradford's head to the side. "Somebody touched himself, didn't he?"

Bradford's dick gives a guilty twitch.

"How many times?"

"Four," he mumbles toward the tile.

"I'm sorry, what?"

"Four times, sir."

"And you're how old?"

"Eighteen, sir."

"And who does that dick belong to?"

A blush climbs his tan cheeks. "You, sir." It's barely a whisper.

"Should an eighteen-year-old be able to keep his hands off a dick that doesn't belong to him?"

Bradford is starting to cry. I long to reach forward and thumb away the tear, let him lick it from my thumb, suckle there like the boy he wants so desperately to be. But Bradford needs something more right now. Men who have always had to be strong and perfect, men like Bradford, don't know how to ask for what they really need. Someone else has to know what's best for them. Someone else has to give it to them.

"Four times eighteen is how many?"

"Seventy-two, sir."

"Then it's seventy-two licks. Get my belt and lean over the bench."

Bradford tries to rise, and I yank his curls again. "Did I tell you to stand?"

Shaking his head as the tears come faster, Bradford begins to crawl.

Shaw touched himself. He was wet. The idea came in a flash, and rather than considering it more carefully, he rolled off the bed. After collecting what he needed, he left the bedroom and padded into the kitchen.

North must have heard him; he didn't look up, but he said, "I've got some of that goat's milk you like if you want to warm it up."

Grabbing North by the back of the neck, Shaw forced his head down to the table. For a moment, North resisted, and then something changed and he yielded. His breathing sounded quicker. His cheek was flattened against the tabletop.

"Well," he said, trying for the dry detachment he so often wore. "This is definitely—"

Shaw's fingers tightened around North's throat, not choking him, but tight enough that the pressure must have been uncomfortable. North's words cut off. Into the silence, Shaw said, "You're not going to talk unless I ask you a direct question. Do you understand?"

North tried to nod.

"That was a direct question. Do you understand?"

"Yes."

Shaw set down the lube he'd brought from the bedroom. He closed the laptop and pushed it to the other end of the table. Then, his hand still tight around North's throat, he tugged. North followed him until the blond man's torso rested completely on the table. Shaw released him, petted him, and smiled at the slightly frantic edge to North's rapid breaths. When Shaw slid a finger under the waistband of North's boxer briefs, North reached back to help strip them off.

Shaw twisted the elastic and yanked. "Did I tell you to move?"

"Oh fuck," North groaned.

Shaw yanked again, harder. "That wasn't an answer."

"N-no."

"Then don't. Fucking. Move."

For thirty seconds, Shaw was quiet, and it seemed to take everything in North's power not to shift on the table. Then Shaw pulled his underwear down, manipulating North's legs to slide the clothing free. North was very, very white. But his ass was extra white. The term *full moon* came to mind. Shaw clutched a cheek in each hand and squeezed, and North made a guttural noise. He slid one hand between North's legs; a thread of pre swung from the tip of North's dick, and Shaw let it coat his knuckles before running the back of his hand down North's shaft. Once.

North groaned and tried to rut into Shaw's hand, and Shaw caught his hip one-handed, stilling him. When he released North, livid spots lingered on the pale skin, and Shaw guessed he might have left bruises. "What the fuck don't you understand about don't move?"

North's breath was reedy. He made a noise that Shaw didn't even know how to describe.

Flipping the cap on the lube, Shaw applied a generous amount to his hand and to North's ass. Then he worked slowly: teasing, then just the tip of one finger, then breaching North. He knew he'd found what he wanted when North's head whipped up from the table and came back down hard enough that the whole table shook. One of North's legs began to tremble.

With his free hand, Shaw petted the trembling leg and stroked that spot again.

The muffled noise might have been a word, but Shaw let it slide. He took his time, spacing out the touches, not wanting to desensitize North too early. He added a second finger and spent his time stretching North. North gasped. Once, he gurgled and sounded like he might have choked on his own spit. When Shaw risked a glance, he saw North white-knuckling the table, the muscles in his arms corded as he fought to keep himself from reacting.

Two fingers, when he pressed down hard on North's prostate, made North scream, "Oh my fucking God."

Shaw withdrew the two fingers. "What did I say about talking?"

North panted.

"That was a question," Shaw said.

"You said—" North seemed to have trouble finding words. "You said—"

"I said don't talk unless I ask you a direct question. Now, you said four words, and you're twenty-six, so that would be a hundred and four licks. I'm going to be very nice and not make you count them. This time."

He delivered the first blow harder than he intended; his palm caught fire, and the shock ran all the way to his elbow.

North didn't make a noise. It was so much worse. He jerked off the table, and the wooden legs skittered over the floor. North stumbled sideways, rounding the table, and grabbed a chair. His eyes were huge. His face bloodless. He stumbled again like his legs might not hold him up, but he kept hold of the chair, interposing it between him and Shaw.

"What the fuck?" he shouted.

"Oh my God, North, I'm so sorry, I—"

"What the fuck?" North screamed.

And then Shaw remembered: Tucker, and the years that North had shown up with bruises, black eyes, split lips, weals broken open on his arms and legs.

"No, I didn't—it was just supposed to be—North, I didn't mean—" Shaw took a step.

North skittered back. The only noises were his rapid breathing and the chair's legs clicking against the floorboards.

"Oh my God," Shaw said, hands tented over his mouth. "Oh my God."

For another moment, North kept his body turned. Shaw understood why: to minimize his outline, to keep as much of himself as possible out of reach. Then, shaking himself like a dog, he nodded. His voice was a bad copy of North McKinney when he said, "Ok. Well, I guess we figured out I don't like spanking."

Shaw started to cry. He turned away from North, away from the look of pain and betrayal etched into his features that, no matter how hard North was trying, he couldn't completely disguise. Shaw had the brilliant plan to run, but he couldn't seem to get his feet to work. He couldn't seem to do anything except stand there, hiding his face in his hands, and sob.

"All right," North said, pulling him against his chest. That only made Shaw cry harder: huge, racking sobs that he was vaguely aware were resulting in a lot of snot and tears in North's chest hair. "Come on, it's ok. You just—you know, you startled me. I know you were just trying something."

But Shaw could feel North's heartbeat going a mile a minute.

"I didn't think—" Frantic gulps for air interrupted Shaw's attempts to explain. "I forgot—Tucker—I never wanted to—it was supposed to be fun!" The last was a wail.

North just shushed him, stroking his hair and pressing Shaw's face to his shoulder. When the worst of the storm had passed, North turned Shaw toward the bedroom, steering him by the shoulders. He sat Shaw on the bed, left, and returned with a warm washcloth. After cleaning both of them up, he tossed it in the corner, bore Shaw down onto the bed with the weight of his body, and pulled the blankets up.

"North, I never, ever, ever—" Shaw tried before tears rolled over him again.

With more of those shushing noises, North nuzzled into Shaw's neck. His fingers combed the frizzy poof of Shaw's hair until Shaw had settled down again. They were quiet together for what felt to Shaw like a long time. Above them, in Mr. Winns's unit, the drone of TV voices buzzed up and down.

Then, sounding marginally more like the real North McKinney, he said, "Is your hair ever going to be long again? I miss it being long."

Shaw sniffled. "There's a horse-placenta balm that will make it grow faster."

"No," North said, turning so that Shaw could finally see his face: the slight redness around his eyes, the fresh hardness in his mouth. But he smiled. "It won't."

"Actually, it's scientifically—"

"No." North shook his head. "It's not."

Above them, TV laughter faded into the *Happy Days* theme song. Shaw's eyes burned again. "North, I—"

"Come on, Shaw. I know. I mean, obviously in the moment, I freaked the fuck right out. But I know you're not Tucker, and I know you weren't trying to hurt me. Although, for the record, you set my ass on fire. Next time we've got somebody who won't talk, I'm going to let you put them over your knee and go to town." He scrubbed at his eyes one-handed. "So apparently I've got some stuff that, you know, I haven't dealt with yet."

"You haven't even processed it yet."

North groaned, head falling so he could bury his face in Shaw's neck again.

"Let alone resolved the psychic trauma."

"Be quiet," North ordered, his breath hot and tickling Shaw's neck. "Go back to crying."

"And you definitely need closure."

"I need closure on this conversation."

Shaw squirmed, trying to move lower, but North hugged him tighter, and it turned into an impromptu wrestling match. Shaw ended up on top, flushed, unable to tamp down the smile that had flared up. He pinned North against the mattress, hands around North's wrists. North's eyes were hooded. An asymmetrical smirk pulled one corner of his mouth.

"You got me," he said very quietly. "Now what are you going to do with me?"

"Love you," Shaw said. "Love you, and love you, and love you. And make you wear cloaks."

North's laughter didn't reach his mouth; it was a scintilla at the back of his hooded eyes. "Can we start tomorrow? I think we both need sleep."

Shaw understood the real question, and he nodded. Then he kissed North, releasing his wrists, and slid his hands to cup North's face.

"I'm sorry—"

North flipped him in one easy movement, and Shaw landed flat on his back, the mattress rocking under him.

"No way," North said, fumbling for the lamp. "No more apologies. If I have to listen to apologies for the rest of my life and wear a cloak, I'll just check the Amtrak schedule and go stand in front of a train." The light went out, and he lay down again next to Shaw, pulling Shaw against him.

Sleep, though, was far off for both of them. Shaw, with his back against North's chest, could feel North's heart still racing a mile a minute.

Chapter 32

THE NEXT MORNING, things were closer to normal, and North was grateful for that. The faster he could bury what had happened the night before, the more dirt he could pile on top of it, the better. Sleep, even if it was only a few hours, had been a good start. He was less grateful for the series of text messages from Ronnie that he'd woken to on his phone—he was trying hard to bury those too.

"We need to talk to Josue," North said as they got into the GTO. The puppy was zipped up inside his coat, his little lion face poking out. "Hear his side of things. I'm having a hard time swallowing this whole thing."

"I've heard that before," Shaw murmured.

"I'm sorry, what was that?"

"Hm?" Shaw's whole face was cherubic innocence.

"Do you have a complaint? Do you need a comment card?"

"I don't have any idea what you're talking about."

North grunted and started the car.

"Completely off topic," Shaw said, "but a lot of porn stars practice with bananas."

North's eyes narrowed. "All right. Challenge accepted. I'm going to make you eat your words."

"At least one of us will be eating something."

"Keep it up," North said as he shifted into drive. "Keep it right the fuck up."

Shaw just smiled innocently, checking his hair in the mirror. He had a real Doc Brown vibe going, and he'd changed into spare clothes he kept at North's: a rainbow cardigan over a fuchsia turtleneck with gold pinstripe trousers. The quilted boots were making a second appearance.

"You're going to give children seizures if you move too fast," North said.

"I like how I look."

"That has literally never been the problem."

"No, no, no. Remember when I had body dysmorphia and an eating disorder?"

"I can't do this. Not with a dog trying to disembowel me," North petted the puppy, who was scrabbling against him inside the coat, and got a lick in return, "and not before coffee."

"I just think you're forgetting—"

"You weighed a hundred and thirty pounds at the time, you ate a whole sleeve of Oreos, and you made yourself sick because you'd been off processed sugar for six weeks. You did not have an eating disorder—"

"I threw up! I was bulimic!"

"—and you did not have body dysmorphia."

"I didn't like how I looked!"

"That's because you spent the morning tattooing your pits with a Magic Marker, and all you were wearing when you puked was a jock that said, *You're going to feel a slight sting next.*"

"I wasn't tattooing my pits. I was trying to map chakra points to open my third eye, and—"

"Everybody saw your third eye when you were kneeling at a toilet, puking in nothing but a jock strap."

"North!"

The tone of scandalized horror was too much; North had to look out the side window because he couldn't hide the smile.

They dropped the puppy at the Borealis office, where Pari screamed with excitement and immediately started crumbling a McDonald's sausage patty and hand-feeding the puppy. Then they drove to the Royal Excalibur. St. Louis on a Saturday morning was even emptier than usual. The day was overcast, and in the washed-out light, the downtown could have been taken from a photograph of a war zone: broken cement, sagging chain-link fencing, a flyer for IMO'S – THE SQUARE BEYOND COMPARE pasted against the tinted plexiglass of a bus stop shelter. They parked in the hotel's garage and hurried inside.

In the lobby, what should have been the con's busiest day was having a lackluster start. People stood in small groups, talking in low voices. No one smiled. No one laughed. Yasmin's friend—North couldn't remember her name—looked defeated: dark bags under her eyes, hair unwashed and flattened on one side, face vacant. Nobody else in the lobby looked much better. One woman stirred her coffee with vicious determination. A pair of young guys, shirtless and wearing pasties with red tassels, looked too broken-hearted even to shake their tits.

"If your eyes fall out of your head from ogling those two," North said, "you're going to find out what a real spanking feels like."

Shaw made an outraged noise, and he managed to close his jaw, but he didn't look away.

From the hotel's main hallway, Jadon and Cerise emerged, bracketing Josue and Brendon. North let out a groan.

"It's ok," Shaw said. "He's probably just got a few follow-up questions, and then we can—"

Jadon pointed in North and Shaw's direction, presumably toward the parking garage, and Josue gave a tired nod.

"So much for that idea," North said. "Fuck. He'll have those two tied up all day."

"Why don't we ask Jadon really nicely—"

North was already tuning out the question, glancing around the lobby, trying to figure out their next move. Leslie, looking even more birdlike than usual in a baggy sweatshirt that hung off her thin frame, moved into the lobby. She was staring at her phone, obviously transfixed—albeit, probably not in the way she wanted—by more porn. Someone ran up behind her, and for a moment, North was sure that it was a friend trying to catch up.

He was looking right at Leslie when the figure in the gimp mask drove a knife into her side.

Leslie's head whipped around in almost comic surprise, and she staggered to the left. Then she started to fall.

North sprinted toward the gimp.

A woman screamed.

Jadon shouted, "Stop! Police!"

"Shaw!" North shouted without looking back.

"I've got them," Shaw called after him.

The gimp was already running back down the hallway. It was the main thoroughfare, connecting the lobby with the Camelot Public House, the Round Table, and the Kayak's Coffee. Even with the convention attendance substantially reduced, the hall was beginning to fill with people, and North had to twist and dart. The Redwings pounded the red carpet. The gimp had a lead of thirty yards, but North, even in boots, was faster.

North's brain tried to catch up with his physical reactions. Someone had tried to kill Leslie. Again. Someone wanted her dead. It wasn't a spree killing. It had to be motivated by fear—fear that Leslie knew something, fear that Leslie could reveal the killer. The gimp's zippered mask hid their features, and a bulky, shapeless coat disguised their body. They were short for a man, average height for a woman, and that meant they could have been just about anybody at this con.

Thirty yards closed to twenty-five. Twenty-five closed to twenty.

Ahead, a woman in Cleopatra getup—kohl, a golden snake armband, a jade pectoral—was being carried palanquin-style in a sex sling. The bearers were extremely well-muscled, extremely hot guys; North registered them long enough to worry that Shaw might have an aneurysm if he saw them. Worse, he might try to arrange his own sex-sling palanquin for his birthday or his grandparents' anniversary or a goddaughter's christening.

"Make way," the woman was screeching. "Make way for the Queen of the Hags."

North darted, trying to avoid the sex sling, but the woman shouted something, and the bearers turned sharply, so that they blocked most of the hallway. North cut hard to the right, caromed off the wall, and barely recovered his balance. He kept running.

Twenty yards had opened to thirty again.

"Stop!" Jadon shouted farther down the hall. "Police!"

More screams rang out.

North tried to hit the gas, but weeks of little sleep and pushing himself had sapped his reserves. His chest burned. A stitch pulled in his side. He was vaguely aware that he was gasping for air, and a tiny part of his brain swore he'd trash the American Spirits stashed in the GTO's glovebox as soon as this was over.

Then he forgot about everything except the tower of diapers that had moved into his path. It was clearly some sort of take on the diaper cakes that, for one unending week, Shaw had been obsessed with on Pinterest. Behind the mound of diapers, a larger-than-life poster showed, on one side, a very attractive young man dressed in a suit and glasses. An incomplete speech bubble said, *Daddy*.... On the other side of the poster, the same young man was now naked except for an adult diaper, and he had a slightly shamefaced look as he tugged on the waistband. The speech bubble finished here: ...*change me!* Four women in dresses that looked like they'd come from the Disney princess line were carrying the diaper cake and poster, oblivious to North.

"Out of my fucking way," North tried to shout, but he was out of breath, and he barely managed a croak. He clipped the side of the diaper tower. Someone squealed. Behind him, he heard the patter of diapers hitting the ground.

"Police," Jadon was shouting. He sounded closer. "Police, what the fuck—move it! Police!"

North made a mistake: he looked back, unable to resist the prospect of Jadon weaving his way through a flood of adult diapers. When he glanced forward again, wearing a smirk inside, he saw the erotic cake. Two young guys, obviously hotel staff, stood frozen in the middle of the hall. Right in North's path. The cake had been shaped and decorated to look like a man's ass, hands pulling apart the cheeks to expose his hole. North had one suspended moment to question what the fuck he had gotten himself into. Then he hit the cake.

The force of his momentum ripped the tray from the men's hands. The cake hit the floor first. North landed on top of the cake, face buried in it. Swearing, he stumbled upright, wiping frosting and trying to blink his eyes clear.

"Fuck, fuck, fuck!" he screamed.

The gimp was gone.

Chapter 33

"HE KEPT TRYING to sneak away," Shaw was explaining, pointing to Brendon, who was massaging his knee. North guessed that was because Shaw had kicked him. "Josue, on the other hand, was a model citizen."

Josue sat with his head in his hands; he didn't even seem to have heard Shaw.

"Is that a—" Shaw blushed. "Do you have a dude's frosted hole on your face?"

North glared, scraping more frosting from his face.

"That's probably not what you wanted to hear right now," Shaw said.

"Not really."

"I should have said, 'Is that a gentleman's iced anus?'"

North pushed Shaw out of his way, leaving a handprint of frosting on the fuchsia turtleneck, and smiled grimly at Shaw's squawking. He crossed to stand in front of Josue.

"Let's talk."

Josue looked up; he was obviously tranqued on whatever cocktail of legal and illegal stuff he'd been able to get his hands on. Glassy-eyed, he mumbled, "Cops want me to go to—"

"The cops are busy right now. They've got a stabbing victim who might not make it." Heated by North's skin, some of the icing was beginning to liquefy, running down into his eye. North flicked it away. "And if you'd asked me fifteen minutes ago, you and your fuck buddy," he waved at Brendon, "would have been at the top of my list of suspects. So get your ass up, and let's have a chat."

"And a shower," Shaw whispered helpfully. Whatever he saw on North's face made him say, "It's the presidential suite. They're going to have a killer shower."

The sugary mess was starting to itch, and North realized Shaw might have a point. While Shaw conducted Brendon and Josue toward the elevator, North jogged back to the GTO and got a clean tee from the trunk. They went up to Josue's suite, and Josue waved North toward the bedroom and the shower.

North threw Shaw a questioning glance. When Shaw rolled his eyes and nodded, North passed through the double doors into the bedroom. Clothes covered the floor. Suitcases lay on their sides. The bedding was a tangled mess. The suite's décor might have been presidential—the damask rose carpet, the expensive wallpaper, the brass fixtures and the chintz sofas and the Pre-Raphaelite knockoffs. But Josue was living like Shaw freshman year. Or, North thought more carefully, like a man sinking into a bottomless grief.

The bathroom continued the slightly outdated but expensive motif: marble, brass, damask roses printed on the towels. North showered with some sort of gel that smelled like sweetened ginger, dried himself, and dressed in his jeans and the clean tee. The Carhartt coat and his other shirt would need laundering, but at least he didn't have to spend the whole day smelling like buttercream and scratching himself like a crazy man. He spent a few extra minutes poking through the toiletries. Three toothbrushes. Three different brands of deodorant. Three travel bags. One of the bags held condoms.

When he went back into the suite's sitting room, Brendon and Josue sat together on a chintz sofa, and Shaw was holding a ceramic lamb.

"—and you get lambchops by cutting here, here. Now, if you didn't know about how Big Meat is putting mind-controlling hormones in your lambchops, you're in for a treat, because I memorized a four-hour lecture on—oh, hi, North."

"How long have you two been boning?"

Brendon jerked his head in an automatic no; Josue stayed still, gaze locked on the damask rose carpeting.

"We already know about Scotty," Shaw said.

This time, Josue flinched.

"Can't you leave him alone? It's bad enough he was tortured by that…by that monster," Brendon said, tossing his head to shake his long, silky black hair out of his eyes. "The police are treating him like a criminal, and the two of you want to drag out everything in his life and put it on display. How would you like that?"

"I don't cheat," North said. "You two got into this mess on your own."

"Oh really? You think you're so much better than us? You don't have any idea what it was like for Josue, being in love with someone who thought you were disgusting, who wouldn't look at you, wouldn't even touch you unless it was a performance—"

"Brendon," Josue said, the word coiled and venomous. "Shut. Up."

Brendon leaned away from Josue, sulking into the sofa's arm.

Josue's eyes came up. North met his gaze, held it, and waited. Outside, the dull roar of a vacuum announced housekeeping's progress along the hall. The white noise went so perfectly with the suffocating, cloistered moment that

North was shocked to realize that it had begun to snow: fat, white flakes falling in dense flurries on the other side of the glass.

"You know?" Josue asked.

North nodded.

"God." Josue shivered. "It's like letting out a breath. Like I've been holding my breath for six years."

"Scotty's been cheating on you for six years?" Shaw said.

The surprise that transformed Josue's face contracted into a smile. "Oh my God. You don't know. You're fishing."

"Karen told us about the affair."

If anything, Josue's smile got bigger, and he waved the words away with one hand. "She's just the latest one. She's actually a fairly decent person. She felt bad about it, you know? The sanctity of marriage and all that." A burst of laughter, shockingly loud against the vacuum's distant hum, broke free, and Josue's smile got wilder. "Some of them got off on that part. On me knowing. On finding little ways to rub it in."

"So how long has Scotty been carrying on with other people?" North asked.

"Since puberty, I guess. He never stopped. We started our relationship six years ago. Got married five years ago."

"And he never stopped seeing—"

"Women," Josue interrupted. His smile was too big now. His eyes manic.

"He was straight?" Shaw said. "But I've seen you guys. Your interviews. Your post-workout videos. You're cute. You touch each other. Scotty is very…hands-on with you."

"What did you call it?" Josue said to Brendon, who was picking at the stitching in the chintz upholstery, eyes focused on his work. With a soothing noise, Josue reached over and took Brendon's hand, squeezed it, and said, "I'm sorry I snapped at you. I'm scared. These meds are making it difficult to feel…to feel things the right way. Don't be mad."

Brendon looked up, jaw set, eyes hard.

Josue kissed his cheek, and Brendon sighed, features relaxing, and squeezed his hand back.

"A performance," Brendon said, shifting to sit pressed against Josue. "Scotty loved to perform. And he knew how to entertain people. How to make them laugh. How to make them love him. How to titillate them."

"Groping me in public," Josue said. The wild excitement in his face had dimmed; he looked tired and glassy eyed again. "Talking about our sex life, which was nonexistent, with the whole world. Sticking his tongue down my throat, humping me, peeling my clothes off. He had no interest in men. Not sexually, anyway. I was a prop. A convenient one."

"Why'd you put up with it?"

"It was an acting job. I'm an actor." His lips twitched in a zombie smile. "Role of a lifetime."

"And," Shaw said quietly, "you were in love with him."

Even buried under the zannies, the heartbreak still shone in Josue's eyes. After a few labored breaths, he nodded and wiped his face. "Nobody knew the real Scotty. When it wasn't a show, when he wasn't turning it on for everyone else. He was funny. He was sweet. He was charming. The first year, I messed up. A lot of times, actually. I kept thinking he was just confused. That he wanted more than what we'd agreed on. But then I realized he really was straight. He didn't want to fool around, no matter how drunk or high he was, not except...not except the one time. But even if he didn't mean to, he made me fall in love with him. And then, even though it hurt worse than anything I'd ever been through, I kept loving him. And then I started hating him, and even then I loved him. And then I realized I had to get out of this. I'd do anything to get out of this."

"What did you do?"

"Nothing," Josue said, shifting on the chintz cushions. "I didn't do anything to Scotty. I can't even begin to process the fact that he's dead."

"It's not that hard to process." North dropped into a chair and leaned toward Josue. "He treated you like shit. You were desperate to end things. He had a fuck-ton of money. You were an out-of-work actor without anything on his resume for the last six years except making Instagram workout videos. Now, by a miraculous coincidence, the guy who tortured you and took your life away for six years is dead, and you're rich and have a hot, new boyfriend."

"No," Josue said.

"Get the fuck out of here," Brendon shouted, rising from the sofa to jab a finger in North's face.

North swatted his hand away. "Come on, guys. You see how this looks. How much have the police already sniffed out?"

"I told them the same thing I told you," Josue said. "They knew about Karen, so I told them."

When North looked at Brendon, he sagged onto the sofa again, nodded, and looked away.

"Well, you're very fucking lucky that somebody decided to do a public stabbing. At the very least, it suggests someone else is involved—"

"We're not involved," Josue said.

"We had nothing to do with any of this," Brendon shouted, half-rising again.

"Sit down, dumbass," North said. After Brendon had dropped onto the sofa again, North said, "The police aren't going to let you go that easily. You're nice, juicy suspects. Right, Shaw?"

"The juiciest," Shaw said with an eager nod. "And Jadon and Cerise are very, very good, which means if you did this, they'll find a way to prove it."

"They're not that good."

"They're very good, North. Remember when Jadon caught that guy who was spray-painting homophobic slurs on houses in Lafayette Square?"

"I surely fucking do remember it," North said. "Because we're the ones who tipped him off about who was doing it. We handed him that arrest on a silver platter."

"Only because it was his birthday!"

"Hey," Brendon said, snapping at them, "what the hell are you guys—"

"Grab your panties and hold the fuck on," North told him. "We're in the middle of something. Shaw, he's not that good of a detective. That's a fact. He's decent looking. Fine. He can have a semi-polite conversation in public. Fine. But let's not go overboard and pretend he's this amazing detective."

"He dug up all that stuff on the Slasher and those dirty cops."

"Yeah, and he almost got himself killed."

"Yeah."

"Yeah."

Shaw waved both hands. "Yeah."

North blew out a breath and slumped back in the seat. "I made my point, then."

"And I made my point."

"All right."

"All right."

"What the fuck—" Brendon screamed.

"Why did Scotty tell Mary Angela that you were bleeding him dry?" Shaw said, the question launched suddenly and unerringly at Josue.

Josue shrank into the cushions, shoulders curved. "I didn't—I wasn't—"

"You threatened him," North said. "How much was he paying you?"

"When Scotty and I made our arrangement six years ago, it wasn't about money. It was about—"

"I'm talking about recently. When you decided to get out. How much were you squeezing him for?"

"You don't have to—" Brendon tried.

"Two thousand dollars a month," Josue whispered.

"Jesus Christ," North said. "That's more than I take home most months."

"That's because you always make us pay the bills," Shaw said. "It's always something. Gas, water, electric."

"Of course I pay them. They're bills."

"Yes, but you pay them every month."

"Do you not understand how utility bills work?"

Shaw raised his chin. "I'm not going to dignify that with a response."

"Will you please tell him?" North said to Josue.

"You—you do have to pay them every month," Josue managed, staring at Shaw.

"Duh," Brendon added.

"If you would just install that waste-water recycling—" Shaw tried.

"No, Shaw. I'm not drinking my own pee. Or your pee. Or anybody's pee, for that matter." To Josue, North said, "You realize that's an additional motive? Scotty was being blackmailed by two people. Mary Angela has an element of logic to her argument that killing Scotty would have been the same thing as killing her golden goose, even though I don't think that really puts her in the clear. You, on the other hand—well, you just took possession of all of your joint property. All those books. All those royalties. Everything. You became an independently wealthy man, and you're free of Scotty. We're right back where we started unless you can give me someone else."

Josue glanced at Brendon; the photographer shrugged and, in a tight voice, said, "You haven't listened to anything else I've said. It's only going to make you look worse."

For a moment, Josue was still. Then he lifted Brendon's hand, which he was still holding, and kissed his knuckles. A reluctant smile splashed across Brendon's face, and then he was serious again.

"Scotty had been having a hard time writing a book," Josue said. He hesitated and added, "You can probably guess why."

"He was a homophobic straight guy," North said.

"I guess. More or less."

"So why was he writing gay romance?" Shaw asked. "I've read his books. I love his books."

"Big surprise," Brendon said, rolling his eyes. "You've got your own life-sized Lars doll."

A flush lit up the sharp triangle of Shaw's face, but all he said was, "I mean, I've read a lot of gay fiction, and I don't agree with Scotty that you have to be a gay man to write it, but…but I mean, Scotty's stuff was good. It felt authentic." His voice slowed, and his gaze sharpened on Josue. "Because you helped him write it."

With a shrug, Josue nodded. "Scotty wanted to be a big deal. He had this fantasy of being a famous author. He'd been writing for years, all sorts of things: space opera, high fantasy, and then more and more literary fiction. It was one of those stories that opened a door for him. The way Scotty tells it, he was experimenting with voice and form; it was supposed to be a take on those old skin-rag confessionals, only told by a 21st-century rent boy. It sold the first place he sent it, and the editor wrote back and asked if he was working on any gay romance novels, because the market was booming. The way Scotty told me, when he approached me, was the industry was going through another of those purges—a big push for authenticity, 'own voices,' that kind of thing. Several women writing under male pen names had been outed. Scotty knew he'd be drawn-and-quartered if he published a gay romance novel as a straight guy, but he was so sure that he could get rich and—more importantly—get famous that he couldn't walk away."

"Cue the fake husband," North said.

"We were 'dating,' which meant we'd go out to dinner and then go back to Scotty's apartment, and he'd write and I'd watch TV. But Scotty couldn't seem to get anything decent. He published two books that didn't really get any attention. One night, I got bored listening to him pounding away at the keyboard. I went into his office, looked at the draft of something he was writing, and I knew how to fix it. I mean, the characters were all wrong. Even the sex was wrong; you could tell he'd just tried reading gay porn and didn't have any idea what he was talking about." Josue's dark skin hid any possible blush, but embarrassment laced his voice. "I offered to let him try, you know, so he could write about it more authentically, and that was the first time he shot me down like that. Hard."

"But not the last," Brendon muttered.

"No, not the last. I helped him with the first three Lars books. They were huge hits. His career took off, and Scotty had everything he wanted. Me, on the other hand. Jesus. I was getting sick from it, from wanting him, from the humiliation, from the constant need to be 'on.' Finally, I told him I was done. I refused to help him with the last Lars book or anything after that."

North's mind went to Heidi's comments about the drop in quality; when he glanced at Shaw, the other man said, "That lines up with when his writing changed."

"I bet he didn't like that," North said.

"At first," Josue spread his hands, "he put on a tough guy act. He was the literary genius, right? He could hammer out a few shitty gay romances. Then, when he couldn't produce anything decent, he begged. Then he threatened to cut me off. I threatened him back. I said I'd expose him. It was a stalemate. Then, for the first time ever, Scotty was the one who gave in. He said he wanted to try it."

"Fucking?" North said.

Josue shifted again, casting quick looks at Brendon. "He said it more...more romantically, I guess. He had a whole lot to say about how much I meant to him. He said he was willing to try to take our relationship to a physical level if it would make me happy. But..."

Shaw made a distressed noise as though he already knew.

"But he wanted to leak a sex tape," Josue said, casting more looks at Brendon, who remained stony-faced and staring out the window, into the vortex of snow. "He said it would jump-start his career. I said no. He kissed me. Not a public kiss. Not the groping and tongue. A real, Scotty kiss. And I couldn't think straight, couldn't...couldn't think at all, really. I said yes. I would have said yes to anything if it meant having him."

"I need some air," Brendon said. He lurched up from the sofa and stalked out of the suite. On his way, he slapped a ceramic Lancelot from a side table, and the tiny knight shattered against the wall.

With a low, long exhalation, Josue watched him go.

"It's only hard for him because of how he feels about you," Shaw said. "You'll make it up to him after."

"Maybe," Josue said. "I don't know anymore. I don't know if I can fix some of the things I've done."

"What happened with the sex tape?" North asked.

"We were at last year's Queer Expectations. Scotty was upset with how things had gone. His books weren't selling. He didn't get top billing, which he thought he deserved. He kept pressing me and pressing me. I said something about getting a tripod, and he said no, he had someone in mind. A fan. She'd be the perfect person to leak it; nobody would think twice about it because she was always doing that kind of thing."

"Leslie," Shaw said.

Josue nodded.

"We've heard two stories about Leslie last year," North said. "In one of them, she got caught hiding in your hotel room, trying to film you and Scotty having sex. In another, she hired a sex worker to seduce an author. It sounds like neither of them is true."

"Actually," Josue said, wringing his hands, "both are. In a way. Scotty wanted her to film us having sex and then leak the tape. He liked—" Josue took a bracing breath. "He liked the idea of performing. Big surprise. And I wanted this. I'd wanted it for years. Then, God, the whole night was unreal. We started out on the bed, dressed, just making out. He was kissing me. Hell, he was touching me. I was shaking; it felt like my first time all over again. But then Scotty stopped. Just right in the middle of it. He walked into the bathroom and shut the door and was in there fifteen minutes. Ok, I thought. Nerves. He came back, we picked up where we'd left off."

"He couldn't get hard," North said.

Josue shook his head. "I said we should try it with our clothes off. I offered to, you know, help. He looked at me like I was the stupidest person he'd ever met. He went in the bathroom again. He was in there almost an hour. An hour. I had to sit on that fucking motel bed and pretend this old lady wasn't there to film me and my straight husband have the biggest bedroom failure in history. Finally, Scotty came out, and he told Leslie to go downstairs and bring up a guy. He'd gotten somebody off an app. He couldn't get hard with me, but he figured a threesome would fix him right up. It didn't hurt that the guy brought some coke."

"But things got worse," Shaw said.

"Yes. Yes, they did. The guy was young, and he wanted to seem tough even though you could tell he'd spent hours on his hair. It was so long. He was pretty. I've thought about it a lot, later, and I wonder if that's what Scotty was going for—the long hair, the big blue eyes, the pink lips. If the guy was pretty enough, maybe he could convince himself he was with a girl. I honestly don't know, though. The coke didn't help; Scotty never really got into it, and then the kid who had brought the coke got mad, and Leslie said the kid and I should fuck while Scotty jerked off. That sent Scotty over the edge. Here he was, his big show, and he couldn't perform." A tired smile pulled at Josue's mouth. "He lit into Leslie. Screamed at her. Took her phone. Threw her out into the hall, and the hookup boy too. People started to come out of their rooms. Someone called the police. Then we had to tell them something, and Scotty came up with the idea of Leslie hiring a hustler."

"Why didn't she say anything?" Shaw said. "We've met Leslie. She's not exactly a closed book."

"I don't know. I know Scotty freaked out when he heard Yasmin had banned her from the convention. He thought Leslie would retaliate. But in typical Scotty fashion, he decided to lean in—change a PR disaster into an opportunity, the way he always did. Scotty must have talked to Leslie, made some sort of deal with her, because the one time he mentioned that night again, it was to tell me that he'd deleted her recordings, and I didn't need to worry about that anymore. But I don't know what they worked out between them. After that night, I was done. I knew it was never going to happen. And I was tired of myself. Tired of being so pathetic. Tired of hanging around for a guy I knew was never going to return my feelings." Laughing, Josue leaned his head back, one hand over his eyes. "In one of Scotty's books, we would have figured it out. I would have threatened him. I would have delivered an ultimatum. And Scotty would have realized what he was losing, and he would have caught up with me on a train platform or at the airport gate. Do you know what he said when I told him I was done? He said, 'If you think you're getting one fucking nickel in the divorce, after all my money you've blown on your fuck buddies, you're out of your goddamn mind.' That was it. And then he told me he needed to work and locked himself in the office."

North leaned back in the chevron-patterned chair, his fingers tracing the carved wood of the arm. "Sounds like an awfully good reason to want somebody dead, Josue. He humiliated you. He rejected you. And he was determined that you'd walk away from the marriage with nothing. Now, instead, you got your revenge and your money."

"I didn't care about the money. At first it was a job, I guess. But then I cared about Scotty. And then I—I just wanted to be away from him. I just wanted to stop hurting and find somebody who cared about me. Brendon's a good guy. He's smart, he's talented, he's ambitious."

"How ambitious?" Shaw said.

"What?" Josue brought his head up sharply.

"What do you mean, he's ambitious? How ambitious?"

"I don't know what you mean," Josue said, but he shifted again on the sofa, casting about. The King Arthur figurines stared back blankly.

"Ambitious enough to kill Scotty?"

"No. God. No, absolutely not! Look, Scotty was pathetic. I can see that now. I feel sorry for him. He lied about who he was to have this blip of attention, and even that wasn't really his. He couldn't write the books he wanted to write. He couldn't even write the books he needed to write. He was trapped, and he was the one who'd set the trap. I think he knew that; he slept a lot, and he'd doubled his Prozac dose—not that he bothered to talk to the doctor about it. I think it must have gotten to him, you know? Living that lie. It was the fantasy he sold everybody else: this is what romantic love is supposed to look like—two hot guys who can't keep their hands off each other, two sex machines, the kind of physical attraction and desire that obliterates everything else. It was an impossible standard for any relationship, real or fake. Honestly, now that I'm a little bit away from it, I'm glad he was able to have some sort of physical relationship with those women. I think—I think those were lifelines, even if they never could keep him above water for long. Even I bought into it for a while. With Brendon, though, I've actually got something real. Sometimes we're in the mood. Sometimes we're not. Sometimes we snipe at each other. Sometimes we need some space. But we care about each other, and we want what's best for each other." Another of those tired, broken smiles. "If I haven't run him off completely."

"Do you think Leslie was blackmailing Scotty?" Shaw asked. "Even without the videos, she could have done a lot of damage to his reputation."

"There's no way this was Leslie. She's kookie. She's probably a sex addict. But she's not dangerous, and she's definitely not a killer. If you want to know what I think…" Josue smoothed the front of his shirt. "If you want to know what I think, I'd say you should talk to Yasmin."

"Yasmin?" North said. "She hired us. Why would she hire us if she was planning on murdering Scotty?"

"Why would she even want to murder Scotty?" Shaw said. "It's ruined the con, and that's her whole life."

"You should talk to her," Josue said again. "But I do know two things: last year, Scotty threatened to ruin her. After that stunt with Leslie, when Scotty had to pretend to be outraged and furious, he said it was Yasmin's fault for not providing adequate security for celebrity authors." Josue rolled his eyes. "Bullshit, of course, and Scotty and Yasmin both knew it. But Scotty also said he'd ruin Yasmin and the con just by running up legal fees. He didn't care if he actually won the suit. They must have reached some sort of agreement because Yasmin's been pimping Scotty's next release like crazy, and I know Scotty didn't pay for all this advertising—he couldn't afford it even if he'd wanted to. The advertising is normally the con's big moneymaker, by the way."

"So all the ads we've been seeing—Yasmin would be taking a hit by letting Scotty have them for free."

Josue nodded. "A big hit. But not as bad as letting Scotty bleed her in court."

"Where were you Wednesday night?"

"Scotty and I had a fight. A really bad one."

"All night?"

A hard shake of his head. "I went out for a walk. I walked for a long time."

"In the cold? At night? In a city you don't know?"

"I went for a walk. I was mad, so I went for a walk. I don't know what you want me to tell you."

North and Shaw tried for a while longer, taking Josue through more questions, versions of the same questions, probing for cracks and gleaning details that he'd skipped on the first telling. But nothing significant came, and eventually, they had to leave, with North carrying a hotel laundry bag that held his icing-covered shirt and coat.

In the hall, North saw no sign of Brendon.

They rode the elevator down. Muzak played from a hidden speaker, a jazzy saxophone rendition of "Greensleeves." A greasy, fast-food smell lingered in the elevator car: oil on the verge of going rancid, something fried and starchy.

"He didn't do it," Shaw said.

"He probably didn't do it." North slipped an arm around Shaw, and Shaw rested his head on North's shoulder. "He's got a decent sob story. But he doesn't have an alibi for Wednesday night. He knew Scotty's favorite brand of water. The storage room was unlocked. He could have gotten inside and tampered with the water. He's got more of a reason than some of the people we've talked to."

Shaw was frowning; North couldn't see it, but he could feel it.

"What?" North asked.

"What was the cause of death?"

"What do you mean? He was poisoned."

"With an amphetamine. That's not a traditional poison. And the other people on the panel didn't die."

The elevator shivered as it stopped at the lobby. "That's a good question," North said. "We'll have to see if we can get an answer. Maybe you can seduce Jadon with your infamous dance of a thousand yaks and—oof." Gasping for breath, North stumbled off the elevator after Shaw. "Hey," he croaked. "Wait up."

The police had cordoned off the site of the stabbing, and a pair of techs had positioned tower lights and were now snapping pictures. What they were photographing, aside from bloodstained carpet, wasn't clear to North. Yasmin wasn't at the registration table, and the exhausted-looking woman stationed there—Nancy? Yancy? Flossy? Flancy?—didn't know where Yasmin had gone.

"I've been handling this stuff all morning," she said, waving at a pile of convention badges, programs, bookmarks, and Scotty Carlson-branded tote bags. "Like I'm the only one who can do her job anymore."

North eyed the empty lobby. "Looks like we beat the rush."

"It's the principle of the thing," Flancy said. "It's not fair. Am I supposed to handle all the new convention attendees by myself?"

Across the lobby, the Royal Excalibur's main doors opened. Snow swirled, settling in a white skirt near the doors, and two men entered. One was tall, massively muscled, with fire-red hair and a star chart of freckles. The other man was average height and slimmer; he wore sunglasses in spite of the storm.

When the men approached the registration table, the smaller man said, "We're here for the Queer Expectations convention. Is this the right spot?"

Flancy made a disgusted noise. "You're late."

"Right. Sorry. I apologize for the massive snowstorm that delayed my flight."

The bigger man patted his arm.

Rolling her eyes, Flancy said, "Names?"

"It should be under Snow."

"What happened?" the bigger man asked, his eyes locked on the techs and the tower lights.

The digital click of cameras was the only answer for a moment.

"It's nothing. Everything's fine."

"Yep," North said. "Everything's fine. Just your complimentary hotel stabbing."

"We call it the St. Louis turndown," Shaw said.

"For a small charge," North said, "we can upgrade you to a poisoning."

"That comes with a suite," Shaw said. "And a robe. Wait. Does it come with a robe?"

"Definitely a robe."

"Someone got stabbed?" the big man said flatly.

"And poisoned?" the other man said with a suspiciously familiar note that North had heard in Shaw's voice once or twice.

"Oh no," the big man said, grabbing the other man's arm and steering him back across the lobby. "Not a chance."

"But we came all this way for the con and—"

"Not a chance," the big man repeated. "And don't look back; clowns like that think eye contact is encouragement. Let's see if we can find a museum. Or an antique shop. Or a padded room."

"He's Bozo," North called after them.

"Yeah, I'm Bozo," Shaw shouted.

The two men walked faster, and in another spindrift of snow, exited onto the street.

"You're not supposed to want to be Bozo," North said.

"Why not? He's got the biggest feet, which means he's definitely got the biggest—um, hi, kids. Where did you come from?"

"Field trip," North said, pointing to the cluster of children in matching purple shirts.

"Again?" Shaw said.

"Looks like it."

"On a Saturday?"

"Looks like it. Come on. Before you get put on another sex offender website."

The teacher, a young black woman who was still struggling to remove her coat, stopped to stare.

"I didn't get put on a sex offender list," Shaw told her with a smile. "I accidentally added myself to a sex offender list."

"Oh my God," North whispered as he tried to put as much distance between himself and Shaw as possible.

They tried The Round Table next. No luck. Then the Camelot Public house. Nothing. They made their way through the convention rooms: Tintagel, Wormelow Tump, Castle Orgulous and Castle Blanc and Castle of Maidens. So many castles. Nothing.

"The storeroom?" North said.

Shaw nodded.

As they moved down the service corridor, North pointed to the open hasp and the missing padlock. "Someone is definitely in there."

"Well, it has to be Yasmin. She's the only one who has a key."

North slowed. He glanced at Shaw.

"Right," Shaw said, and the slender man spun and sprinted back the way they had come.

As North approached the door, he opened the laundry bag, found the pepper gel in his Carhartt, and tucked it into the back pocket of his jeans. Then he counted to a hundred, dropped the bag, and opened the storeroom door.

Yasmin sat crisscross on the floor, and she glanced up at the intrusion. She looked awful: skin sagging, eyes bloodshot, an invisible fug of old smoke and body odor poisoning the cramped room. Between her crossed legs, she was using a screwdriver to pry the cap off a water bottle. On the ground next to her stood several more bottles, the caps obviously tampered with. A plastic baggie held a white powdery mixture with several large pieces—pills, North guessed, that had been only partially crushed.

"No," Yasmin moaned. "No, no, no. Go away!"

"Stay—" North began.

But Yasmin slid onto her knees, waving the screwdriver in North's direction. North reached back slowly. His fingers wrapped around the pepper gel canister, the aluminum smooth and cool, the edge of the ribbed cap resisting for a moment as he popped it off. Yasmin was getting to her feet, still making threatening slashes and thrusts with the flathead.

"Let's calm down," North said. "Whatever's going on here, I'm sure you have a reasonable explanation."

Yasmin made another of those despairing noises, shaking her head, and then she turned and ran. She shouldered through the storeroom's rear door, bursting into the Tintagel banquet hall. Then a quilted snow boot appeared in North's line of sight, catching Yasmin at the ankle. Yasmin tripped, fell, and faceplanted on the carpet. She lay there, stunned.

Shaw emerged from his hiding spot behind the storeroom's back door. He stomped on Yasmin's hand twice until she squealed and released the screwdriver, and then Shaw kicked it away.

"North, look, we got her!"

With a grunt, North shut the service hall door behind him. Then he crossed to the Tintagel door, where he could keep an eye on Yasmin and on the tampered water bottles at the same time.

"That's got to feel good, right?" Shaw smiled beatifically. "You know, on account of your flagging self-confidence, your dwindling libido, the emasculation of letting that gimp get away from you earlier. You've got to feel so much better now that you redeemed yourself by catching Yasmin. With my help, of course."

North stared at him.

After a moment, Shaw swallowed. "You know what? I'd probably better go find Jadon."

"That's why I keep you around," North gritted out. "You're so smart."

Chapter 34

YASMIN DIDN'T CRY OR howl or fight when Cerise placed the cuffs on her. Whatever final burst of energy had driven her to run seemed to have burned off; she looked barely able to stand as Cerise and Jadon Mirandized her. The Tintagel banquet hall—half lit, quiet, with its engrained smells of Italian seasoning and roast beef and chafing-dish Sterno—might have had something to do with that.

"You two can get yourselves down to the station without an escort, I guess," Jadon said. "We'll need statements. And we'll have questions."

"Sure," North said. "How's next Friday? Or, even better, how's March 35th?"

"Shaw?"

Shaw nodded. "We'll head straight there."

And they did, where they then spent the next eight hours. Part of that wasn't Jadon's fault; two women got into a brawl outside the LGBTQ squad room, and separating them seemed to require the efforts of every officer in the building. Screams of "My hair!" and "That's right! That's right! You're a bald bitch now!" trailed away in opposite directions.

When Jadon and Cerise were finally ready to talk to Shaw, he found himself in an interview room with a one-way mirror, cameras, a particleboard table, and chairs. Someone must have puked recently, and Shaw's stomach turned at the smell.

At first, the questions were straightforward: who did you talk to? what did they say? what did you do next? But once the ball got rolling, Jadon and Cerise jumped back and started asking questions that Shaw hadn't expected. They wanted to know about when Yasmin had hired them. They wanted to know about the death threats. They wanted Shaw to describe the threats that Yasmin had shown him. They wanted to know about Leslie—what had Yasmin said exactly about her? Why do you think Yasmin wanted you to pay attention to her?

"Wait a minute," Shaw said. "You think Yasmin poisoned Scotty?"

Jadon rubbed his face with both hands.

"You found her putting crushed-up pills in water bottles," Cerise said. "What do you mean?"

"I mean—I don't know." And then Shaw did know, and it horrified him. "She didn't do this."

After a stretched-out silence, Cerise made a disgusted noise.

"Don't engage," Jadon said, dropping his hands. "It's better that way."

Cerise's gaze didn't waver from Shaw. "What do you mean, 'She didn't do this'? You saw her doing it. Are you changing your testimony?"

"No, but—"

"Oh, so you're telling me that there's a problem with the evidence in that storeroom? You and North went for a smoke break, and while you were gone, somebody put those pills and those water bottles with the broken seals in the storeroom. And poor Yasmin was just so curious that she picked everything up and got her prints all over those baggies and bottles and the screwdriver. That's what happened?"

"Do you really already have fingerprints back?" Shaw asked Jadon.

"No," Jadon said. His eyes were fixed on a spot somewhere above Shaw's shoulder. "I'm not doing this."

"I'm just trying to understand what you think happened," Cerise said. "Or we can go back to the way we were doing this before, when I was asking questions and you were being helpful."

"Jadon, Yasmin did not kill Scotty."

Jaw set, Jadon shook his head.

"Let's go back to Leslie Hawkins," Cerise said. "We're going to make a list of all the times Yasmin tried to direct your attention to Ms. Hawkins, beginning with—"

"Jadon, she didn't. I can feel it in my gut. This is all wrong."

"Oh my God," Jadon breathed. Then those sandy-dark eyes slid to Shaw, and he said, "Shaw, feeling queasy about this, it's natural. You bond with people very quickly—"

"That's not what this is."

"—and you're a very compassionate person—"

"Don't do that!"

"—and those are very admirable qualities. But a bad feeling in your gut isn't enough to create reasonable doubt. You've only known these people for a few days, and you and I both know that you can know someone for years and they can still have you fooled."

Shaw bit the inside of his mouth to keep the next words from escaping. Jadon's former partner and two other detectives on the LGBTQ task force had been involved in drugs and murder, including the attack that had almost taken Shaw's life in college. Jadon knew better than anyone that just about anybody was capable of killing, no matter how they appeared on the surface.

"A bad feeling in your gut," Cerise said, "also isn't enough to get a conviction. You saw Yasmin Maldonado tampering with water bottles. With your own eyes. She was the only one with a key to that storeroom. She had a clear, powerful motive: Scotty was threatening her, threatening to ruin the convention and, by extension, to ruin her. The death threats were an easy way to make herself look like a victim; the first suspect would be whoever had been writing those notes. She even pointed out a possible person: Leslie Hawkins. Nobody can alibi her for the night when Leslie, Clarence, and Karen were pushed down the stairs. Nobody can alibi her for the half-hour surrounding the stabbing today."

"But someone did write those threatening notes," Shaw said. "Why aren't you looking for whoever was sending them?"

Cerise shifted in her seat, body angled toward Jadon. He was quiet for a moment and said, "We found materials in her room that suggest she made those threatening notes herself."

Shaw shook his head. "That doesn't make any sense."

"Of course it does." In her cheap suit, Cerise slouched in the metal chair, one arm across the back. "She got exactly what she wanted: to throw the blame on someone else, and to stir up some excitement for the con. People have been buzzing about the notes for weeks."

"No, she only told—"

"She told everyone. It came up in every interview we conducted: Yasmin told everybody who would listen about the notes, and then she made them swear to secrecy. She knew exactly what she was doing. That gossip spread like wildfire."

"She didn't do this. You're wrong about the storeroom; the service door, the one that connected to Tintagel, it was open all night after Yasmin put Scotty's special water in there. Anybody could have snuck down from their hotel room, poisoned the water and gone back up. And half the people at that convention had Adderall in their bags."

"From what you and North told us, and from what the hotel staff has said, it's a possibility that the door was unlocked all night, although every single staff member denies opening it. But that doesn't matter. You and North caught her right in the middle of it. End of story."

"But why use Adderall? Why use an amphetamine at all? It was just a fluke that Scotty died from it; the other people on the panel were fine. If Yasmin really wanted to kill Scotty, why not use something that would be sure to kill him?"

Jadon's voice was gentle as he said, "We're going to be waiting for a while to know exactly what was in the water, but yes, it was clearly an amphetamine of some kind, and yes, Adderall seems to be the most obvious choice, based on the demographic and the reactions that the other people on the panel described. Do you know what serotonin syndrome is?"

Shaw jerked his head in a no.

"It's when there's an excess release of serotonin in the brain. If it's bad enough, it can cause death. That's how Scotty died. Normally Adderall doesn't produce a drastic change in serotonin. But if someone already has elevated levels of serotonin, the risk is dramatically increased."

"And Scotty was taking double his Prozac," Shaw said. "But—"

"Our best guess is that Yasmin tampered with all of the water bottles for that panel because she couldn't be sure Scotty would get the right one. For the other panelists, the effects would be mildly uncomfortable; for Scotty they'd be fatal. And no, we don't know how Yasmin learned that Scotty had upped his meds. Someone might have told her. Or she might have known that Scotty was on antidepressants and, not knowing he was taking more than he'd been prescribed, still hoped that the drug interaction would be fatal. Anything you can help us with, we'd really appreciate it."

For a moment, Shaw sat there, his fingers gripping the seat of the folding chair, the oil on his skin making the metal slick. "Josue told us. About Scotty increasing his medication without consulting the doctor. I don't think Josue wanted Scotty dead. He loved Scotty. Or he used to love him. I think Josue just wanted to live his own life."

Jadon nodded.

"I guess that's me being naïve again," Shaw said. "Isn't it?"

"We'll look into it," Jadon said.

"Even if Josue only wanted to get away," Cerise said, "he might have said something to the boyfriend."

"No, Brendon wouldn't hurt—" Shaw stopped. He rubbed his eyes, which were burning suddenly. "I sound like a *Care Bears* episode. Can I—can I go? I don't think I can tell you anything else that will help you."

He was vaguely aware of Cerise shaking her head, but no words followed. Instead, metal squeaked on linoleum, and steps moved around the table. A warm hand caught his arm, helping him up, and Jadon walked him back to the squad room.

"What the fuck," North said, rising from the bench where they'd left him, "did you do to him?"

"Nothing," Shaw said. "They didn't—"

"What the fuck is wrong with you?" North shouted.

"Would you keep your voice down?" Jadon said mildly. "I know it's been a long day, and I understand you're upset, but shouting isn't going to help."

"You think I'm upset?" North said. "Pretty boy, you have no idea what I look like when I'm upset."

"We'll make this as fast as possible," Jadon said, squeezing Shaw's arm before releasing him. "Do you want tea? Or I have a seaweed chew that's supposed to be calming?"

"Of course you do," North said.

Shaw shook his head.

For a moment, Jadon stood there. Then he crossed to his desk, rattling drawers as he searched.

North's hand came down, warm and rough, on Shaw's nape. "Are you ok?" North asked quietly.

"Yeah," Shaw said. "Yes."

"God damn it," North muttered.

Jadon came back and pressed something into Shaw's hand: an oblong piece of something green.

"We'll be as quick as we can," Jadon said.

The two men were still bickering as they walked away. Shaw tried the seaweed chew, which had surprisingly little taste and, after five minutes, made his jaw ache. He spat it into a wastebasket. The fluorescents buzzed. Someone burned popcorn. An overweight man, fiftyish, with a buzz cut of graying hair, sat at the closest desk and hummed the same ten-second snatch of "Hotel California" again and again.

When North returned, he was alone, and he helped Shaw stand. They made their way to the GTO, where Shaw slumped against the seat. An ocean of orange-gray light hung above them, hiding the stars. In the closed confines of the car, Shaw sniffed the air.

"Why do you smell like smoke?"

"It's probably from Yasmin."

"No. That was hours ago."

North shifted in his seat. "I went outside for a few minutes. While they were interviewing you. A bunch of uniformed guys were smoking."

"And what? You just went up and talked to them?"

"Yeah, sure."

"Why?"

"I don't know. I was going out of my mind from all the waiting."

"Did they say anything interesting?"

"Yes. One of them is a major fairy and does nude ballet on the top of the Arch."

"Wow, that is interesting."

In the weak yellow glow of the dash, North reached over and stroked the back of Shaw's head. The tires hummed. At the next red light, a Mercedes SLK rolled to a stop next to them. Two tinselly blond girls were hitting their vapes and screaming along with Ariana, "thank u, next." When they light changed, the Mercedes peeled out, fishtailing once halfway through the intersection, Ariana trailing behind them like exhaust.

"Don't you dare try to race them."

A smile glimmered on North's face as he said, "No challenge. Wouldn't be any fun."

"North, she didn't do it."

With a sigh, North nodded. His fingers slid down, scratching lightly at the sensitive skin on the back of Shaw's neck. Then his grip tightened, and he squeezed once. "Jadon said you'd already gotten your teeth into this."

"Do you think Yasmin poisoned Scotty?"

North was silent for the next two blocks. "I think Jadon and Cerise make some good points."

"North, she didn't. I've been thinking about it nonstop. Yasmin's whole thing was that she wanted to save the con. I get it. Maybe she wrote those threatening messages. That's possible; I'd buy that. She was trying to drum up some excitement, add an edge. And yeah, whatever she was doing today when we found her, that was messed up. But even that part doesn't make sense. She'd already poisoned Scotty. Why risk it again?"

"She must have been trying to remove a potential witness. Leslie clearly knew something, and there must be someone else that knows something incriminating."

"Fine. Maybe. But why hire us in the first place? We were even more of a threat than the police. Why bring us into it at all?"

"You have to admit," North said, "that people got excited when we introduced ourselves. They liked it. And her whole angle was to make the con thrilling, to draw people in. Besides, it's the perfect way to remove yourself as a suspect."

"I can't believe this," Shaw said. North turned onto the Benton Park street where Shaw lived and pulled up in front of his house. The ground-floor windows were dark; Pari and Truck must have left the Borealis offices hours ago. "I honestly can't believe that you're—that you're going along with such a stupid explanation for what happened."

"It's been a long day. Take it down a little."

"I shouldn't have to take it down a little. I shouldn't have to be quiet or calm down or whatever you want me to do. You're wrong about this, and I can't believe you're going to take their side when I'm sitting here explaining why it couldn't have been Yasmin."

North was taking deep breaths, nostrils flaring with each exhalation. "I am always on your side. Do you get that? Always. And you know what? I see what you're saying. I agree that there are some irregularities. If you want to keep working this case on the side, that's fine. You know I'll help you. But we've also got a business to run, Shaw. We've got real work to do. We've got bills and employees and we've got other clients depending on us. And you know what? I am actually really pissed off right now because I don't like that you're biting my head off because you had a spat with your ex-boyfriend and you're mad he wouldn't roll over and play nice just because you two used to bang one out."

Shaw grabbed the door handle. Then he stopped. "That's what you think this is about?"

"Part of it, yeah."

Shaking his head, Shaw opened the door. He got out, the cold stinging, and his eyes welled. As he blinked them clear, he bent to meet North's gaze and gestured at the still-running car. "Well?"

"I think we should both get a good night's sleep."

Shaw huffed a breath. "Fine."

"I'll see you tomorrow."

Slamming the door was childish. Shaw knew that. But as he crossed the street, listening to North swearing inside the GTO, he also knew that it had felt very, very good.

Chapter 35

SHAW TOSSED AND TURNED and woke with his jaw aching from grinding his teeth all night. For a while, he lay in bed. His room looked pretty much like it always did: on the wall, he'd hung sixteen pashmina scarves silkscreened with Dolly Parton at sixteen different points in her career; on the floor, a mound of Chucks—rights only—formed a multicolored pyramid topped by a single, metallic rainbow high-top lined with fleece; on his dresser waited his current project, a small keepsake box being decoupaged with historical condom advertisements. All of it reminded him of North, and he went back under the covers for a while.

But he was awake, and the gears were turning, and he couldn't stop thinking about yesterday. It was one thing for Jadon to be wrong about Yasmin; now that Shaw had some distance from the argument, he could recognize Jadon's reasons, even if he didn't agree with them. The fight with North, though, was another thing entirely. Shaw's brain kept rewinding to the cold, compacted anger in North's face, how the yellow light from the GTO's dash raked across his cheekbones. Then it got worse: his brain kept playing back all the nights North was too tired, all the nights one of them wasn't in the mood, all the nights Shaw got caught up in a project and didn't even realize until too late that North had already gone home.

Throwing back the bedding, Shaw sat up. He listened for a moment. The house was old; below him, voices mingled, including the smoldering rumble that belonged to North. Shaw got out of bed. He stumbled into the bathroom, showered, brushed his teeth, and drank water. He found a pair of jeggings and a Cuban collar shirt in leopard print. He shoved one foot into the metallic rainbow Chuck; he couldn't unearth its mate, so he settled for a Sorel snow boot. Then he grabbed a pen and a pad of paper and got to work.

First, he made a list of everyone who might have wanted to hurt Scotty. The list was long—it included almost everyone he'd met at the convention over the last few days. The only people he excluded were Rodney and Jerry, the married couple in Western gear. Then he rewrote the list in order of what he considered the strongest motives. He drew a line under the top five, separating the names into the two groups. In the first set, he had Josue (money and possibly revenge), Mary Angela (to cover up her blackmail scheme), Karen (simply because she was involved in a relationship with Scotty), Brendon (money), and Yasmin (to save the con, plus the very irritating fact that they'd caught her contaminating water).

In the second group, he wrote JD (she had followed him into the bathroom to fight about something, and in spite of her version of events, the possibility of plagiarism still hovered over her), Serenity (her ongoing feud with Scotty, and his public humiliation of her), Clarence (public fights and humiliation), Leslie (revenge for being banned from the con), and Heidi (her negative reviews were the only thing Shaw could think of, but he kept her on the list anyway).

He directed his attention to the top five, sketching out what he knew of their scheduled appearances (relying on the online convention program for this) and details that had emerged in their conversations. The problem, of course, was that no one had a solid alibi for the entire night that the storeroom had been unlocked. Although Karen had admitted to sneaking around the hotel that night, any of the others could have left their rooms too. Without reviewing hours of footage from multiple security cameras—which they didn't even have access to—Shaw didn't have any way of guessing who else might have been wandering the Royal Excalibur. Worse, even if he did get access to that footage and did spot someone roving the halls, there were no cameras in Tintagel that could prove someone had entered the storeroom.

Blowing out a frustrated breath, Shaw ripped the pages free from the pad and set them aside. Then he turned the pad and began sketching the layout of the important rooms: Tintagel, the storeroom, and the service corridor. He spent as much time as he could on the storeroom: the doors opposite each other, the racks of shelves, the location of the water, the cart that Yasmin and Clarence had used to move supplies around the Royal Excalibur.

At some point, the sketching turned into what North called doodling. One corner of the floorplan now featured a man in profile whose jaw and nose and short, messy hair suggested a certain pain-in-the-ass boyfriend. Another corner featured a stick figure with a straight-backed chair, which he was using to fend off a lion who—if lions could be said to resemble people—might have had the exact same eyes as a certain someone Shaw knew. He tore the sheet loose, flipped it over, and began sketching North the way he remembered him from two nights before: barefoot, leaning against the wall, shirtless, the curl of his arm, biceps flexing.

A knock at the door galvanized Shaw. Heat rushed into his face, and he grabbed the papers, trying to cover the drawing. "I'm—it's not—don't come in. I'm—I'm wanking."

The sigh on the other side of the door definitely belonged to North. "Since you're using British slang for spanking your monkey, I'm guessing you're about sixteen hours into that baking show you like. Can I come in?"

"No. And I'm not watching anything. Wait. Yes, I am. I'm watching porn. Really, really messed-up porn."

"Huh." The boards creaked as North shifted his weight. "That sounds an awful lot like shaming someone for their sexual preferences."

"No." Shaw could hear, as the word echoed, the unfortunate note of adolescence.

"I would like to apologize for last night. I was tired, and I was frustrated, and I didn't treat you the way I should have."

"Ok. Fine."

"Shaw, come on."

"It's fine. I'm not mad."

The handle rattled. Shaw jumped, but the lock was set, and North didn't do anything...Northish, like kick the door in.

"I want to look you in the eyes when you tell me you're not mad."

"I can't." Genius struck. "I'm covered in lube. And condoms."

The only sound was Pari's laughter from downstairs.

"Well, Pari and Truck brought in sandwiches from The Daily Bread, and I brought Donut Drive-In, and somebody brought an insulated mug of thistle tea with a four-mushroom immune defense mix-in that cost him forty fucking dollars at Whole Foods, so—" North took what sounded like a deep breath. "We'll be downstairs when you're ready to forgive me. Or tell me what I need to do to make it up to you. Or whatever, Shaw. I'm really sorry."

Heavy steps moved down the stairs, and then more of Pari's laughter floated up. Shaw tried to go back to doodling, but the spell had been broken. He could smell the sandwiches: bacon, eggs, a fresh bagel, a thick slice of gouda. He imagined he could smell the donuts, yeasty with the lingering fragrance of hot oil. And he'd been telling North for weeks about the immune-system benefits of the four-mushroom blend he'd found online, and it was, after all, cold and flu season.

He stopped himself with his hand on the door.

So close.

He went back to bed, grabbed his phone, and texted North: *Nice try*.

The composition bubbles appeared, disappeared, appeared, disappeared. What finally came through was a single emoji of a perplexed face.

You know exactly what I mean, Shaw wrote back, *and it's not going to work.*

This time, the answer came back faster: an emoji of a man shrugging.

Now Truck was laughing, then saying something, and then Pari was giggling. They'd been dating for almost as long as North and Shaw, and from what Shaw could tell, Pari and Truck hadn't had a single fight. The same Pari who threw plates and screamed and had once stood on her desk and placed a sobbing call to the Missouri Department of Social Services, asking that someone do a welfare check on her because Shaw had helped himself to a tiny, tiny piece of her danish—that same Pari took every single thing that Truck did in stride, without so much as blinking. Even the time Truck had made her a hair pin out of a raccoon paw.

This time, Shaw caught himself too late; he was already on the stairs, drawn by the perfume of breakfast food like a cartoon character floating toward a cooling pie. He made it as far as the kitchen and then stopped. Pari was standing at the sink, Truck pressing kisses to her face, hir big hands on Pari's waist: possessive and, Shaw could tell just from looking, also surprisingly gentle.

"Oh," Pari said, pushing Truck back with one hand. "Shaw. Um. Excuse you. We were—I mean if you have to have a sandwich, you can, just, you know, hurry. So Truck and I can—I mean, are you just going to stand there?"

"I don't want a sandwich," Shaw said. Or rather, shouted. He was increasingly aware that he was losing control of the volume of his voice. "And I don't want donuts. And I don't want a four-mushroom mix-in. And I don't want anybody to bother me ever again. And you two make a wonderful couple, and I hope you're really, really happy together."

By the end, he was crying, and he stumbled back upstairs and threw himself on the bed.

A murmured conference was taking place below him. Shaw gritted his teeth, waiting for the familiar tread of the Redwings on the stairs. Instead, though, two sets of footsteps moved toward his room. He pulled a pillow over his head.

"Please go away," he said when the door opened. "I'm fine, I'm just—" Both sets of footsteps crossed the room. "I said go away, please. I don't want—"

A massive weight settled onto Shaw, forcing the breath from his lungs. Someone pulled the pillow away. Shaw blinked up at Pari, trying to catch his breath, which was difficult because Truck was sitting on him.

"Uh," Shaw gargled. "Uh, uh."

"You're fine," Pari said. Perching on the mattress next to Shaw's head, she added, "You're making North very sad. I don't like it when North is sad. When North is sad, he puts on that awful playlist with Poison and Bonnie Tyler and Bon Jovi and all that old-people music, and I have to listen to it for hours. And he's not nice to Truck, and everybody should be nice to Truck."

"He's still pretty nice to me," Truck said. "But North-level nice. Not Shaw-level nice. That's a compliment, by the way."

Shaw managed a gurgled thanks.

"What's going on?" Pari said.

Shaw wheezed.

"If Truck gets off you, you're not going to do anything dramatic, are you? Sometimes you're really too much for me to handle, Shaw."

Shaw had a lot of thoughts about that statement, but all he could manage was a frantic nod. Truck eased off of him, and Shaw took in a gasping breath.

"You broke my ribs," he said. "I don't even think I have ribs anymore. I think you turned them into dust. They're going to have to build me a new ribcage, and I'll probably end up like Iron Man."

"You won't," Pari said. "You don't have the It factor, Shaw. You're a B-lister at best."

"I think he's cute," Truck said. "The kind of cute that goth girls would be really into."

"That's not a comp—"

"What's wrong?" Pari said.

"Nothing. I told you: I'm fine. Just go back downstairs and be perfectly in love and happy and have a million babies together."

"Kingsley Shaw Wilder Aldrich, I am not up here getting older and grayer by the second just so you can tell me you're fine. I ought to be downstairs making out with Truck, but instead I'm here because I'm the best, most loyal friend you've ever had."

"Technically, you're supposed to be working because you're on the clock, not making out with Truck. In fact, I'm not even sure why Truck is here except—"

"Ze's here because ze loves me and it's day twenty-four of our month-long Valentine's. You get one more chance, or I'll ask where North keeps the paddle, and I'll let Truck turn your ass cherry-red."

"I'm pretty good at it," Truck said. "It's all about spreading out the blows and being consistent. You want every inch of ass to get the same—"

"Everything's awful and North hates me and he's already tired of me and I've loved him my entire life and it's over."

In the silence that followed the rapid-fire declaration, Shaw felt blood flood into his cheeks.

"Truck," Pari said, "why don't you go keep an eye on the sandwiches and make sure North doesn't eat another one without paying us for it."

"Ok," Truck said. "Bye, Shaw. Sorry North hates you."

"Thanks, Truck," Shaw said as he pulled the pillow back over his head.

When Truck's steps had faded, Pari said, "North doesn't hate you. He loves you. It's kind of gross, actually, and I honestly don't get it because you have no ass and sometimes when you don't wash your hair there's a definite smell and—"

"Ok, ok. Thanks, Pari. I feel so much better. Bye."

"Why in the world would you think North hates you?"

"I don't know." Inching the pillow down, Shaw squinted at her. "I guess I don't think he hates me. But...but I do think he might be realizing he can do better. I mean, I don't know. I've been in love with him my whole life—"

"No, you've been in love with him since college."

"Fine. But you know what I mean. And I thought if we ever got together, it would be magical and perfect, and instead, he doesn't even want to have sex with me anymore, and when I make an issue of it, the sex is bad because I mess it up, and—" A rush of inspiration hit Shaw. "At this con, the case we've been working, there was this guy. And he liked to throw it in everyone's face that reading romance novels is this escapist fantasy, and people are so desperate to get away from the boring, ordinary shittiness of their real lives that they'll run after these fantasies. And he was kind of right. I mean, he was playacting this fantasy with a fake husband, and everybody bought into it. Even me. And maybe that's the problem. Maybe I've read too many romance novels, and maybe my expectations are too high, and maybe I want something that doesn't even exist in the real world, and I'm going to end up just like he said Clarence did, lonely and desperate and wanting this fantasy of romance that only takes place in storybooks."

The heating kicked on, a draft of warm air from the register stirring Pari's long, dark hair. She combed the strands away from her face, lips pursed in thought. Then she said, "That is the stupidest thing I've ever heard in my life."

"Pari!"

"Well, it is. I mean, you're not a rocket scientist."

Shaw groaned.

"Sometimes I even think you're a little dim."

"Ok, enough helping."

"Like the time I caught you trying to chew through that lamp cord while it was still plugged in."

"I wasn't trying to—Pari, ok, I'm fixed now. Thank you. Go back downstairs."

"But even knowing that you're a little touched up here," she tapped her temple, "I honestly did not expect this level of totally willful stupidity."

"Please tell me when this is over," Shaw said as he pulled the pillow back over his head.

Pari snatched the pillow away. "Sit up."

After a moment, Shaw sat up.

"What's going on here," Pari said, "has nothing to do with romance novels. They're books, Shaw. Unless you are a truly special category of stupid, you're not going to mix them up with reality. Nobody does."

"But I—"

"You already said it yourself: you've been building up this relationship with North for a long time in your head, and now it's reality. And the reality is that North sometimes wears the same socks two days in a row, and they stink. And sometimes he gets the bean burrito at Taco Bell, and that really stinks. And when he eats that one kind of cheddar he likes and then talks to me too close—"

"I get it, I get it."

"I'm not sure you do. He's a guy. He's not perfect. He's not magical. One time I saw hair on his toes."

"Sweet transcendent Padumuttara Buddha, please change me into a grasshopper or a wingnut or an ozone molecule."

"I'm trying to tell you that if you want something with North, you have to build it with the real guy. The one who's here, not the one who's in your head. And you definitely have to talk to him about the socks."

Wiping his eyes, Shaw nodded. "Fine. Maybe you're right. But North doesn't want me anymore. I can tell. The sex is—"

"Oh my God. Did you ask him?"

"What?"

"Did you ask him why he hasn't been ravishing you or plundering your hole or whatever you want him to do?"

"It's a little offensive that you assume he's the one plundering my hole. Maybe I'm plundering—"

"Shaw!" The scream had a definite edge to it.

"Well, no. Not, you know, verbally."

"I'm done." Pari stood, dusted her hands, and added, "I'm sending you a bill. I charge two hundred dollars an hour for therapy. Plus an extra fee for outright stupidity."

Her shoes clicked on the bare boards. Then she was gone.

Shaw sat for a while, turning it all over in his head. He washed his face. His hair still looked like a nimbus cloud, but he patted at the worst of the tufts, trying to get them to lie flat. Then he went downstairs. Pari and Truck were making out on the floor behind her desk.

"I'm deducting this from your therapy bill," Shaw said as he passed them.

When he stepped into the office, North was typing something. He threw a glance over his shoulder, and his hands stilled when he saw Shaw.

"Hi," Shaw said with a tiny wave.

"Hi." North's face seemed to close, and he spun in the chair to face Shaw. "This doesn't look good."

"No, it's just—do you not want to have sex with me anymore?"

Shock rippled through North's features, and a laugh burst out of him. He swallowed the sound after a moment, but a dazed grin lingered as he said, "What?"

"I'm serious."

"Are we talking about right now?"

"No, in general."

Some of the surprised humor faded as North's eyebrows drew together. "I absolutely want to have sex with you. Right now would be a good time for me. Is it a good time for you?"

"Really? Because we haven't had sex in, like, a month."

"It hasn't been—" North cut off. More slowly, he said, "A couple of nights ago...but I guess we didn't really—" He chewed his lip. "Damn. Wait, not even on Valentine's?" A note of despair entered his voice. "Oh my God. What the fuck did we do on Valentine's?"

Shaw shook his head. "We were in Wahredua, trying to track down Billy. You, um, said you were having back spasms from sitting in the car so long on the stakeout, so we just ordered pizza and fell asleep in front of the TV in the motel."

North pinched the bridge of his nose, closed his eyes, and said, "I'm sorry, let me get this straight. Our first Valentine's together, I ordered pizza, and we fell asleep in front of the TV, and I didn't even sex you up?"

"And we combined it with my birthday because you said we were out of town and it might be easier to just combine them this year because my birthday is the day before Valentine's, and you were having so much fun annoying Emery—"

"Holy shit. And you didn't murder me? Ok, you need to break up with me right now so I can come crawling back. Please break up with me. Crawling back is the only way I can make this up to you."

"I don't want to break up with you," Shaw said with a tremulous laugh. "And I don't want you to come crawling back. But—but I know I'm not very, um, experienced, and I guess that gets boring after a while, and I know I've got a lot of hang-ups about sex in general, so I'm sure you get tired of that too. I just don't want you to have to pretend that you're too tired or something, so maybe we can just—"

"Shaw, I am not bored with our—I guess I should say with our sex life. I love you, and I am also very fucking into you. Sometimes, when I've had a bad day, especially when things with Tucker and the divorce get in my head, I might not be in the mood. But for the most part, I've just been tired."

"Oh."

"Maybe that sounds stupid, but I'm being serious. I've been exhausted."

"You have been working a lot."

"I've been working too much. I know I get...focused on work."

"You get obsessed with work."

"Yeah, I guess I do. But I honestly didn't realize it was messing things up between us. I kept telling myself that it was temporary, that if I could just close out the month, things would calm down. And then it turned into a routine. And then, I'm now realizing, it killed our sex life and also made me the shittiest boyfriend ever."

"Not ever," Shaw said. "You didn't try to torture information out of me and then kill me."

"Oh God," North groaned. "Ok, let's go."

"What?"

"Let's go pack your bags. We're leaving today. Somewhere. Anywhere. A vacation."

"No, we've got clients, and we've got—"

"Shaw, I have wanted to be your boyfriend since I was eighteen. Now I find out I've fucked it up to the point that you think I'm bored with you. And I ruined your birthday. And I fucked up our first Valentine's. So, yeah, let's go. Pack a bag."

He was already moving across the room, herding Shaw toward the door. Shaw caught his arms, laughing as he tried to stop North's momentum.

"Slow down," Shaw said. "We don't need to leave on a vacation. Not right now, I mean. But maybe some time off would be good. And maybe figuring out some ways to, you know, make sure we still have time for each other. Time that doesn't have to do with work. Or sleeping. Or eating while we work."

North cupped his face in both hands, turned his head, and kissed him.

Shaw's breath was ragged when North finally pulled back. "We don't have to…I didn't mean right now."

"We surely fucking do," North said. "Right fucking now."

Steering Shaw by the shoulders, North propelled him toward the door. They passed through the office. Pari was now sitting at her desk, while Truck sat on the floor, giving her a foot massage. In the short time that Shaw had been in the office, another dozen roses had been delivered. *To Pari, From Truck* were written in a child's scribble on the card.

"Oh thank God," Pari said. "If I had to hear one more time about his urethra being blocked up from not enough sex, I was going to kill myself."

"My chakra," Shaw said. "My root chakra was blocked, and—"

"Go home," North said. "Fuck, go anywhere. Just get out of here."

"I'm working," Pari snapped as she turned her attention back to her phone.

"Then you're fired," North said.

"You're not fired," Shaw called over his shoulder as North pushed him into the kitchen. "But we're definitely closed for the rest of the day."

"You promised me I'd get time and a half," Pari screeched after them.

Shaw tried to turn, but North had an iron grip.

"Maybe I should make sure she knows—"

"Uh uh," North said.

"—just so she doesn't wipe the hard drives or—"

"Nope. You started this. Now we're going to finish it."

"That sounds a little scary, actually, when you say it that way."

"Good," North said as he strong-armed Shaw up the stairs.

North released Shaw when they reached the bedroom, and Shaw stumbled at the final thrust from North's hands. He caught himself, barely, from tumbling into the pile of Chucks. Then he turned around. North was thumbing the lock shut.

"We don't have to—I just meant—the principle of the thing—if you don't want to—"

Leaning against the door, North studied him. Then he rucked up the Hampton Nursery and Landscaping tee, turning himself out of it, and tossed it to the floor. He worked the Redwings off next, one at a time, and dropped his jeans. He shucked his boxer briefs next. He was hard. The tip of his dick was wet.

"Does it look like I don't want to?"

Shaw had an answer, but it emerged as a raspy noise that wasn't quite a word.

"I know this is still scary for you sometimes," North said as he crossed the room. The movements were slow, confident, predatory. "I've tried really hard not to pressure you. I guess I went too far the other way if I let you get the idea that I don't want to do this every time I'm around you."

"And you've been tired," Shaw pointed out in a whisper.

A tiny smile pulled the corner of North's mouth as he grabbed a handful of Shaw's shirt and yanked him forward, closing the final distance between them. He worked the buttons open. Shaw was surprised to feel a tremor in North's hands. "I'm not tired now, am I?"

"You do still have those bags under your eyes, so—"

North kissed him again. His hand slid inside Shaw's shirt, and strong, rough fingers closed around one nipple. Shaw moaned as North twisted and pulled, gently and then not so gently. North's tongue slid into his mouth.

When the kiss broke, North finished the buttons. He tugged on the waistband of the jeggings, slid his hand down the front of the jeans, and cupped Shaw's erection through the stretchy denim. "I love you," North said, his voice unsteady.

"I love you too."

"And I'm going to fuck you like a crazy man now because that's what I am. You make me crazy. I never thought I could feel so much for one person."

When North's hands reached the waistband again, Shaw closed his fingers around North's, stopping him. "You've been teasing me a lot lately," Shaw said. "Sometimes I think I just annoy you."

North tried the button again, and again Shaw stopped him.

"You like when I tease you," North said, and then he worked the button open and shoved the jeggings down to Shaw's knees. Hands on Shaw's bare hips sent an inferno through Shaw. North guided him back, eased him down onto the bed, and drew the jeggings off the rest of the way.

"Commando," North said. "Again?"

Goosebumps prickled along Shaw's belly and chest as North straddled him. "And you have to be nicer to me," Shaw whispered.

North considered this, stroking himself lightly, his ice-rim eyes already glassy with lust. "Fuck that," he finally said. "You don't want me to be nicer."

"I do," Shaw said, but he whimpered when North's other hand closed around his dick, North's thumb brushing the slit and following the curve of the head. "I want you to be nice. Jadon is always nice to me. I want you to listen to my fourteen-hour playlist of Telanganan tribal instruments, and I don't want you to roll your eyes or tell me it sounds like cats getting their anuses cleaned or anything mean. I just want you to be nice. Like Jadon."

With a thoughtful noise, North nodded slowly. He leaned down, tracing a line of kisses along Shaw's chest until his mouth closed over a nipple. His hand still slid along Shaw's shaft. His tongue caressed the nipple. The hot, wet heat made Shaw moan again.

Then North bit him. Hard.

Shaw squealed. He tried to sit up, but North pressed him back down.

"North, what the hell?"

North kissed him. Shaw was too stunned to resist. Then, after a moment, he twisted away.

North was smirking.

"You are a jerk, North McKinney."

"Just reminding you who you belong to, and that it doesn't have anything to do with being nice."

"I don't belong to anyone. I'm a person, not a thing, and you being objectifying and possessive is not acceptable."

"But it makes you hard as a fucking rock," North said, his smirk growing. His hand moved faster. And then faster. And too late, Shaw realized the rush of endorphins had tipped an already precarious balance, and he rolled his hips up to thrust into the tight circle of North's hand, bucking wildly as he came. One of Shaw's hands clutched North's arm. The other dug furrows into the bedding.

When Shaw came back down, North's hand was still moving lightly, and Shaw had to close his eyes. When he made a faintly distressed noise, North chuckled and released him. Then North's mouth was on him again: butterfly kisses all over Shaw's chest and belly, up and down, until North's lips brushed Shaw's. Shaw's mouth parted, accepting North's tongue again, and when North pulled away again, this time it was North whose breathing sounded shattered.

"I love you so much. I love you so, so much. I love you more than anything ever, in my whole life, and I'm such a fucking piece of shit for not treating you the way you deserve. Please let me make it up to you."

Shaw opened his eyes, and he was shocked to see that North's eyes were red, and tear tracks glinted silver on his cheeks.

"North, it wasn't just you. I know I need to be better about being…direct. Honest, I mean. I need to stop getting in my head and thinking that I can flirt or seduce you into what I want; sometimes I don't know how to tell you because there's only been you and Jadon and Matty, and I feel uncomfortable about expressing that stuff because I had to bury it for so long. And part of me had these fantasies where you were always going to take care of things and make everything better—I don't know what I'm saying. I'm just trying to tell you that a lot of it is me."

"I will take care of you, though," North said. "I will. I'll do better."

"I know you will. But I need to do my part too. And I will." Shaw licked his lips; he still felt wrapped in clouds, hazy in the post-orgasmic rush. He found North's dick and ran his hand along it; the semi turned into a full-on erection in a matter of seconds. "I would really like you to fuck me."

North's eyes were still wet, but he blinked them clear, trying for another smirk. "Yeah?"

"Yes. Fuck me, North."

"God, you have no idea how hot that sounds."

"Fuck me right now."

North kissed him again. One hand slid between Shaw's legs, past his balls, already slick and circling as the kiss intensified. When North pulled back, he got his hand under Shaw's knee and pulled one leg over his shoulder. His finger breached Shaw, and Shaw made a weak noise as he tried to grind against the touch.

"Next time," North said, wiping his cheek on Shaw's calf, his smirk trembling, "I'm going to make you call me daddy."

"You are such an asshole, North McKinney!"

North's mouth was on Shaw's dick then, his finger moving until Shaw gasped and a nova of pleasure ignited behind his eyes. He decided, in the last fragments of conscious thought, that they could have that particular argument later.

Chapter 36

IN SOME WAYS, for North, the after-sex routine was better than the sex itself. Sex with Shaw was phenomenal; it was the best sex of North's life, and a lot of that had to do with the emotional component that had been missing from most of his previous relationships. But North had plowed his way through plenty of hot guys, and good sex was still just sex. Lying in bed with Shaw under his arm, listening to Shaw's heartbeat while Shaw tried to explain the social-justice imperative to never eat potato chips again, was something North had wanted for most of his life and only recently gotten. As far as he was concerned, sex didn't come within a mile of being as good as this.

"Come on," North said as Shaw launched into years 1970-1972 in his racial history of fried snacks. Rolling to his feet, North glanced around for his clothes. "Let's go pick up some groceries. Your fridge is empty, and I'm starving."

"I was just getting to the good part about Andy Capp's."

North pitched the jeggings at Shaw, then the Cuban collar shirt. "I'll give you a quarter for the gumball machine if you're good."

Shaw was already halfway into his clothes when he froze and, with stilted dignity, said, "I'm not a child."

North was still laughing when they piled into the GTO.

They picked up sandwiches and groceries at LeGrand's, a deli that had just enough stock for an emergency run like this, and then they went home. The inside of the GTO smelled like the meatball sandwich North had ordered. Shaw kept leaning into the bag and taking deep breaths.

"If you wanted a meatball sandwich," North said as they parked in Shaw's garage, "you should have ordered a meatball sandwich."

"I—"

"Which is why I suggested that you order a meatball sandwich."

"I don't want a meatball sandwich. I want a Reuben." His tone became a mimicry of North's. "Which is why I ordered the Reuben."

"Just for that," North said as he retrieved the keys from the ignition, "you can walk the long way around."

"What do you—North, no!"

But North had already seized the bags of food and was sprinting for the door. As soon as he was inside, he locked it behind him. Shaw tried the handle and then pounded on the door.

"Open up! This is not funny. It's cold!"

North waited until he heard angry footsteps moving away, and then he undid the lock. Humming, he made his way down the hall and into the kitchen. He started unpacking the cold stuff first, putting away the wedge of English cheddar, the Greek yogurt, the frozen pizza that Shaw had spent four minutes in front of the freezer case explaining was full of butylated hydroxyanisole and sodium ascorbate. He was still stowing the cold stuff when Shaw stomped into the kitchen, chafing his arms.

"Not funny, North!"

North offered his most innocent look.

"I could have gotten pneumonia, and—when did you buy ice cream sandwiches?"

"When you weren't looking. I think you were in the middle of your ecstasy about finding oat milk creamer."

"North, you can't—those are really, really bad for you."

North shoved the box into the freezer, closed the door, and leaned against the appliance. "Oops. But, here they are. I guess I'd better eat them; it's incredibly unethical to waste food with so many starving people in the world."

Shaw's face twisted at the catch-22. He must have decided to change the terms of battle because he said, "You can't lock someone out of the house, North. Not in the winter. I could have slipped and fallen and broken my neck. Or I could have frozen to death. Or I could have been raped by a...by a Yeti!"

"Good fucking luck to the Yeti," North muttered.

"What was that?"

"I said I didn't lock the door."

"You absolutely did."

"Nope."

With a wild noise of frustration, Shaw caught North's arm and towed him down the hallway. He stopped at the door that led to the garage. "This door, North. You locked this door. You thought you were so funny, and you locked me out in an arctic wasteland where I could have been mauled by caribou."

"I didn't lock the door. Look. It's not locked."

Shaw cast a suspicious glance at North and then checked the door. It opened. His mouth formed an O.

"You must have thought I locked it," North said. "I don't know how you got that idea in your head."

"You did lock it. And then, as soon as my back was turned, you unlocked it so you could gaslight me and—" All the color drained from Shaw's face.

North touched his arm. "Are you ok? Hey, I didn't—"

"How did you get the ice cream sandwiches?"

"Look, if you're really upset, I'll throw them out."

"North, how did you get them?"

"I waited until you were looking at the oat milk and then I put them in the basket. I put the frozen pizza on top of them. Why did you—"

"We have to go to the hospital," Shaw said. "It's still Sunday, right? Today is the last day of the con. We have to go to the hospital right now, North."

"What are you—"

But Shaw was already throwing open the door and stumbling out into the garage. Over his shoulder, he shouted, "I know how he did it. I just don't know why."

Chapter 37

THE VISITORS' ENTRANCE TO Barnes-Jewish Hospital led them into a lobby that, at mid-afternoon on a Sunday, was quiet and only sparsely populated. A larger woman, her thinning hair pushed behind her ears, was talking quietly into her phone and, from time to time, turning her face toward the windows. A man with a graying lumberjack's beard was sobbing into a handkerchief embroidered with teddy bears. On the back of the vinyl chairs, someone—North assumed a child—had applied what looked like a full sheet of stickers: stars, rainbows, and hearts.

"Fish," North said, wrinkling his nose as they crossed the lobby.

"It's better than that cheese you buy," Shaw said. "Brain cheese or whatever it is."

"Right, Shaw. Brain cheese."

"May I help you?" The secretary or receptionist or clerk or whatever his title was looked barely old enough to shave. He had paused in the middle of typing, hands poised dramatically over the keyboard, eyes exaggeratedly wide. "Hello?"

"We're here to see Leslie Hawkins," Shaw said. "Have you ever had brain cheese?"

The young man paused again, fingers dangling in the air. Then, with a disgusted noise, he checked the computer. "Ms. Hawkins has requested no visitors. I'm very sorry."

"It's an emergency."

"I'm very sorry."

"Could you call and ask—"

"I'm very sorry," the young man said in a tone that sounded a little more like *go fuck yourself*, and then he went back to typing.

North caught Shaw's arm, and they stepped away from the desk. They found a quiet spot along one wall, next to a fern that looked real and alive, but only barely. Shaw played with the brittle tips of a dead frond. Brown flecks snowed down to the linoleum.

"We have a couple of options," North said. "Even though I'm going to immediately regret saying this, we could call Jadon."

Shaw shook his head. "He's not going to make an exception for us."

"He might if you tell him who the real killer is."

"Not until I have proof."

"Maybe I could help you get proof if you'd tell me who you think did it."

Shaw cocked his head. "Nah," he said after a moment. "I like having you hanging on my every word. I'm going to make a lot of dramatic pronouncements." In a voice that echoed through the lobby, he proclaimed, "Let word go forth, from this day forward, there will be no brain cheese in my kingdom."

"I should try being single," North said, rubbing his eyes. "I should just try it. It honestly can't be that bad."

The elevator doors dinged. A young guy, probably only a few years younger than North, his hair long and in rainbow-dyed 'locs, emerged from the car. The man who followed was much older, shuffling on a walker, his face wasted and drawn.

"—bad enough that you're a faggot, but I have to come home, to my house that I pay for, and find you riding your dildos like you're the queen of Egypt. Up and down and up and down. If God meant you to put something up there, He'd have left an instruction manual."

The younger man stared at the linoleum, playing with his 'locs, and mumbled something about a car. Then he hustled toward the automatic doors.

"My car, you mean," the old man called after him. "You're going to get my car because you haven't paid for a damn thing your whole life."

The automatic doors whooshed shut behind the guy with 'locs. The older man chuffed as he inched forward on the walker. His eyes roved the lobby, obviously trying to catch someone looking at him—either to talk or to pick another fight, North wasn't sure; it was hard to tell with men like that.

"If he makes eye contact," North said, "I'm going to fold up that walker and shove it up his chute. I don't need God to leave me an instruction manual for that."

Laughing quietly, Shaw squeezed North's hand. "Get ready."

"For what?"

"You'll see."

"This is even more annoying than you not telling me what you figured out."

But Shaw shot down the hall, heading deeper into the hospital and darting around the next corner without looking back. Crossing his arms, North leaned against the wall, careful to keep his gaze from intersecting that of the man on the walker. The older man was still puffing and wheezing as he limped across the linoleum. The forced-air heating created its own noise, a steady whisper. North didn't even notice the new sound until it had grown significantly in volume: a whirring that could almost have blended in with the rest of the white noise, except that it had a slightly wet note to it. North had absolutely no idea what it could be.

Then the floor scrubber came around the corner. It was a big, blue plastic beast, a walk-behind model that was obviously self-propelled. Its scrubbers spun wildly, leaving a gleaming track in the linoleum as it moved down the hall at a surprisingly good clip.

"Hello?" the young man at the front desk demanded. The word rose in pitch and intensity. "Hello? Hello?"

The scrubber glided forward.

Drawn by the receptionist's voice, the man on the walker glanced back. He must have come to the same conclusion that North had already drawn— the scrubber was headed for him on a collision course—because he let out a deep-throated, "God damn," and tried to shuffle faster. Either the idea of turning out of the scrubber's path didn't occur to him, or he was just too damn stubborn. Again, it was hard to tell with that type.

"Hello," the receptionist squealed. "Hello, hello, hello." And then something must have clicked because he scrambled out of his chair and chased after the floor scrubber.

For a final moment, North entertained a Loony Tunes-esque fantasy of the scrubber sucking up the old man and spitting him out, shiny and clean, behind it. Then he jogged to the desk, closed the browser tab for a Discord chat about the top ten hottest elves—Legolas, North thought, easy—and found Leslie's room number.

It took less than thirty seconds. By the time he stepped away from the desk, Shaw was ambling down the hall, a huge grin on his face. The receptionist was still wrangling the scrubber; he'd managed to turn it from its collision course with the old man, but now it was plowing through a row of chairs, sending them skittering across the floor.

"There is no fucking way," North said, "you knew you were going to find a self-propelled floor scrubber."

Shaw raised his chin. "I'm a level-five psychic. I have access to fonts of preternatural knowledge the likes of which a mundane like you could never imagine."

"You randomly tried doors until you found something you could use as a distraction."

"I summoned a spirit guide: Old Jonas, the faithful Basset hound companion of Even Older Jonas, who was a janitor here for fifty years until he was killed by his own self-propelled floor scrubber."

"I hate you sometimes," North said as he stalked toward the elevator.

"Yeah," Shaw said, "but I still solved the case first."

Leslie was asleep when they found her. The room was obviously meant to be shared, but the partition was drawn back, and the second bed was empty.

The lights were off. A bouquet of mylar balloons hung above the bed: GET WELL SOON and BEST WISHES and one that North genuinely hoped had been designed for bachelorette parties, THIS BITCH NEEDS DICK. Like so many hospital rooms, it smelled of bleaching powder and distressed bodies.

"Am I supposed to wake her up?" North considered the sleeping woman: her choppy shag of silver hair was matted, and her already thin frame was mummy-like under the thin bedding. "She looks like she needs all the rest she can get."

"Not yet," Shaw said, already crossing the room to a laminate-wood wardrobe. After opening the door, he scanned the contents for a moment, then stretched up on tiptoe to collect a plastic bag from the upper shelf. Dropping back onto his heels, he displayed the bag: a pair of black flats, turquoise stirrup pants, a purse roughly the size of a mail carrier's bag, and a cellphone. "Tada."

North crossed his arm and raised an eyebrow. "You said, 'he.'"

"What?" Shaw's gaze turned to the bag as he opened it and drew out the phone.

"You said, 'he.' You had figured out how he did it. But we're in Leslie's room, and you're acting like that phone has key evidence."

"We already assumed that Leslie knew or saw something that made her a liability." Shaw tapped the phone's screen; it woke to his touch, but it remained locked. "I'm guessing that it has something to do with her phone; we know Leslie had something of a fetish for videos. If I'm wrong, we'll wait until she wakes up and ask her a few questions." He tapped the phone again and showed the passcode prompt.

"That's an older model," North said. "It'll take her fingerprint."

With a grin, Shaw carried the phone over to the bed. He turned Leslie's hand, extended her index finger, and touched it to the home button.

The screen stayed locked.

"Other hand," North said.

"I know, I know. They must have her on something good; she's out like a light."

This time, the phone's display changed to its home screen. Shaw tapped a few times until Leslie's stored videos were displayed. He played the most recent one.

The sound of gagging, choking, and spitting filled the room.

"Yeah, bitch," a familiar voice said. North couldn't quite place it; based on the slight echo from the stainless panels, he judged that the video had been recorded inside an elevator. "Take that cock."

More gagging was the only answer.

The video panned and tilted, and all of the sudden, Nacho was on the screen. He still wore the shirt and jacket of his hotel uniform, but his trousers and underwear were conspicuously missing. Not that there was much to see, because Nacho was using two hands to skullfuck a very skinny white boy who was kneeling in front of him.

"Yeah," Nacho grunted. "Yeah, choke on my dick."

"Looks like he has a type," North murmured.

Shaw cleared his throat.

"That could have been you if I'd left you alone for five more minutes."

"Oh please," Shaw said.

"Your breakout role."

"You are so immature sometimes. Nacho and I are just friends." A frown creased Shaw's mouth. "I don't recognize the other guy, although it's hard to tell from the back of his head. Does he look familiar to you?"

Before North could press the issue, the elevator doors dinged, and then the sound of them rattling open filled the background. The car rocked under the weight of a step, and then a man said, "Oh. Oh!"

Nacho didn't seem to have noticed; his pace didn't falter, and the frenzy contorting his face didn't relax.

Something hit the floor of the elevator car, making a boom.

The camera panned left.

"I'm sorry," the man stammered. "I had no idea."

On the phone's screen, a water bottle rolled across the floor. A man darted in to snatch it up. For a moment, all North could see was thinning brown hair and a boxy blazer. Then the man stumbled back, out of frame.

The camera kept panning.

Clarence O'Neill stared into the camera as he shoved the water bottle he had retrieved into a swag bag. Horror twisted his features. Then the elevator doors slid shut, and the camera panned back toward the sound of grunts and gagging and flesh slapping flesh.

Chapter 38

ON THE DRIVE to the Royal Excalibur, North pressed the GTO as hard as he could, sliding between cars that seemed stationary on I-64. Clouds congealed on the horizon, turning the day gray and thinning the winter sunlight.

"Try him again," North said.

"I am trying him again. He's not answering."

With a grunt, North shook his head and accelerated. "That feels about right: Jadon was popping up like a jack-in-the-box until we need him."

Shaw only bent over his phone and kept trying.

When they got to the Royal Excalibur, hotel staff were dismantling the Queer Expectations registration station: loading the folding tables onto rolling carts, stacking chairs, taking down the banner. On a Sunday afternoon, the only other person in the lobby was a bored-looking young woman at the front desk who was teasing out her hair in a compact mirror.

North took off toward the banquet hall, with Shaw at his side. The double doors to Tintagel were closed, but an amplified voice still reached North. A woman was speaking, and he thought he recognized the voice—Heidi, the blogger. When he yanked open the door, the smell of fish rolled over him (with notes of lemon, Sterno, and overwarm bodies), and the words became clear.

"—tragedies this year, most of all the loss of one of the clearest, brightest voices in our genre," Heidi was saying from a podium on the far side of the room. The lights had been dimmed, and on the wall behind her, a projector displayed the words *Queer Expectations Awards Banquet*. A row of chairs was lined up next to her on the portable stage, but only one was occupied: Clarence sat, legs crossed, smoothing his thinning hair with one hand. "Thank you, all of you, for pulling together. We're a family, and supporting each other, especially during hard times like this, is what we do."

Shaw's gaze roved the room. Without a word, he took off at a run, sticking to the perimeter to avoid the maze of tables and chairs. North moved in the opposite direction, following one wall of the banquet hall as he approached the stage.

The text on the projector changed: *Queer Expectations – Lifetime Achievement Award.*

"Tonight, though," Heidi said, "we're here to celebrate the contributions and impact of someone who helped the gay romance genre coalesce into what we know today. He's been writing in this genre longer than most people have been reading it." With a grin, Heidi added, "For that matter, he's been writing in this genre longer than some of us have been alive."

Clarence mugged for the room, a mock grimace. Rodney and Jerry sat near the stage, Rodney (or was it Jerry?) snapping pictures of Clarence fanatically. A chuckle rippled through the audience at Clarence's expression, but the faces were tired and strained, and with swaths of empty seats separating them, the clumps of friends and cliques had never been clearer. Nothing like a little murder and mayhem to make people draw lines around their little tribes, North thought. He was still twenty yards from the stage. He gave the room a quick scan, but he'd lost sight of Shaw.

"If you haven't read a book by Clarence O'Neill, you're missing out. Clarence writes a little bit of it all: sexy, sweet, funny, heartwarming. My personal recommendation, if you're looking for a place to start, is his Home on the Range series. On a blog review, this is where I'd include five eggplant emoji, because those cowboys get into some delectable trouble. But that's just a jumping off point. Clarence's work spans subgenres. He's got a lifetime's worth of series and standalones. And I'm sure there's more great stuff to come; for those of you who are joining us for the first time, you might not know that agents and editors attend our awards banquet. I see a few familiar faces out there, and I know they'll want to talk to Clarence tonight and congratulate him—and maybe fight each other for his next book."

Another titter. North spotted a couple of the faces he thought Heidi was referring to: a woman in an ill-fitting jacket, her eyes locked on her phone, fingers flying; a tired-looking man in a plum-colored cardigan that Shaw would love. North stopped at the stairs up to the stage.

"Without further ado, I give you Clarence O'Neill, winner of the Queer Expectations Lifetime Achievement Award."

The applause was generous if not overwhelming. The woman in the ill-fitting jacket looked up long enough to slap her hands together once. The man in the cardigan leaned forward in his seat as he clapped. Clarence smiled, smoothed his hair again, and stepped toward the podium. Heidi handed him a trophy that North thought might have been an abstract representation of two men kissing, and then she hugged Clarence and stepped back. The applause died out quickly as Clarence moved toward the mic.

"Thank you so much," Clarence said. "This is an honor, and I'm proud and pleased to be recognized by the readers and writers of this genre." Shifting the trophy to the crook of one arm, he reached into his jacket with his free hand and produced a stack of notecards. "I'm a writer, so I took the liberty of writing down exactly what I wanted to say. You only get one chance at a lifetime-achievement award, after all."

A trickle of indulgent laughs answered him.

"When I began to write romance, I did so because I believed that the ability to imagine a happy ending for fictional characters is the first step toward finding our own happily ever after. That ability to imagine the inner world of another person, fictional or not, is one of the things that sets humans apart from animals. To then take that understanding of another person and to use it to tell a story about a world that's better than this one, a world where good people find love and belonging, where bad people receive their just deserts, a world that reminds people that to be human is to seek out meaningful relationships that make us more than we could be on our own—well, I think that's quintessentially human as well. My first book—"

He cut off at the sound of North's boots ringing out on the platform. Then his gaze cut toward Heidi. Heidi's face was blank with confusion for a moment. Then she stepped to the side and stage-whispered, "Mr. McKinney, I'm not sure—"

"Sorry, folks," North said. "We're just going to take a minute of your time, and then you can finish up your meal and the banquet and the convention."

"I don't understand," Clarence said, the words split between North and Heidi. "What is he—"

"You can keep that statue thing if you want," North said, "and I'll even give you five seconds to wrap up your speech. Then we're going."

A large man at the back of the audience barked a laugh and then went silent when his neighbor elbowed him.

"What?" Clarence said.

"Time to go, Clarence. You came pretty close to getting away with it, but you overreached when you tried to get rid of Leslie."

Speakers overhead squawked, and North—along with everybody else in the room—flinched. Then Shaw's voice boomed out: "Overreaching is the classic error of villains—and tragic heroes—in classical literature."

Massaging one ear, North said, "Not that Shaw would know, since he got an F on his Oedipus paper."

"I didn't get an F. I had to rewrite it because the instructor didn't tell me beforehand that sexually explicit images were not part of traditional literary criticism."

Clarence was frozen, his face sallow and waxy.

"What are you talking about?" Heidi said. "Mr. McKinney, you need to leave, or I'll ask hotel security to—"

"I'm talking about Clarence killing Scotty Carlson."

Clarence rocked back on his heels. "I didn't—I never would have—" With visible effort, he tried to pull himself together and said, "Even if I'd wanted to, I couldn't have—"

"You could, and you did. You'd been carrying a grudge against Scotty for years, but it reached a turning point when Scotty got that editor job at Bolingbroke. Your writing career was over; oh, sure, you still turned out books, and you might have even been planning that suspense series you told us about, but you weren't really selling in significant numbers anymore. That must have frustrated you. It must have made you crazy, actually. Here you are, one of the founding authors in mainstream gay romance, and nobody's buying your stuff. And then Scotty comes along, and not only does he outsell you exponentially but he also humiliates you, time and again, every chance he gets. He's young. He's successful. And he's the one Bolingbroke chooses as the editor for their new imprint. Not you."

"This is ridiculous. I'm not a lunatic; I wouldn't kill someone over something like that. Honestly, it was kind of a relief. I can focus on my own writing." Then, passing a shaky hand over his mouth, he added, "Anyway, Yasmin did it. They caught her. You caught her."

"We caught Yasmin putting something in water bottles. But she didn't kill Scotty Carlson. She was making a last-ditch effort at publicity, trying to save the con by turning this whole thing into a stunt. The same reason she'd invented that story about the death threats and hired Shaw and me in the first place. She needed this year to be a huge success, and she thought a spectacle like death threats and private investigators could give the con exactly the jolt it needed. Of course, she didn't realize that she was giving you the perfect cover. As soon as you heard about the death threats, you saw your opportunity to kill Scotty. Everybody would be thinking about the death threats; nobody would look twice at you.

"No! I couldn't have done—"

"Sure, you could have. You were with Yasmin the night she bought Scotty's preferred brand of bottled water. You were with her when she locked it up in the storeroom. After that, it was easy. You waited until everyone had gone back to their rooms. You hurried back to Straub's and bought more of the same water. You took it up to your room, and you crushed up Adderall and added it to each bottle. Then you put the tampered water in your swag bag; everyone is carrying a swag bag, so nobody would look twice. The next morning, you took the service elevator to avoid running into anyone from the con. You walked into the storeroom with Yasmin. You knocked a bottle of cleaner off the shelf, and while Yasmin was busy cleaning it up, while her back was turned, you pulled the water out of your bag and put it on the cart, swapping it with the bottles she had bought. The perfect switch; she never noticed. The same thing with the locked door to the banquet hall. You made sure she saw you lock it the night before, and the next morning, when she wasn't looking, you unlocked it. That way, if anyone checked, it would look like the door had been open all night, which meant anyone could have gotten access to the water. You knew Scotty was taking antidepressants. You knew the

Adderall would interact with his medication. All you had to do was sit back and wait."

"I didn't. I didn't do that. I didn't do any of that." Clarence glanced around, as though appealing to the crowd. Heidi took a step back, her face frozen with horror. "I did not do this. Yasmin did it, Yasmin did—"

"No," North said. "Yasmin didn't research this as carefully as you did. She was opening each bottle, breaking the seal. You couldn't take that risk; you removed the caps whole and then replaced them. There are plenty of YouTube videos that show how; it's easy. That way, the seal remained intact, in case anybody happened to check. Karen did notice, by the way, and the other authors must have as well, so that was a smart move."

Clarence was shaking his head.

"Shaw?" North called out.

Behind Clarence, the projection changed, and the video from Leslie's phone began. There was no sound, but sound wasn't really the point. Gasps ran through the audience at the graphic sex. Then a few nervous giggles. And then, when the camera panned across the fallen water bottle and Clarence, shocked silence.

"You took the service elevator," North said again, his voice pitched only for Clarence now, "because you didn't want to bump into anyone from the con. But you hadn't planned on Leslie. You hadn't planned on her talking Nacho into filming an impromptu porno. And she saw everything. Worse, she recorded everything. You must not have realized what that meant until later because you still swapped the water, but once you understood that she was a threat, you had to eliminate her. You threw yourself down the stairs at the costume party, taking Karen and Leslie with you. There wasn't anyone in a gimp mask. Then, when that didn't work, you went after Leslie the old-fashioned way, with a knife. You still didn't get the job done." With a smile, North added, "When I knew you were behind this, I have to admit, I was a little embarrassed that you got away. Then I remembered: you run marathons."

Clarence gave one last, abortive shake of his head. Then he began to cry, wiping his face with his free hand, hugging the trophy tight with the other. It took him two tries to get the words out.

"I didn't mean to kill him."

Chapter 39

THEY SAT IN THE hotel security office while they waited for Jadon and Cerise. It was a cramped space, stinking of Funyuns and musty fabric upholstery. In addition to filing cabinets, a desk, and a bank of monitors that showed rotating feeds from security cameras, the hotel's head of security—a tiny woman with a short, graying afro—had added only a single personal touch: what Shaw guessed was an original poster for the 1971 film *Shaft*.

"Just so you know," North said, "it's going to be a lot easier for you if you confess. You don't have to say anything to us, but keep that in mind."

Clarence nodded, his face vacant.

Dropping into the seat next to Clarence, Shaw said, "I read your book. The one about the prank wars, where the guy puts a laxative into his neighbor's workout shake. That's what this was supposed to be like, wasn't it?"

After a moment, Clarence gave another nod. One corner of his mouth quirked. He wiped his face with both hands. "That's all it was supposed to be. That's all. He laughed at me. He'd been laughing at me for years. And last year, he laughed at how angry I got, at how my hands were shaking. I went back to the hotel that night. I couldn't sleep; I kept turning it over and over in my head, all the things he'd said to me about being old and pathetic and lonely. The idea popped into my head. It was like a lightbulb turning on; the simile couldn't have been more perfect, this sudden, bright understanding. I knew that higher doses of Adderall could make people aggressive. In some people, it produces tremor. I'd read all about it before I decided to start using it to help me focus. I wanted people to see the angry Scotty—not the cool, amused, sniping anger he was always performing, but out of control. The mean, petty, tantrum-throwing Scotty behind the scenes, who terrorized Yasmin and anyone else who came within his private orbit."

"And then?" North said.

"And then I fell asleep, and the next day, it was like a hallucination. I couldn't believe I'd been considering it. We finished the convention. I went home. I kept writing. I didn't have anything to do with Scotty. Then, a few months ago, one of his posts showed up in my feed. He'd gotten the job at Bolingbroke, the same job I'd applied for. I lost my mind. It was like that night in the hotel again: part of my brain turned on, and all I could do was think about how I could humiliate Scotty."

"What about the death threats?" North asked. "The ones Yasmin was telling everyone about?"

"I didn't have anything to do with those. What you said earlier, about Yasmin creating them herself, seems likely. When I heard about them, though, it was like a sign. I realized I could do this. I could make Scotty look like a fool, make him look like a shaky old man who'd lost his mind, and I could walk away, and nobody would ever look at me. A high enough dose, and he'd make a total fool of himself. It was petty, I know that. But Scotty was petty. He brought out pettiness in everyone around him."

"But you didn't just poison Scotty."

"I told you: I was out of my mind. There was this thing in me, this animal, and all I could think about was every slight, every jab, the ways all of them had mocked me and insulted me and trashed my work. You've met them; you know how vicious they all are. Besides, it was the only way to keep from drawing attention to myself."

The hum of the PC's fan was the only answer. Then North said, "I call bullshit. You knew exactly what you were doing, and you knew exactly what it would do to Scotty."

Clarence shook his head. "I'd read about serotonin syndrome, of course. That was another thing that I'd learned in my research before I started using the medicine myself. But I'd completely forgotten about it."

"Selective memory," North said. "Convenient."

"Even if I'd remembered, why would I have suspected that Scotty was using a prescription antidepressant? Why would I have had any reason to believe he was unhappy? His performance for the whole world was that he was the perfect gay: young, attractive, athletic, an artistic genius, sexually voracious but in a healthy monogamous relationship. I didn't think Scotty was depressed; if anything, my motivation came from believing exactly the opposite, that he was happy and successful in spite of how poorly he treated everyone around him."

North made a noise in his throat that was the nonverbal equivalent of calling bullshit again.

"What did you do?" Shaw asked. "Here, I mean. At the convention."

"You got most of it correct. I was with Yasmin when she bought Scotty's preferred brand of water Wednesday night; she complained about it, and I can't say I blame her, so I knew who the water was for. I could have figured it out anyway, though—I had volunteered to help her with everything, and I knew Scotty would make excessive demands for star treatment."

"Did you know he was blackmailing Yasmin for free publicity?" North asked.

"No. Although I did wonder why he had purchased so much of our advertising space—that isn't usually Scotty's style."

"And after you learned that the water was for Scotty?" Shaw said.

"As your friend said, I went and bought more of it that night. It's not really that difficult to remove the caps with the seal intact. I added a double dose to each bottle, and then I replaced the caps. I stored the bottles in my swag bag. The next morning, I tried the service elevator." A shocked laugh burst out of him. "Leslie was there. And those men. And I was so surprised I dropped my bag. One of the bottles rolled free. I grabbed it without thinking. Leslie turned to see what was happening, and as I was grabbing the bottle, I saw her phone. I knew she might connect me to the water later, but that's one part you got wrong: I wasn't worried at the time because, of course, I thought it was just going to be a prank."

"When Scotty had that terrible reaction, though," Shaw said, "things changed, didn't they?"

"Yes. I thought I could play up the angle of the mysterious person writing threatening notes. That's why I did what I did at the party, and that's why I made up the story about the man in the gimp mask."

"Endangering two women's lives in the process," North said from where he slouched against the filing cabinets.

"Then I found out Scotty had died, and—and it was like I was in that hallucination again. Nothing seemed real. Or maybe, I don't know, maybe it all seemed too real, the way dreams are all-consuming when you're dreaming them. I knew Leslie could link me to Scotty's death. I knew she had to…she had to be neutralized." North made another of those noises, but Clarence's blank façade didn't shift. "I still can't believe…" His breathing was raspy, and his head came up, his eyes suddenly fixing on Shaw. "She's ok, isn't she? She's all right?"

"Why'd you stay?" North asked. "You wanted to run; did you stay just for the award ceremony?"

Clarence waited, as though still expecting an answer to his question. After a moment, he said, "Yes and no. For the meeting after the ceremony, actually."

"With the agents and editors?" Shaw said.

"It's one thing to send them a cover letter and tell them you won an award. It's another thing entirely to be in the same room, to shake hands, to smile and describe your next book and why you think it'll go to auction, with every major publishing house bidding for the rights. I thought the death threats and the attack on Leslie had bought me time, and then Yasmin did something unbelievably stupid, and suddenly I was in the clear. I could breathe. I slept like a baby last night." He seemed to hear his own words, and a patchy flush covered his cheeks. "It didn't seem like a risk, staying."

The door to the security office opened, and Cerise stepped into the room, followed by Jadon. Shaw's gaze skated away, studying the *Shaft* poster, Richard Roundtree's sideburns, the mean streets of Harlem lit up in orange behind him. When he looked back, Jadon's sandy-dark eyes were still hard and waiting for him.

"Tell him what you told us," Shaw said quietly.

Clarence didn't answer; the color had drained from his face, and he looked much, much older.

"Come on," North said, guiding Shaw out of the room with a hand on his shoulder.

When the door closed behind them, Shaw withdrew his phone, ended the recording, and emailed it to Jadon. Jadon's response was immediate: a smiley face and a thumbs-up.

"God," Shaw said. "They're going to hit him hard."

"No less than he deserves," North said, urging Shaw forward again, his hand still big and warm on Shaw's shoulder. "He's a psychopath."

"I think he was telling the truth, North. I don't think he meant to kill Scotty. In fact, I think that's partly why this case was so hard—so much motive, but no intention."

North grunted. "Maybe. But you heard him: Leslie had to be 'neutralized.' He can't pretend that was an unfortunate accident."

Shaw was silent as they moved down the service corridor, heading for the parking garage.

North's phone buzzed, and the bigger man fumbled it out of his pocket and silenced the alarm.

Shaw groaned.

"I'll do it myself," North said. He kissed Shaw's temple, scrubbed a hand through the poufy hair, and added, "I want you to go home and feel better."

"I'm not going to feel better. I'm going to feel miserable. I liked him, North. And I liked his books. And I agreed with a lot of what he said. And he did awful, awful things."

"I know," North said. "So I want you to go home. I want you to take a hot bath and squirt goat's milk straight from the teat all over yourself and have Truck give you a massage."

"Pass. Truck's massages get way too sexual. I had to use four safety pins on the towel last time."

"Of course that's the only part of that scenario you object to," North murmured.

"What?"

"Nothing. Are you sure you want to do this?"

"I'm very fucking sure. Let's go bust Tony Gillman." In a thoughtful voice, Shaw added, "I'm going to kick him in the balls. I think that's going to make me feel a lot better."

Chapter 40

BUT SUNDAY NIGHT WAS a bust; they followed Gillman in the boxy Toyota he retrieved from the second parking spot in his garage, and he led them to a stretch of south Grand where he clearly liked to cruise. Shaw was bait, standing in the black, February cold for three hours before North called it off, with no sign that Gillman had done anything but drive the street over and over again, looking for prey. Then it took Shaw all night to get warm again, even curled up inside North's arms, wearing an adult snowsuit and lying under an electric blanket.

They tried again on Monday. Sitting in the GTO, Shaw gave himself a once-over, tugging on the sailor-stripe crop top, the bedazzled denim cutoffs that barely covered his balls and featured the words *Plug It* on the rear end, and a pair of North's old Redwings (which were much too big for Shaw). An old hoodie lay across his lap.

"You are literally going to freeze your tits off," North said.

Shaw cupped himself suggestively and then said, "Don't say tits. It's sexist."

North beckoned him over.

Rolling his eyes, Shaw leaned in for a kiss, which North delivered. It was surprisingly slow and sweet until it ended with North twisting Shaw's nipple. Viciously.

"North, dammit! Oh my Jesus, Mary, and Buddha. I think you ripped it off."

Massaging Shaw's chest gently, North laughed and kissed him again. "I like your tits where they are," North said when he pulled back. "I don't want them freezing off. I'll be the bait tonight."

Shaw couldn't help it. He started to laugh.

The surprise on North's face slowly transformed into outrage. "Is there something funny about what I just said?"

Somehow—Shaw wasn't sure how, exactly—he managed to suppress the laughter. "No, of course not. It's just, we asked Jadon about his previous victims, and he basically told us I'm Gillman's type."

"His type isn't expired twinks with hair like Scooby Doo got plugged into an electrical outlet while he was still wet."

"See, that kind of lip is just one more reason why you'd make a terrible rent boy. Hustler. Sex worker. God, all this tit talk really got in my head; you're a bad influence."

"I would be a fucking fantastic rent boy. What the fuck is wrong with you? Cars would be lined up for a fucking mile with johns wanting to pick me up."

"Yeah, definitely." And then, in an artificially deep voice, Shaw said, "First I'll drill you, then I'll drill your sink. Fifty dollars."

The outraged expression on North's face deepened. "Is that supposed to be me? That doesn't even make sense. Nobody drills a sink, Shaw. And fifty dollars?" He made a strangled noise. "Get your ass over here so I can rip your other tit off."

In that same voice, Shaw said, "You need Daddy to lay some pipe? Copper or PEX?"

"You are un-fucking-believable."

Grinning, Shaw slipped out of the GTO. The cold was a slap that made his eyes sting; a few snowflakes swirled around him. He shut the door, waved, and strode up the block of south Grand. North rolled past in the GTO. Shaw was pretty sure North was trying to give him the finger before he pulled away.

Tugging on the hoodie, Shaw checked the can of pepper gel in its pocket. Then he picked a spot near the end of the block. Even with the extra layer, the cold bit into him, and the bare skin of his legs burned. On the opposite corner, in the salt-and-ash swirl of snow under a streetlamp, another boy was working. He looked much younger. Too young, shifting his weight in white sneakers, standing too far back from the curb, groping himself halfheartedly through faded Levi's when a flatbed rolled past. The headlights picked out his features, raking light across his face: soft brown skin, soft brown eyes, tape across the bridge of his nose. Then the flatbed was gone, and the street was dark again.

Shaw knew he needed to stay in position. They had followed Gillman here again; Gillman would make a pass soon, checking out the boys on offer. Gillman had resisted the temptation last night, but the urge would be growing, rising, getting stronger. Would he be able to resist again tonight? Shaw doubted it. He tried to drag his mind away from the boy on the opposite corner; he told himself to stay focused.

But thirty seconds later, Shaw was jogging across the street, the oversized Redwings causing him to slip in a slushy patch near a manhole.

"Hey," he said.

The boy jerked his chin in acknowledgment. Up close, Shaw realized he couldn't have been more than fifteen. He wore expensive-looking Nikes, and he had a gold chain around his neck.

"Shaw." He pointed at himself.

"Nikshay. Nik."

"Cool," Shaw said, chafing his arms through the hoodie. The breeze kicked up again; particles of snow and ice whipped against Shaw's bare legs like embers. A boxy car rolled toward them, and Shaw's heartbeat accelerated. He glanced at Nik, who shrugged, and Shaw moved to the curb. He shouldered free of the hoodie, exposing of much as himself as he could, and tugged on his balls through the denim. The car slowed and then sped up; through the glass, Shaw glimpsed a woman who had to be in her mid-sixties, mouth forming a horrified O.

"Fuck," Shaw said as he rejoined Nik. "Not really my type anyway. I like them to have those really, really dangly balls."

Nik snorted a laugh, and he looked surprised by his own reaction.

"You're new at this, huh?"

One eyebrow went up in silent question as Nik tried to harden his expression.

"The shoes," Shaw said. "And the chain. You haven't hocked them yet. Or had somebody take them."

After a wide-eyed moment, the kid shrugged and looked away.

A minivan rolled to the curb; the apron of light from the streetlamp offered a faint impression of the driver, with his undercut hair and his white tank and a tribal tattoo on one well-developed bicep. Behind him, even more faintly, the light picked out twin car seats.

With a challenging glance at Shaw, Nik approached the minivan, obviously trying for the casual hustle that he must have noticed in other boys. The driver took a long look and rolled his window down a crack. He said something that Shaw couldn't hear, and Nik shook his head. The driver said something again, and Nik answered, and then the driver pulled away from the curb with a screech of tires.

When Nik came back, he was hugging himself. "White-bread suburban daddy wants to pay fifteen bucks to get sucked off. Fuck him."

The whine of the minivan's engine faded into the tinsel of lights farther up Grand; the cloud of exhaust was sickly sweet, hanging in its wake.

"Do your parents know you're out here?" Shaw said.

Nik looked him up and down. "You're blowing up my spot. Go work the other side of the street."

"Better to stick together. Sometimes these guys, they like options. Sometimes they want two at a time. And sometimes, stupid people won't do stupid things if they're outnumbered."

"Yeah? I can take care of myself." Angling his body away from the street, Nik unfolded a pocketknife, the dusty light glancing off the steel.

"Ok."

Nik tucked the knife away again. For a moment, they both stood there, the wind picking up enough to chase a clamshell takeout container down the street. Nik shifted his weight from foot to foot.

"My parents are dead, anyway, so fuck them."

"Oh," Shaw said. "I'm really sorry to hear that."

"Who fucking cares? I can take care of myself."

The cold cut through Shaw's hoodie; his legs felt like they were ice. Even the glittering lights on distant blocks were cold. The only warm thing seemed to be their clouds of breath mingling. A dusting of fine dark hairs covered Nik's upper lip, and Shaw wasn't sure if that was because Nik didn't have a razor, or if he thought it made him look older, or if he was really so young he hadn't started shaving.

"Yeah," he said. "I can see that. But don't you have a guardian or something?"

Nik threw him a furious look.

"Or your own place to stay or something," Shaw said hurriedly.

A few heavy, sullen moments passed before Nik said, "Yeah. My Uncle Pranith. My parents left everything to him, and the first time he caught me sucking Lucas's cock, he threw me out. Fuck him. I've got friends. I can figure it out."

"You know, he's probably supposed to hold that money in trust for you. It's not just his."

"Yeah?" Nik sneered. "What are you, some kind of sex accountant?"

"Oh my God, why is North missing this conversation?"

"Who's North?"

Shaking his head, Shaw said, "Never mind. Listen, I'm not an accountant. And I can't promise I can do anything. But I—I have a friend who might be able to help. You should call. Or stop by his office. Borealis, can you remember that?"

Nik gave a one-shouldered shrug. Fifteen, aching, scared, and alone, and still too cool to care.

"Seriously," Shaw said. "And if you need a place to crash tonight—"

But then a boxy sedan rolled out of the darkness, and Shaw forgot what he'd been about to say. Light flashed across a familiar logo. Toyota. Then the weak ambient light offered the outline of the man behind the wheel, a familiar silhouette after the nights of watching him driving into his Clayton parking garage.

When Nik took a step forward, Shaw caught his arm. "My turn."

"Fuck that, I saw him first and—"

"Trust me," Shaw said. "You don't want this one."

The boy was still trying to figure that out when Shaw jogged to the curb. He slipped the hoodie down from his shoulders, turned three-quarters of the way, and shot his hips so that the streetlight's glare would sparkle across the bedazzled words on his ass.

The window rolled down.

"Hey," Shaw said with what he honest-to-God hoped was a seductive smile.

Only the rumble of the Toyota's engine.

"Forty bucks," Shaw said, "and you can shoot in my mouth. Or if you want—"

"Yeah."

Shaw's pulse pounded in his ears.

"What the hell are you waiting for? An invitation?"

"Sorry," Shaw said, grabbing the door handle. "Thanks."

He slid into the car. Warmth blanketed him, and he closed the door firmly and rolled up the window. The smell of sweat, CVS aftershave, and stale cigarette smoke came in on his next breath. The man in the driver's seat was Tony Gillman. He matched the photos Ronnie had provided—the dark hair, the bags under his eyes, the slight bulldog cast to his features. He was staring at Shaw.

"For fuck's sake, don't tell me you're new at this." He spread his knees. "Get to work."

"Could we go somewhere private?"

"We're going somewhere private. Don't worry about that. I want your mouth on my cock, and I don't want to feel your teeth."

"But the kid," Shaw said, glancing over his shoulder. "I mean, I don't want to do it here."

Gillman's posture changed: knees drawing together, shoulders tightening, a dark intensity to his eyes. "Ok," he said. "We'll go someplace private. How does that sound?"

"Yeah, great."

"Put your hand on my dick."

Trying to hide a grimace, Shaw reached over and palmed Gillman, not quite hard, through his pair of chinos. Gillman grunted. His eyes hadn't left Shaw's face.

"That's it?"

"Um." Shaw cast about. "It's so big," he tried.

Gillman was silent.

"Daddy?" Shaw offered, and he sent up a silent prayer to whatever numinous spirit was in charge of his sex life that North McKinney would never hear about any of this.

With a growl deep in his throat, Gillman shifted into drive, and they pulled into the street. Shaw tried to pull his hand away, saw the flash of irritation in Gillman's face, and gave Gillman's dick a few light pats.

"Just keeping this guy awake and interested," Shaw said in answer to the look Gillman shot him.

To Shaw's surprise, Gillman barked a laugh. "Jesus. You are really going to earn those forty dollars, cunt."

"Oh. Boy. Well, I'm not super good at dirty talk, but, just so you know, that's a really offensive word. Like, it's not just a nickel-and-dime one. So you probably shouldn't use it."

Another laugh came back in reply, Gillman shaking his head. "I'm going to have fun with you."

"Yep," Shaw said, giving Gillman's now fully erect dick another friendly pat. "We're going to have lots of fun."

They went down the next side street, and then Gillman cut down an alley, pulling to a stop on a narrow asphalt parking strip that was tucked behind a clapboard building with the washed-out signs for a Russian Orthodox church and a laundromat. The spot was perfect for what Gillman liked to do, Shaw realized. It was completely hidden from the street. Even somebody turning down the alley was likely to overlook them on this tiny parking pad.

"Now," Shaw said, "forty dollars is the base, but if you go up to sixty, I'll put on lip balm, and for eighty I'll hum 'Yankee Doodle' while I—"

Gillman was faster than Shaw expected, one hand shooting out to seize Shaw's hair. For an instant, Shaw assumed that Gillman had decided to move things along, dragging Shaw down to his cock. That was a mistake. Instead, Gillman slammed Shaw's head against the dash. Taken by surprise, expecting Gillman to pull instead of push, Shaw never had a chance to resist. He managed at the last moment to turn his head, catching the blow on the side of his head instead of breaking his nose, but the force of impact still made his vision explode with stars. He threw an elbow, but his position made it impossible to do anything more than thump against Gillman's arm. Gillman pounded his head into the dash again. And then again. And then again. And then again.

For a moment, Shaw's world was a series of white strobes. Then he came back, shocked by the sound of ragged breathing that he only distantly realized was his own. One side of his head was wet. His ear felt huge and inflamed. But worst was the disorientation and the pain that made it difficult to think clearly. So difficult, in fact, that for a moment, he didn't remember where he was. A car. Someone's car.

The door opened. Cold air rushed in, electrifying, and a strong hand grabbed Shaw by the hoodie and hauled him out of the seat. Gillman's face rushed into view. Gillman. Shaw remembered part of it now. The car. The frozen darkness of South Grand. Then Gillman threw him to the ground. Broken pieces of glass and asphalt bit into Shaw's cheek, his hands, his bare legs. He glimpsed something long. A baseball bat. He rolled, moving from instinct now.

The first blow from the bat caught him on the shoulder, Shaw understood dimly, instead of the back of the head. That probably saved his life. The pain was distant, still coming down the line, barely more than a long white lick. Shaw kept rolling.

The next blow caught him on the upper arm, glancing off muscle. Shaw kept rolling, scrabbling at the ancient asphalt.

The next blow caught him on the thigh, and then another in rapid succession, low on the back. They didn't have as much force behind them. Gillman was panting. Shaw came up against clapboard siding. He tried to squirm away, but the bat came down again.

This time, the side of the building saved him: the bat clipped the boards, which slowed its passage so that when it connected with Shaw's ribs, it only drove the breath out of him instead of shattering bone. Shaw's eyes and chest burned. He wheezed, flopping on his back, trying to get air into his lungs.

Gillman loomed over him. He was still drawing those rapid, overly excited breaths. His bulldog features were trembling. He licked his lips. He brought the bat up again.

Shaw kicked out, catching Gillman in the side of the knee. He felt something pop, and Gillman's face went blank. Then he screamed. Stumbling, he tried to support himself without putting additional weight on his injured knee. Shaw took the opportunity to scoot along the side of the church, putting distance between himself and Gillman. He fumbled in his pockets. The pepper gel was gone. He'd lost it rolling across the asphalt, or maybe when Gillman had yanked him out of the car. Shaw scanned the parking pad.

Then his fingers closed over the canister, still safely in the hoodie's pocket—he'd missed it somehow in that first, panicked search. Drawing out the canister, he retracted the plastic safety lock that covered the trigger. He aimed the gel at Gillman, who was hopping on one foot, still screaming. With a steadying breath, Shaw depressed the button, and pepper gel hit Gillman in the shoulder, the chin, the cheek, the eye, the nose. Shaw held the button down until the canister was empty. The fumes, even at a distance, made his eyes water.

For a moment, Shaw sat where he was, his head leaned back against the clapboard church. Then, with a shuddering breath, he got onto his knees. Then he got to his feet. As adrenaline ebbed, pain was rushing in, and he had to shuffle to the alley as his hip and thigh and shoulder protested every movement.

The GTO was rolling sedately along the side street; North would have assumed—apparently foolishly—that everything had gone according to plan. But North must have seen Shaw, must have understood that something had gone terribly wrong, because the GTO leaped forward, engine roaring. It slewed to a stop at the edge of the parking pad, and North burst out of the car.

"Are you all right?"

"Yeah." Shaw waved at Gillman. "He—"

Shaw never had a chance to finish. North gave him a final, assessing look, and then turned and sprinted toward Gillman. He hit him at full speed in a flying tackle that sent both men to the ground. Gillman screamed again. When they skidded to a stop, North was on top, and he reared back and landed a right hook that snapped Gillman's head to the side.

Sirens blared.

North threw another punch; the crack of Gillman's nose breaking ricocheted back from the clapboard.

Lights swept along the side street.

"North, get off him." Shaw stumbled forward, body already stiff and likely to get stiffer. "We've got to get pictures."

North's face was twisted, inhuman with rage. He didn't seem to hear anything. When his fist came back, his knuckles had split, and blood ran to his wrist.

"Get off him," Shaw said, catching North's arm before he could land another blow. North twisted, and for a moment, Shaw thought North meant to hit him instead. Then understanding penetrated whatever was fogging North's thoughts, and his features relaxed slightly. Shaw shook his arm and said again, "Get off him."

"Fine," North muttered. Road rash covered one temple where he had hit the asphalt when he tackled Gillman. "Take a picture, and then I'll go back to beating him to death with my bare hands."

As soon as North was clear of the frame, Shaw began snapping pictures on the phone: Gillman, bruised and bloody; then, after North toed the bat and rolled it next to Gillman, more pictures of Gillman and the bat.

Shaw passed over his phone. "Now me," he instructed as he lay down on the asphalt, face turned away from North and the camera's lens. The parking pad was freezing, and without the rush of adrenaline to buffer him, it felt like instant frostbite against all the acres of exposed skin. Broken pieces of asphalt, loose stones, beads of tempered glass—they bit into Shaw's belly and thighs.

"Holy shit, Shaw," North said. "I don't know how you're walking on that leg."

"It's fine. I'm fine. Just take the pictures."

For a minute, the only sound was Gillman's whistling breaths, the occasional splat of a bubble of blood bursting as he tried to breathe through a broken nose, and the tap of North's finger against the phone's screen.

"Ok," North said, one warm hand on Shaw's arm. "We got plenty."

He helped Shaw stand, and then he pulled Shaw into an embrace, his arms loose and cradling as though he feared he might break Shaw. The warmth was incredible. The smell of Irish Spring and American Crew gel and leather and blood. His lips, chapped, rasped against Shaw's cheek.

"When I saw you," he said. "When I saw you." And then a shudder went through him.

Shaw shushed him and rubbed his back; North's faced dropped to Shaw's shoulder, wet and hot through the crop top's thin cotton.

Snuffling, North lifted his head. "I'm going to beat him to death now. Go buy yourself a hot chocolate."

"It's those damn boots," Shaw murmured, clasping North around the waist, refusing to let him go when North pretended to struggle.

"Good idea. I'll curb-stomp him first."

"No. I think it's those boots that make you act so macho. I think you'd be much more bearable if you had to do your job in ballet flats or those big, fuzzy granny slippers you keep under your bed."

The sirens were drawing closer now, cones of blue and red light sweeping the alley.

A squad car pulled in, and its sirens cut off with a squawk. The swirl of red and blue continued. A young woman got out, one hand on her holstered sidearm as she studied the scene. Then she leaned back into the car and said something into the radio.

"Sir," she said, "I need you to show me your hands."

"She's talking to you," North said.

"She's talking to you," Shaw said. "I don't look like a sir. I look like somebody's sexy college-age brother."

"No, you think you look college age because you smoke a tremendous amount of weed, which is, not coincidentally, exactly what you did in college. In reality, you look like a past-his-prime rent boy."

"Sir," the officer tried again.

"No," Shaw said. "No. No. And anyway, you look like—you look like you're forty, North. Forty. And in that Carhartt coat and those boots, you look like, um, Pete. From the garage."

"Thank you. That's a compliment."

"No, Pete's fifty-three. I saw it on that nudie calendar he keeps behind the desk."

"And he's a hot-as-fuck polar bear. So, yeah, Shaw: thank you."

"Sir," the woman shouted, coming around the car now. "I need you to show me your hands and separate right now."

"I told you she was talking to you," Shaw said.

"I'm talking to both of you!"

Grimacing, Shaw limped free of North's embrace. "Then you probably should have said 'sirs' because there are two of us."

"And your response time is shit," North said. "I called you ten fucking minutes ago."

"Show me your hands," the woman snapped, "and sit over there. Right now."

Hands in the air, Shaw dragged himself a few feet down the parking pad. North did the same, moving in the opposite direction. When the cop moved to check on Gillman, North produced his phone and began snapping pictures again. After several shots, he stowed his phone before the cop noticed what he was doing.

"Officer," Shaw said, a sudden wave of nausea making his stomach clench. "If it's not too much trouble, could I maybe call my spiritual advisor and ask him to draw me a healing bath of yarrow, arnica, and comfrey. I think I'm going to—"

He didn't manage to finish; the puke came up hot and fast, and when it was over, Shaw was glad he'd turned his head in time.

"Or, instead of all that horseshit," North said, "you could get him an ambulance."

Chapter 41

NORTH'S HANDS WOULDN'T STOP shaking, and he kept sloshing water over the rim of the thin paper cup someone had given him at the hospital. Eventually he abandoned the water and settled for gripping a rolled-up magazine. *New Mothers' Monthly.* "Baby's First Boo-boo: You Might Cry Harder than She Does!" He wanted to laugh, but the sound caught in his throat felt more like a scream.

He kept replaying the same moments again and again: turning down the alley, the GTO's headlights picking out Shaw, the stark brilliance exposing the pain and lingering fear in his face. Knowing in his gut that things had gone wrong, that Gillman had hurt Shaw. And then the world had gone white for a few minutes. Glimpses of a few fragmented seconds here and there: the jolt of his fist connecting with Gillman's cheek; seeing the shadow of a bruise already darkening the back of Shaw's thigh; the late awareness of the ache in his shoulder after a shitty tackle. But mostly, it was those heart-stopping seconds when the lights had bleached Shaw's face, leaving only the pain and fear and the knowledge that North had left him alone.

"North," Shaw mumbled from where he was stretched out in the hospital bed. Under the thin sheet, he was wearing a too-large Saint Louis University sweatshirt and pink jogger bottoms, donations from a pair of nurses who had, of course, immediately fallen in love with him.

North wiped his eyes, surprised to find they were dry. "Yeah?"

"Maybe you should pull your chair over here and hold my hand."

This time, North's eyes stung, and he had to blink them clear. After a moment, he managed to say, "Yeah."

He dragged the chair next to the bed and took Shaw's hand. With his other hand, Shaw traced the bandages taped across North's split knuckles. North squeezed his eyes shut against another hot rush, and Shaw's hand came up to rub the short, stiff bristles on the back of North's head.

The noise caught in North's throat wasn't a scream, he realized. It was a sob, and he barely managed to hold it back.

"It's ok," Shaw said. "I'm fine. I feel pretty good, actually. Whatever they gave me, it might even be better than my yarrow bath."

North cleared his throat. "Yeah." Then he forced himself to make an effort and added, "Tylenol is a wonder drug compared to dirty plant water."

Doctor Hull was being paged, and in the next exam room, a woman was shouting about back spasms, demanding a refill on her tramadol.

They had been held at the scene, Shaw in the back of the first police cruiser, North in the back of the second when it arrived, until Jadon and Cerise had gotten there. The ambulances had pulled into the alley about thirty seconds after Jadon. Jadon had released them to go to the hospital together, ordering them to wait for someone to come and question them. And then the trickling minutes had turned into a fluorescent-bright nightmare.

The exam room's curtain parted, and Jadon stepped into the room. He looked bad, and North felt a guilty satisfaction at the thought: his features drawn, his skin sallow. Still beach-bum pretty, but now he looked hard used.

"Where's Garfunkel?" North asked after a moment.

"He's Garfunkel," Shaw said, fingers still teasing the short hairs on the back of North's head. "She's Simon."

"That makes sense; Garfunkel was the talentless hack. Ow! Shaw, for the love of Christ."

Petting the hair he had just pulled, Shaw said, "Whoops."

"Let's hear it," Jadon said.

North told the version they'd hammered out, bare bones bullshit: they'd been hitchhiking after the GTO wouldn't start, and Gillman had picked them up and taken them to the parking pad, where he'd attempted to beat them to death with a baseball bat.

Jadon stared at the linoleum for a moment, breathing slowly. Without looking up, he asked, "The same GTO that was parked in the alley?"

"Oh, yeah. I went back and got it after we put Gillman down. It started up like a charm; must have been vapor lock."

"So, I'm supposed to believe this was all self-defense."

"It was self-defense," Shaw said.

Jadon turned to him; his expression softened. "Some of it was self-defense, maybe. But you did a stupid thing, putting yourself in danger like that. And it's hard to argue that self-defense extends to kneeling on top of a guy while he's down and punching his face in."

"He was beating the shit out of street kids," North said. "He was going to kill one of them, eventually. He was working up to it. And now you've got him wrapped up with a bow; you ought to be thanking us."

"If forensic evidence from the other victims comes back on that bat," Jadon said. "If I don't have to put you two yahoos on the stand and watch Gillman's lawyer rip your story apart." He shook his head. "You can go." He reached for the curtain and stopped. "Are you all right?"

"Fine and fancy free, thanks oh-so-fucking much."

Jadon didn't respond.

"I'm all right," Shaw said quietly. "The doctor said I don't have a concussion, just some bad bruising."

With a nod, Jadon strode out of the room.

"Asshole," North muttered, but he felt intensely grateful to Jadon. The sparring, as short as it had been, had steadied him, and he was able to unroll the copy of *New Mothers' Monthly* and toss it onto the seat next to him. "I'll find a nurse and see if we can leave now that Detective Jadon Reck has given his blessing."

Shaw squeezed his hand in answer, and North squeezed back before heading for the hall.

A shadow on the other side of the curtain stopped him. Short, squat, goblinish through the thin fabric.

In spite of himself, North took a step back.

"What—" Shaw began.

The curtain rattled on its rings, and Ronnie pushed his way into the room. His tropical shirt was a virulent lime color today, patterned with fronds, and he was patting the bowling-ball bulge of his stomach contentedly as he stepped forward.

North retreated again, his body between Ronnie and the hospital bed.

"North, my lad, apple of my eye. How are you?"

"Not great, Ronnie. Not good at all, actually. We had a shit night doing your shit work, and we want to go home. We can talk about this in a few days."

But Ronnie didn't move. His bushy eyebrows threw deep shadows over his eyes. Pineapple air freshener and Vitalis mixed with the disinfectant smell of the hospital air.

"Why are you here?" Shaw said. "How did you even know—"

"One of my friends told me." Ronnie leaned to peer around North, waving at Shaw. "Hello, Shaw. Lovely to see you again, young man. Well, well, well. Somebody had a rough night, didn't he?" Ronnie gave a chuckle, patting his belly again. "Yep, looks like you're still a scrapper. That's good, that's really good. You've got to know how to fight for what matters to you. Take care of it. Make sure nothing bad happens. Isn't that right, North?"

"Ronnie—"

"Life is all about making smart choices," Ronnie said, his voice tight now. "Smart choices are how you take care of the things that you love best in the whole wide world. And the opposite of smart choices are stupid choices. Stupid choices are bad, bad, bad. Bad for you. Bad for the people you love. Stupid choices like bringing the police into a personal matter. If you're doing a favor for a friend, and if that friend has told you he wants to leave the police out of it, well, by gum, you leave the police out of it."

North's pulse hammered in his throat. He couldn't breathe.

"North?" Shaw said.

"Now," Ronnie said. "Here's what you're going to do. You're going to tell the police this was all a big misunderstanding. You don't know what happened. You don't know how poor Tony ended up there. Probably a carjacking. You came across him when you were out for a walk; maybe you even saw someone running away. That stretch of Grand has had its troubles; it's a shame when an upstanding citizen like Tony Gillman gets dusted up like that, but it's nothing more complicated than a carjacking."

"That bat—" North began.

"I'll take care of the bat."

Someone was paging Dr. Hull again. Dr. Hull. Dr. Hull. Dr. Hull, North thought, pick up the fucking phone.

"No," North said. Then, more clearly, "No. I'm done with this."

The page for Dr. Hull ended. Down the hall, rubber squeaked against linoleum.

"Shaw," Ronnie said, "you have such a nice home."

"Thank you," Shaw said slowly.

"I hope you're very careful about your stairs. Stairs are a real hazard in a home. You might leave the vacuum out. You might trip on the cord. You could fall and break an arm or a leg. You could even break your neck."

The ringing in North's ears took on a cymbaling shimmer. And then it was gone, and he took a deep breath.

"Back the fuck off," he said, his voice dead, "you fucking little troll."

Shock rippled through Ronnie's features, a pebble tossed in dark waters, the disturbance total and then gone. "Bow wow wow," he said with a hard little grin. "North McKinney, all bark and no bite."

"We're done. I don't want to see you again. I don't want to hear from you again. I paid up in September, and as far as I'm concerned, we're square. If you so much as look at Shaw, I'll come after you and put you down. Do you understand?"

Ronnie drew out his phone, tapped the screen once, and then again. His hands shook slightly—rage, or maybe just age. North wasn't even sure he knew how old the man really was, but right then he looked very old, shrunken and wizened, his pate an oily smear of reflected light.

A recording began to play. A man's voice. North's father's voice.

"—that's what I'm asking for." The same rough, grating weariness that North remembered in David McKinney's words since he'd been a child. "So?"

"I'm still not sure I understand." That was Ronnie's voice. A note of glee was buried deep in the words.

"I want you to make it so he walks away from this without his life wrecked. Whatever it takes. Talk to whoever you have to talk to. Pull in favors. Make sure twelve dumbshits in a box don't ruin my son's life—whatever he hasn't fucked up himself."

Ronnie tapped the screen, and the voices cut off. "That's jury tampering, my lad. That's a felony. Seven years in prison. Ten thousand dollars. And that's not even dipping our toes in the stress—and cost—of a trial. All that publicity. All that shame. Your father's not a well man, North my boy. If court doesn't kill him, do you really want him spending his last years behind bars?"

North was throwing the punch before his brain had caught up with his body, but the blow never connected. Something—Shaw, a tiny part of his brain recognized—had hauled him back, out of reach of Ronnie. Ronnie didn't flinch, didn't move. He had that impish smile, almost childlike and grotesquely out of place on his tired, old features.

"Now." He pocketed the phone. "I'm going to have to spank your bummy for this debacle, North. I don't like it, but I'm going to have to do it. I'll give it some thought, and when I've decided, I'll let you know. And the next time I come to you and tell you what I want you to do, you're going to do it. Isn't that right?"

North was silent. He was still trying to move forward, still pulling against Shaw's hold on his coat.

"Say yes," Shaw whispered, yanking him back another step. "We'll figure something out, but just say yes for now."

"No." Then, more loudly, "No. Fuck you, and fuck that recording. I know a bully when I see one; I grew up with a fuck ton of them around me, and that includes my old man. I was married to one. You want to do something? Do it. But I'm sick of bullies. Go fuck your ancient ass with that recording, and get the fuck out of my sight."

Ronnie's lip drew up in a silent snarl. His small hands tightened into fists. He swallowed, and for a moment, it looked like he might say something else. Then he relaxed, and a specter of his usual façade floated into view: your buddy Ronnie, the guy in the tropical-print shirt who could have stood in the background of a hot dog commercial, turning wienies on a grill.

"North, North, North. I just want what's best for you. I want what's best for everybody. We'll talk later, after you've had a chance to cool down, get some sleep, screw your head on straight. You boys have a nice night. And Shaw, mind those stairs!" He giggled, twitched back the curtain, and was gone.

Chapter 42

IN THE BOREALIS OFFICE Monday afternoon, Shaw shifted in his seat. North's gaze snapped toward him, and Shaw suppressed a sigh.

"Do you need something?"

"No." And because the pain was a lot worse today—and, maybe, because it was the fiftieth time he'd been asked in the last two hours—Shaw had to struggle to add, "Thank you."

"Water?"

"No."

"Tea?"

"No."

"One of those honey buns Pari keeps locked in her desk?"

"God, no. She'd murder me in my sleep."

"I'll get you a different cushion. You've got about sixty percent of your weight on your right hip; let me find one that will give you better support."

"No!" When Shaw had been growing up, his mother had indulged herself with a Jack Russell terrier, whom she had promptly named Terror. And Terror had followed his mother everywhere, yapping. He yapped when she went outside to get the mail. He yapped when she brought in the groceries. He yapped like a motherfucker, furious at being excluded, when she shut the door so she could use the bathroom. "I mean, I'm fine. It just hurts to sit on that side, that's all. And you already found me a cushion; the cushion is great."

Technically, North had bought him seven cushions. And then he had stood, watching, until Shaw had tried them all.

"You're overdoing it. You don't need to work today. You should be stretched out upstairs, resting."

"If I have to lie in bed for five more minutes, North, I'm going to start chewing the blankets. I'm fine. I want to work. I want to do something."

North was quiet for a blessed fifteen seconds before he asked, "What about a bath?"

Shaw tried and failed to suppress a groan.

"I bought some healing bath salts this morning. They've got lavender and juniper essential oils in them. They're fair trade and organic. They're supposed to help with pain and inflammation."

"I don't need a bath. And I don't need to be babied. And it was my idea to be the bait for Tony Gillman, so you don't need to feel bad just because he handed me my ass."

Shaw heard, too late, his own words. The silence that followed crackled like spring frost. North turned slowly in his chair, swiveling to face him.

"I mean—"

"I like babying you." The words were flat, challenging, delivered in North's low, smoldering rumble.

"Well, you're not very good at it." Then, before Shaw could stop himself, he said, "You tried to tuck a napkin into my collar at breakfast."

"I just need more practice."

"Any more practice and you'll go full Munchausen-by-proxy on me."

North's eyes narrowed. He stood up. Shaw bent closer to his computer, fighting the urge to scramble away from the desk.

Moving slowly, North stepped to stand behind Shaw. His hands came to rest on Shaw's shoulders—one hand tracing, just barely, where Shaw's shirt covered the massive bruise, the other gripping his good shoulder firmly, thumb digging into tight muscle in and then twisting into the beginning of a massage. The moan slipped out before Shaw could stop it.

North didn't say anything, but satisfaction radiated off him as he continued the massage: one hand gentle, barely more than a warm presence over the bruise, the other hand digging deep into tight muscle, working out knots and kinks that Shaw hadn't even known were there.

"About that bath," North said very quietly.

Shaw managed to make two noises that, while not quite words, were still a kind of agreement.

"And then you're going to take more Tylenol."

The massage dragged out more of those agreeable noises.

"And then you're going to lie down."

Shaw's head bobbed on an invisible string.

"And I'm going to take as long as I want getting you off."

"Oh shit," Shaw managed to get out.

"In fact," North said, spinning Shaw in the chair so they were facing each other, "I think I'm going to start right now. Get you hot and bothered before your bath so you have plenty of time to think about how long I'm going to spend taking you apart."

"No, North, don't—" He swallowed. "Don't be mean."

"Sorry, baby," North whispered, kneeling liquidly. "It's like you said: I'm shit at taking care of you."

"Never said—"

But North's hands were already on Shaw's knees, spreading them, and his mouth was already on the front of his sweats, damp heat transferring through the cotton. Shaw's dick twitched in response and then lengthened. North sucked harder, just enough for the wet fabric to drag across the sensitive head. Then he pulled off with a pop, running his tongue along his lower lip. On his knees, pupils blown, he stared up at Shaw.

"These are in the way, don't you think?" North asked, fingers curling over the elastic waistband.

Shaw nodded frantically.

North lowered the sweats inch by inch, covering Shaw's thighs in kisses, but when Shaw tried to shove down the black jock he was wearing, North caught his wrists and made a stern noise. His mouth covered the cotton pouch, so much more intense than when the sweats had been between them and still nowhere close to what Shaw wanted. After a few minutes of the frustrating scrape and abrade of the cloth, North moved Shaw's hands to his mess of blond hair, squeezing once in a silent message for Shaw to keep his hands there. Then North spread Shaw's legs wider. He popped off Shaw, lips puffy now, the jock wet and clinging, and spat in his hand before taking the cotton in his mouth again.

"North, North, North—oh shit." The last two words were pitched so highly that Shaw thought maybe only dogs could hear them. The slick pad of one finger pressed against him and then slid inside easily. When North found that spot inside him, Shaw's back bowed, and his fingers spasmed in North's hair. "Don't make me come like this, don't make me come like this, oh fuck, North," then, in a wail, "I'm coming."

North's free hand yanked the cotton down, trapping it beneath Shaw's balls, and his mouth captured the head of Shaw's cock as Shaw began to come. The orgasm was intense, almost a blackout, and still somehow wildly disappointing. As Shaw slumped against the chair, breathing raggedly, trying to force his fingers to relax so he could release North's hair, he guessed dimly that that had kind of been the whole point.

Leaning back on his heels, North drew the back of his thumb under his lower lip, catching the drool and come that glistened there. His eyes looked almost black with the pupils swollen to the edge of the iris. "Oops."

"Jerk," Shaw panted.

"I forgot; I'm shit at sexing you up too."

"Oh my God."

"Sorry about that."

"Oh my God," Shaw said again, turning his head into his arm.

"I'm just so bad at this."

"Oh my God," Shaw uttered desperately.

Chuckling, North kissed one knee, then the other. His hands settled at Shaw's waist. "Let's pull up your pants so we don't have a sexual harassment lawsuit on our hands, and then we're going upstairs, where I'm going to fuck you very slowly and very gently. Very, very slowly, Shaw. Because I don't want to hurt you."

The threat made Shaw pull his shirt up over his face and whimper. He tried, a last-ditch effort, "The bath—"

"But you said you didn't want a bath. Maybe you need something else. Maybe you should tell me what you need, like we talked about, so I don't feel like an utter fucking failure as a boyfriend."

"You're going to kill me. You realize that, right?"

North tugged on Shaw's shirt, and it slid down so that he could see the smile on North's face. "*Fucked to Death*," North said, with only the tiniest hint of a smile at the corners of his eyes and mouth. "*The Shaw Aldrich Story*."

"Put, *He died a happy man*, on my tombstone."

The lust and desire in North's face blew out like a candle, and he pressed a slower, softer kiss to the inside of Shaw's leg. Then he turned, his face feverish against Shaw's thigh, and was very still.

"I'm ok," Shaw said, carding his hair. "I'm right here. I'm fine. He got the jump on me, that's all."

"Yeah." But his voice held a note Shaw couldn't understand. North sniffed once and sat up, his face flushed.

"North," Shaw said. He hesitated, and then he took the plunge. "I want to talk to you about the business."

Settling back on his heels, a tiny smile quirking the corner of his mouth, North nodded. "Yep. This seems like the right time to do that."

"It won't take long. I just—I want to start doing some jobs to help people. People from the community. I mean, our community. I met a kid, Nik, and he's on the street because I think his uncle stole his inheritance, and he's super gay but he has no idea what he's doing, and—" Shaw could hear himself going off the rails. He took a breath. "I know we've worked really hard to build up the agency, and I don't want to risk that. I'm not asking you to turn away paying clients, and I'm not asking you to change our business model. But I want to start doing work that feels like I'm helping people, so I think I'm going to take some cases independently. On my own time. They won't interfere with Borealis at all, I swear to God."

"No."

Outside, a car roared past—too loud and too fast for this street. Shaw counted his breaths and waited until the sound had died.

"I'm sorry you feel that way, but—"

"I meant no, absolutely not, no fucking way are you going to do that on your own. We'll do it together. And that means we'll have to cut back some of our paying jobs because we're already working too much as it is." North pressed another kiss to the inside of Shaw's thigh. "But it's the right thing to do. And we'll do it together, Shaw, because we're a team. As long as you can accept that our work isn't always going to be noble and heroic and fun and interesting. Sometimes it's just work, and we still have to do it."

"Yeah." Shaw had to blink to clear his eyes, and the smile hurt his face. He managed to say, "Thanks. Thank you. That makes me really happy."

North just smiled.

"I do feel like I have to point out that I'm not accountable to you for my choices, and the toxic masculinity that makes you think you could say no to my—"

"God, Christ, whatever. Let me wash my hands, and then I'm going to shut down the computer. We're taking the rest of the day off."

"Is it a federal holiday?"

North stared at him.

"Is it Christmas?"

"Very funny, smartass."

"Is it the Second Coming of our Lord and Savior, which in the North McKinney employee's handbook merits a half day off?"

Slapping Shaw's calf, North got to his feet. "You want to know why I'm so bad at babying you? It's because of this shit. You're always so busy indulging yourself that I never get a fucking chance."

"If you really want to baby me, you can get me that SeaCell blanket I told you about."

North was already halfway to the door as he called back, "You can buy your own fucking seaweed blanket, thanks."

Once North was out of the room, Shaw didn't have to hide his grin. He pulled up the jock and the sweats and powered down his computer. He was rolling toward North's desk when he heard a woman's voice from the front door, and Pari answering. Then steps clicked across the floor toward the office.

Today, the bindi was flamingo pink. "Yasmin Maldonado is here to see you," Pari said in her best professional tone. "She gave me a check to settle up her account, but she asked to speak to you and North."

"Thanks, Pari. You can send her in."

Pari moved away, and a moment later, Yasmin was stepping into the office. She looked exhausted, dark circles under her eyes, the skunk stripe in her black bob a mile wide, and the heel of one Reebok flapping like a dog's tongue on each step.

"Sit down," Shaw said, coming around the table to pull her into a hug— today, there was nothing stale about the smell of cigarette smoke. "Talk about a few bad days. I bet you're ready to get on a plane and then sleep for a week."

Yasmin's hug was surprisingly tight, and when Shaw made to release her, she didn't let go. Then she began to cry quietly. He tightened his arms until the storm passed, and then she stepped back, wiping her eyes with a wad of tissues.

"Sorry. That's been happening on and off for the last two days. I don't even know when it's going to start; it just hits me."

"Sounds pretty normal after everything you've been through." Then, as gently as he could, Shaw said, "I'm very sorry about Clarence. And Scotty. And Leslie. The whole thing is awful."

Waving a hand, with a forced air of lightheartedness, Yasmin said, "Leslie will be fine. She was trying to get a male nurse to, in her words, 'plow that pretty orderly,' when I left her room today. She's like the Terminator of sexual objectification; nothing's going to stop her for long. She did tell me, by the way, what Scotty promised her in exchange for silence: her own book, with as many sex scenes as she wanted. He never delivered, but the promise was enough. That woman loves her porn." She paused and drew a deep breath, touching her eyes with the tissue again. "Clarence, on the other hand. I heard what he told you and I believe him. I really do. He never would have wanted to hurt anyone, but…but it's all just so horrible. And Scotty. And Josue. None of it seems real."

"I think you'll need a lot of time to process everything. I think everyone will." Shaw drew a deep breath. "Yasmin, what were you thinking?"

A sad, tired smile crossed her lips. "Nothing smart, apparently. I kept telling myself I'd take a page out of Scotty's book; he always knew how to fall into shit and come out smelling like a rose. First it was faking the threats. Then it was hiring you. Then it was spinning the poisoning into something exciting. And then—I don't know. Somehow I thought I could amp up excitement by making myself the next victim, drinking water that had obviously been tampered with and letting someone find me. It sounds asinine now, but at the moment—well, the next thing I knew, I was sitting on the floor of the storeroom with a bag of crushed-up Tums."

North appeared in the doorway, drying his hands on his jeans, and cocked one eyebrow. Before Shaw could speak, though, Yasmin said, "Oh, North, good. You're here. I wanted to talk to both of you."

"Everything ok?" North asked as he took a spot next to Shaw, sliding an arm around Shaw's waist to tug him close. Shaw rested his head on North's shoulder.

"God, aren't you two adorable? Everything is what it is, I suppose, and that's the best we're going to get right now. First thing, I wanted you to know that I recommended you to everyone. Absolutely everyone. Plenty of our con-goers are local, and I know at least a few of them will have work for you. I already talked to one couple who's absolutely desperate to hire you. Something about their cat going missing. So, you can expect plenty of work to keep you busy this year."

"Because we were slow before," North muttered; he grunted when Shaw elbowed him.

"Second, I'm very happy to tell you that you are Queer Expectations' first honorary lifetime members."

"Oh my God," Shaw said.

"That's right. You'll be welcome to attend every future convention for free. And we hope you'll come. You're going to be celebrities, at least among this crowd, for a long time."

"Oh my God!"

"Did you hear that, Shaw?" North said. "Celebrities."

He grunted a little louder because this time Shaw elbowed him a little harder.

"But what I really wanted to talk to you about in person was your life story rights."

"Oh my God," Shaw whispered.

"I'm sorry," North said, "our what?"

"You don't have to make a decision right now," Yasmin said, opening a tote bag to withdraw a thick manila envelope, "but I've been looking for the right project to get me back into writing, and historical M/M just wasn't doing it for me anymore. Everything that happened at the con, well, I think it's got a lot of potential to make an amazing romantic suspense novel. Lightly fictionalized, of course, to smooth out some of the rough patches." She gave an uncertain smile tinged with embarrassment. "You did spend an awful lot of time bumbling around, not that that's a bad thing!"

"We do tend to bumble," North agreed, and he flinched when Shaw pinched the skin above his hip.

"Please take a look. I can pay you five hundred dollars each for the rights, and then we'll do some initial interviews for me to get the details down. I honestly think this could be the start to a great series. Every year you'd get to solve another crime at a gay romance literature convention."

"Sounds like bestseller material," North said.

"I know!" With a crow of triumph, Yasmin passed over the envelope. "Get back to me as soon as you're ready; I'd love to start working on this project before somebody else gets the jump on me."

"I already know my answer," Shaw said as he reached for the envelope.

But North snatched it first. "Our answer is, we're going to sleep on it."

"North!"

"Now," North said, "if you'll excuse us, Shaw is still recovering from getting banged around on another case. I'm going to get him settled upstairs, and then we're closing for the day."

"Oh my God," Yasmin said. "Of course, of course. Are you all right?"

"I think so. For a little while, I was running a real risk of death by suffocation. Smothering, you know?"

This time, North was the one who pinched, and Shaw let out string of swears.

"Sorry," North said. "He's still in some pain."

They got Yasmin out the door; Pari had already left, and the reception area was empty. After turning off the lights and locking the door, North helped

Shaw up the stairs, and Shaw let out a breathless thank you at the top. A light sheen of sweat covered him. He could have done the stairs on his own, probably. It would have just taken longer. A lot longer.

"Maybe you should stay at my place for a few days," North said as eased Shaw down onto the bed. "Save yourself all those trips up and down."

"Yeah," Shaw said. He tugged the comforter up and played with one corner. "Um, if that would be ok."

"I just suggested it, didn't I?"

"I know, but—"

North dropped onto the bed next to him. His hand ran over the comforter, found Shaw's thigh, and stroked his leg. "We were roommates in college. It's not like we haven't lived together before."

"I know, I know, but now we're, you know."

"Dating?"

"Well, yeah."

North made an amused noise and bent to kiss him. Then he pulled back, and his hand stopped on Shaw's leg. "She kind of killed the mood, huh?"

"Sorry."

"Christ, don't be sorry. Want some of that cheesecake? Some tea? Do you want me to bring you some books?"

Shaw flopped back in bed, wincing at the throb in his shoulder, and pulled a pillow over his face. Voice muffled, he said, "Please don't start—"

Then North's hand was there, pressing down on the pillow until Shaw slapped his arm. North laughed and pulled back, and Shaw tossed the pillow to the side.

"Jerk!"

"Damn, was I smothering you again? I just can't help myself."

"You are a real jerk, North McKinney."

North was still laughing as he clomped down the stairs in those godawful Redwings.

While the sound of dishes and glassware clattered below, Shaw propped himself up against a mound of pillows. He grabbed his phone and started a new book by Clarence—he'd downloaded all of them that morning, in a flurry of purchases that he didn't completely understand. *Castling the Rookie* was a best-friends, secret-lovers, nerd-jock romance about a US college soccer team that traveled to Scotland, spent three weeks at a training camp operating out of a real castle, and mostly centered on the relationship between the team's student manager and a red-shirt freshman. Two pages in, Shaw was hooked, and when he emerged from the story in odd moments—when he took the Tylenol and drank some of the kukicha tea that North had put on a tray next to him, or when he devoured the wedge of cheesecake in three huge bites—he felt a pang for Clarence, who had written beautiful, happy things.

Stretched out next to him, Shaw was vaguely aware that North was reading too, flipping through papers and interrupting himself with a series of increasingly frustrated noises. At first, Shaw tried to dive deeper into the book. Then, dropping the phone onto the bed, he looked over.

"What?"

North made a questioning noise without looking up. Then, with another of those disgusted sounds, he flipped the page onto the growing stack next to him.

"North Prophylacticus McKinney—"

"Not my middle name."

"—what is going on? You sound like a water buffalo. A grumpy one. And I'm trying to read."

For a moment, it looked like North wouldn't answer. Then he raised his head, waving the remaining pages at Shaw with one hand and gesturing to the pile next to him with the other. "This is bullshit!"

"I thought you said we were taking the rest of the day off. Whatever Truck and Pari messed up in the paperwork, it can wait—"

"She made me Norton!"

Shaw cocked his head. "Am I having a stroke? Or are you?"

"She made me fucking Norton. Yasmin." North shoved a sheaf of pages at Shaw. "Norton and Shaun. Those are the names of her characters. Norton is the big, drooling dumbfuck who's always getting everything wrong, and Shaun basically leads him around by the dick. And Shaun is this brilliant, athletic, charming billionaire who solves crimes for his own fucking amusement. This is the biggest crock of shit I've ever seen."

"Well, there's always an element of—" Shaw stopped at the look on North's face. "You're right. It's a travesty."

"It's not just that. There's no make-up sex. There's no sex at all."

"Some romance novels don't have sex. Or if they do, it's fade-to-black. They have all these different heat levels, and—"

"Yeah, it's that fade-to-black shit. Norton fucks up a major piece of evidence, and Shaun comforts the big fuck by revealing that the brilliant Shaun knew that Norton was going to fuck it up all along, so he planned for it, and then they start kissing, and right when it's about to get good, nothing."

"Some people prefer—"

"And they don't fight. And they don't threaten to break up. And they don't bang it out for fourteen pages in epic make-up sex. What kind of romance novel does she think she's writing?"

"I thought you didn't read—"

The look North turned on Shaw was so intense that Shaw forgot the rest of the sentence. It took Shaw a moment to recognize the emotion in that look, and then his body responded. He pushed the comforter down; his erection was visible through the thin gray sweats.

"I think we should break up," Shaw said.

North shoved the tea tray out of the way, the cup rattling on its saucer. He crawled across the bed to Shaw and caught Shaw's jaw, gentle but firm. "What the fuck did you just say to me?"

"I'm starting a fight. A big one."

"Yeah, you are. You have no—" He cut off, stifling a noise as Shaw pressed a hand against his crotch. After a moment of internal struggle that mapped itself across his face, North thrust into Shaw's hand. Shaw undid the button and zipper, drawing North's dick out, stroking him. North tried to suppress a whimper. "You have no idea—oh fuck. You have no idea what kind of..." He trailed off into heavy breaths.

"But maybe," Shaw said, pausing as he leaned forward to lick the head of North's cock, smiling as North failed to stop a moan, "since I'm injured, we can skip the rest of the fight and go straight to the fourteen-page make-up sex?"

"Fuck yeah," North said, shimmying out of the jeans. "That sounds like the perfect ending."

MISDIRECTION

Keep reading for a sneak preview of *Misdirection*, book two of Borealis: Without a Compass.

Chapter 1

KINGSLEY SHAW WILDER ALDRICH was trying to finish his story, but he had to compete with the bass line of a Weezer song.

"—and that's when I knew I could do it because the power to achieve my dreams had been inside me all along."

North McKinney, his boyfriend, sighed, spun his beer, and said, "The power to buy pre-shelled pistachios had been inside you all along?"

"Don't say it like that. It was a very enabling revelation. Societal pressures have been holding me back for years. Understanding that the power had been—"

"Please don't keep saying 'inside me.'"

"—inside me all along was life-changing. I'm going to write a book. I'm going to free people from their chains." Shaw leaned back and stole a cheesy fry from North's plate. "And you didn't have any complaints about me using the phrase 'inside me' last night."

A pair of very young, gym-bunny gays was passing the table right then, and they shared a look and burst out laughing.

North's cheeks reddened, but his only answer was to drag his plate closer and curl an arm around it protectively, glaring at Shaw.

"Also, that cheese is mostly preservatives," Shaw said, "and it's hardening inside your small intestine, and you'll probably get a blockage and die."

North's eyes narrowed.

"A slightly smaller portion—"

"No."

"Or if you shared—"

"There it is. No. No. No. No fucking way, Shaw. Nibble on your lettuce."

"If you'd be nice to me, maybe I'd nibble on your lettuce."

North covered his face with one hand, but he didn't relax the protective curl of his arm around the cheesy fries.

The Unicorn Trough wasn't officially a gay bar, but with a name like that, it had a hard time being anything else. At least half the couples were men; of the remaining half, some were women, some were straights, and a few were clearly enby. A banner over the bar limply announced 90'S NIGHT, but that only seemed to refer to the choice of music—nobody else had gotten into the spirit of it. Colored lights spun and swiveled, illuminating patches of the haze that floated over the dance floor; a handful of couples were dancing, all of them young and clearly looking for an excuse to grind on each other.

"My parents would have killed me if they'd found out I came to a place like this," North said as he dragged a fry through the cheese sauce and glanced around. "Not that that ever stopped me."

"My parents would have cried with joy if I'd asked to go to The Unicorn Trough," Shaw said. "They made me do the whole gay-straight alliance thing in school after I came out. They were literally waiting for me to tell them; my mom had made t-shirts ahead of time."

"They made you join the GSA? That seems like a bit much."

Shaw shook his head. "They made me start it."

North rolled his eyes. "Parents have some fucked up ideas about knowing what's best. Exhibit A."

He didn't have to glance across the room for Shaw to know what he meant; Exhibit A was Nicci Lesperance, the woman they were following that night. Nicci had a chop of purple-gray hair and was probably too full figured to be wearing nothing but a leather vest (on the back, the name of her yet-to-be-discovered band, Bathtub Punchout) and leather leggings. She was a middle manager at Aldrich Acquisitions, which was the company owned by Shaw's father and which supplied most of the work for North and Shaw's private investigation agency.

Nicci's father, Ralph Lesperance, was an executive at the same company, and he had asked that North and Shaw look into a younger woman with whom Nicci was having an affair. Kelly Cann—fifteen years younger, with blond ringlets and cherry-red lipstick—was, from all North and Shaw had been able to discover, about what you'd expect from the lead-singer-slash-genius behind a band called Bathtub Punchout: no steady job, no education, heavy use of recreational drugs. The subtext when Ralph had given them the job had been to get rid of Kelly, and Shaw couldn't exactly blame the man—but that didn't make him blind to North's point either.

Fanning aside the sweat, artificial smoke, and skunky weed that cobwebbed the air, Shaw grimaced and said, "I'm going to have asthma from breathing all this glycol or glycerin or whatever it is. I'm going to need lemongrass and sage and—"

North took a long pull from his Schlafly—their pale ale, tonight. It was his turn to watch the women, and he was frowning.

"—ginger root and gingko biloba and—"

North lifted a finger from the Schlafly's brown glass, and Shaw went silent. Then, with a tiny shake of his head, North said, "Never mind. They're just getting more comfortable in the booth." He took another, quicker pull on the beer. "And you're not getting asthma."

"I might be getting asthma. I definitely feel like I'm getting asthma. My throat's all scratchy—"

"Because you've eaten four bowls of bar mix, and it's mostly pretzels."

"—and my tongue feels like corroded battery terminals—"

"Because you've had six Cokes."

"Four, North! I had four. You cut me off, remember?"

"I remember very fucking well, thank you. I also remember that you flirted with the piece of meat behind the bar and got two more while you thought I was in the bathroom."

"You can't—I didn't—" Shaw struggled to sit up straight. "First of all, trust is very important in a healthy relationship, and—"

North made a face as he retrieved his phone.

"Thank you, Vishnu," Shaw whispered.

When North saw the caller, his expression disassembled into a deadly blankness that Shaw had come to recognize over the last few months. He stared at the phone, unmoving. In Shaw's ears, the music became a background of pounding white noise—surf washing everything away.

Fighting the urge to close his eyes, Shaw said, "You can take it."

"No." But North kept looking at the phone. "No, he knows we're only supposed to communicate through our lawyers now."

"So don't take the call."

North sat there, staring at the illuminated screen that flashed with Tucker's name. "He's drunk. And he wants to scream at me. Or he wants me to think he's drunk and he wants to scream at me. Or he doesn't think he's as drunk as he really is, but he wants me to think he—"

"I'm going to get some water," Shaw said, sliding down from the stool.

Behind him, North's voice was low and hard as he said, "What the fuck do you want, Tucker? What the fuck don't you understand about 'no contact'? Are you too fucking stupid to understand—" North broke off and resumed more fiercely, "I'll talk to you however I fucking want, you fucking imbecile. We're not—"

And then The Smashing Pumpkins were singing about tonight. Shaw kept his gaze on the bar, refusing to look back. He wormed his way through the press of bodies, flagged down the bartender, and ran a hand through his auburn hair—long enough now that he could hold it back with a scrunchie, which was a nice change from the crazy cloud of curls that North had described as Bob Ross-bred-with-a-poodle (the little yippy kind, he had clarified).

"Hey, beautiful," the bartender said, leaning on his elbows, a white towel crisp against his black shirt. He couldn't have been older than twenty, sandy haired, and he still managed to look boyish even though he must have spent a couple of hours at the gym every day. He had an inner bicep tattoo of a distorted clock and writing in what Shaw thought was Sanskrit. "You're making my night better and better. I'm glad you came back."

"Thanks," Shaw said, checking over his shoulder; North was bending over their two-top, one hand cupped around the phone, probably so he could eviscerate Tucker more thoroughly. "You're beautiful too. I bet you're a Pisces."

"Can I get some service?" a salt-and-pepper bro at the end of the bar shouted.

"What's Pisces?" the bartender said, smiling as he pulled the towel from his shoulder and flapped it at the bro. "What dates, I mean?"

"February 19th to March 20th."

"No way. March 1st."

"I knew it. It's because you're so pretty. And I bet you have a really beautiful soul. Have you ever had your chakras read?"

The bartender blinked. Then his smile got bigger. "No, but I'll try anything once. Do you want to—"

"Hey, buddy." Daddy-bro was shouting again. "Trawl dick on your own time."

The bartender shot him an angry look and turned back to Shaw. "I've got to, you know. Can I get you anything? Another Coke?"

For a moment, something nasty snapped its teeth inside Shaw, and he almost said yes. "Just a water. And another Schlafly, the pale ale."

When the bartender set the drinks next to Shaw, he took Shaw's wrist in one hand. His touch was warm and soft. His thumb traced the vein visible under Shaw's pale skin. "I'd really like to keep talking to you."

"I'd really like to keep talking to you," Shaw said with a smile. "And you know what? I'm really glad you said that I'm making your night better because now you're making my night better. North, that's my boyfriend, is being such a jerk. It's not like he tries to be a jerk. Well, sometimes he does. Like one time, he came home when I was using one of those as-seen-on-TV back shavers, and he told me if I really wanted to manscape, I could start, well, down there, because, quote, 'it's like getting lost in the pubic Amazon,' which was really rude, and I said—"

The bartender released Shaw's wrist and straightened. "You've got a boyfriend."

"Oh, yeah, he's the one over there who's trying really hard to look butch with the henley and—"

The bartender shot toward the other end of the bar, saying something like *wasting my fucking time* under his breath.

"I didn't give you the name of my psychic," Shaw called after the young man. "If you want your chakras read. It's Master Hermes!"

"Dude," one of the guys next to Shaw said, covering his ear.

At a more normal volume, Shaw repeated, "It's Master Hermes."

"Yeah, whatever, quit yelling in my fucking ear."

Shaw was carrying the drinks back to the table when Nicci got up and headed toward the bathroom. Kelly played with her glass, gaze fixed on the appletini in front of her, until Nicci had disappeared down a narrow hall. Then she grabbed Nicci's purse, slid out of the booth, and shot toward the door.

North was still whispering furiously into the phone.

"Something's happening," Shaw said, touching North's elbow.

With an inarticulate cry, North ripped the phone from his ear and hammered it against the table. When he pulled it back, he said, "No, you listen to me, you abusive piece of shit—"

"She's running," Shaw said.

"You want to talk about unfair? You want to talk about what's unfair, Tucker? What's unfair is every fucking minute I had to spend standing behind you, smiling and looking supportive—"

Shaw grimaced, set the drinks on the table, and went after Kelly. She was moving at a fast walk, sliding through the crowd without glancing back. Shaw copied her. She hit the door and disappeared into the night, fingers of artificial smoke curling after her. Shaw was five yards behind her. The April evening was cool, the air shockingly clean and sweet with spring after the weed-and-glycol haze in the Trough. A couple of guys were making out hard, pressed up against the Trough's brick façade. A woman in a matted fur coat smoked at the curb, the security light washing out her face so she looked like a picture from an old book.

Kelly was already halfway down the block, disappearing between the aprons of light from the streetlamps, and Shaw took off after her. She was wearing biker boots to go with the leather leggings and the leather vest, and they made her steps solid, heavy, the only sound in the universe. At the next alley, she jinked right, swallowed up by the yellow, fluttering light from deep between the brick buildings.

When Shaw came around the corner, she punched him, aiming for the face. He had good reactions, honed by sparring in the smattering of martial arts he'd picked up and then abandoned, and he managed to dodge so that the punch only clipped his ear. It still stung, and the rush of adrenaline narrowed his vision to a tunnel and sent his pulse racing. She kicked before he could recover, catching him in the hip, and Shaw went down. He landed on the cracked pavement, chips of cement slicing his palms.

Kelly came after him. A part of Shaw's brain told him things had gone wrong—she should have run again; now was the perfect opportunity for her to escape—but things were moving too quickly for him to figure out why. Her boot came down in a vicious stomp intended for Shaw's head. He rolled and came up against a dumpster.

The movement had reversed their positions: now Kelly stood at the mouth of the alley, and Shaw scrabbled backward, deeper into the cleft between the brick walls. Bringing back Nicci's purse as though intending to use it as a club, Kelly leapt forward. Shaw grabbed a broken section of pallet, driving splinters into his hands, and tossed it. It caught Kelly at the legs. She swore, stumbled, and almost lost her balance.

That delay gave Shaw time to regain his feet. This time, when Kelly lunged, Shaw was ready. He threw a jab that was meant to catch her in the solar plexus, but the uneven cement caused Kelly to lose her balance. Shaw's fist connected with her breast. Kelly's eyes got huge, and she screamed.

Shaw had already committed himself to the uppercut, launching up with as much force as his body could produce, focusing all of it behind his clenched hand. The blow caught her on the jaw, a perfect bell ringer. Silence. Lights out. Then the soft scuff of clothing as she slid to the ground.

Behind Shaw, in the alley, a man's voice said, "Jesus Christ, sorry I'm late. Toss me the wallet so you can get back in there before the bitch realizes—"

Shaw spun. Through red clouds of adrenaline, he was aware of his hand throbbing, his heart hammering in his throat. He locked eyes with a man who had at least six inches on Shaw and a hundred pounds. Bald, tiny eyes, and the evolutionary trade-off of a neck for shoulders that looked big enough to do some serious smashing.

His steps slowed. His tiny eyes were little black chips of confusion. "Kels, what…what did you do to her? I'm going to—"

"Hey." That was North, speaking out of the darkness near the bar's fire door and stepping into the middle of the alley. "Bozo."

Tiny-eyes lumbered around.

North grabbed a length of two-by-four and cracked it across the back of the big guy's head before he'd gotten farther than a quarter-turn. Again came the soft thump of flesh hitting cement. North tossed the broken length of wood aside, standing up straight, shoulders back, deep breaths making his chest rise and fall. The orange glow from the security light touched the mess of short blond hair, the pale eyes the color of ice. He was trying not to smile. He put his hands on his hips and glanced down at the big guy.

"Very het," Shaw called, shaking out his hand. Adrenaline was leaching out of him, and pain from his hand and a dozen scrapes and bruises was rushing in.

The half-hidden smile on North's face went out, and he scowled.

"No, seriously. It was super het. I'm really proud of you. I thought you'd still be busy on the phone, and then boom, 'Hey, bozo!'"

"Pretty big talk from a guy who just beat up a girl," North said, squatting next to the big guy to roll him onto his back. He patted him down, stopped when he uncovered a knife, and tossed the weapon into a dumpster. Rising, North added, "You must be really proud of yourself too, knocking her around like a frat boy who can't get his dick up."

Shaw sat down crisscross applesauce on the broken cement. He emptied Nicci's purse onto the ground: Marc Jacobs mascara, a pack of face wipes, a baggie with several latex dental dams, crumpled tissues, and the wallet. As Shaw opened the wallet and began taking out credit cards, he said, "First of all it's the twenty-first century."

North's only answer was a grunt.

"Women have every right to get beaten up in a fair fight."

The clip-clop of those massive Redwings.

"And she started it."

A noise that might have been a laugh.

"And if I hadn't punched her, I would have been treating her differently because she's a woman, so basically it was a feminist imperative that I, you know, beat the shit out of her."

Kneeling next to Shaw, North made a very angry rumble in his chest, but his touch was soft as he tilted Shaw's head.

"I'm trying to do something," Shaw whispered, but he'd forgotten about the wallet.

North took Shaw's hands next, turning them up, and he released a blistering string of swears when he saw the cuts and broken bits of glass and cement embedded in his palms.

"Where'd she get you?" North asked.

"I was stupid; I came around the corner, and she was waiting. She just got me on the ear, and the rest of it is mostly from the fall."

"This ear?" North asked. Then he kissed Shaw's ear lightly, his lips brushing the inflamed tissue. He kissed Shaw lightly on the lips and leaned back on his heels. "I really fucked up."

"No, that was the right ear."

"I mean in there. I shouldn't have gotten distracted. I shouldn't have let you go after her alone."

"It's fine. I knew you'd have my back."

"But I—"

"I knew you'd have my back, North." Shaw shrugged. "I trust you. Besides, I can handle one skanky bitch on my own."

"That sounds like the feminist imperative talking."

"The feminist imperative is a real thing."

"Sure. And I'm sure that's what you were thinking about when you titty-punched her."

Shaw shrugged again. "At least I didn't pull her hair."

Kelly made a soft, groaning noise.

"Wake up, Sleeping Beauty," North said. To Shaw, he asked, "Anything?"

"Two Amex, three Visas, a hundred and sixty-three dollars in cash—"

"Jesus."

"—and the grand prize," Shaw flourished a card on a lanyard, "an Aldrich Acquisitions secure-access ID."

"What the fuck?" Kelly mumbled.

"Stay down," North said when she tried to sit up; either the words or the tone convinced her, or maybe she just didn't have the strength, because she fell back against the cement. "Police are on their way. What was this? Some sort of identity-theft scam? You toss bozo her wallet, and then you gaslight Nicci until he finishes copying everything? Nicci gets her purse back before the end of the night, none the wiser until she learns that somebody ordered eight thousand dollars' worth of Xboxes on her Mastercard?"

"Who are you?" Kelly said. "What the hell is going on?"

North made a disgusted noise. "You've got some fucked-up priorities, lady. Nicci seems nice. She seems like she really cares about you. But her dad was right about you—you're garbage. You're going to throw away a chance with a decent woman for a few credit cards that will get canceled by the end of next week."

Kelly gurgled. It took Shaw a moment to realize that the sound was laughter. The words came more slowly, and Shaw was starting to realize he might have caused some damage with the uppercut. "Her dad?"

Shaw glanced at North.

More laughter. Kelly rolled onto her side, curling up slightly, but the muffled words kept coming. "Her dad's the one who hired me in the first place." She laughed again, raised herself up on one elbow, and spat blood across the cement. "Nicci was having a mid-life crisis. Nicci lezzed out, wanted to start a band. Daddy's little girl got wild, and that wouldn't look good to the board." The short, declarative sentences dissolved into huffing breaths.

"Her father hired you?" Shaw asked.

Kelly nodded. Her pupils were huge; the cone of orange light barely reached her face.

"To—what? Steal her identity?"

"To fuck her life every way from Sunday." This last sentence seemed to take the rest of her energy; she slumped against the cement, lines of tension relaxing in her body.

Shaw began returning everything to the wallet. North watched silently. Disapprovingly. When Shaw had finished with the wallet, he returned it to the purse along with the rest of the contents he'd dumped on the ground. Then he stood.

North caught his elbow. "He's the client. He paid."

"He's a monster. He's conducting this psych-ops warfare on his own daughter because he doesn't like her life choices and wants to scare her back into submission."

When Shaw tried to step away, North's grip tightened. "We're private investigators. We aren't going to like every job we're hired to do. We don't have to like the jobs we're hired to do."

"And we started our own agency so we didn't have to answer to anybody else. So we could help people. Is that what this feels like to you?"

"No, but he didn't ask us to—"

"He wants pictures of Nicci with Kelly so he can hold them over her head. And he told us to run Kelly off because he figured we'd be more receptive to that. Do you think this is the right thing to do?"

North didn't answer. He held Shaw's gaze, his face coloring, and then he broke and looked away.

Shaw reached for the hand still clutching his elbow. He had half a mind to rip North's fingers away; instead, he was surprised to find himself taking North's hand into his own, squeezing.

"Compromise," North said, his voice rough. "She tells Nicci what her dad was up to, and then she leaves, and she never talks to Nicci again. We tell her dad we couldn't get any decent photographs, but we managed to put a scare into her, and she won't bother his daughter again."

"That doesn't solve the problem, North. He's going to try again."

"We can't solve all the world's problems. We're solving this one, right now. That's what we can do."

Shaw's eyes stung; he closed them for a moment. North's fingers tightened around his own, and after a moment, Shaw gripped him back.

When Shaw opened his eyes, he was looking at Kelly. She was still punch-drunk, her mouth loose, her breathing soft and shallow.

"Tell Nicci the truth," Shaw said. "And don't do anything like this again, or I'll punch you in the other, you know."

"Titty," North supplied.

Shaw sighed and headed back to The Unicorn Trough. North's hand, warm and solid, found the back of his neck.

"There are seventeen reasons," Shaw said, "why you shouldn't say tit or titties. Number one, it's sexist."

North squeezed the back of his neck and sounded suspiciously like he was laughing.

Chapter 2

NORTH DROVE THEM BACK to Shaw's house in Benton Park, on the south side of St. Louis. It was, for the most part, a quiet area, although with lower income and higher crime than the western neighborhoods. They passed Hodak's, windows dark beneath its green awnings (best fried chicken in the city). They passed the Dollar General, where a scrawny white man was trying to lift a motorized shopping cart onto a city bus. The April breeze chased a Big Gulp down the gutter. With the windows down, the smell of hops and malt and yeast from the Anheuser-Busch brewery floated into the car, and the 1968 GTO's engine rumbled pleasantly at the light.

Instead of dropping Shaw off, North took the alley and parked in the garage. The door rattled down behind them. Neither man moved. The automatic light flicked off. The air was cooler here, kept cold by the dark and the concrete slabs, and North shivered.

"I'm really sorry. About Tucker. About taking that stupid call. It's like— it's like he's in my head, and he knows exactly what to do to make me insane. I can't even think straight." North let his head fall back against the seat. "I swear to God, if he keeps trying to drag out the divorce, I'm going to drive over there one night and murder that son of a bitch."

The noise Shaw made was much, much sadder than a sigh.

North found his hand in the darkness, and Shaw hissed as their fingers slotted together.

"Christ, I forgot. I'm sorry." North thumped his head against the seat once. "Fuck me, I cannot believe I let you do that alone. I can't believe I let you get hurt."

"North, it's fine. It's—"

"It's not fine. It's very fucking not fine, Shaw." North turned in the seat, got into an awkward kneeling position, and lifted Shaw's hand to his mouth. He kissed the swollen knuckles. He kissed each fingertip. He turned the hand over and kissed each scrape and cut, gossamer kisses. Shaw shook himself once and let out a harsh breath. "I." He kissed the inside of Shaw's wrist. "Am." He kissed a few inches higher up Shaw's arm. "So." Another kiss, this one to the sleeve bunched at Shaw's elbow. "Sorry." He kissed Shaw's shoulder. Then, as gently as he could, he kissed Shaw on the lips, his tongue flicking until Shaw parted and let North in.

When North pulled back, Shaw's mouth hung open. Just a little, sure. But it did nice things to a guy's ego.

"Here's what we're going to do," North whispered. "We're going to go inside. I'm going to get a bath ready for you. I'm going to ice your hand while you soak in those healing salts. I'm going to tape up the worst of these cuts when you're nice and relaxed. And then I'm going to ride your dick like Paul fucking Revere."

As North leaned in for another kiss, Shaw said, "But you probably want to sleep in your own bed tonight."

North froze. Pulled back a quarter inch.

"You've been working so hard," Shaw said. "And I move around too much, and I elbow you, and I snore. So you probably want to sleep in your own bed tonight." Shaw groped blindly for the door handle.

Gathering a handful of Shaw's jacket, North said, "I do not want to sleep in my own bed tonight."

Shaw pulled the handle; the door popped open.

"Where do you think you're going?" North asked.

"You probably need to get home to the puppy. He needs you. He needs your full and undivided attention. He needs you to take him out to go the bathroom. He needs you to get his food and water. He needs you to play with him even when your boyfriend is trying to tell you about the psychosexual Mormon homoeroticism underpinning seasons one, three, and five of *Battlestar Galactica.*"

North drew back another quarter inch, studying Shaw. "The puppy is with Pari and Truck. What the fuck is going on?"

"And you've probably got to take another phone call." Shaw would have slid out of the car, but North's grip was too firm. "And I'd hate to be a distraction when you've got to take an important phone call."

North's eyes narrowed. "You petty little bitch."

"North! You can't say bitch anymore either because—"

Shaking him by the jacket, North said, "Oh no. You're refusing to give me dick as a punishment? That is fucked up, Shaw. That is seriously fucked up."

In an easy, practiced movement, Shaw grabbed North's wrist and broke his hold. He slipped out of the car and slammed the door.

"Hold on one fucking minute," North said, throwing open his own door.

Shaw was already sprinting toward the door into the house, laughing.

North had to skirt Shaw's Mercedes SLC 300, which slowed him down, and he barely got to the door before Shaw could lock it. They played that game for a while, Shaw laughing uncontrollably as he tried to force the door shut and set the deadbolt, North growling and swearing and shoving just enough to keep Shaw from winning. Finally Shaw gave up, bolting down the hall. The main floor had been given over to the Borealis offices; North flew past them without even a glance, buttonhooking through the reception area at the front and following Shaw into the kitchen.

Shaw let North catch him at the top of the stairs.

North grabbed his ankle, dragged him down, and climbed on top of him. He trapped Shaw's wrists, pinning him; Shaw was still laughing. His auburn hair had come loose in the tussle, and now it formed a crazy cloud. For a moment, North just enjoyed the view: the refined features, the slender eyebrows, the sharp triangle of cheekbones and jaw that made Shaw more than handsome, more than beautiful. His hazel eyes were bright with amusement.

"Not fair," Shaw said. "I'm injured. You never would have caught me otherwise."

North made a noise low in his throat. He bent his head, nuzzling aside Shaw's collar and kissed the sensitive skin there. Then he bit. Shaw groaned, hips coming up, the beginning of his erection rubbing against North's belly. North ignored the silent request, sliding his mouth to Shaw's neck, kissing again.

"Not—" Shaw gasped. "Not fair. Not fair, North. I—" He made a high-pitched noise when North bit his collarbone, and this time, his boner was steel as he rutted up. North rocked back to meet him, coiling Shaw's hair around his fingers, turning his head to attack his neck again.

Unable to help himself, North bent down, his voice a low, hot whisper: "Still think I should take that phone call?"

Shaw shook his head wildly—or as wildly as he could, with North still clutching his hair. Then he froze, one hand on North's chest.

North froze too. "What happened? Shit, you got hurt worse than I realized, didn't you?"

Shaw's phone buzzed in his pocket; the faint notes of "Girls Just Wanna Have Fun" floated into the air.

Shaw's slender eyebrows drew up into innocent arches.

"Ignore it."

"It might be important."

North rubbed the bulge of Shaw's erection. "I'm going to be so nice to you. Ignore it."

Swallowing, Shaw blinked glassily. But he whispered, "It might be really, really important. Sometimes I get these important phone calls, and I have to drop everything else."

"You are a vengeful prick," North growled, yanking open the waistband of Shaw's pants. He hooked his fingers around the waistband and hiked the pants down to mid-thigh. As usual, Shaw was commando, and his dick sprang up and slapped the underside of North's chin wetly. Shaw groaned. He made another, more animalistic noise when North took the head in his mouth. Just the head. Suckling.

With what sounded like genuine pain, Shaw slid free and dragged himself up a few more steps. Pupils wide, he wrenched the phone from his pocket and met North's gaze.

"Don't do it," North said.

"It's my mom."

"At half-past eleven?"

"She'll be worried sick if I don't answer."

"This is the same mom who bought you a one-way ticket to London when you were sixteen?"

"She won't stop calling."

"She'll be just fucking fine for ten minutes."

"Ten minutes? That's all?"

"Fuck you, Shaw. Fuck—"

"I knew you'd understand. About taking important phone calls, I mean."

North dropped back on his heels, eyes narrowing, and Shaw accepted the call.

"Hi, Mom. No, no, you didn't wake me. Now's a very good time. I have fourteen new kinds of wallpaper paste I need to tell you about."

Shaking his head, North rose, and he gave Shaw a hand up. Shaw did an awkward, hopping dance to try to tuck away his erection and keep his pants from sliding down. North took advantage of the opportunity to deliver a cracking, one-handed smack to Shaw's bare ass. The noise echoed in the stairwell, and Shaw yelped.

"No, Mom—holy shit—no, I just stubbed my toe. I don't know; that must have been on your end."

"Tell your mom hi," North whispered.

Shaw rolled his eyes.

"Hi, Mrs. Aldrich," North bellowed.

"You heard him? Ok, maybe now he'll leave me alone."

"Did she say hi back?"

Grimacing, Shaw gave North a fake push, and North pretended to topple down the stairs. Shaw just made an even more aggravated expression and turned away.

With a grin, North ruffled Shaw's hair and headed through the bedroom and into the bathroom. He brushed his teeth—real brushing, which involved using the tube of Crest he'd hidden under the sink instead of the coconut oil, for pulling, that Shaw had decided was going to cure his invisible goiter or Christ only knew what. He flossed. He washed his face, considered a shower, and decided he was too tired. When he got back to the bedroom, Shaw was stretched out on the bed, still on the phone with his mom. North lay next to him, head on Shaw's chest, and Shaw curled an arm around him and scratched his back lightly.

A text came from Haw Ryeo, their contact—and nominal boss—at Aldrich Acquisitions: *Attempted break-in at Nonavie. Be ready in case I need you.*

North texted back: *Any idea who it was? Security cameras get anything?*

But Haw didn't reply.

North checked their business banking accounts; he had nothing better to do. Johanna Griffin was a client who had hired them to find her missing father, who suffered from dementia. Her check had bounced the week before, and when North had called, she had told him it had been an error and the check would clear if the bank processed it again. When it bounced a second time and he'd called, she'd promised an electronic transfer and hung up on him. Surprise, surprise, the bank account showed that Griffin's payment hadn't arrived.

Shaw was still talking. He sounded different when he talked to his parents. Nothing easy to pinpoint. It wasn't like his vocabulary changed, or even the content—sophomore year, when Shaw had been living at home and recovering from being stabbed, North had walked in on Shaw and his mother debating dildo lengths, girths, and materials. With samples. But maybe a slight shift in manner, a hint of education and money that Shaw had dropped early in freshman year—one of the things, North remembered, that had made him hate Shaw at first sight.

Now, he burrowed deeper into Shaw, smelling the cigarette smoke and the slight musk of his hair product, Shaw's hand warm and comforting and possessive around him. Shaw's voice rumbled in his chest as he talked. North ran his hand over Shaw's ribs, tracing them, then pushing up the shirt to caress the wiry muscle and the dusting of auburn hair. He turned his head just enough to kiss Shaw's bare skin. In spite of his own best efforts, North was hard again. Really hard.

When Shaw ended the call, his hand came up to the short mess of North's hair, playing with it. North rolled onto his stomach, kissed Shaw's belly again, and pushed the shirt higher. He followed it with another kiss, leaning down to rub himself against Shaw's leg. Then he realized Shaw was soft.

He let out a slow breath, rested his chin on Shaw's abdomen, and looked up the length of that slim body. "You ok?"

"What? Oh. Yeah. Sorry."

North stroked more bare skin in slow, calming movements. "What's up?"

"Oh, nothing."

"Great."

"Yeah," Shaw mumbled.

North crawled up the length of his body and then let himself drop, flattening Shaw against the mattress.

Shaw's breath whooshed, and he grunted under North's weight. Then he slapped North's hip. Then he tried to buck North off. Then he tried to shove him.

"North, come on."

"What?"

"Will you get off me?"

"I'm comfortable. I might fall asleep."

"This is so juvenile."

North took slow breaths that alternated with fake snores.

"You are a child. Do you realize that? You're a teenager at heart. A delinquent."

More fake snoring.

"A…a hooligan."

"Could you keep it down, please? I'm trying to get some shut-eye."

"I'm fine, ok? I'm totally, perfectly fine. It was just a bummer of a conversation. My mom is really stressed about these students in her studio, and I still haven't figured out what to get my mom and dad for their thirtieth anniversary, and they won't stop talking about—" Whatever he'd been about to say, he changed it at the last moment. "—the party, and then I had to hear about how my great-aunt's chemo port keeps coming out."

North turned his head, scruff dragging on Shaw's cheek, and kissed his jaw lightly. "What's the one you're worried about the most?"

"My aunt, I guess. She's eighty-three."

"Are you close?"

"Yeah. She's always been so nice to me. And now she's sick and miserable and nothing has gone right with the treatment."

Sliding onto his side next to Shaw, North said, "Maybe you should take a couple days off and spend them with her."

"I don't know." Shaw shook his head, staring up at the ceiling. The next part burst free, although he seemed to try to stop it. "And why can't they just drop it about the party? I don't—I don't know why I have to keep hearing about it. It's their party. It's for them. For their anniversary. Why am I involved at all?"

"I don't know. Why are you?"

"I don't know."

"How are you involved?"

"I don't know!"

"Ok, ok." North considered the stubborn-as-a-fucking-mule set of Shaw's jaw, prayed inwardly to whatever saint protected fools who got involved with complicated, beautiful men who owned an entire drawerful of assless chaps, and tried a different angle. "Should I be expecting an invitation? Delivered on a silver platter of course."

Shaw rolled off the bed. "I'm going to brush my teeth."

"Hey, I was just joking."

"I know." He delivered the words while walking, without looking back.

"Will you tell me what the fuck is going on?"

The answer was a slammed door.

Whatever the hell coconut oil-pulling involved, it apparently took a lot of time. North finally turned off the lights, crawled under the blankets, and closed his eyes.

Soft steps. The blankets being drawn back, the whisper of cool air, and then a warm body. One arm across North's waist. Shaw's head on his shoulder.

"I want you to go to the party with me."

"Great."

"It's a week from Saturday."

North didn't say anything about the preparations, about how long a family as rich as Shaw's might have spent planning and ordering and inviting and arranging. More than a few fucking days, that was for sure. All he said was "I'll get my day planner."

"I'm sorry I'm being a pill."

North grunted. He had kept his eyes closed through this whole exchange, but now they opened. In the faint light from the window, the room was blue-black, bruised. He didn't mean to say it out loud. He definitely didn't want to say it out loud. But it slipped out anyway: "You know I'll be on my best behavior, right? I'm not going to get drunk and make a scene or pick a fight with your Uncle Al or look down your Aunt Suzy's dress. If you promise me treats, I bet I could even do some nifty tricks like use the right fork and drink out of a glass."

The silence had a heartbeat pulse to it.

"My Aunt Suzy got really good implants," Shaw finally said, his tone suggesting a joke to smooth everything over. "So if you're into that thing, you actually probably should look down her dress."

North bit back the swear words. He bit back the reply. He couldn't help the rest of it, though: he rolled onto his side, his back to Shaw, and closed his eyes.

Chapter 3

IN MOVIES SOMETIMES—the kind North watched, the kind North made Shaw watch, even when there was a perfectly good four-hour QVC spot on empowerment gemstones—a guy stepped on a landmine, and then he froze because he knew if he moved at all, if he even scratched his nose, he'd get blown to Kingdom Come.

The next morning, Shaw knew how the poor bastard felt. Unfortunately, he couldn't seem to stay still.

The bed was empty when Shaw woke. It was a Monday, so Shaw found North downstairs, in their office, but North would only reply in grunts and monosyllables. He refused the coffee Shaw brought him. He ignored the slice of cherry danish. When Shaw tried to kiss him, he stood abruptly and left the room. When he came back, he moved his chair away from the desk, under the pretense of kicking up his heels and reading a sheaf of documents. When Shaw moved his chair back, so that they were sitting side by side, North made a noise and rolled his chair closer to the desk. When Shaw rolled his chair back to the desk, North looked over, wild-eyed, and dumped the cherry danish in the trash.

"Now you're making me mad," Shaw said.

"Good."

"I know I hurt your feelings last night, but you won't talk to me, and I want to apologize, and that was a perfectly good slice of danish!" Shaw lost it a little on the volume at the end.

North stood and pushed back from the desk so hard that the chair caught an uneven floorboard and tipped over. He stomped out of the room; when he came back fifteen minutes later, he smelled like cigarettes. Shaw caught his eye and opened his mouth, but the look on North's face made him reconsider.

It might have gone on like that all day, except Pari rapped on the door. She used what Shaw considered her professional voice (in contrast to her normal, I'm-going-to-harangue-you-into-an-undeserved-raise voice), which meant that a prospective client was in the reception area.

"There's a Mrs. Chittenden here to see you."

"We're not doing walk-ins today," North said without looking up. "And if it's your fault because you forgot to put her on the fucking calendar, you can apologize to her and find a better time for her to come back."

Stepping into the office, Pari shut the door behind her. She lowered her voice and said, "If the two of you could pull yourselves out of whatever high school relationship drama you're tangled up in for fifteen seconds and act like professionals, you might be interested to know that Mrs. Chittenden is a state senator from Dore County. In other words, a very important person. And she wants to hire you. Although God only knows why; she'd be better off hiring the cheer squad."

North didn't exactly look at Shaw, but his voice was gruff when he said, "You'd probably better send her in, then."

Pari didn't reply; the look on her face said it all. A moment later, she was ushering a blond woman into the room. Shaw's first impression was of a waxwork Kim Novak—and not at the best point in her life. The short, tousled curls. The dark eyebrows. The high cheekbones. Her real age was most visible near her ears—and, of course, in her hands. She wore a navy suit under a scarlet jacket. A dark-haired young man pranced at her heels; Shaw had seen pieces of toast with more personality.

"Mrs. Chittenden," North said, coming around the desk to shake her hand. "And—"

"We'll have espressos," Mrs. Chittenden said, shrugging out of the jacket, which the young man caught like a relic. "Gavin, hold my calls."

"We actually don't have an espresso machine," Shaw said as he approached, "because North decided that only 'rich twats who have never done an honest day's work' own their own espresso machine, which was a jab at me because I had two in my dorm room." North's eyebrows were arching sharply now, so Shaw hurried to add, "We don't even have a Nespresso machine because the pods are so bad for the environment. But we do have coffee, if the coffeemaker isn't broken again, and we have a thistle tea that I brew, and—"

"Actually," North said, "we don't have thistle tea."

"No, we do. I picked all those weird, white twigs off the bush in the backyard, and if you pack it into a tea infuser, it tastes just like thistle tea."

"Oh my God," North whispered. In a stronger voice, he managed to say, "Coffee?"

Mrs. Chittenden gave each of them a long look. "Gavin, take their girl and get us some espressos. A double for me. For you?"

"Well, I like mine unicorn style—" Shaw began.

"A double is fine," North said, shooting Shaw a look.

Gavin, who Shaw now noticed wore a headset, was whispering furiously into the microphone as he pranced out of the room again. He pulled the door shut behind him, cutting off his words as he snapped at Pari, "Come on, I don't have all day."

North winced. Just barely.

"He's going to be lucky if she only rips out all his hair," Shaw whispered.

They got Mrs. Chittenden settled, and when they were seated behind their desks again, North said, "How can we help you?"

Mrs. Chittenden was examining the room. Success had made it possible for North and Shaw to update the room: comfortable chairs for clients, accent tables, a muted landscape painting they'd bought at the Francis Park art fair together. North's desk, as usual, was perfectly organized: the chrome in-out trays with their neat stacks of documents, the high-def monitor, the organizer with individual compartments for paperclips and binder clips and tacks and staples. North had shouted himself hoarse the one time Shaw had dumped it out to borrow it for his antique button collection. Shaw's desk, on the other hand, had a less traditional organizational system. Today, for example, was day seven of his exploration of metal racking and shelving systems, so he had a spread of trade magazines and sales catalogues spread across the desk. On top of those was the homemade kilt he was still working on, for which he had used a combination of black vinyl and rayon that was a color North described as "grandma's stirrup pants." The one bare spot was where Shaw had set a copy of the *Kama Sutra*, but when North had looked at it and then looked at Shaw for fifteen seconds, Shaw's whole face had caught fire, and he'd shoved the book in the bottom drawer of his desk.

Eyebrows drawing together, Mrs. Chittenden bent over the accent table next to her seat, picking up a figurine of dried pasta to examine it.

"That's elbow-macaroni Emery Hazard," Shaw said. "He's my best friend."

North pinched the bridge of his nose.

"Not the elbow-macaroni version. He's not a real person. I know that."

"Now," North muttered. "After fifteen conversations."

"I mean the real Emery Hazard. He's basically my best friend in the whole universe. He's got a boyfriend who's really sweet, and his name is John-Henry, and I was going to make an oatmeal-cream-pie John-Henry because, well, Emery is so stiff and prickly, and John-Henry is so sweet and gooey, but North told me I couldn't. North is always telling me what I can and can't do. But I just go along with it. I thought it'd be really nice to give elbow-macaroni Emery Hazard a boyfriend, but North said no, and I always do what North tells me to—"

"For fuck's sake, you said you were going to, quote, 'cream-pie John-Henry,' and when I said absolutely not, because God help me if I understood what you actually meant, you sulked for three days and then made the damn oatmeal cream pie anyway. And then you ate it."

"Oh," Shaw frowned. "Huh. I forgot about that."

"Are you the ones who caught the West End Slasher?" Mrs. Chittenden said, leaning forward, clutching the elbow-macaroni figurine without seeming to realize it.

"Yes," North said. "We had help, of course. And the police—"

"And that man who ran the youth shelter, the one who went missing?"

Shaw nodded.

"And there was something recently, an author who was murdered?"

Elbows on the desk, North leaned forward. "The official charge was manslaughter, I think. Mrs. Chittenden, are you in danger? Because—"

"The job is simple. My son Philip made a very stupid mistake. As a result, he is required to report for weekly drug testing. Since he has proven himself unreliable, you will pick him up at his school, accompany him to be tested, and take him home. I understand you typically require a retainer, so I've already written a check for five thousand dollars. Gavin will give it to you when he comes back."

Shaw glanced at North. "We appreciate the offer," Shaw said slowly, "and we recognize that you're placing a lot of trust in us."

"Unfortunately, we currently have a full case load." North tapped a key on the keyboard. "I'd be happy to refer you to—"

"No." The word was brittle. Color mottled her cheeks, red patches climbing her neck. Her knuckles were white around elbow-macaroni Emery Hazard. "I'm hiring you. I've researched your agency extensively. I'm impressed by the work you've done." A big, white smile broke out across her face; that was the politician, Shaw knew, poking her head out for the first time in this conversation. "My son means everything to me, and I'll be happy to pay your priority rates or whatever you believe is necessary."

"Mrs. Chittenden—"

"Celia."

North took a breath. "Celia, what you're asking us to do, it's not our specialty. If you want transportation, there are car services, luxury ones, who will do what you're asking and do it very well. We've used a couple in the past, and I can recommend them."

"Unless it's more than that," Shaw said softly. "Unless you're worried about Philip for some reason. Do you believe he's in danger?"

"Don't be stup—" The smile slipped, and Celia plastered it back on. She was still white-knuckling the pasta figurine. "Don't be silly. Philip is perfectly fine. He attends The Gouverneur Morris School, which I'm sure you've heard of."

"It's very small, isn't it?" North asked. "Very exclusive?"

"Very rigorous," Shaw added. "All the students there still learn Latin and Greek."

"It's also very safe," Celia said. "I'm not worried about trouble finding Philip. I'm worried about Philip finding trouble. He's a very good young man.

He's...he's almost perfect, in fact." The iron rigidity of her voice flexed. "I don't want to see him mess up his life. I don't need to hire a bodyguard, and I don't need to call him an Uber. I want you."

"Why?" Shaw asked.

The waxworks chill was back in her face as she turned her full attention on him. The silence dragged out a moment. And then another. Then the sound of the front door opening broke the stillness, and a pair of footsteps moved through the reception area.

"I'm sorry you've wasted your time," North said, "but you're asking us to babysit. That's not our specialization, and it's not the right fit for us as an agency. As I said, I'd be happy to put you in contact with—"

Her cry began wordless and low, but it climbed to an earsplitting pitch. Celia's hand tightened around elbow-macaroni Emery Hazard until the figurine cracked and broke. The bottom half fell and shattered against the floor, a starburst of macaroni spinning across the boards. Then Celia's shriek ended, and for a moment she sat there, shoulders hunched, chest rising and falling as she sucked in air.

The change, when it came, reminded Shaw of those stupid Transformers that North liked: twist a piece here, push this that way, fold that. Celia's back straightened. Her shoulders rolled back. Her chin came up. She opened her hand, shaking out the broken pieces of pasta that still clung to her flesh.

"I seem to have cut myself," she said. "Do you have a tissue?"

Both North and Shaw were frozen for a moment. Shaw moved first, grabbing a tissue from the box he kept in his desk. Celia accepted it, dabbing at the blood. She fixed her senator smile on them. Forget Transformers, Shaw thought. Forget landmines. This was Shark Week.

The door opened. Gavin minced into the room, holding a Shameless Grounds cup that he handed to Celia with what almost looked like a bow—there was certainly some kind of animal body language, some kind of groveling, that Shaw would have loved to analyze further. He didn't have a chance, though; Pari stormed into the room, a swirl of black hair and flashing eyes, the bindi a screaming red today.

"For my boss," she said, gritting her teeth in what was probably supposed to be a smile as she slammed a Shameless Grounds cup down in front of Shaw. "And for my other boss."

Then she clicked out of the room, her heels sounding like the promise of nail gun to the forehead.

Gavin pranced away.

The door clicked shut.

Silence, and the perfume of good espresso.

"I think this would be a good point to end our conversation," Shaw said.

Celia sipped her espresso, made a face, and set the cup down.

"I'm sorry we couldn't help you," North said. "I hope you have better luck with another agency."

Smoothing the navy skirt across her legs, Celia watched them with glittering eyes. "Philip's first testing appointment is this afternoon. I've already spoken to the head of school, and she knows that you'll be helping out for the next few months. Gavin will provide your girl with the address for the school and a recent picture of Philip."

"She's technically not our girl because you can't own a human being and because Pari would probably bury me in fire ants if she ever heard someone describe her as—"

"There seems to be a misunderstanding," North said, "so I'm going to be frank. We're not taking this job, Mrs. Chittenden. It's time for you to leave."

"Celia," she said with that glad-handing smile. "Please." Then she stood. "And you absolutely will do this job, and you'll do it perfectly well, because if you don't, the next time your private investigator licenses come up for renewal, I will make sure your applications are denied. You'll be out of a job. Now, isn't a little bit of carpool duty better than that?" She walked briskly toward the door. "Gavin will leave the check with your girl."

Acknowledgments

My deepest thanks go out to the following people (in alphabetical order):

Austin Gwin, who pointed out that Michigan isn't for lovers, taught me that all Acuras are front-wheel drive or all-wheel drive, and was vigorously in favor of the convention paying them in poppers.

Steve Leonard, who pointed out the need for more background information about Jadon, who remembered where North's bedroom was in *Declination*, and who weighed in on boxers vs. boxer briefs.

Cheryl Oakley, who gently notified me when she caught me repeating myself, who helped me eliminate a wandering (and pointless) husband, and who encouraged me to make the cameo couple easier to identify.

C.S. Poe, who reassured me when I was worried about stepping on toes, who kept me updated on the emotional rollercoaster, and who leant me her boys for a cameo visit.

Tray Stephenson, who caught so many little errors, who helped me reconsider which book Scotty was editing (and why), and who provided all this help while going through some pretty major life stuff of his own!

Dianne Thies, who caught me doubling down on swag, reminded me about Irish Spring soap, and made me debate Shaggy versus Scooby Doo.

Jo Wegstein, who helped me keep track of fingerprints, who taught me the proper way to take off a pair of Redwings, and who pressed me on the issue of tamper-proof bottle caps.

Wendy Wickett, who offered her usual gentle nudges about italics, who helped me cut back on superfluous words, and checked me on thumbs and index fingers for phone security.

About the Author

Learn more about Gregory Ashe and forthcoming works at
www.gregoryashe.com.

For advanced access, exclusive content, limited-time promotions, and insider
information, please sign up for my mailing list at
http://bit.ly/ashemailinglist.

Made in the USA
Las Vegas, NV
27 August 2021